THE
LIES
WE
LIVE

THE LIES WE LIVE

A Homefront Mystery

Liz Milliron

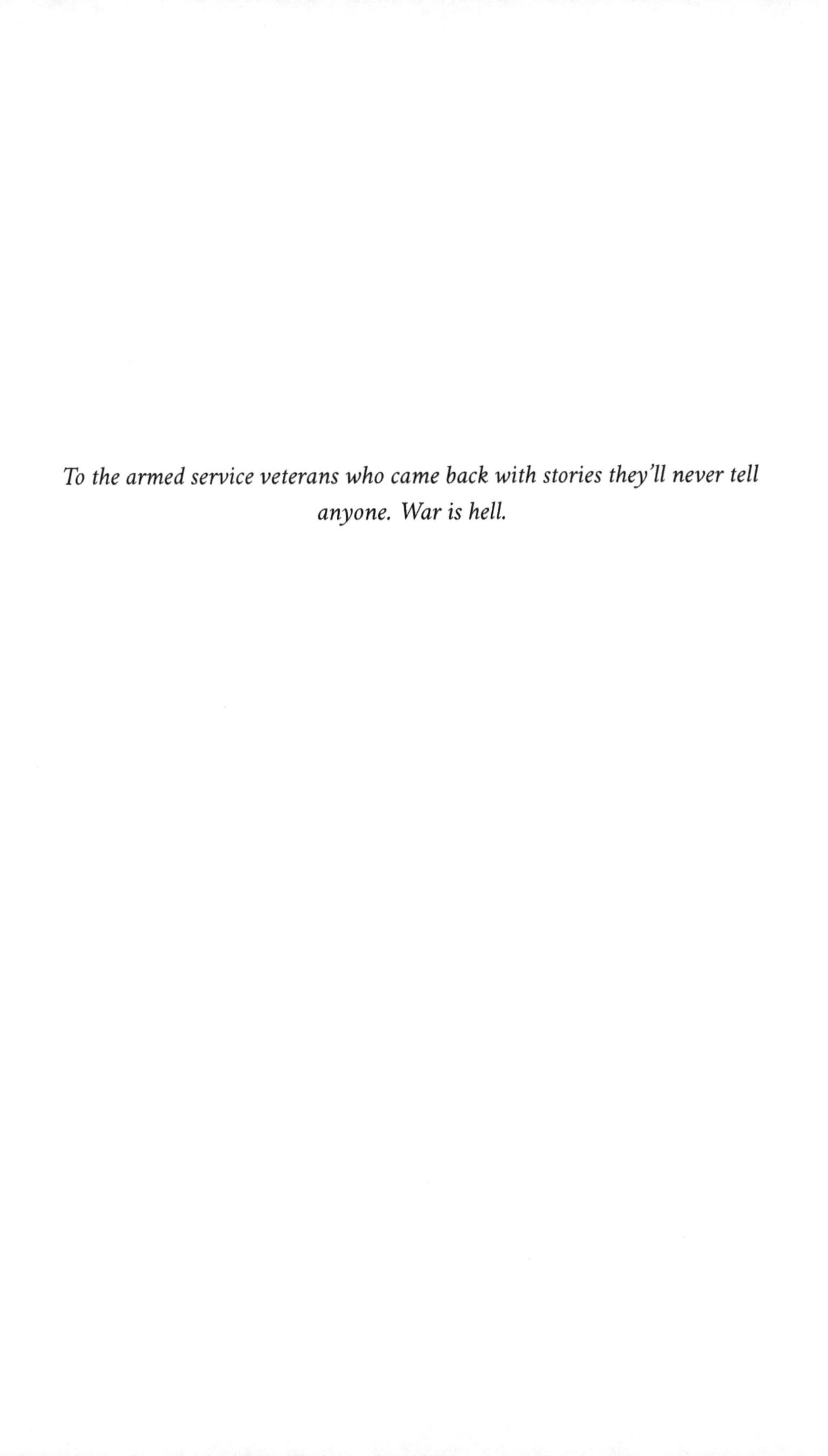

To the armed service veterans who came back with stories they'll never tell anyone. War is hell.

Praise for The Lies We Live

"Betty is back, and this time she has an office, a Girl Friday of sorts in friend Emmeline, and a case from an unexpected client. Author Liz Milliron presents a nuanced and sensitive exploration of wartime America, and a compassionate portrait of trauma in men back from war. *The Lies We Live* is a mystery with a capital M, and a triple R for the trifecta of a nuanced exploration of Race, Relationships, and Redemption."— Gabriel Valjan, Shamus Award-winning author of the Shane Cleary Mystery series

Chapter One

September 1943

Lies are a part of life. Most of the time, it's little white ones. You tell Grandma that you love her meatloaf, even though it's dry as dust. Or you say to your best friend that her new dress is the bee's knees when the color makes her look a little washed out. They don't really hurt anyone. Other times, it's a little more serious. Like saying your brother broke Mom's favorite vase when it was really you.

But every once in a while, you get stuck in a whopper. A lie so big it takes over your life. It forces you to tell one after the other, until you're stuck like a fly in a gigantic spider web. You can see the danger homing in on you, trouble looming clear as day in every one of those five eyes. But you're powerless to get away or stop what you know is coming.

Lies like that get you in big trouble. They also get you killed.

I turned slowly in one spot, taking in my surroundings. Thanks to two big cases, business was coming in a steady flow. I could afford to hire Emmeline part-time. I also had the dough to rent our own digs. We'd been looking for an office for a month or so. I didn't need swanky. Just a little place to meet clients instead of doing business out of Teddy's Diner. Judy would be disappointed, but hey, I was a professional now. I needed to have the whole package. And I could still stop at Teddy's every morning for a real cup of coffee with a side of neighborhood gossip.

This place had potential. There was a small front room with space for a desk. That could be for Emmeline or a receptionist, although that hire was way in the future. A heavy oak door led to a bigger office where I could see my desk, some filing cabinets, and a chair or two for clients. A tiny closet with a counter offered a place to put a percolator coffee pot and maybe even a water cooler.

I had no idea if I could afford that last item, but dream big was my new motto.

The only bump in my plans was my fiancé, Tom Flannery, who was overseas with the 1st Armored Division. In the last letter he'd sent me, dated in May, he'd made it pretty clear he didn't approve of my new career. But with no end to the war in sight, I had time to decide what to do about him.

I waited for Emmeline to finish her inspection. "What do you think?" I asked.

"I like it." She brushed dust from her hands. "It's the perfect size. It has a good location. We're close to downtown. We'll be easy to find, but not in the heart of it, so it shouldn't be as expensive. I love the big windows in your office. No one wants to work in a cave."

Her thoughts mirrored mine. I'd be able to grab breakfast at the diner, jump on the bus, and be to work early. If I saved enough dough to buy a car, I'd be able to park it nearby. 'Course I had to get a driver's license before I could even think of buying one.

We opened the door, which we'd shut so we could talk privately, and went back to the front entry. I faced the landlord. "How much?"

"Forty dollars a month." His self-satisfied smirk gave away his thinking. He was faced with two dames too stupid to know what a thing should cost.

Emmeline and I exchanged a look. "You've gotta be joking," I said. "This place isn't worth more than twenty."

His smirk faltered. "I might be able to do thirty. It's a prime location."

Emmeline shook her head, her expression one of woe. "I doubt that, sir. This space has been open for months. How prime can it be if no one wants to move in?" She paced, mumbling to herself as though doing a calculation. "It's not a lot of square feet, either. I don't know, Betty. For thirty bucks, I think we can get twice the space somewhere else."

"If you say so." I grabbed my coat. Buffalo was stuck in a nice bit of late summer weather, but you never knew what would blow off Lake Erie this time of year. "Thanks for your time. We'll be going."

"Wait." The landlord held out a hand. "I can tell you ladies are smart cookies. I'll give you a deal. Twenty-five dollars a month, and I'll throw in the water cooler the last tenant left behind."

I smothered a grin and held out my hand. "Mister, you've got a deal."

* * *

After making arrangements to come in and sign the lease, Emmeline left to go fix her schedule at the Buffalo Public Library. Starting next week, she was gonna work at our agency in the morning and the library in the afternoon. I caught the next bus back to the First Ward and made my way to Teddy's for a late breakfast. "Hey, Judy? What's shakin'?" I tossed my jacket on the bench and slid into my booth in the back, the one she kept reserved for me until noon every day except Sunday. "The usual, please."

She set down a white ceramic diner mug and filled it. "How'd it go with this one?" She knew all about my search for professional digs.

"We got a winner. Good location and we bargained him down to a reasonable price." I sipped the java and relished the taste, as I always did.

"I still don't know why you have to give up coming here." Judy took out her cloth and gave a quick swipe of the tabletop. "Bill doesn't care, and I'd save this booth for you all day."

"Who said I wouldn't come in to see you? Where else would I get my joe?" I might have space for a percolator, but I'd still be makin' chicory. "I'll be here every morning, eight on the dot. If a client happens to show up, that's okay, too." I patted her arm. "I'm not gonna abandon Teddy's. I promise."

"I s'pose that's jake." She jotted my order in her pad. "I'll go put this in. It'll be up in a jiffy."

"Thanks. By the way, I'm expecting a potential client any minute. Send her back if you see her."

"What does she look like?"

Good question. "Not sure, but chances are she'll ask for me."

Judy rolled her eyes and walked away.

I took out the notebook where I'd been keeping my budget numbers. Pop had helped me work it all out. What I needed to earn to afford what I wanted to spend, including rent and Emmeline's salary. I'd figured out that I could get a telephone. Emmeline could answer it when she was there. Now I had to hammer out the details and cost of an answering service for when we were both out. There wasn't any sense in having a phone if no one was around to take messages. I looked at my numbers. It would be a little tight, but I could do it. If I could pick up one or two more cases a month, it'd be better. I reasoned that having a telephone would help with that. It would be good if I could spring for a small box ad in the *Courier-Express*, too.

A soft cough sounded at my shoulder. "Excuse me. Are you Betty Ahern?" The voice was soft, barely louder than the clatter of the diner.

I looked up. A slim colored girl wearing a neat cotton dress stood next to my table. The robin's-egg blue of the fabric, with the white buttons down the front, set off light brown skin. A gold necklace with a charm on it was framed by the squarish neckline, which also exposed delicate collarbones. Her dark hair was smooth, bobbed at her chin, and tucked behind her ears. Small gold earrings adorned her earlobes. Her eyes were dark brown with a soft expression like a doe. She couldn't have been more than eighteen.

"That's me." I held out a hand. "What's your name?"

"Nancy Washington. I left a message for you here? You said we could meet."

My potential client. I didn't know she was a colored girl. Buffalo didn't have the Jim Crow laws of the South, but there were few Negroes in the city. Pop worked with a couple of coloreds at Bethlehem Steel. Lee said one or two were at General Motors. Mostly they lived in the houses near the East Side, William Street, between Michigan and Jefferson, in the neighborhood known as the Fruit Belt. "Right. Please, have a seat."

She slid into the booth.

Judy came over and lifted her eyebrows at me. I gave her a small nod.

"Would you like coffee?" Judy asked, holding up the pot.

"Real coffee?" Nancy's eyes widened.

"Sure thing. We don't serve anything else." Judy snapped her gum.

"I thought everything was chicory." Nancy's eyes were cast down as she played with her purse strap. "I don't have money to go to many diners."

Judy's gaze softened. "It's okay, honey. Now you know. We get the real deal here." She poured a mug full of dark, steaming liquid. "Milk and sugar? Betty here likes it black, but I can get some if you want it."

Nancy seemed stunned. "A little milk would be very nice, thank you."

"You got it." Judy grabbed a container of milk from another table. "You want anything to eat?"

Nancy's cheeks reddened. "No, I'm okay."

I wondered if she was embarrassed. Maybe she didn't have money for diner fare. "A client's first breakfast is always on me," I said.

She looked up, the gratitude undeniable. "Scrambled eggs and a slice of white toast with butter."

"Comin' right up." Judy wrote the order. "I'll bring it out with yours, Betty." She swept up the menus and left.

Nancy fidgeted with her purse. "Do you eat here a lot? The waitress seems to know you."

"I've been working out of Teddy's since I started my business. Been a couple months now, although I'm gonna sign the lease on a real office tomorrow." I sipped my coffee. "Where do you live?"

"On Bennet, just off William Street."

I'd been right. "What brings you all the way to the First Ward?"

"I called a couple of other detective agencies. They were either too expensive or they didn't want to work with so—" She broke off. "Work with me."

She'd been about to say "someone like me." I was sure of it. The various neighborhoods in Buffalo rubbed along okay. Sure, the Germans made fun of the Irish, who made fun of the Italians. Everybody made jokes about the Polish. But we were all white. The Negro population was new and folks looked on them with more than a little suspicion. Pop said all the ones he worked with were solid men, honest, and put in a good day's work for a good day's wage. Lee said the same. But both admitted not everyone felt that way. It was the same in the Army. Tom had made mention of 'em. Coloreds served in their own outfits, a lot of times in non-combat roles. Most men got along. I guess when you were in a foxhole, the color of a person's skin wasn't that important. But Tom had also written of occasional fights, usually between soldiers from the South and the Negroes.

"That doesn't explain how you found me." I sat back as Judy laid our plates on the table, put out a selection of jams for the toast, and whisked away with her typical briskness.

Nancy looked at the various flavors, her tongue caught between white teeth, and selected the strawberry. "The brother of a friend of mine works at GM. He said a man named Lee Tillotson told him to tell me to find you. Lee said you'll work with anyone who needs help."

Good old Lee. My best friend since childhood, Lee's gimpy leg had kept him out of the service. It hadn't stopped him from helping me a time or two, though. He didn't accompany me on investigations so much these days. But he jumped at the opportunity to make a referral any time he could.

"Lee's a good friend of mine." I drizzled maple syrup over my flapjacks. "Tell me, Miss Washington—"

"Nancy."

I dipped my head. "Nancy. What seems to be your trouble?"

"It's my brother." Nancy paused while she spread strawberry jam on her toast. "Stevie is only sixteen. Too young to go overseas, not that he didn't try to lie about his age and enlist. Thank goodness they didn't believe him."

"War's no place for a child, that's for sure."

She nodded. "He's dropped out of school. That broke Mama's heart. He's such a bright boy. I suppose it wouldn't have been too bad if he'd gotten a job. Plenty of places are hiring. But he doesn't have any interest in factory work." She took a bite, chewed, and swallowed. "Mmm, that's so good."

"You don't get jam where you live?" It would be precious, but it was around. Especially in the summer with the farmer's markets, when folks from the Southtowns came in to the city to sell their produce and things.

"We can't afford it." Nancy still sounded a little abashed, but she was either getting more comfortable with me or the hearty meal was making her lower her guard. "Just the margarine from the ration books. And there's not much of that to go on a slice of toast, either. I got six brothers and sisters. Daddy's serving in Europe as a cook. Mama has to make ends meet best she can."

"What does she do?"

"A little cleaning for white folks in Delaware Park. And some sewing. She's a real fine seamstress." Her face shone with pride.

I wondered if Lee's mother, who did a little housecleaning of her own, could lend a hand. I made a note to ask Mrs. T. 'Course that assumed Mrs. Washington would accept the help. "You were saying about Stevie."

"Right. Well, the thing is, like all bright boys, Stevie needs to keep his hands busy. Idle hands are the devil's tools, that's what Grandmama used to say." She loaded her fork with eggs and ate.

"Let me guess. When Stevie is bored, he gets into trouble. Which is why you've come to me."

"Yes. It's awful, Miss Ahern. He won't tell me what he's up to. Stevie and me, we're not quite two years apart in age. We've always been close. But lately?" She sighed. "I don't know what he's up to, but it's no good. I'm sure of that."

"Call me Betty. It's only fair we both use our Christian names." I took a sip of coffee. "What makes you think he's in trouble?"

"He keeps late hours. He goes out at nine, well after dark. Then he doesn't come home until three or four in the morning. He tries to sneak in, but I hear him." She pushed her eggs around with her fork. "That's bad enough, but he's suddenly got money and he won't say where it's from. I'm not talking about a few dollars. I've seen him with tens and twenties. He bought Mama a new pair of shoes. Brought home a roast for dinner that must've cost a fortune. I've tried to get him to open up, but he won't talk to me. 'Best you don't know,' he says and winks."

I could see why she was worried. If one of my brothers acted that way, I'd be giving them a tongue-lashing that would peel the skin off their hides. And that was after Mom and Pop finished with them. Michael and Jimmy were as full of mischief as any boys of twelve and thirteen. But they wouldn't dare do anything illegal. It didn't sound like the same could be said of Stevie Washington. "What is it you want from me?"

Nancy's eyes were full of anxiety. "Find out what he's up to. I don't mean stop it. I know that might not be possible for you. But if I knew exactly what he was doing, and who he was doing it with, Mama and I could go to the police, or, or…well, do something."

I thought about it. I'd have to tail Stevie, take notes, and maybe a few pictures. I'd bought a small camera, a Kodak 35, and it had come in handy for a few of my cases. If I could get snaps of who Stevie was meeting, I could talk to my buddy, Detective Sam MacKinnon in the Buffalo police, and get some names for Nancy and her mother. "I think I can do that. But you gotta understand. If I witness Stevie committin' a crime, I'm gonna have to call the cops."

Nancy's answering smile was like a ray of sunshine on a gray winter day. "I understand. I hope it don't come to that."

For her sake, I hoped so, too. "Let's talk money. My rate is fifteen dollars for the first week, plus expenses. After that, it's five dollars a day, also plus expenses."

The sunshine dimmed. "I'm sorry. I've wasted your time. Thanks for breakfast." She gathered up her purse and made to leave.

Wow. I knew for a fact my price was lower than most gumshoes in the city. "Hold on." I put out my hand. "What can you afford?"

She opened her purse. "I've managed to save ten dollars doing odd jobs and a little rough sewing. It's all I have." She laid a five, and five ones on the table.

Emmeline would give me a lecture for sure. But I couldn't turn this girl away. She was so young. Her brother was the same age as my sister, Mary Kate. If I were in Nancy's shoes, wouldn't I want someone to help me? "It'll be enough." I swept up the money. "Give me the week. How do I get in touch with you?" I pushed over my notepad. "If you have any names, or addresses I could use, it sure would help."

"Oh, bless you, Miss Ahern. Betty. You are an angel." She scribbled the information on a sheet of paper. "That's the number of a pay phone at a grocery store near my house. If you leave a message for me, Mr. Jones will make sure I get it. It's our community phone." She scrambled out of the booth and kissed my hand. "Thank you so much. Mama thought I was chasing moonbeams for sure. 'White folk don't care about us,' that's what she said. Wait until I tell her we're finally going to know about Stevie. Goodbye!" She hastened out of the diner.

Swell. I was getting less than half my usual fee, and my client thought she had a guarantee of success.

How did I get so lucky?

Chapter Two

I grabbed my cup of java. I hoped against hope Stevie wasn't involved in anything criminal. My instinct warned me that prob'ly wasn't the case.

A movement at the corner of my eye caught my attention. I looked up. Frank Hicks sat at the counter. He waved to me. "Good morning." He grinned, showing the dimple that made my heart go pitter-pat.

"Hey there. Come join me."

He hopped up, mug in hand, and slid into the recently vacated seat.

I took a moment to appreciate his looks. I'd met Frank Hicks while working a case. He was charming, intelligent, and Jimmy Stewart-handsome, with dark brown eyes you could get lost in and a dimple that stole my breath away when he smiled. "When did you get here?"

"About twenty minutes ago."

Judy swung by and topped off both our mugs. We nodded our thanks. She threw me a wink as she tipped her head in Frank's direction before she hustled off.

He continued as though he hadn't seen anythin'. "You were with that girl, so I grabbed a seat at the counter. Is she a client?"

"Yeah. Her brother might be gettin' himself into some trouble. She wants me to find out."

"Ah." Frank didn't ask any further questions. He respected my work, both my ability to be a detective and my clients' privacy.

I appreciated that. "You come all the way over here just to try the pancakes?" Frank lived near Buffalo State Hospital, which was across the city. Since he was a Quaker and a conscientious objector to the war, he worked there. His status as a conchie had put me off when I first met him. That and I also thought he might be a murderer, but we'd gotten past that.

He smiled. "Hardly. I didn't think it appropriate to call your house, but I wanted to know if you'd like to have dinner with me. We can continue the process of getting to know one another."

The idea of dinner with Frank warmed me down to my toes. We'd had lunch together a few times over the summer and he'd become a good pal. I knew he wouldn't object to being more. But I still had a ring on my finger and my heart wasn't ready to write a Dear John letter. "Do you mean tonight?"

"I was thinking of Friday. I have to work and tomorrow, too. There's a place near where I live that is quite good." He took a drink. "I don't go there often, but I thought it would be nice to do so with a friend."

"I'd like that. It's a date." The heat rose in my cheeks. "I didn't mean, well, oh shoot."

"I know exactly what you meant." He looked at his watch. "I have to run. If I miss the bus, I'll be late to work." He got up and leaned over and kissed my cheek. "See you Friday at five at my apartment. We can walk to the restaurant from there." He left.

The spot on my cheek fairly tingled. I knew it was a simple gesture, nothin' more. Frank and I got along, despite our differences in background and views on the war. It'd be nice to have a quiet meal together.

Judy stopped at the table. "Who was that? He's a looker for sure."

"A friend of mine."

She raised her eyebrows. "Really? Seems to me like he wants to be more than that."

I refused to meet her gaze. "I'm engaged."

"Uh-huh." She leaned on the table and stared until I lifted my head. "Don't play around with me, sister. Tom is over there, this guy is right here. You gotta be thinkin' about it."

The diner suddenly felt stuffy and hot. I stood and threw some money on the table. "Keep the change." I headed outside. I'd done nothing but think of it ever since Frank saved my bacon that night in Front Park. Trouble was, I still didn't know what I wanted to do.

* * *

After leaving Teddy's, I headed home. I wanted to run the rental agreement past Pop, to be sure I wasn't missing anything. He wouldn't be home from the steel plant for a few hours. Lee was at work. So was Dot, my other best friend, who still worked at Bell Aircraft. I could spend my waiting time coming up with a strategy for Stevie Washington. His sister had given me the address for his local hangout as well as the names of some of the guys he'd been spending time with. I called Sam, but he was out workin' the street. I said I'd call back later.

Cat, my adopted stray, came running up the sidewalk on Mackinaw to greet me. I scooped him up and nuzzled his gray fur. I remembered how ratty and thin he'd been when Mary Kate found him. He looked almost domestic these days. Except for the fact he never went inside. I suspected that was more 'cause Mom had to draw the line somewhere than any reluctance on his part.

"I've got an office now, buddy. Wanna be my work cat? Greet the clients when they come in?"

He blinked. *Meow.* I took that to mean, "I'll do anything if I get fed for it."

I scratched his ears. "That means I'd have to find a way to take you back and forth. You'd prob'ly have to ride the bus with me. Maybe in a bag? What do you think of that?"

He twisted in my arms and leapt to the ground. After landing gracefully on all four paws, he trotted off, tail in the air.

Guess that answered that. Office work was fine, but no bags—or buses—for Cat.

I entered the house. "I'm back. Mom? You here?"

She came out of the kitchen. "How'd it go?"

"Good." I told her about the office and a little about Nancy Washington.

"She's a colored girl? Why'd she come all the way to the First Ward?"

I shrugged. "Seems I've got a reputation for being a sucker."

She flicked the towel at me. "You're no such thing. You're a good-hearted girl who'd rather help people than make money. And that's not a bad way to be." She paused. "But you be careful on this one. It's not a good area of the city."

"Mom, I'm surprised. Pop knows coloreds from work. So does Lee. They're okay."

"Mmm." She returned to the kitchen.

I followed. "What?"

She stood at the sink, washing dishes. "It's not the people, so much. It's a new community. Some people, they're suspicious. They think the Negroes are going to take their jobs. There's always a little friction when a new group tries to find its place. It happened with the Irish and it happened with the Italians." She placed a dish in the drying rack. "All I'm saying is to keep your eyes open when you're over there."

I picked up a dish towel. "I always do, Mom. Don't worry."

We worked side by side for a bit, her washing, me drying. We talked about the younger kids, Mom's frustrations with Michael in school, and her opinion of the boy Mary Kate liked. The jury was still out on that one. A knock on the front door interrupted us.

"I'll get it." I set down my towel.

Mom grabbed the kettle. "I'll start water for tea."

I whistled as I went to the front door. In the middle of the day, I didn't expect anything serious. If something had happened to Pop or one of the kids, we'd get a phone call, not a visit.

Mrs. Flannery, my fiancé Tom's mother, stood on the front step. She clutched a crumpled piece of paper in her hands.

I recognized it as a telegram. Last I heard, Tom was in North Africa with the 1st Armored Division. I hadn't had a letter from him since early summer, and that one had been dated in May. I gripped the door. "Mrs. Flannery? Is that what I think it is?"

She held it out. "I've gotten a telegram about Tom."

Chapter Three

A telegram about Tom? That could only mean one thing. My knees sagged. I struggled to breathe. In my mind, the sunshine dimmed, and the soft breeze turned cold. I struggled to speak.

Mom came to the rescue. "Betty? Who is it?" She saw Mrs. Flannery. "Margaret! How nice to see you." She stopped and her gaze went from Mrs. Flannery, to the telegram, to me. Her voice turned brisk. "Come in, right now. Betty, you too. Close the door."

She led Mrs. Flannery to the living room and settled her in a chair. "Sit." She pointed at the other chair. "I'll be right back."

I obeyed. A telegram about Tom. There'd always been the possibility of this. I knew that. It was still a shock. What would Lee say? Or Dot?

I thought about that morning. Frank invited me to dinner. I'd accepted. At the time, I hadn't thought anything of it.

But a telegram changed everything.

I wrenched myself back to the present. Mrs. Flannery sat on the other chair, tears running down her face, but her smile was broad, almost joyful. Her expression was odd. If I didn't know better, I'd think she was relieved. Even a little happy.

Just what was in that message anyway?

Mom returned with a pot of tea, the sugar bowl, and a bottle of whiskey on a tray. She poured a cup, added a splash of spirits, and handed it to Mrs. Flannery. "Here. Drink this." She made a second cup and handed it to me. Then she sat. "Now. What's this about a telegram?"

Mrs. Flannery held it out while she accepted the doctored tea. Both her hands shook so hard, the china cup rattled against the saucer. "It's Tom."

I found my voice. "He's dead?"

"No." She clasped her hands. "He's coming *home*."

What? I set down my cup, took the telegram, and read it.

Regret to inform you your son, Corporal Thomas Flannery, was seriously wounded in action on 7 May 1943 in Tunisia. You will be advised as reports of condition are received.

I looked at the date. The telegram had just come. But he'd been injured this past spring. "Mrs. Flannery, this isn't recent. Why are you just getting this now?"

She took a hasty sip of tea. A little sloshed out. "I don't know." Her cheeks reddened. "The news makes everything seem like it's running like clockwork, but I remember when Mr. Flannery was in the Great War. It was chaotic. Maybe they couldn't identify Tom right away because he lost his dog tags, or there was some clerical error. But we know now."

"This doesn't say he's coming home. Only that he's hurt."

"That arrived this morning. Then there was a letter in this morning's mail." She drew another piece of paper out of her apron pocket and held it out. "It seems the original telegram was delayed."

I took it. The seal of the United States Army was large and bold at the top. Underneath, in fancy letters, it said "Honorable Discharge." I scanned it. All it said was that Tom was honorably discharged after faithful service. "Did they say why? What does seriously wounded mean? It says here he's been in a hospital in England, but where?"

She set down her cup. "I don't know where he was while he was in the hospital. It doesn't matter now."

I glanced at Mom. "When is he gettin' back to Buffalo?"

Mrs. Flannery paused. "He arrives, well, tomorrow. I know, it seems a terrible rush. I get the feeling a lot has happened and the mail service is barely keeping up. Mercy, I'm glad the poor boy won't be alone in the station, wondering why no one is there to greet him. Lee is taking me, since William is working. I hope you can come too, Betty."

Tomorrow? The U.S. Army was sending home a wounded soldier, and they weren't organized enough to let us know more than a day in advance? It was baffling. Then again, they had thousands of men to account for. Maybe I shouldn't be surprised one slipped through the cracks.

But Mrs. Flannery was avoiding my gaze. Why? She knew somethin' and was holdin' it back. "Mrs. Flannery, what do they mean by seriously wounded? Please don't tell me you don't know, 'cause I think you do. It's bad or else you woulda said somethin' when I read the telegram."

She folded her hands in her lap and stared at them. After what seemed like forever, she lifted her face. "There was another page to the letter. I didn't bring it. His tank took a hit. Because of the shrapnel, they had to amputate his left leg below the knee."

I nearly dropped my tea. My fiancé was coming home. As a cripple.

* * *

I waited until after supper, when I knew Lee would be home from work. I rushed down to the Tillotson house, puffing on a Lucky Strike Green while I went. I didn't worry about telling Dot. She and Lee had gotten together earlier this year. Where I found one, I'd find the other.

I didn't know what worried me more. Tom was on his way home, safe although not whole. The decision I'd been puttin' off could wait no longer. I knew what Lee would say. He'd stick up for his best friend. Dot, on the other hand, knew how tormented I'd been, wonderin' who I would choose. Frank or Tom?

Should I have written Tom earlier? Would he even have gotten the letter while he was in the hospital, or would it have gone astray? He thought he was comin' home to a steadfast lover, and I might have to break his heart.

I should have bucked up and been honest in the first place. If I'd only known what had happened.

I pushed the thought aside. I couldn't have written that Dear John letter if I knew Tom was hospitalized instead of on the front. But I would have put more effort into figuring out where my feelings stood instead of thinkin' I had all the time in the world to get my head on straight.

Now I had to do it by tomorrow.

I found Lee in his backyard, bent over the engine of his dad's old car. As expected, Dot sat on the ground near him, handing up tools. Lee had often joked about how good it was to have a girlfriend who knew what he meant when he asked for a three-eighths wrench. Fact was, she coulda fixed things as easily as him. She preferred to play the role of helper.

She looked over at the sound of my steps. "Betty! We didn't expect… What's wrong?" She got up.

"Tom's coming home. Tomorrow." I told them about my visit from Mrs. Flannery.

Dot gaped. "That's wonderful. Isn't it great, Lee? All of us together again." She watched him. "Lee?"

I took in the sheepish expression on my friend's face. "You already know." I tossed aside my smoke.

He held up his hands. "Now, don't snap your cap. Mrs. Flannery stopped here this morning. It's not like I knew a week ago or anything."

I clenched my fists. "You gimpy-legged dope. Why didn't you tell me?"

"Mrs. Flannery made me promise. What was I s'posed to do, huh? She's my best friend's mother. I've been listening to her like she was my own mom since I was that big." He held his hand about two feet off the ground.

I exhaled slowly and uncurled my fingers. "You're right. I'm sorry. I've been runnin' around the city. You wouldn't have found me anyway."

He seemed relieved. He lit up a Chesterfield. "How bad is he hurt? That's the one thing she wouldn't tell us."

"Bad." I sagged to the ground. "He lost his leg."

Dot gasped and covered her mouth with her hands.

Lee let loose with a couple words he didn't use in front of his mother. Not quietly, either. He must not have cared if she heard him. "Did Mrs. Flannery say anything else? How's he feeling?"

"I don't know. But it can't be good." I looked up at Dot.

Sympathy shone from her eyes. She knew for sure what I was thinkin'. "Have you told anyone else?" She meant Frank.

I shook my head.

"And here just yesterday we were all happy about Ike's announcement about the Italians surrenderin'."

"Yeah, shows you what we know." I stared at a crack in the cement. "What am I gonna do?" I raised my head to look at her.

She and Lee exchanged a knowing look. In a split second, I realized I'd been stupid to think my secret was safe. Of course she'd shared it with her beau. To his credit, Lee hadn't given me a clue. She'd prob'ly threatened him if he did, which would scare anyone who knew her well. Sweet-natured and pinup pretty, Dot rarely got angry. When she did, you'd better hold on to your hat 'cause she'd let you have it. "When is he arriving?" she asked.

"Tomorrow on the three-fifteen train from New York." I stretched out my legs. "I've got a new case, but I'm gonna meet Mrs. Flannery there."

Lee took a drag off his smoke. "I'll take half a day off and be there, too. If he's hurt that bad, you'll need help with his trunk. There are the redcaps, but I think it'll go better if I'm with you."

I looked up. "What's that s'posed to mean?"

"I know Tom. This is gonna hit him hard. I think he's gonna need a sympathetic shoulder." He drew Dot to him.

I bristled. "You think I'm not enough? Or you think I'm gonna say something I shouldn't?"

"That's not it at all, Betty. Dot's told me a bit about Frank Hicks and what's goin' on there."

Dot flushed.

He continued as though he hadn't noticed. "I haven't said anythin' to Tom, and I don't think you'll hand back his ring right there on the platform. I just have a feeling that Tom will appreciate having another person there who understands what he's goin' through."

I caught his eye. "Who understands bein' a cripple, you mean."

Lee lowered his head.

It was somethin' I hadn't considered. All my focus had been on me, my feelings, and what this meant for my decision. I hadn't given a moment's thought about how Tom would be feelin' about his new life.

More evidence that I was not exactly the world's best fiancée.

Chapter Four

The next morning, I put the lease agreement in my purse before I left home. Pop hadn't seen anything wrong with it. I planned to swing by the landlord's office after I took care of some business, but before I met Lee and Mrs. Flannery at Central Terminal. I had no idea what I was gonna say to Tom when I saw him. Perhaps I should have planned it, but playing things by ear was all I could think of.

I skipped Teddy's in the morning, instead opting to go to Moe's down by police headquarters. The reason was simple: I knew Sam often grabbed a bite there before he went to work. I wanted to catch him early, both to pick his brain about Stevie Washington and see if he could call Stevie's school to ask some questions. They would hang up on me, but a police detective couldn't be ignored. Stevie was young. Maybe he was up to the normal hijinks associated with young men with too much time on their hands.

Instinct told me it was more than that.

I quickly spotted Sam at the counter and sidled up next to him. "Morning."

He looked up. "Didn't expect to see you here. What brings you downtown?"

"You, of course." I held up my hand and ordered coffee, scrambled eggs, hash browns, and bacon.

"You skipped breakfast for me?" He patted his mouth with a napkin. "I'm flattered."

"I didn't skip anything. Didn't you hear me put in my order?" The waitress set down my joe.

Sam peered at me. "What's wrong?"

"Who said something had to be wrong?"

"You don't look right. Did you sleep last night?"

I'd tossed and turned, playing out possible meetings with Tom while thoughts of Frank kept intruding. What was I gonna do? I s'posed it depended on what happened with Tom. Around and around my thoughts went, until I finally gave up.

I wasn't surprised Sam noticed my sandy-eyed condition right off. I also didn't want to start my morning chewing old soup. "It's nothing. Let's get down to brass tacks. I got a new case." I gave him a sketch of what I knew about Stevie. Technically, Sam and I weren't partners. But we'd developed enough of a working relationship that I was comfortable giving him details, especially if I was askin' for his help. I never gave him dope that was too personal, and he respected my boundaries.

"Stevie Washington? The name doesn't ring a bell." Sam used his biscuit to sop up some gravy from his corned beef hash.

"What about the neighborhood over around Jefferson? Is it a problem?" The waitress set down my plate, and I dug into my eggs.

"No more than some, much more than others." He finished his coffee and signaled for a refill. "Compared to Delaware Park, it's a hotbed for crime. But when you look at someplace like the Hooks, down by the canal, it's almost as peaceful as Eden."

"Mom tells me a lot of colored people are settlin' there."

He nodded. "The population is small so far. Mostly people coming from the South looking for work. Just like with other immigrant populations, industrial jobs bring folks from outside the region."

"Which brings trouble."

"I always said you were a smart cookie." He pushed away his plate. "Seems it happens every time a new group arrives."

"Mom told me as much." I forked up a mouthful of hash browns, relishing the greasy, salty crispness of the fried potatoes. I'd never say this to Judy, but Moe's made better hash browns. It had to be the seasoning. "What kind of trouble? Murder?"

"A couple. Robberies, too. I wouldn't be surprised if they're organizing their own gangs, just like the other ethnicities."

I ate for a minute, thinking. "But Stevie Washington isn't a name you know? He'd be a young guy, a kid really. He ought to be in school."

"Nope, hasn't crossed my desk. But unless he's been connected to a homicide, he wouldn't. Are you asking me to poke around or call his school for you?" Sam nudged my arm.

"If it won't get you into trouble, that'd be swell. I'm gonna do my own digging, of course. But it'd be nice to know what I'm walking into."

"I'll call your house and leave a message."

"Oh, that reminds me." I pulled out one of my business cards and a pen. "I'm signing a lease on an office this morning. This is the address. I'll have a telephone number to go with it soon. In the meantime, you can still call home." I slid the card over.

Sam looked at it. "Congratulations. Work must be good."

"Steady enough to pay the rent and hire a part-timer."

"You're moving up. Nice job. I'll see what I can do." He pocketed the card. "Are you going to tell me what's bothering you?"

I tried to avert my face. Sam was too good at reading people. "Who said I'm bothered?"

"I can read it in your eyes, Betty. And it must be personal. You've got a new office, a part-time employee, and you're getting your own telephone. Business is, as they say, booming for you." He spun on his stool. "I'm a friend, not just a colleague. What is it?"

I weighed my words. "Tom's coming home. Today." I filled him in on Mrs. Flannery's visit yesterday.

"You're caught between a rock and a hard place." Sam knew all about Frank. "Want some advice?"

"Always."

"You're overthinking it. It's been months since you've seen Tom. More than a year, right?"

I nodded, mouth full of eggs.

"Find out his feelings first. He's going to be dealing with a lot. I know men who've been in his shoes. Oh, maybe not injured as badly. But it's a hard thing to move back home and leave Army life behind you. Tom has to do it with a serious injury. Be patient with him."

I set down my knife and fork. "And if I make up my mind? What then? How do I tell him? Either of them."

Sam patted my hand. "Be honest. That's the best thing you can do in this—or any—situation."

Oh, how I hoped it would be that simple.

Chapter Five

I left Sam and hopped a bus that would take me over to Jefferson. While I rode, I checked my camera. I didn't think I'd have the opportunity, or the need, to take any pictures, but you never knew.

The weather was warm and sunny, with just the slightest breeze off the lake. The leaves had not yet started to change. That didn't come to Buffalo until later in the month, sometimes into October. For now, I enjoyed the kiss of the sun on my face. It was almost enough to distract me from my appointment at Central Terminal this afternoon.

Almost.

I got off the bus and walked east. As I did, a sensation I'd never felt before settled over me like a heavy blanket, blotting out the pleasure of the day. It puzzled me at first, but it didn't take me long to put my finger on the reason. I stuck out worse here than I had in Delaware Park. Up there, I obviously hadn't been one of the swells, but once you got beyond the clothes, everybody looked like me. Most of the people I saw on Jefferson had skin in various tones of brown, some almost so dark as to be black. They stared at me openly, some with curiosity, others with hostility. The skin on the back of my neck tingled. I was a bug under a magnifying glass, an unusual butterfly to be regarded with suspicion until they decided whether or not I was a threat.

It was a feeling I'd never experienced before, no matter where I'd gone in Buffalo. For the first time in my life, I didn't belong. I couldn't allow myself to be distracted by the thought, but I knew I didn't like it.

Head up, shoulders back. I took a deep breath. Pop always said that the first step toward not being taken advantage of was to look like you were a person who *couldn't* be overwhelmed. There was no reason for me to be quakin' in my shoes. They were just people, same as me.

I rapidly learned that might be true, but they were people who didn't want to talk to me. Oh, most were polite. They knew the Washingtons, but they weren't in a hurry to flap their gums with a stranger. Even among the friendlier ones, I sensed a reluctance. This was their neighborhood. A stranger with questions should hop a bus and be on her way.

I stopped a man walkin' down the sidewalk. "Excuse me, sir."

He shot me an unfriendly glare and kept goin'.

I tried again with a woman leading a little girl. "Good morning. Would you be able to spare me a couple of minutes? I'm a private detective. I have a few questions about a boy who lives around here."

The woman stopped, a sympathetic smile on her face as she clasped her little girl's hand. "I'm sorry, I got things to do. You say you're a detective?"

"Yes, ma'am."

The woman clucked her tongue. "Ain't no one around here gonna talk about a neighborhood boy to a white girl. You best give it up now and get." She hurried off.

It wasn't a promising start. Perhaps Nancy shoulda hired someone closer to home.

A knot of boys who couldn't be much older than Lee approached. One in the front of the group, tall, lanky, with close-cut hair and wearing denims and a white T-shirt, stepped to the front. "Hey, girl. You sure are a fine one. What're y'all lookin' for? Maybe we can help y'all out."

His buddies sniggered. Boys were all the same.

I detected a slight accent in his voice. Was that what a Southern drawl sounded like? I'd heard it done in the movies, of course. But I'd never come across it in real life. There was a little more of what I could only describe as slurring to it. It wasn't at all like the crispness of a Buffalo native. It was also less exaggerated than an actor. "I'm looking for someone. Perhaps you can help me."

They laughed. "Oh, we can help you all right."

I took a step back. "Do you know a boy named Stevie Washington? Maybe he's a friend of yours?"

The group advanced. Out of the corner of my eye, I could see we were getting looks from others. But no one seemed willing to step forward and put the young men in their place. "Stevie? Don't rightly know. Maybe you and we can go somewhere quiet and figure it out."

I was at a bus stop, but luck was against me. There wasn't a bus in sight. I had my pocketknife in my purse, but I didn't fancy my chances against a gang of five, 'specially since they were all bigger than me and prob'ly had their own knives. My older brother Sean, who was away in the Pacific, always said fighting was a numbers game. When they were stacked against you, don't get involved. I continued to back up. "Why aren't you serving? You all look healthy to me and over eighteen. Most joes I know are in some kind of uniform."

One of them snorted. "Draft board didn't want us."

"Then why not enlist?"

"If they don't want to draft us, why should we join up?" another one replied.

I wasn't liking my chances here. Why had I come? Because it was the middle of the day, and I hadn't expected such behavior. Surely, if the group rushed me, someone would come to my aid. Not wanting to talk to a stranger was one thing. Standing by while a young woman was attacked was a completely different story.

Right?

A stout woman stormed across the street, heedless of traffic. She wore a red housedress not unlike my mother's, with a knitted shawl over her shoulders. One hand held a half-full bag. The finger of the other wagged ferociously. "George Henry Vickers. You stop right there, boy. Yes, you. And the rest of y'all. Shame on you. Is this how you spend your time? Harassing young women? You boys wait until I tell your mammas what it is you get up to during the day. They're off working to keep clothes on your backs and food on your tables, and this is how you thank them?"

I wasn't surprised when every single boy hung his head. It was the same sort of speech a grandmother in the First Ward would have delivered to a bunch of hoodlums cruising down Louisiana. I told myself not to smile. I had a funny feeling it wouldn't be understood in the way I meant it.

"Now, scoot! I see you out here again, I'll drag you down to the recruiting office myself. By the ears, if I have to." She planted her fists on her ample hips. "Of course, I wouldn't blame the Army if it wouldn't take you. Bunch of layabouts. Maybe you can get a night job sweeping the floor at the steel plant."

The boys fled.

A man who must have been Pop's age, maybe a little older, came out of a store fronted by a display of late-summer vegetables. "What's all the ruckus?"

"George Vickers and his ruffians, gettin' up to no good again." The woman shook her head. "You okay, dear? They didn't hurt you none, did they?"

"No, ma'am. But thank you for your help," I said. "I admit, I was feelin' more than a bit out of my league there."

"You lost, miss?" the older man asked.

He must think that was the only reason a white girl would be in the neighborhood. I needed a friendly face. I fixed a smile on mine. "No, sir. My name is Betty Ahern. I'm a private detective. Nancy Washington is a client of mine. Do you know her?"

The man and woman exchanged a meaningful look. "Why would a detective be lookin' for Nancy?"

"It's not her I'm after. She hired me." I wished I'd brought the contract to show them. "She's worried about her brother, Stevie."

Another look, this one heavy with meaning, passed between the two adults. The man beckoned to me. "You'd better come inside."

Chapter Six

The inside of the store was dim, lit mostly by the sunshine through the front windows and a few light bulbs. The earthy smell of root vegetables greeted me. A bin of rosy apples rubbed shoulders with one of green pears, and another holding small baskets of blueberries. The standard late-summer fruits of Western New York. "You grow all this yourself?"

"Not by a long shot, miss. Hard to grow a garden in the city. I get it from here and there, sell it to folks in the neighborhood who can't grow their own. Which is most everybody." He chuckled.

Along one wall was a table stacked with loaves of bread and other baked goods. "Is your wife a baker?" I waved my hand.

He sat and spit into a brass pail near the register. "Wife, mother, sister, and Miz Alva. She's the woman who rescued you. They bake, I sell."

"She left before I could get her name. Please thank her again for me. You didn't introduce yourself, either."

"Rodney Jones." He held out a weathered hand. The dry, wrinkled skin matched his seamed face, but his grip was as strong as Pop's. "I hope them boys didn't give you the wrong impression. We ain't all like that."

This was the man with the communal telephone. I shook hands. "Trust me. Before the war took 'em all away, we had groups like that in the First Ward, too. Boys seem to be boys, no matter what color their skin is."

Mr. Jones cackled. "You got that right."

I wandered the aisles. "I'm surprised people around here don't go to the Broadway Market. Well, not you personally, but others." I examined a jar of hard candies. "It's not that far away."

"Some do. Others are more comfortable staying close to home. Not everyone in Buffalo has welcomed us with open arms."

I always thought of my neighbors as being friendly people. But even in the First Ward, when someone who wasn't Irish wandered in, there was a slight closing of the ranks. "I understand. It's hard to get used to people not like you."

"That it is." He watched me. "You want a piece?" He reached for the jar of candy.

"What is it?"

"Horehound. Try one."

I took one of the slightly sticky rounds and popped it in my mouth. It wasn't sweet, not exactly. There was a slightly bitter taste as well, like the cough medicine Mom forced on me when I was a kid. "Interesting flavor."

Mr. Jones grinned. "Takes some getting used to. Now." He squinted at me. "What's this about Nancy and Stevie? She didn't say she was gonna go to no detective."

Experience taught me people didn't give up information easily without a reason. "I'm sure you understand, but I have to protect my client's privacy. What's Nancy to you? The way you talk, it makes me think she's more than a girl you know from the neighborhood."

He slapped his thigh and let out a hearty laugh. "You're a smart one, ain't you? Not as trusting as I thought."

"Maybe not, but I did come in your store." I hadn't gotten an eerie vibe off the older man. That didn't mean I trusted him. "You answer my question, I'll answer yours."

His weathered face split in a wide grin, showing a mouthful of crooked, slightly yellow teeth that showed evidence of a tobacco habit. "Shoot, 'course I know Nancy. She used to work the counter for me, 'fore she got busy workin' with her mamma. She's a good girl." He looked around. "Her mamma is my baby sister. When her husband went off to war, well, you might say I took it upon myself to look out for Clementine and her young'uns."

Family. That explained his interest both in Nancy and her brother.

He pulled out a worn billfold from which he took out a faded linotype picture. "That's Clemmie and me as kids."

I looked at the barefoot children, both with wide smiles. "She's very pretty. Her daughter takes after her."

"Nancy gets a lot from Clemmie. Including her need to be a mother hen." He spat more tobacco juice into the pail. "Your turn."

"I already told you she came to me about her brother." I gave Mr. Jones the rest of the details about Stevie, as far as I knew them. "She thinks now that he's not in school, he's taken a wrong turn on the path of life, as my grandmother might say."

"Smart woman, your grandmamma. Where she from?"

"County Cork, Ireland. Her parents fled during the Famine. She was a little girl. They went from New York City to Buffalo. My family has been here ever since." I shifted the candy in my mouth. The taste was growing on me.

"Irish, huh? I heard they had their own problems when they first arrived." Mr. Jones crossed his arms over his chest. "No Irish need apply and all that. She knows about not being wanted."

"She does." I waited. I wondered if knowing that story would be the thing that sealed Mr. Jones's decision. He'd either keep talking or tell me to get lost.

Eventually, he nodded. "Nancy ain't wrong. Stevie, he's not in bad trouble yet, but it's just a matter of time."

I took out my notepad and a pencil. "What do you mean?"

"It's like she said. Stevie is a smart boy. He was good with his figures in school. Good enough that I let him run the register when I needed a break. Usually, I just let the kids stock shelves, things like that." He leaned back against the counter. "Then, when he was about fifteen, things changed. He wasn't interested in working no more. The war broke out and he said he was gonna enlist. Go see the world. I told him he was too young. He didn't listen. Those Army men, they ain't dumb. They saw through his story 'bout being eighteen as easy as anything."

Nancy had told me the same thing. "His sister said that didn't make him happy."

"No, miss, not a bit." Mr. Jones took a candy for himself. "Instead of going back to school, or even tryin' to get a job in one of the factories, he figured he'd make himself a quick buck. I told him. Only way to get ahead in this world is hard work, clean living, and fearing the Lord. He didn't listen. Ran after Georgie Vickers. When Georgie laughed in his face, he took up with some men I don't like at all. Got a bad reputation on the street."

"What kind?"

"Schemers. Gambling, fighting, and worse. From what I hear, Stevie isn't at the top of the ladder, but he works with them as is. I wouldn't be surprised if they was grooming him for something bigger in the future." He pushed off the counter and picked up a towel.

"It doesn't sound like you've seen this first-hand, though. It's all rumor."

He wiped his counter. "But I heard it more than once. The boy suddenly got money, and he don't tell nobody where it came from. That ain't good." He fixed me with a stare. "When he was little, he was honest, just like his sister. What makes a good child like that turn all secretive and sullen? Nothing worth doin'; you mark my words."

I had to agree with him. I hadn't been on this case long. But it seemed certain that whatever Stevie Washington was into, it wasn't gonna turn out to be on the right side of the law. I had enough experience to know it wouldn't end well. Not for him and not for his family.

* * *

I stepped out of Mr. Jones's store into the warm September sunshine. I checked my watch. It was slightly after one. I didn't want to be late to meet Tom, but I had some time. Normally, I would have walked up and down Jefferson, tryin' to find someone who would talk to me. Or I'd have staked out Stevie's address to see if he was home, then followed him if he came out.

It didn't take me long to figure out this case required a different strategy. It seemed that Miz Alva had gone before me, spreading my bona fides. People seemed a smidge friendlier, at any rate. But the minute I asked anything close to a probing question, they clammed up. Claims of ignorance were the most common responses, but I also talked to a few people who remembered last-minute appointments or swore they heard someone calling for them, and they hurried away.

A stakeout was just as impossible. I'd done a few of 'em. One of the important things in a successful watch was not to be noticed. You didn't want passers-by to remember or be surprised by a girl who didn't move for three hours. And you certainly didn't want your mark to spot you from three blocks away and decide to beat feet before you could do anything.

There were plenty of good spots where I could watch for Stevie. The problem was I had to be the only white person in a three-block area. Definitely the only white woman. News of my presence and purpose would spread like wildfire, if it hadn't already. If Stevie didn't see me himself, he'd catch word long before he came into view.

This would require a different, more creative approach. I hopped a bus and headed back downtown to see one of the most creative people I'd ever met.

Chapter Seven

I breezed through the door of the *Courier-Express*, one of Buffalo's two bigger newspapers. As always, the joint was hoppin'. I wondered if there was an hour of the day when it wasn't. Prob'ly not. Just like crime didn't take nights or weekends off, neither did the news.

I went over to the receptionist. "Afternoon, Myrtle. What's shakin'?"

"Hi, Betty." She held up a finger and answered the phone in a brisk voice. "Thank you for calling the *Courier-Express*. How may I direct your call? One moment, please." She put the call through the switchboard and focused on me. "You here to see Melvin?"

"Who else?" Melvin Schlingman, one of the *Courier's* busiest news reporters, was a friend of mine. We'd met on the same case that had brought Frank into my world. At the time, Melvin'd worked for a local tabloid rag, and my opinion of him started pretty low. But over time, he'd cleaned up his act, personally and professionally. Now he was one of my best sources. Him and Sam. "Is he here?"

"He's in the newsroom. You know the way, right?" She laid her hand on the phone, which had rung again.

"It's jake. Catch you later." I tapped her desk, and she gave me a wink before answering the new call.

I climbed the stairs to the third-floor newsroom where all the reporters made their home. The overwhelming noise of fifty typewriters filled the air. The first couple of times I'd come, I couldn't take two steps without some man wondering who let the unknown broad in. Now they all knew me, even the errand boys.

A man wearing a white shirt rolled up at the sleeves, a lit cigarette dangling from his mouth, leaned back in his chair and hooked his thumbs behind his suspenders. "If it isn't the girl detective. When are you gonna ditch the string-bean and come hang out with me, honey?"

"Just as soon as your wife says it's okay, Larry." I stopped at his desk. "It goes like this. Irene and I are friends." Irene, a nurse at Our Lady of Victory Hospital, was Melvin's girlfriend. I credited her with half of Melvin's turnaround. She gave me props for the other half. We got along swell. "She knows when Melvin spends time with me, he's workin' and not steppin' out on her. I'm not sure your wife would feel the same way."

He sat forward and ashed his smoke in a metal dish already overflowing with butts. "You got a point. He's in the corner."

"Thanks." I threaded my way through the desks until I spotted Melvin. He'd put on a few pounds, but he was still rail thin despite the fact that I'd never seen him eat anything less than three helpings at a meal. Like his colleagues, his shirt was rolled at the sleeves, his tie loose. A pencil was tucked behind his ear, another in his fingers as he read a sheet of copy. A second page, half-filled with type, was in the newish-looking machine next to him. "Melvin."

He didn't move.

I waved my hand directly in front of his face. "Hello?"

He looked and blinked. Then a grin spread over his face. "Heya, Toots. Sorry I didn't notice you. Trying to get this story written. Pull up a chair."

I looked around. "From where?"

"Anywhere as long as someone's keister isn't in it." He took a drink from a cup of coffee that had to be cold, given the lack of steam. "Ugh, let another one go to waste. What brings you here?"

I pulled over a wooden chair and pointed at the typewriter. "That looks new."

"You like it? It's one of those newfangled Remingtons. Supposed to be noiseless. Not that I can tell since there's always such a racket in here." He put aside the cup. "A little birdie told me you finally have an honest-to-Pete office."

"Don't know why you'd be keepin' track of that, but yes. I signed the lease this morning."

"I like seeing my friends go up in the world."

I rolled my eyes. "You like knowin' where to find me in case I'm workin' on an investigation that could turn into a juicy scoop."

"That too." He twirled the pencil in his fingers. "Enough chit-chat. What's cooking?"

"Maybe I'm stopping by to say hello. Could be I'm the one looking for leads on any new situations I could make some dough on." I crossed my legs at the ankle. The room was full of men, but that didn't give me leave not to be ladylike.

"I don't think you need me to feed you work. Not if you can afford rent." He tossed the pencil on his desk. "Time is money, Toots. Talk."

I needed to up my banter game with him. "I'm lookin' for your help."

His eyes sparkled, and he sat forward. His nose practically twitched with excitement. "What's in it for me?"

"For cryin' out loud." I threw my hands up in an exaggerated gesture. "Just once, can you give me a hand without angling for a story? Just who is feeding work to who, here? I can't be your only source of leads."

He grinned. "You gotta admit, Toots. You've given me some good ones."

I had. A couple of murders, wartime espionage, and a long-lost woman tied to a society family. It was a pretty good record. Irene was right: I'd done a lot for Melvin's career. "Right now, I don't have anything like that. I'm lookin' into a boy for his sister. I don't have any hard facts on anything newsworthy. You really would be helpin' me out of the kindness of your heart."

"But you'll tell me if you get one, right?"

I held up my hands in surrender. "I'll call you first. But are you sure you don't want to hear what it is before you jump on the wagon?"

He tilted his head. "Fair enough. Shoot."

"My client and her brother live over in the Fruit Belt. I managed to talk to one person this morning." I spread my hands. "The rest of the neighborhood didn't exactly welcome me with open arms."

Melvin's expression sobered. "No, I don't suppose they would. What are you searching for?"

"Without goin' into details, my client is worried her brother is gettin' corrupted."

"By who?"

"That's just it. I don't know. My source from this morning said he's heard rumors about a gang. Well, a group of criminals. I don't know what else to call 'em, but I doubt it's like the Italian Mafia gangs." I withdrew my notebook. "He also mentioned some hoodlums that run around the neighborhood, but you prob'ly don't have much on a bunch of teenagers."

"Not unless those teenagers are into shenanigans way beyond their tender years." Melvin held up a finger. "Also, may I offer a clarification? It might not look like the Mafia *yet*. Give them time."

I acknowledged his point. "My source mentioned gambling and fighting. I'm here to ask if you or your buddies have written any stories that would put names to those activities."

Melvin raised his eyebrows. "You haven't asked your cop buddy, Detective Sam?"

"I talked to my source after I saw Sam this morning." I scanned my notes. "Be flattered. You're my first stop."

"Oh, I am." He tapped his thumbs together. "I haven't written anything but hold on." He put his fingers to his lips and whistled. "Roger! Over here."

A heavyset older man with thinning black hair lumbered over. He smelled like fried bologna and onions. "Yeah?"

"Roger, meet my friend Betty."

Roger held out a beefy hand.

Melvin continued. "She's looking for news about any criminal activity over in the Fruit Belt."

"Specifically, the area between Main and Jefferson," I added. "Maybe a little east of Jefferson, but not by much."

Joe's massive shoulders moved up and down. "Why should I talk to some broad? I know she's a detective, but who's to say she won't run to my sources and rat me out?"

I'd expected this. I didn't know why Melvin had bothered calling over his buddy. I opened my mouth to say so.

Melvin cut me off. "Betty's jake. She's not gonna ruin your network. I'll vouch for her. All she wants is a direction."

Roger gave me a sly look. "And what do I get?"

"Reporters. You're all the same." I blew out my breath. "Same as Melvin. This turns into a story, I'll call the newsroom. You two can fight about who gets the byline." I flipped to a clean page and licked my pencil. "You got names, or am I whistlin' Dixie here? As Melvin is so fond of saying, time is dough."

The two men exchanged a look. "The Negroes ain't as organized as the Italians, or the Sicilians, or whatever they call themselves," Roger said. "Not even as much as the Irish. But when any group gets together, you get at least one less-than-savory element. Most of the time, a couple battle it out for who gets to be cock-of-the walk. That's kinda what's happening now over in that neighborhood."

This was more like it. "Names?" I asked.

Roger ran a hand over his head. "Two guys. Alonzo Coates and Moses Gainey. I hang out at the cop shop a lot, and those are the names that come up most often."

"What for?" I jotted down the names.

"A few hold-ups, nothing major. No banks. But the cops are starting to get wind of a protection racket, hitting local businesses up for dough. In one report, a store owner had gotten hit up by both of them."

"I don't s'pose you got a name for the businessman."

Roger tugged his ear. "Common name. Jones, Smith, something along those lines."

How many of those could there be in that neighborhood? Here I'd thought Mr. Jones and I had gotten along so well. "Anything else?"

"Gainey has been connected to a bare-knuckle fight ring. Lots of gambling done at those. Fighters don't got to be colored. They take all kinds." Roger spread his hands.

It was a good start. "One more question. Your stories ever mention anybody named Stevie Washington?"

Roger frowned. "Like the president? No, that's a name I'd remember."

Melvin had strung some paperclips together in a chain while he listened. He set down his creation. "Thanks, Rog." He faced me. "That enough?"

"Enough for a start." I put my notepad and pencil back in my purse. "Thanks very much, gentlemen." I stood.

Roger aimed a finger at me. "Remember."

I raised my hand in a half-hearted gesture. "Yeah, yeah. You get the scoop."

Chapter Eight

Melvin talked me into lunch. It was even on his dime. We spent an hour or so talkin' about city politics. Now that I had digs downtown, Melvin thought I needed to know a lot more about City Hall and its devious antics. After he was done, I half-wished I'd gotten an office in the Southtowns or at least the First Ward. Sure, City Hall policy affected us there, but it felt more removed. I s'posed Buffalo was better than Tammany Hall, but that wasn't saying much. A shyster was a shyster, no matter where he lived.

I left Melvin around quarter to three and hot-footed it over to Central Terminal. I passed the stuffed buffalo, the one people touched for luck before their journey, 'specially guys heading overseas. Both Tom and Sean had done it. How much had it brought Tom?

He was coming home alive. Not in a box. That had to be worth somethin'.

I checked the arrival board and went to the platform where Tom's train was expected. There were a ton of people milling around, but no train. I spotted Lee's head, wearing his trademark squashy cap. I weaved my way through the crowd to join him.

He and Mrs. Flannery were standing off to the side. Lee flicked away the spent end of his Chesterfield when he saw me. "You're right on time. Tom's train should be pullin' in any minute now."

I reached out to touch Mrs. Flannery's shoulder. "How you holdin' up, ma'am? You look a little peaky."

She gave a wan smile. "My boy is coming home, Betty. He's not in one piece. Or he's missing a piece is a better way of saying it. But he's alive. I'm better off than other mothers or wives in that regard. I can't completely believe it until I see him. Then I'll be overjoyed, no matter what."

"I'm sure he'll be happy to see you, too."

She twisted the handkerchief in her hands. "I hope he's okay in his mind. So many men who came home from the Great War were angry. Not that they were home, mind you. But some were never the same, even if they hadn't been wounded. I saw it with Mr. Flannery's friends." She bit her lip.

"Don't borrow trouble. That's what Mom would say." I hugged her. "We gotta take what comes and make the best of it."

A train whistle split the air.

Lee pointed. "Here it comes."

Brakes shrieked as the three-fifteen from New York rumbled to a stop next to the platform. The doors opened, and conductors leapt out to put stairs in place. Passengers disembarked. Older men, those past draft age. Women, some with children, some alone. But no young men in uniform. Where was Tom?

Then I spotted him. I could see his head, topped by the narrow hat worn by the enlisted men, same as Private Lake had worn. His khaki uniform peeked out from under his greatcoat. The conductor held out a hand as he maneuvered his crutches out of the carriage.

Mrs. Flannery cried out and waved her hankie. "Tom! Over here."

He looked over through the thinning horde of passengers.

My breath caught in my throat. Even from a distance, I could see the sallowness of his skin. The clothes hung loosely on him. His face had the pinched look of someone who had recently recovered from a long illness. Gone were the cheeks flushed with health, the body that radiated strength and vitality. What had happened to him?

Don't be a ninny. He might not have been sick, not in the traditional sense, but how did I think he'd look after weeks in the hospital?

The people moved aside, and I was able to see him from head to toe. He gripped the crutches tight, his gaze darting around to make sure no one would bump into him. His right leg was straight, foot planted in a dark black Army-issue shoe.

The left one ended just below the knee. The empty fabric of his khaki pants was pinned up behind his thigh to keep it from trailing on the ground.

The crowd watched as he moved toward us, and most of 'em stepped outta his way. Those who didn't got pulled aside by others. The men doffed their hats. Some of the women turned away, as if embarrassed by the sight. Tom didn't react. It was as if he didn't see any of it. Or he didn't want to acknowledge it.

I couldn't hold back the sob or the small gasp that escaped from my lips. I'd spent weeks wonderin' if I still loved Tom enough to marry him. In that moment, it didn't matter. Even in the low light of the station, the dark, haunted look in his eyes was obvious. Tom Flannery might be back. But the boy I'd sent off to war had not come home.

Lee musta heard me, 'cause he squeezed my elbow. "Steady. Don't go to pieces on him."

"I won't." I didn't look at Lee, but I was sure he would know how grateful I was for his presence.

Mrs. Flannery pushed through the crowd, Lee in her wake. I stayed a few steps behind 'em. I wanted to give his mother the opportunity to greet her boy. Not only that, I hadn't figured out exactly what I was gonna say.

Tom stumped over and met us in an empty space the other people on the platform made. A redcap trailed behind him with a trunk. "Mom." He let her kiss his cheek. "Lee. You didn't have to come. What about work?"

"Did you honestly think I'd let my best pal come home from the war and not be here to greet him?" Lee tugged his cap. "That all your luggage?"

It seemed I'd have to be the first to speak. "Hi, Tom."

He stared, eyes dead. "Betty. Good of you to take the time." He didn't attempt a kiss or lean in for one.

The words stung. Take the time? I knew he wasn't thrilled with my new career. Did he honestly think I'd stay away? "You look…well."

"You don't need to patronize me, Betty. I'm a wreck and I know it." He resettled the crutches under his arms. "I'll be fine, though. You don't need to worry."

It didn't take Sam Spade to see Tom's pain, right under the surface, raw like freshly burned skin. "I wasn't patronizing you. I'm sure you need a few home-cooked meals. I think any soldier who'd been living on field rations would jump at that. But we're all here for you. You'll be good in no time."

He looked away.

Lee covered the awkward silence by moving to the trunk. "I'll ask again. This all you got? I borrowed a car from a guy at work. I can drive you, your mom, and Betty back to the First Ward, then head off to GM."

"I don't need your pity either, Lee." Tom's voice sounded harsh. "You must feel pretty good. You may limp, but at least you got both your legs."

Lee's face reddened. "That's not fair. I never thought that. Not once."

Tom ignored the protest. "The redcap can carry the trunk. We'll take a taxi." He crutched off. "Come on, Mom. I'll need your help to get in the car."

Mrs. Flannery found her voice. "Oh, Betty. Lee. I'm so sorry. You must forgive him. He'll get over it. He needs time. Come with us. I'll talk to him. Lee, you went through all the trouble of borrowing a vehicle, and now this." She gave a limp wave in Tom's direction.

"No, Mrs. Flannery. It's jake. Go on. I'll drive Betty home." Lee hugged her. "I think it best we leave you two alone, at least for tonight."

She kissed Lee's cheek, then mine. She hurried after her son, who was still moving, not even sparing his best friend and his fiancée a backward glance.

I gripped Lee's hand and we exchanged a mute look. It sure wasn't the homecoming either of us expected.

\#

I stared out of the front window while Lee drove his friend's car to the First Ward. I toyed with the idea of having him drive me over to Frank's neighborhood, but decided runnin' to see another Joe when my guy cut me off wasn't the best thing to do. After all, Tom and I were still engaged. "Were you expectin' that?"

Lee sighed and flicked ash off his cigarette out of his window. "I'd hoped for a better scene, but yeah, I knew it might happen the way it did."

I twisted in my seat. "Why?"

"A couple of guys at work, includin' the one who owns this car, warned me." Lee took a drag and blew out the smoke.

"But why would he be mad at us?"

"Don't know." He threw away the butt end of his smoke. "Don't beat yourself up, Betty. He'll come around."

"Maybe."

He dipped his head. "Hopefully."

I hesitated for a moment before continuing. "Do you think I should go over there?"

"When you get home?" Lee stopped at a light. "No. Let him be."

"I don't understand it." I crossed my arms over my chest. "You've limped for ages, and it doesn't make you mad. It's not like we're gonna ditch him or anything."

"But those who don't know him might think differently. You saw the looks at the station."

I flipped my hand. "When did he start carin' about what total strangers think? Do you?"

"Not anymore. For a while, yeah." He paused. "I was too young to be mad when my leg got messed up. I almost don't remember *not* having a limp. But if you don't believe having that recruiter tell me I wasn't fit for service didn't hurt, you aren't as smart as I thought." He shot me a look. "Thing is, I could still go out and do stuff. I know my work at GM is important to our boys, and that helps. With Tom, it's different."

"I s'pose." I nibbled a thumbnail. "You can get him a job, though, can't you?"

"Prob'ly, if he gets a prosthetic leg, and I'm sure he will. But he's gotta be able to stand for eight hours unassisted 'cause he needs to use his hands." We stopped to let a woman with little kids cross the street. They gawked at the car. "He can't do that on crutches," Lee added and pulled forward.

I hadn't thought of that, and I should have. "Do you think his dad will help him out?"

Lee's laughter had a cynical overtone. "Mr. Flannery? Are you nuts? I know it's been a while since you talked to him, but don't you remember how he is?"

I did. Mr. Flannery was a good man. He went to church and provided for his family. He didn't drink to excess, and he didn't beat his wife or children. He didn't chase other women. But he wasn't what you'd call a warm person. He believed life was tough and any adversity had to be met with a stiff upper lip. Tom wouldn't find a lot of sympathy, 'specially if his dad thought he was feeling sorry for himself.

Lee made the turn off Louisiana onto Mackinaw. "I know who could help him." He gave me a pointed look.

"Who? You said I should stay away."

"Your pop." He pulled to a stop in front of my house. "He's got a way of seein' people through things. Of makin' them understand they're stronger than they think without puttin' 'em down. He did it for me after what happened with my dad."

Lee had found himself head of the family after his dad, who'd become an alcoholic, died this past spring. I'd kept Lee from bein' convicted for murder. Pop helped him settle into his new role. "I'll talk to him. He may not wanna get involved yet."

"I trust him. And you." Lee chucked me on the shoulder. "You got something to keep you busy in the meantime?"

"Between movin' into my office and my new case, yeah. I won't be sittin' on my hands, that's for sure." I grabbed the door handle. "Say, you know anyone at GM who lives over in the Fruit Belt? That's where my client is from."

"There aren't a lot of Negroes at GM. A few. I don't know 'em that well, though."

"Any chance you can strike up a conversation and get a little dirt? I need to know who the troublemakers are. 'Specially if they've heard of Stevie Washington, Alonzo Coates, or Moses Gainey."

He took off his cap and scratched his head. "I dunno. I'll see, but it might be awkward. I assume you don't want me to sound like I'm interrogating them."

"No. Only talk to 'em if you can do it and sound natural."

He settled his cap. "I'll try."

I leaned over and kissed his cheek. "You're the best, Lee. Dot's a lucky girl."

He grinned. "She is, isn't she?" The expression faded. "So are you, Betty. It'll work out."

I slipped out of the truck and waved as Lee drove off. Ever the optimist, that was Lee. But I knew in my gut it wouldn't be that easy.

Chapter Nine

I could tell Mom wanted to know what had happened at Central Terminal. She dropped it pretty quick when I made it clear I wasn't gonna talk about it, but was still as curious as Cat when he was checkin' out the garbage.

I shut myself up in my room. To divert my mind, I focused on work. First, I made a list of all the things I needed to scrounge or buy for the office. Two desks, at least four chairs, a filing cabinet, a percolator, and office supplies. I had to set up telephone service. The cabinet and furniture would be the toughest things to find. But necessary. Emmeline and I couldn't meet with clients while we were sittin' on the floor. I decided to search the Salvation Army, church sales, and second-hand shops for the bigger items.

I turned my thoughts to Nancy Washington and her brother. It was a familiar story, one I'd seen in the First Ward. Boys too young to serve, bored with school, and too smart to be left on their own. Nine times outta ten, they got in a jam. You had to give boys that age a purpose, something to do. Could be school, could be work. But something. Otherwise, trouble was sure to pop up.

After talkin' to Nancy and Mr. Jones, that sounded exactly like what had happened with Stevie. Speaking of Mr. Jones, I needed to go back and talk to him again. He hadn't mentioned anything about Coates or Gainey. Had he been covering for Stevie? Did he know more than he'd told me? It was a good bet.

That brought me to Stevie. It'd be hard to follow him around. I'd put out feelers with Lee and Melvin. Sam wouldn't have come into contact with

Coates or Gainey, but he might know people in other departments who did. I made a note to go back to him.

I didn't like relying so much on other people, though. Could I engineer a meeting with Stevie? Maybe, but not in his neighborhood. It had to seem accidental, and I didn't think I could pull it off over there. But maybe I could locate either Coates or Gainey, follow one of *them*, and hope they'd lead me to Stevie. Preferably outside the Fruit Belt, where I would stand a better chance of blending in. Melvin's co-worker, Roger, had mentioned the bare-knuckle fights. If I knew the location, I could stake that out. "It might work." I tapped the pencil on my notes.

Mary Kate's voice came from behind me. "What might work?"

I hadn't heard her come in. "Nothing. Something for a case. Can I help you?"

"Pop just got home. Mom sent me to say to wash up for supper." She peered over my shoulder. "What are you tryin' to do?"

I fought back a sigh. At sixteen, Mary Kate was at the age where she thought she could butt in on anything. Sometimes, it was easier to humor her. "I need to meet this guy. But he's a colored boy. I can't hang out in his neighborhood and cross my fingers."

"Because they'd spot you for sure. Maybe even bully you out." She nodded. "Well, he's gotta leave his street sometimes, right? We've gotta go out of the First Ward to buy things and stuff. Michael and Jimmy leave Mackinaw to go to church or play with friends. Find out where and see him when he's there."

She made it sound so easy. Then again, maybe it was. "Thanks. You're a peach."

She tried to look modest and failed. "Glad to help. Now come to the kitchen before Mom loses her temper."

After we ate, Mary Kate and I did the dishes. Then I went to the living room, where I found Pop sittin' in his favorite chair, pipe and paper in hand, radio tuned to the evening news program. Mom was on the couch with some mending. I sat at his feet. "Pop, can I ask you something?"

He let the top half of the paper drop. "Of course." Blue smoke trailed from his pipe, leaving a warm, sweet smell in the air.

I'd always found that comforting. "I have a challenge with my latest case." I outlined the problem. "Mary Kate suggested meeting him somewhere else. But where?"

He puffed. "You're right about being alone in the neighborhood. Not just for safety, but you'd be conspicuous, and I don't believe that's a good thing for a private detective."

"No."

"What if you're with his sister? You'll still stick out, but being with her would give you a reason to be there."

I ran my hand over the rug. "But wouldn't that maybe get her in trouble? Fact is, the two groups don't mix a lot. Whites and coloreds, I mean."

He pointed his pipe stem at me. "People are people, Betty. Haven't I told you that before? Seems to me you had a case not that long ago that was about this exact thing."

He was talkin' about Edward Kettle. "Gosh, Pop. It's not like that at all. Nancy seems like a swell girl. It's nothing against her or her people. I don't wanna put her in danger if her brother is mixin' with the wrong sort." I watched him settle back into his chair. "Do you have colored friends at the steel plant?"

He worked his pipe to make sure it was still lit. "There are a few. I would call them work friends. Not close enough to invite to the house, but we get along. One or two have joined us at the bar near the plant for a beer when the shift whistle blew." He blew out a smoke ring. "Can you get in touch with this girl?"

"She gave me a phone number and said it was communal, so I can try."

"I'd do that. She may know more than she realizes." His piercing gaze was shrewd. "But that's not what's really bothering you, is it? Given time, you'd have come up with this solution on your own. Tell me, my darlin' girl."

That was Pop. He knew me better than I knew myself. "It's Tom." I told him all about the disastrous reunion at Central Station. "Pop, he's so angry and bitter. Lee thinks you'd get through to him."

"Ah." He smoked for a long moment, silent as he stared into space. "I wouldn't want to trespass on Mr. Flannery's rights."

"You won't be. Lee and I, we don't think Mr. Flannery is the type to be real sympathetic, if you know what I mean."

Mom clucked her tongue but said nothing.

Pop knew the man, so he surely caught my drift. "I'll try. I can't promise anything."

I knelt and hugged him. "Understood. You're the best. I love you, Pop. I'm very lucky to be your daughter."

He patted my back. "And I'm lucky to be your father." He pulled back. "This will be painful, Betty. You might lose him."

I couldn't bring myself to say that I was afraid I already had—and that I wasn't certain if that should be a relief or not.

Chapter Ten

The next morning, I called Nancy at the phone number she'd left with me. A woman answered, but didn't question when I asked for the girl.

"A place to meet?" Nancy asked with a note of confusion.

"Somewhere we can sit and talk without drawing too much attention." I pictured her expression, a bit surprised, perhaps even hesitant. "I want to be able to observe people."

"Like Stevie."

"Yes, and others."

There was a long pause. "There is a soda shop down on Main Street, near the corner of East North. White folks go there, but coloreds, too. We wouldn't stand out too much if we ordered a milkshake and sat for a while. Just two girls talking."

It was perfect. I got her to agree to meet me around noon by telling her I'd buy the shakes and lunch.

Next, I borrowed Pop's measuring tape, the good metal one that was six feet long. There was no sense getting furniture unless I was sure it would fit through the doors and in the space. But before I went to the office, I stopped at the Flannery house.

"He isn't here, Betty," Mrs. Flannery said when she opened the door.

I double-checked my watch. It was barely nine. "When did he leave?"

"Almost two hours ago." She wrung her hands. "I tried to get him to take it easy. It's his first day home. He's not strong, despite what he says. But he insisted."

That sounded like Tom. "Where'd he go?"

"Looking for work. That's all he'd say." She sighed. "I think he's going to be disappointed, but Mr. Flannery told me to let him go. It's part of getting back to normal, he said."

I thought of Lee's words from yesterday. Tom was like Lee and me. He didn't have office skills. He knew how to labor, to fix things. Working on a tank wouldn't teach him how to do bookkeeping. With his injury, that was all that would be available for him until he could stand without crutches. But I didn't say any of this. I didn't need to add to Mrs. Flannery's worry. She had plenty of her own. "It'll be okay. I'll stop by later this evening."

She murmured a goodbye, and I left.

* * *

When I arrived at the office, a man was already there, painting my name on the window as stated in the lease. He'd outlined the words in a simple, bold black lettering. Ahern & Associates, Private Detective. Pride surged in my chest, thoughts of Tom shoved to the back of my mind. This was a day I'd dreamed of when I decided to get my license. My own place. Sure, I only had the one associate right now, but I'd grow.

The painter paused while I unlocked the door and ducked inside. Once there, I set my purse on the floor and began measuring, jotting numbers on a sheet of paper as I went.

I'd finished the reception area and moved to the main office when I heard a man's cough behind me. I looked over my shoulder. "Sam, how'd you know I'd be here?"

"I didn't." He pushed his fedora back on his head. "I stopped at Teddy's. Judy said you hadn't been in for breakfast. I figured you'd either be here or walking the beat. This isn't too much out of my way, so I took the gamble."

I leaned back on my heels. "Do you like it?"

"Hard to say since it's just two empty rooms." He put his hands in his pockets and strolled around. "This where you're going to meet clients?"

"Yep. I plan to have a desk and chair for me, plus a couple of chairs for clients. File cabinet against the wall. I don't know what else I'll need." I pushed my hair back.

"To start, that'll cover it." He nodded. "How big for the desk?"

I looked at my notes. "I don't want it more than forty-eight inches long, and it can't be more than twenty or so inches wide. Any bigger and it won't get through the door."

He pursed his lips. "I have an old desk of my father's in storage. It'll be about right. Got a chair, too. I'll figure out how to get it to you."

"How much?"

"You can have it."

My cheeks warmed. "Gosh, Sam. You don't have to do that. I got a little dough."

He waved his hand. "You'll be doing me a favor taking it off my hands. It doesn't fit in my house, and I don't want it."

"Geez, Louise. First, you pay for my correspondence course, now you're giving me furniture."

"Lucky you met me, huh?" He took out a notepad of his own. "Speaking of help, you asked about Stevie Washington. Want the skinny?"

I got to my feet. "Yes. Let me get my notebook." I paged to a clean sheet. "Go ahead."

"Stevie doesn't have a record, not even a juvenile one. I called his school. What your new friend told you is true. They said up until last year, Stevie was a model student. He had top grades, never missed a day, and his teachers said he stayed out of trouble."

"What happened?"

"Over the school year, his grades slipped in all his classes. He would be absent for days at a time. He was unengaged, or worse, unruly in class. The principal said it was like night and day. At the beginning of this year, he didn't return. When they called his mother, she had no explanation. She thought he was going to school every day." He looked up.

I mused on that. "Then he was lyin' to his mother, too. Nancy knew he was up to no good."

Sam consulted his notes again. "What he does have are some sketchy friends. Moses Gainey, in particular."

It was one of Melvin's names. "I've heard of him. What's he done?"

"Quite a bit for a man who's only been in Buffalo for two years." Sam ticked the crimes off on his fingers. "Racketeering, extortion, assault, and he runs a backstreet bare-knuckle fight ring over off Best. I'm sure plenty of illicit activity goes on, but the fighting itself is not illegal so we can't do anything."

"How does a teenager fit into that?"

"Every crime leader needs an errand boy. Someone who can be trusted to transport money and messages." Sam put his book into the breast pocket of his coat. "My guess is this Stevie is a runner. It's entirely possible that Gainey is grooming him for a bigger role, but you're right. At sixteen, he's not going to be visiting people and busting kneecaps."

I wrote all this down. "But you said Stevie hasn't been arrested."

"No. Word from my friend in Vice is that Stevie has been seen in Gainey's company at least three times. My buddy described it as an employer-employee relationship, so unlikely that Stevie is a mark. Once is a coincidence. Three times is a pattern." Sam sat on the radiator.

I'd have to ask Nancy about it later. "What about a man named Alonzo Coates? You heard of him?"

Sam whistled. "Where'd you get that name?"

"Melvin Schlingman at the *Courier.*"

"Coates is a little bigger fish." Sam took off his fedora and spun it on his finger. "Same crimes as Gainey, minus the bare-knuckle. But Coates might also be linked to at least one and possibly two murders. Both victims were Negroes. They definitely knew Coates. We're having trouble with the exact connection. If your boy Stevie is working for Coates, his sister has a right to be worried."

I tapped my pencil against my lips. "How much cabbage are we talkin' about? For the brawls, I mean."

Sam's shoulders went up and down. "A bare-knuckle fight can bring down a couple hundred in betting. One or two of those a night, every Friday and Saturday, I think we could easily be talking a thousand bucks. Add in everything else and you could be in the neighborhood of five large a month. I think the Mafia is bigger fish, but it's a respectable amount for what is essentially a start-up business."

Plenty to turn a young kid's head. "I think I know the answer, but what would Coates or Gainey do if they found Stevie skimming?"

Sam's expression said it all. "It wouldn't be good for the young man's health."

Right. "Thanks, Sam. I owe you. For the dope and the furniture."

He tugged on his fedora. "I'll measure that desk and deliver it. Might take me a couple of days, but a friend of mine is a mechanic and he has a truck." He paused, as though he wanted to say something but was afraid to do so.

"What is it?"

He took a breath. "How was the reunion with Tom? Did you two talk?"

"Barely." I dropped my notebook into my purse and gave Sam the rundown. "I stopped at his house this morning, before I came here. I think Lee's right, and Tom's not gonna have a lot of luck today. I'm afraid of what that'll do to him."

Sam rubbed his chin. "What's his temper like? I mean, is he stubborn, rash, or patient? At least before he went off to war."

"He's Irish." I said it like it would explain everything. "He's proud, too. I've never seen him back down from a fight. Having doors slammed in his face isn't gonna help him."

Sam came over and put his hands on my shoulders. "I hope you understand this is a situation Tom has to figure out for himself. You can be there for him, but if he chooses to push you away, you'll only make it worse if you fight him." He took away his hands. "I'll call your house about that desk."

I watched the door shut behind him and stared at the backside of the frosted glass for a long time after. Sam was right. I'd focus on what I could do, and that was work Nancy's case. Whatever was gonna happen with Tom, I could deal with it later.

Chapter Eleven

From the office, I went to the main branch of the Buffalo Public Library to talk to Emmeline. I found her at her usual post in the stacks, where they kept all the back issues of newspapers and magazines.

"It's all set with my boss here. She said that since it's my first day, I can leave a little early. I'm going to go shopping for office supplies after I leave, and then I'll head to the office," she said, a pile of newspapers in her hand.

"We can wait on the stationery. I got something more important for you to do."

She set down the newsprint and picked up a pad. "What is it?"

"Search back issues of the *Courier* and *The Buffalo Evening News* for mention of Alonzo Coates and Moses Gainey. You might find them in the police beat. Also look for who they were with. We're interested in a boy named Stevie Washington." I briefed her on the new case. "I'm meetin' his sister for lunch."

She finished writing with a flourish. "What then?"

"Write up your usual report for me." I thought of something. "Also, call the phone company and ask when they can set up a line. I was gonna do that this morning and got sidetracked."

"Got it." She made another note. "Is there a desk for the phone?"

"Sam stopped and offered me his dad's, but I'm still lookin' for yours. You stumble across one, let me know. You're familiar with the budget." Worst case, the phone could go in my office, but that wasn't really my first choice.

"Look for the desk." She set down her pad. "Is this Stevie person tangled up in fishy business?"

"Possibly. That's what his sister is worried about. I'm meeting her so I can do a little reconnaissance and see if I can identify any other Joes he's hanging out with."

"I can go with you."

I pushed off the desk. "Not this time. It's nothing to do with your abilities. I need help blendin' in." I told her about the challenge. "Two white girls would be worse than one."

"I understand. I'll do some work here and then go to the office. There might not be any furniture, but it's the perfect time to give the place a good scrub." She tapped her chin with her pencil. "My sister is giving me her old Underwood. She says it gives her an excuse to buy a new one."

"You can type?"

"I'm not fast, but I get the job done." She leaned on her elbows. "Are Coates and Gainey the only suspects?"

"Right now, yes. I might learn more at lunch." I looked at the clock. "Speaking of which, I better get goin.'"

* * *

The soda shop where I'd arranged to meet Nancy was on Main, right on the edge of her neighborhood. As soon as I got off the bus, I could tell why she'd picked it. The people on the street were a mix of white and colored. Neither of us would stand out.

She was sitting at the counter when I walked in. Booths ringed the walls, with red-covered benches and chrome edging on the tables. But most people seemed to prefer to grab a stool. A jukebox played "That Old Black Magic" by Glenn Miller. A boy who looked to be about Mary Kate's age wiped the tables and cleared the dirty dishes. It was a nice neighborhood joint, the kind that welcomed people to sit a spell and enjoy themselves.

Nancy moved her purse off the stool next to her. "I saved you a seat."

"Thanks." I studied the layout. "Let's grab one of those booths in the back."

"What's wrong with right here?"

"We don't want to be conspicuous. The booth lets us be out of the way and still see everything that happens." I walked off and picked a seat.

"Oh." She followed me and slid onto the bench across from me.

I gave the place one last check and grabbed a menu. "Order whatever you want."

"Are you sure?" She sounded hesitant, as though she didn't quite believe me.

"Yes. I told you, we want to blend in. If we don't eat, people will notice." I studied the offerings. It was standard soda shop fare.

An older, colored woman came to take our order. "Nancy, honey. Been a long time. Who's your friend?"

"This is Betty. She's helping me with—"

"Math." I broke in before Nancy could spill the beans. "I graduated last year. Nancy's worried about passing algebra."

The woman patted Nancy on the shoulder. "That's right, honey. You study hard. Your mama will be so proud. Maybe you can get into that university in Washington, the one for colored folks."

Nancy blushed. "Oh, I don't think I can get into Howard."

"Why not?" The woman waggled her pencil. "Education is the way to get ahead. You don't want to be me, do you? Fifty-three and still on my feet ten hours a day 'cause I don't got no skills. I bet this young lady agrees, don't you?" She fixed me with a hard stare out of a sparkling dark eye. It reminded me of a bird sizing up a particularly fat worm.

"Yes, ma'am." I didn't dare say anything else. "I can't afford college myself, not with all my brothers and sisters to take care of, but I think Nancy here could get a scholarship."

The woman looked triumphant. "See? Don't you be goin' down the same road as your brother, girl. Now. What y'all want?"

I ordered a strawberry milkshake and an egg sandwich. Nancy opted for grilled cheese and a vanilla malt. "Say, ma'am." I wiggled my menu back into the holder. "What do you mean about Stevie? Nancy told me he's a bright boy. Why couldn't he go to Howard?" I'd never heard of the school, but obviously it meant a lot to this woman.

Her expression darkened. "He is, but I don't think much of his new friends. Bunch of hooligans, you mark my words. They dropped outta school. All they do is run around, taking money from little kids, terrorizing old folks, and stealing from the five and dime. I saw Georgie Vickers with a bottle of corn liquor and a pistol the other day. He was in the back alley, drinking and shooting empty cans. Stevie don't need that kind of influence in his life."

Georgie sounded like another boy. "Have you ever seen Stevie with men named Moses Gainey or Alonzo Coates?"

Her expression became guarded. "How does a white girl like you know about them?"

Oh shoot. "Nancy mentioned the names when we talked earlier. I got the impression they aren't very nice. Forget it. I've always been told I'm too curious for my own good. But I have brothers. They get into a lot of hijinks, but no real trouble. People keep sayin' how smart Stevie is and how he used to be real helpful. He must've gotten in with some bad types to make that change."

"Lord willing, he ain't that far gone." My answer seemed to satisfy her because she said, "I ain't never seen Stevie with them. I know who they are, and they're bad news. Stevie got enough problems being friends with Georgie. Sweet Jesus, I hope I never see him with the likes of those men. I'll be right back with your sandwiches." She ambled off.

I faced Nancy. "Who is Georgie Vickers?"

"He's an older boy, even older than me. Dixie is right. He dropped out of school. He more or less runs the street gang around here." She held up a hand. "Gang isn't really a good word. Like Dixie said, they're hoodlums. Bullies. They like taking money from little kids, lifting fruit from Mr. Jones's outdoor displays, stupid stuff. I'd call them troublemakers, not hardened criminals."

Yet Georgie had a pistol, according to Dixie. "Is Stevie friends with him? Georgie?"

"Depends on how you define friends." Our milkshakes arrived and Nancy sucked on her straw. "He idolizes Georgie the way younger boys look up to the older ones. But they aren't pals or anything. Georgie lets Stevie tag along because it makes him feel important, but that's it."

The bells over the door jingled. Four young colored men entered the shop. I recognized three of 'em from my encounter yesterday outside Mr. Jones's store. I nudged Nancy with my foot and tipped my head toward the group.

She took a quick look and went back to staring at her shake as though it had the answer to the meaning of life. "The one in the front, that's Georgie. The short one in the back is Stevie."

I leaned my cheek on my right hand so I could study the newcomers. Stevie was my height, five-eight or so. He was skinny as a rail, like a kid who'd recently grown. His pants were a little short in the leg, which made me think I was right. He wore a T-shirt and jacket, like the other boys, but he looked a little like a scarecrow. He'd grown in height, but he still had a ways to go to fill out. His skin was a couple of shades darker than his sister's, but his curly dark hair and dark eyes looked exactly like hers.

I shifted my attention to Georgie. He was the one I'd talked to when I came yesterday. I could immediately see why he was the leader and Stevie's role model. He reminded me of Charlie O'Donnell from the First Ward. Both boys gave off an air of being hip and in charge. Georgie couldn't do the Cary Grant-style side part with his tightly curled hair, but he'd opted for the crew cut that was so popular with the military. I thought again about what Georgie had said, that the draft board didn't want him. Why not? I'd have to ask Lee or Pop. All the boys wore white T-shirts and blue jeans with saddle shoes in various stages of wear. Georgie's clothes were the newest. The rest of his gang obviously took their cues from him.

"Shakes and burgers for my boys," Georgie said in a brash voice.

The boy at the register did a quick count. "That'll be four dollars and sixty cents."

Georgie turned a cool look on him. "I think your math is wrong."

The cashier's brown skin turned ashy. "I, I mean it's on the house."

"That's more like it." Georgie strutted toward our booth. "Nancy, lookin' fine as always. Who's your friend? She come to play on the dark side of town?" He faced me. "Hey, I know you. You was talkin' to Old Man Jones yesterday. What you come back for? I thought I made it plain that a cracker like you ain't wanted down here." He stepped toward me.

Nancy laid a hand on his arm. "She's with me. You better behave or I'm gonna tell Miz Alva and she'll beat your hide."

Georgie studied me with a hard-eyed look for a long moment. Then a lazy grin spread across his face. "All right, Miss Thing. I'll give you a pass this time 'cause you with Nancy here. But I warn you. Come into the Fruit Belt again, and it won't be good." A dark-handled switchblade appeared in his hand. He flicked it open. The light played along the blade.

I didn't move. I'd seen this kind of thing before, boys thinkin' a knife made them dangerous. Thanks to Lee, Sean, and Tom, I knew I coulda stripped Georgie of his weapon in a jiffy. He was holdin' it loose. But I wasn't there to make trouble. Not this time.

When I didn't say anything, he closed the knife and slipped it back into his pocket. "We'll talk later, Nancy. I came into some dough today. We'll go to the pictures tonight. Heck, maybe we'll even watch a little bit." He laughed, a coarse sound, and sauntered back to his gang.

Throughout the whole exchange, Stevie hadn't moved. But he'd kept his gaze on us. I paid him a little more attention now. He had the expression of a younger brother who didn't like the older boy's attitude toward his sister, but who was too overwhelmed by his idol to do anything. "Nancy, you'd better get on home," he said. His voice started out deep but cracked halfway through the sentence. He cleared his throat. "Mama'll be worried."

"It ain't me she's worried about." Nancy focused on her brother. "Stevie, please. Stop this. You know better."

He wavered a bit. Then the cool mask came back. "I know what I'm doin'. You go on back with the women, where you belong." He went back to the gang of older boys, tryin' to imitate their strut and not quite doin' it.

Nancy pushed away her half-melted shake. Dixie brought out our food, but Nancy only played with the square of golden bread and gooey cheese.

"Eat up." I took a bite. The egg sandwich wasn't half bad.

"I'm not hungry." She folded in on herself. "Can we leave? Although I'm not sure they'll let us through."

"You might not want food. I'm starved." I slurped some of my shake. "Don't worry. We'll get out."

She looked up, dark eyes big. "If Georgie pulls that flick knife again, what are you gonna do?"

I wiped my fingers on a napkin. "Nancy, I may be white. But the First Ward isn't Delaware Park. You think we don't have boys like that?" I waved my hand toward the gang, now positioned near the door, laughing loudly at their leader's jokes. "We can leave any time we want to. Now eat your sandwich before it gets cold."

She picked up a triangle. "But you see what I mean about Stevie, don't you? He's in over his head."

I shot a glance to the front. Stevie was on the fringe. I could tell he wanted to be part of the gang, but he wasn't there quite yet.

Which was usually the most dangerous place of all.

Chapter Twelve

Nancy and I stayed in the diner and dawdled over lunch. Georgie and his gang didn't leave and played at the pinball game in the corner. I watched them. While they were technically taking turns, it seemed Georgie's time came up a lot more often than the others. The older boys indulged Stevie, but it was clear he was not quite an accepted member of the group.

Every once in a while, Nancy glanced over at them. "What are we doin'?"

"Watching. Focus on me, not them."

"They're makin' me nervous. I want to grab Stevie and march him home."

One of the boys looked over. "Laugh." I giggled.

She stared at me like I was nuts.

"We're two girls gossiping over lunch. Do it." I pushed her hand.

She obliged. It was weak, but it'd do.

The boy looked away.

She played with the straw in her empty milkshake glass. "I don't understand what we're doing."

I poked at my own glass. "We can't stop 'em seeing us. But we can make 'em ignore us. If they think we're two brainless dames talking about nylons or boys, they won't pay attention."

Georgie slapped the machine. "That's it. I'm outta nickels. Gimme yours, Stevie."

"If I do, I won't have it for my turn." Stevie clenched his fist.

Georgie faced him down. "Gimme the nickel." He held out his palm, eyes hard as stones.

Stevie held out for a moment but faltered. He shoved the coin at the older boy and dashed out.

Nancy half-rose, but I stopped her. "Wait." I grabbed our bill and tossed a quarter on the table for a tip.

"I need to go after him."

"If you rush out, you'll be conspicuous." I did a slow count to fifteen. "Now we go. Nice and easy."

We called our goodbyes to Dixie and went to the register to pay. We edged past the boys, who were once again absorbed by the pinball.

George reached over and brushed Nancy's arm. "I'll be seein' you later, girl." He leered at her.

She flinched and I stepped between them. "You'll be leavin' her alone, if you know what's good for you."

He turned his attention to me, a mocking tone in his voice. "Oh yeah? What's a white girl gonna do 'bout it?"

Unlike Nancy, I didn't pull back. "Bother her again and you'll find out."

We stared into each other's eyes. I wasn't gonna blink first. I'd had a lot of experience with boys like Georgie. My money was on him backing down. I was right.

"Ain't worth the trouble." He went back to his gang.

I nudged Nancy outside to the sidewalk. "I can't believe you did that," she said.

"He's not the first bully I've run into, and he won't be the last."

She looked both ways, searching for her brother. "Where is Stevie? I don't see him."

I did a quick scan. Stevie was heading west, hands stuffed in his pockets. "There he is."

She moved like she was about to run.

I grabbed her arm.

She didn't pull away, but her eyes got as big as dinner plates.

I let go. "He's not walkin' fast. Easy. All we gotta do is keep him in view." I could tell she didn't like it, but she slowed her pace. The sun was out, with only a few clouds here and there in the blue sky. Since it was warm, there were plenty of other people on the sidewalk, and I was able to keep enough of 'em between us and Stevie that we wouldn't be spotted if he turned around.

We continued back into the Fruit Belt along East North Street. We passed block after block of businesses. Finally, Stevie made a right turn on Michigan. "Now we can hurry a bit." I dodged and weaved through the crowd, Nancy hot on my heels. Once on Michigan, I searched for Stevie. He was about half a block ahead of us. He stopped and looked around.

I grabbed Nancy and pulled her against a building for a moment. A group of old biddies passed us. Then I ducked out. Stevie wasn't in sight. I ran up to the spot where I'd seen him pause. Two shops crowded together, one closed up. They were separated by a narrow space where there were trash cans. It was empty. I stepped back and swept my gaze over the area. I didn't believe my eyes. I had only lost sight of him for a second. Stevie should be in sight.

But my peepers weren't lying. Stevie was flat-out gone.

* * *

For a moment, I couldn't do anythin' 'cept stand dumbfounded and stare down the empty area. Then I shielded my eyes against the sun and looked around.

Nancy came up beside me. "Stevie, what—" She gaped. "Where'd he go?"

"I dunno."

"You lost him?" Her voice went up an octave.

"That's one way to put it." I kicked at some loose dirt. "Another way is he vanished. He was here, right here. We looked away, and he disappeared."

She crossed her arms. "That's impossible."

"You got a better idea?" I turned. "Let's ask inside the store."

Bein' in the Fruit Belt, there were several Negro customers, but no sign of Stevie and no one copped to seeing him, either inside or outside.

I returned to the last spot I'd seen Stevie, followed by Nancy. Even though I knew it was useless, I searched the entire area. There was a space for the store's garbage and a padlocked door. I yanked on the lock. It didn't give. There wasn't an entry to the other building. Except for one chipped concrete square at the sidewalk, the ground was dirt.

Nancy watched me with narrowed peepers. Finally, words burst from her. "Now what? You gonna search until the sun goes down? He's not here."

I rose from where I had knelt to examine the concrete. "I know." I dusted my hands. "Go home. We've done all we can." On instinct, I snapped a couple of pictures of the gap and the concrete square. Then I put away the camera, shouldered, my purse, and lit a Lucky.

She threw her hands up. "I don't get it. Why aren't you more upset? What are you gonna *do?*"

"Don't flip your wig." I blew out a cloud of smoke. I understood her frustration. We were talkin' about her brother after all. "We got a lead with Georgie. Stevie is hanging around that gang, and I don't think they spend all day playin' that pinball machine. We saw Georgie with a flick knife, and we have the information from Dixie."

Nancy blinked. "That Georgie has a gun?"

"Right." I puffed again. "I'm as baffled as you are about what just happened, but sometimes an investigation goes like this. One step forward, two back." I tapped ash into the gutter. "Go on home. I'm not giving up, I promise. I got a couple other things to look into." I headed off in the direction of the nearest bus stop.

She followed. "Like what?"

She'd heard me ask Dixie about Coates and Gainey. But I didn't think it was a good idea to tell her I thought it was a real possibility, not just an idle question. "I'm not ready to say. I gotta do a little more research first." I reached the stop and spied the bus. "I'm goin' back to my office. I'll be in touch."

She bit her lip and looked every inch of her eighteen years. "Betty, I'm scared for him."

"I know." The bus screeched to a halt, and the doors thunked open. "Be patient. I'll get to the bottom of this."

I said nothing about whether she'd like the answer.

Chapter Thirteen

After I left Nancy, I headed downtown. It was a little after four, and the painter was gone. I stopped to admire the crisp black lettering on the glass. Once the place was finished, I'd have to bring Pop over. He'd be tickled pink to see his girl set up as a professional private dick.

Inside, Emmeline was on her hands and knees, a bucket of soapy water next to her. She whistled a tune, not anything recognizable from the radio, as she worked. She looked up at the sound of the door. "There you are."

I stopped. "What on earth are you doin'?"

"What does it look like? I'm washing the floor." She rinsed her cloth and wrung it out before moving to a new section.

"Why? We're detectives, not a diner. You don't have to eat off it."

"We'll never get a better opportunity to have it really clean. Once we fill these rooms with furniture, it gets more complicated." She used her left wrist to brush hair from her forehead. "My mother would tell you it's a good way for a fresh start. Jews clean the house before Passover. Don't Catholics do something?"

"The altar is cleaned before Good Friday."

"Exactly." She scrubbed another spot. "Both were times of renewal for our people. The Jewish freedom from slavery, what you believe is the resurrection of Jesus. Aren't we starting fresh? I mean, we're late for spring cleaning, but it's the idea of the thing."

She was so earnest, I kinda felt bad interrupting her. "If you want to. Did you get the research done?"

"Of course." She pointed to a neatly stacked pile of paper in the corner.

"Don't worry. It's not wet. I haven't gotten over there yet."

I stepped carefully and picked it up. As usual, there were pages of notes, but Emmeline had put her report on top. "Pretty slim pickings."

"I didn't find much that we didn't already know. The most interesting thing to me is that Stevie isn't mentioned, but he is in a picture. In the background."

"Where?"

"Page one of the city section in the May 13 issue of the *Courier-Express*."

I flipped to the clipping. There was Moses Gainey and some dame, all dolled up for a party. Lurking in the background, looking for all the world like he'd taken a wrong turn, was Stevie. He was a baby compared to the men around him. What had he been doin' there? He wasn't even old enough to drink. "I'm gonna take this. If he won't talk to me, I'll ask his sister if she knows anything."

"Did you learn anything at lunch?"

"That gangsters aren't the only ones Stevie pals around with." I told her about the incident at the soda shop. "If Mr. Jones is payin' protection, I don't think he woulda mentioned it to her. I'll go back tomorrow."

"Knock, knock." Frank peered around the door. "May I come in?"

My heart did its normal pitter-pat. "Why wouldn't we let you?"

"It appears Miss Schechter is cleaning. I wouldn't want to ruin the fruits of her labor."

"It's okay." She glanced from him to me. "Go over near Betty. I'll do the other side."

I sidled over to make room for him. "What are you doin' here? I thought we were meetin' at five."

"My shift ended at three, and I didn't want to wait. I went to the First Ward, and I saw Dot as she was getting home from Bell. She said you weren't home and that this was the only other place to look." He examined the space. "If you weren't here, it was likely you were out following a lead and, quote, would probably be home with the cows." He raised an eyebrow. "I didn't know Dot had farm experience."

Emmeline giggled.

"She doesn't," I said. "It's a saying from her great-grandfather, who worked a farm in Ireland." Trust Dot to be direct.

He went back to eyeing up the office. "I think my parents have a desk that would work in here."

Frank's family owned a furniture store in Orchard Park. "You know I can't afford to shop out there."

"It arrived damaged. Wobbly leg and a scratched side that's too deep to fix. They can't sell it off the floor." He patted his pockets as though he was looking for something.

"I'm not a charity case, either." I puffed up. "I already got my friend Sam insisting I take an old desk of his dad's for my office. I can't furnish the place on handouts." Well, I could, but I didn't want to feel beholden to more people than I had to.

He found what he was looking for, a scrap of paper and a pencil. "I wasn't talking about a handout. I'm sure Mom and Dad would work out a reasonable price with you. They may even allow you to make payments over time if you don't have the full amount. But they will offer a deep discount." He wrote. "Take this note to them. Mom in particular likes you, so it won't be a problem."

"Thanks." I stuffed it in my pocket. "Sorry for snapping."

He waved away my apology. "Are you ready to go to dinner?"

When we had made the plans, he said he was gonna take me someplace nice. I'd been out all day. I wanted to check in with Mrs. Flannery. I doubted Tom would unburden himself to me, not in his current mood, but she would give me the dope. "I don't know if it's such a good idea right now." I hesitated. "I haven't had a chance to tell you. Tom is home."

Frank watched me. "Oh?"

"Medical discharge. He lost his left leg below the knee."

He laid a hand on my shoulder. "I'm so sorry. Is he all right otherwise?"

Emmeline cleared her throat. "You two gotta move. It's dry enough over there."

We obliged. "I don't know. I only saw him a bit at the station. He didn't want to talk about it." At least not to me.

Frank seemed to understand what I didn't say. "It must be hard, for him and you. Perhaps I should talk to him."

I forced a laugh. "I think you're prob'ly the last guy he'd want to grab a cup of coffee and flap gums with. No offense. Not that he knows anything about you, but still."

"That may be why I'm the best person. I'm a stranger. He doesn't have to pretend anything with me." Frank shrugged. "Think it over. You know him best. If dinner is no longer an option, at least let me accompany you home."

It was one of the things I liked about Frank. He didn't take things personally and respected me when I spoke my mind. "I'd like that. Thanks."

Chapter Fourteen

Frank and I got off the bus a good two blocks away from Mackinaw. I faced him. "I'll walk from here by myself."

He bent his head. "I can go with you. It's no trouble."

"It's not that." I put my hand on his chest. "I don't think it's a good idea."

"Ah." He watched me, those deep brown eyes filled with concern. "You mean with Tom home, it might not be appropriate for you to be seen walking home with another man."

We stared at each other, neither of us moving. It had the feel of a movie ending, one where the hero plants a deep, passionate kiss on the lips of his lady love as the film fades to black and the credits roll.

I knew that wasn't my role to play.

The mood broke as the sound of Dot's voice cut the air. "Betty. Oh, thank goodness you're home."

I forced myself to look away from Frank and at her. "Is something wrong with Lee? Or my family?"

"No. It's Tom. Mrs. Flannery is in a tizzy. Lee isn't home yet. Neither is your dad. I don't know what to do." She studied Frank and me. Her worried expression gave way to thoughtfulness as she bit her plump lower lip. She was usually an open book, but in that second, it was impossible to know what she was thinkin'.

"What's he up to?"

My question snapped her back to the current problem. "He's drunk as a lord. He refuses to come home." Dot wrung her hands.

I glanced at Frank, then looked back at Dot. "He at the Fiddle?" The Harp

& Fiddle was the neighborhood bar. When the men wanted to celebrate, or wash away a bad day, they went to the Fiddle. But Paddy, the owner, had no problem tossin' guys out when they'd overstayed their welcome. I didn't understand why he hadn't done that to Tom.

She shook her head. "O'Malley's."

That explained everything. I'd been there once, on a case. Pop had insisted on goin' with me. Good thing, because it was no place for "nice folks." They'd let Tom drink until he ran outta dough and maybe even let him rack up a tab. "Let me guess. His job huntin' didn't go well today."

Dot must've moved on from thoughts of Frank, 'cause she looked close to tears. "Mrs. Flannery said he came home all hot under the collar. Plenty of places are willin' take him, but not until he is off the crutches. She doesn't know exactly how long that will be, and he isn't sayin'. From what I understand, he told her something about since he was a useless cripple, he might as well drink himself stupid, grabbed some cash, and left. I guess she screwed up the courage to go to the door of O'Malley's, but—"

"No one there was willing to toss him out." It was exactly what I'd been afraid of.

Frank crossed his arms. "I take it this O'Malley's isn't for the faint-hearted."

"No." I checked my purse for my knife. It was there, but I didn't exactly want to battle my way outta the joint. "You might say it's more than a little rough around the edges."

His dark eyes shone in the light. "But you're going to go there anyway."

"I have to." I took Dot's arm. "As soon as Lee gets home, you send him over, you hear me? Unless, by some miracle, I get Tom outta there."

She nodded.

Frank straightened. "I'm coming with you."

Dot frowned. "Aren't you a Quaker? You don't fight. It's why you're a conchie. That's what Betty told me."

I shushed her. Now was not the time to be debating Frank's moral beliefs or her opinion of conscientious objectors.

"I am. But remember, I work at Buffalo State Hospital. If you think some of the patients there can't get as rowdy as a drunken man, you're mistaken."

He folded his arms. "I will not strike another person, but I'm more than capable of dealing with Tom should he prove difficult to reason with."

What a nice way of saying if he flat-out refused to leave and threatened me. That was Frank and his college education. "All right. Come on." I patted Dot's arm again. "But send Lee along just in case."

* * *

We walked in silence to O'Malley's. I figured I didn't need to tell Frank how to behave. He was right: If he could handle violent mental patients, he'd be able to take care of one sloppy drunk.

I was quite sure Tom would be exactly that when we found him.

I took a deep breath and pushed open the door to the bar. Tom was at the bar, a glass of whiskey in front of him. How many had he had? His crutches were propped next to him. He tossed back the booze and slammed it on the bar. "Again."

The bartender lifted the bottle. "On your tab?"

He waved his hand.

The bartender poured. He looked up at me. "It ain't couples night. You folks are in the wrong spot."

"No, we aren't." I pointed at Tom. "I'm cuttin' him off."

"No, you ain't." Tom blinked at me. "Dot's sent the cavalry, huh? Think you can do better than my ma, Betty? I didn't leave for her. I'm sure not gonna for you." He slapped the bar. "I said gimme another."

In two strides, I was at his side. I grabbed the glass. "You should be ashamed of yourself. Your mother is worried sick. It's time to come home and sleep it off. You had a bad day. You got sloshed. Fine. Now let's go." I lowered my voice. "These men aren't your friends, Tom."

"Sure, they are." He threw out his arms. "That's Donny. He bought the first round. And Billy. He bought the second. Over there"—he peered through the gloom—"well, I don't remember that guy's name, but he's swell. They're all my pals. Society don't seem to want me, but I've got a home here." He tried to push me aside.

If he'd been sober, it might have been more of a contest. He'd always been bigger and stronger than me. But whiskey had robbed him of any real strength, and I'd spent too much time wrangling airplane parts around on the assembly line to be easily moved. "Only because you've been buying rounds for them." I waved Frank over. "Get your crutches and let's go. Before Lee gets here and really lays into you."

Tom snorted. "Like I care what another cripple does. He thinks he's a big man, huh? He's got a job and I don't. I'll tell you something." He leaned in, his breath sour with alcohol. "I'm gonna be meetin' a guy who knows you don't need legs to be useful. Just brains, and I got those in spades."

Frank took firm grip on Tom's upper arm. "I believe your fiancée said we're leaving. I'd rather not carry you out, but I will if she says to."

Tom tried to push him away. "Who the hell are you?" His gaze swung to me. "I see how it is. I go away, come back half a man, and you've got someone else already, huh?"

"Tom, this is Frank Hicks. He's a friend of mine." I tried to ignore the leers from the men around us. "That's all. I'm still engaged to you, see?" I held up my left hand so he could see the ring.

He pushed it away. "Wearing a ring don't mean nothing. You've been steppin' out on me, haven't you? Admit it." He leaned over and nearly toppled off his stool.

Frank held him up. "No, she hasn't. I'm going to tell you one more time. We're leaving. Betty, hand me those crutches."

Tom swore, words I'd never heard him speak before. "You think you can run off with my girl? What are you, eh? Why aren't you in uniform? You one of those yellow-bellies who doesn't like fightin'? Take that." Still on his seat, he swung, a wild haymaker that upset his balance. His right leg hit the floor, but with no left, he teetered.

Frank coulda let him fall, but he didn't. He grabbed Tom from behind, arms wrapped around Tom's chest. "You're not in any condition to fight me, friend. Please don't try."

Tom wriggled. "Lemme go and we'll see 'bout that."

Frank looked at me.

I nodded.

He spun Tom around, flexed his knees, and lifted. Tom went up and over his shoulder like a sack of potatoes. He pounded on Frank's back, but as with me earlier, the blows were feeble. Frank gripped him tightly, preventing him from twisting free. "I think it's time to go."

"You can't carry him the whole way home. What if he pukes on you?"

"I only have to go to the sidewalk. I think I can get him out before he vomits."

I tossed a dollar on the bar. "Hopefully, this covers his tab. I'll be back in the morning, and you can tell me if it doesn't." I grabbed the crutches and led Frank to the door. My eyes stung with unshed tears. Most of the patrons ignored us, but a few shot Tom a look of pity. That was worse than bein' ignored.

I hated doing this to Tom, but I wasn't gonna leave him at O'Malley's, drunk as a skunk and easy prey. Maybe I'd get lucky and he'd pass out before we got him home. 'Course, then we'd have to figure out how to move him.

Outside, I handed back the crutches. "I'm so sorry I dragged you into this," I said to Frank, pitching my voice to be heard over Tom's string of profanity. "I don't know what's got into him. Wouldn't he have seen a head doctor before comin' home?"

"I did." Tom slurred his words. "They told me all sorts of stuff, like how I'd get a prosthetic and be able to go about my life. I told 'em to stick their fake leg up their—" He staggered and nearly fell into me, but Frank grabbed him and held him upright.

"Why would you say that?" It had to be the booze talkin'. "Don't you want to walk on two feet again?"

"I want my damn leg back!" Tom fixed me with a baleful, red-eyed stare. "Uncle Sam wants you, boy. Go overseas, risk your life, get your limbs blown off. Here's a medal for ya." He fumbled with a crutch.

I lowered my voice and spoke to Frank. "Is this normal? Or is it 'cause he's sloshed?"

Frank studied Tom, but the sympathy in his eyes didn't cut me the same way the pity from the other patron had. "I'm no doctor, but I think it's common. Magnified by the alcohol, of course. You don't get over an injury like that in a couple of months. Maybe Tom started to heal, but it's a process. He'll be angry for some time." He caught sight of my face. "Not every day. But it will come and go."

Still mumbling curses under his breath, Tom took off for home. At least, he tried to. In his state, he stumbled after one step. Once again, Frank caught him. He spoke to Tom in a low voice, prob'ly like he used with his ornery patients. Slowly, the two men walked off.

I trailed behind. I couldn't live with Tom, not with his anger like this. At the same time, how could I let myself add to his pain by telling him to leave?

Chapter Fifteen

The next morning, I grabbed breakfast at Teddy's, then headed into the office. Emmeline was already there. So was a man from the telephone company, who was installing a second telephone in my office. I looked at Emmeline. "No library today?"

"Not on the weekend."

I looked at the telephone worker. "You didn't get us two lines, did you? I don't think that's in the budget."

"Not two lines, just two telephones." She looked up from her seat on the floor. "It didn't cost much more. I was thinking that since I only work half-time, there will be days when you'll be by yourself. You don't want to run out here to answer a call. Not only that, you might want to handle one in private. It would be better if you have your own phone."

It was good thinkin'. "I knew I brought you on for a reason."

She set a wooden board in her lap. "I hope that's not the only one." She made some notes.

"What are you doin' down there?"

"Until we get another desk, this will do."

I smacked my forehead. "I didn't call Frank's parents yesterday. I'll do that as soon as the telephone guy is done."

The man from the telephone company came out. "You're all set. Here's your number." He tipped his hat and left.

Sam walked in. "Good morning, ladies. Betty, I have that desk downstairs for you."

My office had turned into Central Terminal with all the coming and going.

"You didn't have to come and deliver," I said. "I coulda gotten Lee to help me pick it up."

"It's no problem. I know a guy with a truck. But before I get someone to help me bring it up, I have to talk to you." He gave Emmeline a pointed look. "Alone."

His seriousness reminded me of his visit to my house to tell me my last client had been arrested. "Why do I get the feelin' I'm not gonna like what you have to say?"

Emmeline watched us. "I'll call Hicks's. I think you'll be busy. Besides, I'd like to see the desk for myself, especially if I'm the one who's going to be using it."

I handed over a slip of paper with the store phone number. Then I took Sam to my office and closed the door. "I'd offer you a chair, but all my furniture is in your friend's truck." I crossed my arms. "What gives?"

He twirled his fedora on his finger. "Stevie Washington is dead."

* * *

My mouth dropped open. "When?" I would have to call Nancy. If she'd been worried before, she'd be devastated now that her brother was dead.

"Early this morning or late last night, depending on how you look at it. We got a call about a disturbance around two. When officers got there, they found Stevie. He'd been shot in the chest."

"Where?" I searched for my purse and my notebook.

Sam picked them up off the floor and handed them to me. "Over on Wadsworth Street."

"Wadsworth?" My hand paused over the paper. "Are you sure?" Wadsworth was separated from the Fruit Belt by several blocks and was in the middle of a white neighborhood. A colored boy had no business bein' there at any time of day.

"The location of a dead body is not generally something we're vague on." Sam cracked a grin. "You look surprised."

"I'm kinda shocked he went so far afield." Why would a kid go so far from home? "I don't s'pose there are witnesses."

"Not at that hour. We're questioning people in the neighborhood, as well as along the bus route. No one says they saw Stevie, day or night."

In that neighborhood, Stevie woulda been noticed. "You find the gun?"

"No. Nothing on the ground. The boy had a key in his pocket, but when I notified his family earlier this morning, it did not match the front door of his house. His mother and sister have never seen it."

"Is that all?"

"There was another person there." His voice was neutral.

That worried me. "I'm gettin' a bad feeling here, Sam. Do I know this person?"

"You're engaged to him."

"Tom?" That wasn't possible. Frank and I had taken him home. We hadn't tucked him in or anything, but he'd been so drunk he couldn't talk straight. We'd left him on his bed, moaning. I twisted my engagement ring. "He doesn't know Stevie."

"Maybe not, but he was there, on his knees, crutches off to the side. He was blubbering and smelled like a distillery, although I think the body scared him sober." Sam took out his notes. "His hands were covered in blood, which we assume was the victim's because Flannery wasn't wounded. Aside from his missing limb, that is, and that didn't happen in the alley."

"What did he say?"

Sam read. "Nothing that made a lot of sense. He said he didn't do it. He'd been there to meet Stevie for a business arrangement and found him in the alley. We asked what kind of business. He gave us a story about deliveries but wouldn't get specific. He insisted he barely knew the victim and had no reason to kill him."

My chest was tight, and I shivered despite the mild temperature. "Did he have a gun on him?"

"No. And that's the only thing keeping him out of jail right now. We tested his hands for gunpowder." Sam flipped his notebook shut. "He was smart enough to clam up when we took him to the station to question him. All he'd say is he'd met Stevie the previous afternoon and they were going to do some business together. He got all shifty when we asked what kind of business." Sam raised his eyebrows. "I don't need to tell you that the fact they were meeting in the dead of night doesn't lead us to believe anything they were up to was legal."

Of course it wouldn't. I didn't blame Sam in the slightest. I needed to see Tom.

"Did you see him yesterday?" Sam asked.

There was no reason to lie. Sam would get the story from the O'Malley crowd. "Yes, earlier. Maybe around six." I told Sam about how Frank and I hauled Tom outta the bar, stinkin' drunk. "There's no way he woulda been able to shoot straight."

"Not then, but hours later? He might not have been completely sober, but remember, he was a soldier." Sam leaned against the wall. "It wouldn't have been a hard shot, either. They were right next to each other, although the crutches were a couple of feet away, almost like they'd been tossed aside." He cocked his head. "Did he say anything about Stevie?"

I tried to remember. "No. He was yammering about not being able to get a job. But…" I hesitated.

"I'll find out, Betty. It's best for both of you to come clean."

He was right. "Tom said somethin' about how he'd met a guy who was gonna help him. That the job didn't need legs, just brains. An opportunity, he called it." I leaned forward. "He didn't get specific, Sam. I swear. If you want, you can interview Frank Hicks. He'll tell you the same."

He raised his eyebrows. "Why were you with Frank?"

"We had dinner plans." After one look at Sam's face, I hurried to explain. "He asked before I knew Tom was comin' home. It was just friends. Nothin' serious."

He didn't say anythin', but he didn't have to, either. I could read the warning—and sympathy—in his eyes. "Do you think Stevie was recruiting him for someone?"

"Hard to believe Tom would go to work for a teenager." I didn't want to know, but I had to ask. "Is he a suspect?"

"He might be. No gun, no real connection to the victim. It could be coincidence. But I want to know why he was in an empty lot on Wadsworth at two in the morning." Sam took off his hat and jacket and rolled up his shirtsleeves. "Let me see if I can round up a couple of your neighbors, and we'll get that furniture up here."

After he walked out, I sagged against the wall. Sam's question was one I planned to ask Tom myself.

* * *

Not only had Sam brought me a handsome desk, but a matching chair on wheels, a blotter, and a lamp with a green shade. When I protested, he waved me off. "I have no use for the blotter or the furniture, and I always hated that lamp. But you're on your own when it comes to finding chairs for your clients."

After he left, I sat and stared into space as I swiveled back and forth in my seat. I didn't know what disturbed me more. Scratch that. I did know. What was Tom doin' in the middle of the night with a dead guy? Not only that, it was a place way outside the First Ward. I'd left him drunk and mumbling on his bed. Obviously, he'd sobered up enough to leave. He couldn't have been too quiet about it. I'd talk to his mother.

First, I needed to call Nancy. I grabbed the telephone and dialed her communal number. I couldn't help it. I ran my hand over the desk as I listened to the ring. There were still some things to get, but I had my own office. I was steppin' up in the world.

The woman who answered grumbled a bit, but I heard the thunk as she set down the blower to get Nancy. Less than a minute later, the girl's trembling voice came over the line. "Hello?"

"Nancy, it's Betty Ahern. A detective came and told me about Stevie. How're you holdin' up?" Dumb question, but I needed to lead with something.

"Honestly, we're all in shock, 'specially me and Mama. I was afraid Stevie was in a bad way, but I didn't think it would get him killed." She broke into sobs.

I waited. If I'd been there in person, I might not have been so off-kilter. Then again, maybe I would be. I had no idea what the mourning rituals were for Nancy's folk. What if family was sittin' vigil or somethin'? I'd feel out of place in the parade of mourners.

She recovered. "Thank you for calling. Is there something you need?"

"First, do you want me to continue the investigation? Murder is a police matter, after all. You'll get the answer you came to me for and it won't cost you a dime."

"Yes, please. You need to stay on the case." Her words came in a rush. "I don't trust the police. Where I come from, they don't care about colored folk. I don't want Stevie's killer to go unpunished." Her drawl was a little more pronounced as she said "poh-leece."

Where she came from? It dawned on me. She meant the South. "I understand. You should know that I'm friends with the detective in charge of your brother's murder." I thought of Sam. "He'll do his best, trust me. But I'll keep at it if you want. It won't be the first time I've looked into a killing."

"Oh, thank goodness. Yes, please." She paused a beat. "When the police came, they said a white boy was with Stevie when he died. Is he a suspect?"

I didn't want to say yes or no. Heck, Nancy might not even want to keep me on the case once she learned the person with her brother was my fiancé. "It's early stages. Look. We need to meet. I need to know as much about Stevie's movements yesterday as you know." I could leave now. "Should I come to you?"

"I don't think that'd be a good idea. Boys in the neighborhood, they're pretty riled up." She sniffled. "I can come to the diner again."

"I've got an office now." I rattled off the address. "Can you be here by three this afternoon?"

"Better make it four. Neighbors keep coming by. Mama will need me. By that time, they'll be leaving to make supper and take care of their own families."

It was later than I'd like, but I'd work with it. "One more thing. Do you think you can get Mr. Jones to come with you? I've got new information and I'd like to talk to him."

"I doubt it. He doesn't close his store until six, and there's no one he can leave in charge." She blew her nose.

"I'll have to come to him. Don't bother with the office. If you can, meet me at his store. If you can't, I'll catch up with you later."

"Betty, I told you. Boys aren't happy over this."

"It'll be jake. I can handle myself." Perhaps I could get someone to go with me. Like Sam. He had to be lookin' into Stevie's connections with Coates and Gainey, same as me. "Just think all day about what you can remember about Stevie's friends, where he was yesterday, people he's been around lately. What about the people he knew before he quit school?"

"I don't see those kids a lot, but some of 'em might talk to you."

"Swell. Make a list of names. I'll be there this afternoon."

She said her goodbye and hung up. I grabbed a pad of paper I'd brought from home, one bigger than I could carry in my purse. I wrote down my list of suspects. Coates and Gainey, the wanna-be gangsters. Georgie Vickers, the neighborhood bully-boy. Not a bad start. Who else had Stevie Washington known who coulda gotten him killed?

Was one of 'em the guy Tom had been goin' to meet?

Chapter Sixteen

While Emmeline busied herself in the outer area, I made lists of tasks for what had become the investigation into Stevie's murder. Which of the lies he'd told had cost him his life?

I also called Melvin at the *Courier-Express* and gave him my new telephone number. He was suitably impressed. 'Course, now I had to find an answering service that wouldn't cost me an arm and a leg. That couldn't be too hard.

I scrounged up one chair for clients. It was a battered old wooden one someone had put out for trash, but for now, it was better than nothing.

It was around one when Emmeline stuck her head through the doorway. "Sorry to bother you. I'm going to Orchard Park to take a look at that desk."

"Remember, don't—"

"Break the bank. I know." She glanced behind her. "You have a visitor. Two of them. I think one wants to hire you."

I hadn't been in the building for a full day, and business was boomin'. "Send 'em in. I wonder how they got my name. I haven't put the ad out."

Lee appeared behind Emmeline. "We didn't need advertising."

I wasn't positive who he meant by "we," but I had a strong suspicion.

Emmeline practically ran through the door.

I heard a thunk. Lee moved farther into the office. Behind him, Tom held tight to his crutches, lookin' for all the world like my brothers when they'd been caught red-handed in some misdeed.

His appearance was worse than when he'd gotten off the train. His clothes were rumpled, leading me to think he'd slept in 'em. His hair needed a comb, and his eyes were bloodshot. It didn't take a genius to see that he was sufferin' from a massive hangover.

I exchanged a look with Lee. His expression was firm and solemn. He pointed at the chair. "Sit down." He wasn't talkin' to me.

Tom obeyed. The chair creaked, but it stayed together.

Thank goodness.

I read the tension between the friends. Tom didn't want to be here. Lee had forced him. That was clear. I wondered what he'd held over his friend's head to ensure obedience. I'd ask Lee later. "Sorry I don't have a place for you to park it."

He leaned against the wall. "I'm fine."

Tom rubbed his hands on his thighs. He'd propped his crutches against the desk. "This wasn't my decision. I want to get that out in the open." He wore a blue jacket with a suspicious square lump in the pocket. A bottle?

I steepled my fingers. "Why'd you come, then?"

He cast a nervous look at Lee, who'd crossed his arms over his chest. "Lee said I didn't have anything to lose. He told me how you helped him when his dad died."

"How she saved my bacon is what I said." Lee's voice was flat. Clearly, he wasn't gonna let Tom downplay anything.

I wouldn't either. "What does that have to do with you?"

Tom glanced again at his friend. "I, um, think I need the same thing. You know."

"No, tell me."

His skin, formerly a little pale, flushed. "I want to hire you. To keep me outta jail."

Better. "Detective MacKinnon was here earlier. He told me about findin' you with Stevie Washington's body."

Tom's head jerked up.

"The detective's a friend." I leaned back. "I brought you home around six. You were dead drunk. When did you leave?"

"Later." He wouldn't meet my gaze.

"Where did you go?"

"Here and there."

I exchanged a look with Lee before focusing on Tom. "Sorry. I want to help you, but I can't. Not if you won't be straight with me."

Tom swore. He musta picked up that language in the Army. "You'll get cozy with the movie star look-alike, but you won't give me a hand. Swell. Don't bother denying it. I wasn't so far gone I couldn't notice you two last night, mooning over each other." He fumbled for his crutches.

Lee moved faster than I thought he could. "You stay put." He snatched up the sticks. "I guess you didn't understand me the first time. You're gonna hire Betty to clear you. Stop acting like a baby."

Tom removed a stainless-steel flask from his jacket.

Lee grabbed it. "No booze. No swearing. You're in a pickle. Your mother is sick with worry. I know your father, and he's not likely to help. It's down to me and Betty. And Dot."

Tom jerked his thumb at me. "Have you seen the guy she's runnin' around with? Huh?"

"He's a friend. Nothing more." Lee swatted the back of Tom's head.

I owed Lee for that. I knew he didn't like my relationship with Frank, but he stuck up for me anyway.

Lee limped back to his corner, flask in one hand, crutches in the other. He leaned the props against the wall and pocketed the liquor. "Now answer her questions, nice and polite."

Tom rubbed his face. "After you and Handsome dumped me off, I passed out. I woke up around eleven, maybe closer to midnight. I wasn't completely sober, but earlier that afternoon, I'd arranged to meet Stevie to discuss an…opportunity he knew about."

I pulled over my pad and took notes. "How'd you meet him?" This story already smelled fishy. A fifteen-year-old kid was offerin' him a job? But I stayed mum.

Tom shrugged. "I spent most of yesterday goin' around lookin' for work. Most of the places, well, they were sympathetic and all. Said they'd be more than happy to hire me once I had, you know." He looked away.

A prosthetic leg. "I thought you didn't want one. That's what you said last night." *When you were so drunk you couldn't stand up without Frank's help.*

"Why are you givin' me a hard time?" He clenched his fist. "I shoulda had one already. Another Army paperwork mess. Do you wanna hear my story or yap about my leg?"

I let it go. "Then what? You musta met Stevie somewhere."

"I'd gone pretty far from the First Ward." He rubbed his thighs again. "It was later in the afternoon. I'd skipped lunch, and I was real hungry and stuff."

"You wanted a drink." I tried to keep my voice level.

He glared at me. "I went into some bar. Don't ask me where or what the name was. They didn't have much on the menu, but I did get a whiskey. Maybe two."

Lee huffed but said nothing.

"When the bill came, I was short. I offered to wash dishes or something, but Stevie paid my tab. We got to talkin'. He asked how long I'd been home. I told him how I wasn't havin' much luck on the job front. Then he said he knew of an opportunity I'd be perfect for. One that didn't need two legs, just quick thinkin'."

"What kind of opportunity?" I asked.

"He didn't say. Told me to meet him in that lot at two that morning and he'd fill me in." Tom fidgeted. "I knew it had to be shifty. Who does legitimate business at that time? But I was half-drunk and I didn't care. No one else wanted a cripple." His lips twisted, words bitter.

I raised my eyebrows. "You didn't wonder why a kid was in a bar?"

"I was drunk. I coulda seen my mother there and not given it a second thought." Tom's shoulders twitched. "Stevie gave me a couple bucks, said it was an advance 'cause he thought I'd work out fine and be able to pay him easy. I went back to the First Ward, bellied up to the bar at O'Malley's, and, well, you know the rest from there."

Where I'd found him three sheets to the wind. "Tell me about goin' to the vacant lot."

"All this talk is makin' me thirsty." Tom shot a look at his friend.

Lee didn't move. "Doesn't look like the water cooler is set up yet."

Tom scowled but continued, although he wouldn't look at me straight on.

"It was like I said. I woke up around midnight or so. I crept outta the house, quiet as I could. You saw Mom made up a bed for me in the back room, so I don't have to do the stairs. She and Dad are both sound sleepers. They didn't make a peep, not that I heard. I took a late bus to Wadsworth. When I arrived, there was Stevie, lying on his back. I went over to him. I knew he was dead, shot in the chest. I was gonna run when the cops showed up." He turned a wide-eyed stare to me and leaned forward. "I swear before God, Betty. I didn't kill him. I barely knew him!"

It wasn't the whole story, not by a long shot. But there was a germ of truth. "Did you see a gun anywhere near the body?"

"No. I s'pose it coulda been in one of the trash cans. Not like I went lookin' for it."

I tapped my thumbs together. I glanced at Lee.

He raised his eyebrows. *Your call*, the gesture seemed to say.

"All right. My rates are fifteen bucks for the first week, plus expenses. It's five dollars a day after that, again plus expenses. I'm workin' on gettin' real contracts drawn up, so for now we'll have to shake on it." I held out my hand.

"But I'm your fiancé!"

"About that." This was gonna crush Tom. It hurt me, but I had to do it. The thought had come into my head as I listened. Maybe if he was honest I wouldn't, but I knew he'd left out parts of the story. Important parts. I pulled the engagement ring off and pushed it toward him. "Until this is over, I think we should end our engagement. Nancy Washington is also my client. You're a suspect until I find proof otherwise. I think it's best we keep things professional for now." I also couldn't marry a Joe I didn't think was bein' honest with me, but I figured sayin' so wasn't helpful.

Tom pulled back as though I'd slapped him. "You're ditching me?"

My resolve wavered a bit at the look in his eyes, but I held onto it. "Ditching is the wrong word. But yes, I'm callin' off the wedding. For now."

"Forget I even came. Gimme the crutches. I'm goin' back to the bar."

Before I could respond, Lee pushed off the wall. "What's wrong with you? You oughta be on your knees, thankin' Betty that she'll take your case. I've been over there listening to you whine and moan the entire time we've been here. No wonder she won't marry a sad sack like you. I wouldn't either. Take the ring, pay her, and deal with the engagement once this is over. It wouldn't hurt if you'd sober up, either."

I'd rarely heard Lee talk to his friend like that. I kept silent. Maybe he'd get through where I hadn't.

Tom glared but swiped up the ring and put it in his pocket. "I don't have that much cash on me."

"It's okay. I know where you live. I'll come get it later." Once again, I reached out to shake hands.

His grip was callused, whether from the war or from the crutches, I didn't know. It wasn't as strong as I remembered, but then again, nothin' about the Tom sittin' in front of me was exactly like the boy I knew.

I read over my notes. "I'm goin' to meet with Nancy so I can keep working on her case. Here's hopin' she doesn't find out I'm workin' for you at the same time. She might flip her wig." I looked up. "Anything else you want to tell me?"

He kept his lips zipped. It didn't matter. It had happened to me before, clients not telling me the entire story. I'd find out eventually. "That's it then. I'll come over tonight for the dough."

Tom's gaze moved between Lee and me, a little like an animal trapped between two predators. "That's it? You'll take that page of scribbling, skip off, and I'm s'posed to believe you'll solve the case?"

Lee cracked the first smile I'd seen since he walked in. "You don't understand, pal. This is what she does."

Chapter Seventeen

By the time Emmeline returned, I had multiple pages of notes, some for Tom and some for Nancy. I added a bulletin board and thumbtacks to my list of office needs. For now, all I could do was spread the paper out on my desk.

She came into my office and removed the scarf from her head. "Did those two bring a new case?"

"They did. Fortunately, it's connected to the one we already have, so the same research will help both." I tapped the sheets with my pencil. "Is the desk gonna work?"

"Oh yes. It's a nice, medium-sized secretary's desk. It's got a big scratch on the side, but a little Murphy's Oil Soap and some elbow grease will make it less noticeable. And there's a little wobble in the leg, but we can fix that." She patted down her hair. "They'll deliver it on Monday."

I winced.

She must have noticed. "Don't worry. They let the desk go for a song and threw in the delivery for free since they have to come downtown for another customer anyway. They like you, Betty. Remember, you helped their son."

This was true. "Swell. That's most of the furniture taken care of."

She came around my desk. "Who was the young man on the crutches? I recognized your friend, Lee."

I almost brushed her off, but she was my partner. "My ex-fiancé."

She raised an eyebrow.

I told her Tom's story, from when he got off the train up until he left the office. "The key seems to be Stevie Washington. Since it's pretty much one case, I couldn't say no."

Her expression softened. "You took him on because of who he is. Don't say otherwise, Betty."

She was right, so I didn't respond to that. Instead, I said, "I am kinda second-guessing my decision to give him back his ring. He brought a flask to the meeting and I get the sense he's been drinkin' a lot. That's not him. I hope I didn't make it worse."

"You did the right thing. Keep it professional." She took my notepad. "Tom's not being honest—with you or himself—and that's not good for a marriage. You also aren't responsible for his drinking. I saw Lee's face. He won't let his friend drown himself in a bottle."

Her words helped, a little. I pointed at the pad. "What do you think?"

Emmeline read my pages of notes. "Is there any way Tom could be guilty?"

"I s'pose." I laid down my pencil and leaned back. "Sam told me they didn't find a gun. That doesn't mean Tom couldn't have gotten rid of it and play-acted finding Stevie dead. 'Course, if he left to throw away the gun, why come back to the body?"

"You're assuming he threw it away somewhere else."

"The cops woulda found it. I'll have to ask Sam if the gunpowder test will be accurate if Tom's hands were all covered in blood."

"Don't sell Tom short. I'm sure he had to get really creative overseas, stashing things so they wouldn't get caught in an inspection. He could have done it that night." She moved a page. "What would be his motive?"

She was right about Tom's ability to hide things. That went all the way back to his childhood, never mind the Army. "Motive's my other problem. Stevie was offering to help Tom, or so he says. He's only been home for a couple of days, which means there's no long-standing argument between 'em. I s'pose Tom coulda been drunk and somethin' Stevie said set him off, but it feels like a long shot." I swiveled the chair back and forth.

"Or they argued over the split of the money. Greed plus booze is a powerful combination." She handed back the pad.

I stood and stretched. "You doin' anything?"

"What are you planning?"

"I'm goin' back to the Fruit Belt and take another crack at talkin' to folks."

She pursed her lips. "They didn't exactly welcome you with open arms last time."

"True, but there's a difference." I grabbed my things, snapped off the lights, and closed the door behind us. "Now Stevie isn't in trouble. He's dead."

* * *

I got off the bus around four. There were still hours of sunlight left, but the late-afternoon slant of the light and a stiff breeze off the lake made me glad I'd brought a sweater. My first stop was Mr. Jones's store. The old man stood in the back, stocking canned goods. He looked over at the sound of my footsteps. "Miss Ahern. You come back for more of that horehound candy?" He tipped his head at the jar.

"It's tasty, but no." I watched him. Nancy wasn't around. She must have had to stay with her mother. "I assume you know Stevie Washington died last night."

"I do." He didn't pause in his work. "Word is he got himself shot. Miz Alva been round the neighborhood. She's organizin' folks to help Mrs. Washington and Nancy."

I picked up an apple. "Have the cops been by?"

"Some man in a fedora. Called himself a detective." He shot me a look. "Help yourself to an apple."

I polished the fruit on my sweater. I'd leave a coin before I left, although I knew he meant for me to have it as a gift. "Sam MacKinnon?"

"Sounds 'bout right."

"He's a good man." I took a bite. "Did Nancy tell you we followed Stevie yesterday?"

He hoisted the empty box and walked to the back. "She did. Said he disappeared."

I walked behind him. "Yep. Into thin air." I told him where. "Got any idea how that coulda happened?"

"Don't rightly know." He stacked the box and went back to the front of the store. "Why are you here?"

Once again, I trailed him. "Alonzo Coates and Moses Gainey."

"What about 'em?"

"Did either of 'em ask you to pay protection?"

He sighed. "They both did."

"You didn't mention that when I was here yesterday." I leaned against the counter next to the register.

He grabbed a mop and bucket. "Didn't think it mattered."

"Everything matters. What happened?"

Mr. Jones dunked the mop, wrung it out, and swabbed the floor. "Pretty much what you think. Them boys said how I needed to give 'em money so's I'd be safe from the other. I told 'em I could take care of myself. Been doin' it a long time. I don't need help from a youngster, no matter how tough he thinks he is."

"What did they say?"

He chuckled. "They weren't happy, I can tell you that. That night, the front window of the store got broke. Each of 'em blamed t'other and said it proved I needed them to look out for me. I said next time someone showed up to smash my windows, I'd introduce 'em to Lizzy."

I licked apple juice off my lip. "Who's she?"

He jerked his chin toward the counter. "The double-barrel shotgun I keep under the register. She's the only protection I need. That made them boys back off quick." He cackled. "I come from Alabama, Miss Ahern. I lived out in the country so's I know how to use a gun. I been keepin' myself safe from white folk with a grudge for a long time. These city boys ain't got no idea."

I looked around the store. "I know Stevie was tied up with Coates and Gainey. Well, at least Gainey. I've seen a picture of 'em together. I think he was tryin' to get in wherever he could, which means he easily coulda switched to working for Coates."

"Mo Gainey wouldn't like that one bit."

I nodded. "I also know Stevie idolized Georgie Vickers."

Mr. Jones snorted. He went around the counter and held out a small pail.

"That troublemaker. Boy's too big for his britches. His daddy died when he was a young'un. Mama never remarried. Thinks he knows how to be a man by watchin' films like 'The Public Enemy.' The men in them pictures is white, but they sure do act tough. Georgie thinks he can be like that."

"I wouldn't call 'em great role models." I tossed the core in the pail and accepted a towel to wipe my fingers.

He set down the pail. "Forgive me, but you sound like you're still lookin' into what Stevie was up to. Ain't this a police matter now?"

"Nancy asked me to keep at it." I took out my notepad. "Like you, she doesn't quite trust the cops, even though I told her Sam MacKinnon is jake. Anybody else got a beef with Stevie?"

Mr. Jones leaned on his mop. "This could be dangerous for you. Unless you got your own Lizzy tucked away in that handbag."

I flashed him a smile. "I've done this a time or two. I know how to keep my skin in one piece."

He sighed. "Then I'll tell you somethin' I didn't tell that detective. This happened maybe two weeks ago. A couple of white boys came into the neighborhood. They was lookin' for Stevie. From what they was sayin', they'd lost money to him in a card game and they thought he was cheatin'. Guess they was comin' for revenge or somethin'."

"What did they look like?"

Mr. Jones frowned. "One was real stocky. Dark hair, buzz cut like the boys wear now. He had a scar, right here." He touched his chin. "The other one was taller and skinnier. Same haircut, but it was either dark blond or light brown. Hard to tell. I think he mighta had the pox at some point 'cause his face was all marked up. Both of 'em were wearing t-shirts and dungarees. They had to be draft age, so I don't know why they're roamin' the streets of Buffalo instead of out shooting Germans."

I wrote both descriptions. They meant nothing to me, but with any luck, they hadn't come because of a casual game of cards. I knew many bars had standing back-room games, although from the sound of these two, my money was on a roaming street game. The buy-in could be high, but if Stevie had dough from his work with Coates or Gainey, that wouldn't be a problem. It could also explain why he'd arranged to meet Tom in an empty lot. I could check the area for any bars that hosted games. "Anyone else?"

"Not that I know of. I ain't holdin' back on you this time." Mr. Jones studied me. "I like your grit, Miss Ahern. You be careful out there."

"I intend to." I took a quarter out of my change purse and held it out.

He waved me off. "That's way too much for a single apple."

I pressed the coin into his palm. "It's not just for the fruit."

Chapter Eighteen

The minute I came out of Mr. Jones's store, I was face-to-face with the considerable person of Miz Alva. She swelled like a bullfrog. "Come with me."

It didn't even occur to me to decline. "Yes, ma'am."

We walked a block down Jefferson. Miz Alva blazed a trail through any people we encountered while I trailed behind her. Those we passed cast curious looks in our direction, no doubt wonderin' what business a white girl had with the Fruit Belt matriarch. But no one stopped us. She turned onto High Street, strode past a neighborhood church, and made another turn onto Rose. I didn't bother askin' where we were goin'. I didn't get the sense she'd tell me until she was good and ready. She'd saved my bacon before, but I kept my eyes peeled for trouble, in case her opinion of me had changed.

We arrived at a small box-shaped house painted white with black shutters. An American flag hung beside the door. Some marigolds in their last bloom butted up next to a small Victory garden and lent a little color to the place. She opened the door. "Come inside and sit a spell. We can have tea like civilized folk and talk."

I slowed. "Ma'am, I'm very grateful for you steppin' in with those boys yesterday. But I barely know you."

"Lord have mercy, child." She threw her hands up. "If I'd'a wanted to hurt you, I coulda had it done before we ever left Jefferson Avenue. All I had to do was snap my fingers." Her smile showcased a gap in her top teeth along with the crooked bottom front ones. "I want to talk to you, but I thought this would be better than standin' on the corner, like two old biddies gossiping the day away. If you'd rather do that, we can go back."

I took stock of the neighborhood. It was quiet. A few young children played in the street, but there were no teenage boys in sight, and nothing that looked like gang activity. Mr. Jones said Miz Alva ruled the roost. I decided to trust his recommendation. "Tea would be swell. Thanks."

The inside of the house was neat as a pin. Mom woulda approved. A colorful quilt draped over the back of the couch. Several framed photographs clustered on the aged but well-polished tables. I picked one up. "Stevie and Nancy?"

Miz Alva entered the room holdin' a tray with the tea things. "As young'uns. I never married. My brother married Clementine. That's her, in that one."

I set down the picture of the kids and turned my attention to the second one. It showed a man and a woman on what musta been their wedding day. "They're a good-looking couple."

"John, God bless him, couldn't stick to a job much. Now he's gone off to war. Rodney, that's Mr. Jones, and I did what we could, but it's been a tough row for her to hoe." She put down the tray and settled her bulk in a chair. "Milk and sugar? We pool our coupons around here, so I got both."

I sat in the chair opposite. "No, thank you. I take it plain."

"Suit yourself." She handed over a chipped cup. "As I said, I been lookin' after Clemmie and her children a long time. This is the second day you been in this neighborhood. You may have noticed, there ain't a lot of White folk around. What's your business here?"

I blew on my tea to buy time. I didn't know how much Nancy had told her aunt, and it wasn't clear Miz Alva would approve of an outsider buttin' in on family business. I had to respect my client's privacy. At the same time, I sensed Miz Alva could be a valuable ally. "I'm sure you know Nancy was worried about her brother. She thought he'd gotten himself into hot water."

Miz Alva doctored her own tea. "Clemmie, Rodney, and I were all worried about that boy. Other folks, too. We're God-fearing people, Miss Ahern. We don't hold with the sort Stevie had been runnin' around with lately."

"Please, call me Betty." I sipped my tea. "At first, that was my only job. Now Stevie is dead, I'm lookin' into his murder."

"What qualifies you for that? Excuse me for sayin' so, but a slip of a girl like you don't look like she oughta be out doin' such things. You better not be takin' my Nancy's money and giving false promises in return."

I smothered a smile. "I'm a licensed private detective, Miz Alva. I have an office and everything. You come downtown and I'll show you the paper." I set down my cup. "I've solved murders. I used to work at Bell Aircraft. Trust me when I say I'm no lightweight. I'm not conning Nancy outta anything."

Miz Alva seemed satisfied. "What have you learned so far?"

I took out my notepad and gave her the skinny on my findings. "Have you ever seen Stevie with either Alonzo Coates or Moses Gainey?"

"Not in the flesh, but I heard the stories. Too often for there not to be at least a grain of truth in it." She stirred her tea. "Stevie, he's a good boy. Or he used to be, I should say. I think as he got older, he felt the loss of his daddy more and more. He didn't want to be dependent on women or an old man like Rodney. But goin' to school, maybe college, well, that was too slow. He wanted to take care of his mama and sister, and he wanted to do it right now. Not in ten years. It woulda been easy for men like Coates or Gainey to turn his head, flashing their money around, showin' off their fine clothes."

"Then they *have* been in the Fruit Belt."

"I used to wonder how they got away from the draft board. Gainey, he's the slick one. Coates makes you think he's like everybody else, but he ain't, not by a long shot." She drank. "Given the kinds of things they've been tied to, I don't want to know why the Army don't want 'em."

This was the second time I'd heard about coloreds not getting drafted. "What kinds of things?"

"Gambling, fights, theft. I know for a fact both of 'em hit up Rodney for money." She refilled her cup. "An old man was killed when his house was broken into earlier this spring. No proof, but I heard folks say he'd gotten on Gainey's bad side. Lost money at Gainey's fight ring and couldn't pay. You heard about the fights, I expect."

"I did." I consulted my notes. "What about Georgie Vickers?"

"Bah." She huffed. "Nothing wrong with Georgie that a stint in the Army wouldn't cure. Or a good thrashing. Another one who growed up without a daddy to show him how to be a man. I caught him with a gun earlier this summer. I told him to get rid of it before he blew his fool head off."

A gun, huh? Miz Alva prob'ly couldn't tell me what kind, more's the pity. "What was it?"

"A short one."

I'd already figured it was a handgun. "Mr. Jones told me Stevie followed Georgie around a lot."

"Like a puppy. Georgie always got cash, but he never paid much attention to Stevie. The others, Coates and Gainey, they use young boys all the time for runnin' errands. Nobody suspects a teenager might be carrying drugs or money or whatever. I'm pretty sure Stevie worked for one or both men, maybe at the same time. That's how he made the dough he used to try and impress Georgie."

If Coates and Gainey were rivals, they might have used Stevie as a spy as well as a runner. "When I was talkin' to Mr. Jones today, he mentioned two white boys came to the Fruit Belt." I described them. "Have you seen anyone like that?"

"No, but gambling, you say? Stevie loved games of chance. 'It's all probabilities,' he'd say. A real head for figures that boy had." Miz Alva sighed. "He'd have thought it a challenge and if you could pick up some money, more's the better. But I've never seen boys like you describe." She finished her tea. "I did see him with another white boy recently, though. Looked like they were makin' plans. At least the boy nodded, so he musta been agreein' with Stevie on something."

"Did you overhear his name? Or did Stevie tell you?"

"No. It was on the edge of the Fruit Belt, outside one of the businesses up on Main. Too much chatter from the crowds, and the boy took off right quick. So did Stevie. I didn't speak to him."

I held my pencil, ready to write. "What did this boy look like?"

"Thin, a little sickly looking, to be honest. Dark hair. I thought he was almost certainly a soldier home from the war. Even injured like he was and out of uniform, a boy who's been in the service has a certain bearing." She gathered up the tea things.

My heart sank. "What kind of injury?"

"Poor thing. He was on crutches." She tsked. "The lower part of his left leg was clean gone. He was real good with them crutches, though. Moved faster than I woulda thought he could."

Was Stevie tryin' to recruit Tom for either Coates or Gainey? Or did he have his own game on the side? It sounded like Stevie had his fingers in a lot of pies and played in a lot of games.

All I had to do now was figure out which of 'em got him killed.

Chapter Nineteen

I said good-bye to Miz Alva and headed straight to the First Ward. I bypassed home and went to the Flannery house, but Tom wasn't there. "I think he's out looking for work again, Betty," Mrs. Flannery said. "He's pushing himself too hard. Maybe you or Lee can convince him to rest up a bit."

I doubted Tom spent the day makin' the rounds of local businesses. Not after what I'd learned that afternoon. I also didn't think he'd listen to a word Lee and I had to say. I couldn't tell any of this to Mrs. Flannery though. She was worried enough as it was. "I'll try. If he comes home, tell him I'm lookin' for him, will you please?"

She promised to do so. But just as I didn't believe anything I had to say would matter to him, I didn't hold out a lot of hope he'd come to see me of his own choice.

After dinner, I went to the Tillotson house. From the back, I heard the snick-snick of the lawnmower blades and smelled the fresh-cut grass. I headed that way.

Lee pushed the mower across the yard, a lit cigarette dangling from his lips. "Gimme a minute."

I went to the back, sat, and lit my own smoke. Cat appeared from behind the garage and leapt up into my lap. I stroked his back while I tried to figure out my plan for the evening.

Eventually, Lee finished his chore. "You look fit to be tied. Let me put this away, and you can tell me what's wrong." He replaced the mower in the garage and came over. "Shoot."

I spilled the story of my day, winding up with Miz Alva's report of Tom and Stevie meetin' on the street. "There may or may not have been a job. I'll have to pin Tom down on that. But I bet one of the things he and Stevie talked about was those travelin' card games. Why else would Tom have been in that lot?"

"I wouldn't take a wager like that." He tossed aside the butt of his Chesterfield. "I told him to be patient. Wait until he got his prosthetic leg and I'd help him get a job. He said he didn't need me and that he had a line on something. I don't know who's the bigger dummy. Him for doin' it or me for believing him."

"He's your best pal, Lee. I'd have bought his tale too."

"I don't know if he was talkin' about one of these gangster types or the cards."

"Could be both." I ashed my Lucky. "I don't s'pose you know where we can find tonight's game, huh?"

"I wouldn't know where to start lookin'. I don't mind a hand or two of poker with the guys from work, but we play for pennies. When you got a job, two sisters, and a mother to take care of, high-stakes gambling isn't your scene." He leaned against the house. "They move those games all the time so the cops can't find 'em. Not only that Tom could be playin' cards or dice."

I stared into Cat's eyes. "Too bad Cat can't talk. I bet he'd know where to go."

Cat licked his paws in a decidedly self-satisfied manner.

Lee ran a hand through his hair. "What are we gonna do? Roam the streets? Would your detective buddy know where to look?"

"I think that's a waste of time." I stood. Cat leapt down and stared at me, tail swishing back and forth. "Wherever he goes, he's gonna have to walk down Mackinaw to get to his house."

Lee tilted his head. "Are you suggestin' what I think you are?"

"Yep." I brushed off my hands. "We're gonna stake out the front of his house tonight and wait for him. Bring a thermos of coffee. It could be a long night."

* * *

Lee and I waited under the massive maple tree in front of the Flannery house. We didn't smoke, since we didn't want Tom alerted by the glow of our cigarettes. We didn't talk much, either. I was busy wonderin' how honest Tom would be with me when I called him out. Lee's face remained stoic, not betraying his thoughts, but I figured they couldn't be good.

It was after midnight when I heard the unique clunk of a single boot hitting the cement and a sound that mighta been the rubber of the crutches. I could barely make out Tom's shape as he made his way down the sidewalk. His low, off-key whistle floated through the night air.

Lee waited until Tom was only a couple of yards away before he stepped out from under the tree. "Have a good night?"

Tom jerked his head back. He threw the right crutch at us and dove onto his yard. He came up on his knees, second crutch clutched in his hand like a baseball bat.

Lee and I darted aside to miss the flying wood. "It's us, you dope!" Lee held up his hands.

Tom blinked. "Jesus, Lee. What the heck were you thinkin', scaring me like that?"

I willed my heartbeat to slow down. "We sure weren't expectin' you to clobber us."

"The last time someone jumped out at me like that, he was carryin' a rifle." Tom used the single crutch to struggle to his feet. "This what you do now, lurk in the night waiting to ambush an old friend?" He held out his hand for the other crutch.

"We didn't think of that." Lee picked it off the ground and gave it to him.

"Yeah, well, you should have." Tom settled them under his arms and moved forward.

I moved to block him. "We came by earlier, but your mom said you were out lookin' for work. Your reaction just now? I can understand that. Did the Army also teach you to lie to the people who care about you? Or did you pick that one up on your own?"

He muttered an oath.

"You've picked up some bad habits." I crossed my arms. "Swearing and lying? To think you were once an altar boy."

He scowled. "You were once a nice girl who supported her fiancé. Sounds to me like you've picked up some bad habits of your own. Oh wait. You jilted me. I guess I'm fair game for your henpecking." He tried to push past me.

Lee grabbed him by the shoulders. "Oh no, you don't. Where've you been? Don't give me any guff about job hunting, either."

"It's none of your business."

I poked him in the chest. "But it is mine. You hired me, pal. You want me to do the job? You gotta be straight with me. Otherwise, hit the road and good luck to you."

"I don't need a dame to bail me out."

Lee snorted. "Are you kidding? You need all the help you can get."

"Says you."

"Yeah, says me." Lee poked him. "Stop bein' a dummy and come clean."

Tom ran his tongue over his lips. "I've been honest."

"No, you haven't. Nobody goes to a job interview at two in the morning. You're a lousy liar, Tom Flannery." I looked him up and down. "Show me your wallet."

"My what?"

I snapped my fingers. "You heard me. How much dough you got in there?"

"Look." He shifted his grip on the crutches. "I've been out with some guys, all right? I don't see what that has to do with anything."

I sighed. "Lee."

He reached around and plucked Tom's billfold out of his back pocket. He opened it and counted the bills. "You got a couple hundred cash here. Where'd you get it?"

Tom hesitated a smidge too long. "I've been saving. Not too many places to spend money in North Africa."

Lee and I exchanged a long-suffering look. Then I focused on my ex-fiancé. "Cards or dice?"

Tom held out for a moment but crumpled under my stare. "Dice. I'm broke."

I didn't believe him. "What happened to the money you got when you were overseas?"

He closed his eyes. "I sent my pay home when I was over there, so I have dough." He opened his peepers. "Ma won't give it to me, so I'm on my own if I want some spending money. I think she's afraid of what I'll do with it if she does."

"She's got a good reason." I jerked my head toward his house. "Let's sit before your arms give out."

He followed me, Lee right behind him. "Now you're concerned for my comfort?" Gripping the iron railing, he lowered himself to the top step.

Lee took the crutches. Then he took out his pack of Chesterfields and held it out to Tom, who took one. Lee lit both his smoke and his friend's. "I think it's time you told us the real story."

I pinned him with my stare. "How did you meet Stevie Washington?"

"What I told you before is true. Well, the first part." Tom blew out a cloud of smoke. "I spent all day lookin' for work. When I struck out, I went to a bar. It wasn't around here. That's where I met Stevie. He seemed on the young side, but he was savvy when it came to the streets, you know?"

I waited.

"He asked how I lost my leg. We got to talkin', one thing led to another, and he said how it sounded like I could use a night on the town. He knew a traveling card game happenin' that night and would I like to come as his guest." Tom puffed again.

"That's the evening I found you in O'Malley's," I said.

"Yeah." He tapped ash from the cigarette. "The next part is what I told you. After you and Mr. Handsome took me home, I slept for a few hours."

"Frank. His name is Frank Hicks."

Tom waved his hand. "I waited until my folks were asleep. Then I snuck outta the house and met Stevie at a game over on Wadsworth, in the basement of an old building. We played blackjack for, I dunno, a couple of hours." He studied his smoke, refusing to meet my gaze.

"How'd you get there?"

"How else? Bus." He took a drag. "After one of the hands, Stevie left to take a leak. A few minutes later, I heard two gunshots."

I had my doubts about his transportation, but for the moment, I let it pass. It prob'ly wasn't that important. I leaned forward. "Did anyone else hear them?"

He looked up. "They laughed, said something about people lettin' off end-of-summer firecrackers. But I knew better." He swallowed hard. "Once you've heard gunfire, you can't mistake it for anything else."

I glanced up at Lee, who gave a slight twitch of his shoulders. I took it to mean Tom hadn't opened up to him about his experiences on the front. "What happened then?"

"I went to check out the noise," Tom said.

"What about the others?"

"They kept playin'." Tom rubbed his chin. "That's when I found him. Stevie. He was lyin' on his back, staring straight up at the sky. Didn't take a field surgeon to see he was in a bad way. I went over to check on him. Not long after, the cops burst into the scene. I guess someone in one of the houses musta heard the noise and called 'em."

I had an easier time believing this story than one about meetin' Stevie for a job interview. "Think. Did you see anyone run out of there? Or maybe climb a fence or somethin'?"

Tom shook his head. "It was a good couple of minutes before I went out. I...I don't move as quick as I used to." He stared at his Chesterfield. "Stevie was alone. Maybe he saw someone. Well, he had to, didn't he, 'cause he didn't shoot himself in the chest." He exhaled and closed his eyes. When he opened 'em, he held my gaze. "Swear to God, Betty. I'm sorry I fibbed, but that's what happened."

"Is that all you did, played cards? Stevie didn't say anything about who ran the game?" I watched him. He'd moved pretty quick just now when Lee and I saw him. 'Course he wouldn't be able to spring up from a table like he used to. Maybe that's what he meant.

"No."

Another question sprang to mind. "Do you think Stevie was cheating?"

Tom averted his gaze. "I dunno. I was payin' attention to my cards, not his."

It wasn't the truth. Again. "Make a guess."

Tom took a drag and exhaled. "He wasn't wearing the kind of shirt or a jacket where you could hide cards. He didn't win a ton. Some. He'd lose a couple of hands, then win a couple. I think he woulda made a good buck if he'd lived out the night, though. I said something about his luck, and he said it was all probability."

There was that word again. What did it mean? The two mooks who'd come looking for him definitely thought he was cheatin'. Then it occurred to me. Mr. Jones had said Stevie was good at math. I turned my attention to Lee. "Could he have been countin' cards?"

Lee gave me a sharp look. "Maybe. Depends on what they were playin'."

I checked with Tom.

"I told you, blackjack," he said.

Lee gave a nod of satisfaction. "Could be. You only shuffle in blackjack once you've gone through the deck, so he'd be able to keep track of what had already been played, too. If he has a good memory and is aces at math, he might be able to do it."

"His sister said he was. Good at math, that is. How's it work?" I asked. I was gonna need a blackjack lesson, but it wasn't the time to ask. I'd do it later.

Lee scuffed his foot. "Fifty-two cards, four of each. If Stevie could remember what was gone from previous hands, he'd know what was on the table in the current hand and what was left with the dealer. From there, it's mathematics to make an educated guess on the odds of getting one of the remaining cards. Smart kid. Too smart." He took one last drag and flicked his cigarette away. "Countin' cards is not exactly cheatin'. But people don't like it. 'Specially the house."

A smart boy who got into trouble. I focused on Tom. "The game tonight. Was there a stocky guy with a scar on his chin or a skinny one with a pockmarked face?"

Tom thought a moment. "No."

"Were either of 'em there the night Stevie died?"

Now he flushed. "I, uh, don't remember."

"You expect me to believe that?"

He refused to meet my gaze.

I stood. "You got anything else to tell me?"

He hesitated. "No."

I knew he did. I wasn't gonna win this argument. Not in the middle of the night. "You'd better get to bed. Is there another of these games soon?"

He glanced at Lee. "They play most every night. Wednesday is the next time it'll be near enough to the First Ward that I can go."

"You're going." I checked with Lee. "Can you be there?"

He ran his hand through his hair. "I'll make it work."

Tom heaved himself to his feet. "I don't need a babysitter."

"Maybe not. But I need a second pair of peepers to look for my suspects. Someone who won't get so drunk he can't see straight." I stood and brushed off my pants. "Goodnight."

I headed home. I'd rather go to the game by myself. But that was too dangerous. With Lee at my side, I knew he'd have my back. And Tom's, if it came to it.

Chapter Twenty

I went to early Mass with my family, as I did every Sunday. After the service, I lit a candle for Sean. I paused a moment, then lit one for Tom. Yes, he'd returned home. But he wasn't whole, and I didn't mean his missing leg. When Lee and I cornered him last night, he'd been worn down. Ashamed. I replayed the talk in my head. The way he'd told the story reminded me of a little boy caught in a lie, not a man being honest. At the same time, I hadn't missed the undercurrent of anger in his voice. At Lee and me for grillin' him and showing no mercy? Or at himself for his behavior?

Maybe a little of both.

Once home, I walked to Conway Park. I'd worn a light coat earlier against the chill of the morning, but the sun had warmed the air, and I left it at home. The park was nearly empty, which suited me just fine. I needed space for my thoughts. I sprawled on the grass and stared at the wispy clouds dotting the sky.

I couldn't focus on my case, though. Tom had changed. He and Lee had grown up good Catholic boys. So had Sean. But that didn't mean anything out in the world. I was dead certain Lee's language and behavior was a lot different at GM than it was when he was around his family and friends in the First Ward. I hadn't spoken to Sean in nearly a year, but I was sure how he talked and acted aboard the *USS Washington* was not the same as when he'd been at home.

No, I didn't worry about what Tom had done overseas, when he'd been surrounded by his fellow soldiers in the deserts of North Africa. He hadn't been broken there. I remembered his early letters. They'd had a lightness to 'em, 'specially when he talked about everyday life. It was what I'd been lookin' forward to seein' again.

It was what I missed now.

I stared at my bare left ring finger and the little dent in my skin. Emmeline told me I'd done the right thing. What she couldn't see was how it had almost torn my heart out to do it. Would I ever put that ring back on?

I forced myself to be honest, if only in my mind. If the new Tom was here to stay, we were through. Everybody kept tellin' me to be patient, but how long was I s'posed to wait? I couldn't, *wouldn't*, sign up for a life with a bitter, broken man.

I also refused to believe the boy I knew wasn't in there. Buried deep. I desperately wanted to pull him out.

Then there was Frank. He'd made it clear he was interested in something more than friendship. How long would he wait? It would be mean to string him along forever. Frank had some odd beliefs, but he was a good guy. Not to mention his dimple and his Jimmy Stewart smile. He liked me for who I was. He didn't make bitter comments about me not stayin' the same girl.

Could I grow old with him? I wasn't sure. I thought about when he'd helped me bring Tom home from O'Malley's. "I won't strike a person," he'd said. Even earlier this year, when we'd faced down a killer in Front Park, I'd been the one who had to bash the creep over the skull and save our skins. Frank hadn't lifted a finger. He wouldn't.

Bein' a private detective could be dangerous. I needed someone who would actively help me, not just cheer me on. Tom would prob'ly not have an issue hitting a person who deserved it. But I couldn't trust him. Not the way he'd been actin' lately.

I groaned.

"I was gonna ask how you were feelin', but that was one of the most awful sounds I've heard lately, so I guess I know."

I sat up. Dot had come into the park. She bent to pick a late dandelion out of the grass. "How long have you been standin' there?" I asked.

"Long enough to read your face like a book." She sat next to me. "Lee told me about what happened last night."

I leaned back on to my hands. "I hardly recognize Tom. I wouldn't marry that man if he was the last Joe in Buffalo."

"At the same time, you're wallowing in guilt."

She knew me better than I knew myself. "Maybe I should hop the next train outta here and start over in another city. I hear Cleveland isn't bad. Or Pittsburgh. I like mountains."

"You won't do that." She bumped my shoulder with hers. "I have no advice for you 'cept to be patient. Ask the Virgin Mary for help. It'll work out."

"I think I'd be better off with Saint Jude."

"Tom's not a lost cause, and neither are you."

I lay back on the ground. Dot was right. I wasn't at that point yet.

She tickled my nose with the flower. "Lee did say you might have gotten a little information for your case, though."

"I s'pose." Tom confirmed Stevie's involvement with gambling, but not the identity of the boys who'd come lookin' for him. However, if there was even a semi-regular game in that neighborhood, there had to be a way of findin' out who was involved. After all, players would need to know where and when to show up. "You have plans this afternoon?"

"No." She grinned and her eyes twinkled. "But somethin' tells me you do."

"Seems like a fine day to go walking." I stood and held out my hand. "How 'bout you join me? For old times' sake."

* * *

The first thing I noticed about the neighborhood near Wadsworth, the scene of the crime, was the houses. They were smushed together, some with wide porches. It would be hard to hide any noise here. Then again, kids ran down the street, makin' a racket. I could easily imagine the same youngsters settin' off firecrackers or something similar. Maybe such noises weren't so uncommon, even when it was late.

Someone had called the cops, though.

The second thing I noticed was the lack of colored folks. There was no way Stevie Washington had strolled down the street unnoticed.

Dot must've thought the same thing. "I can't see Stevie comin' here to gamble. He'd have stuck out for sure."

"It was the dead of night, though." I wandered toward the address Sam had given me. "Fewer people out to see him."

Dot followed. "Maybe, but still. Would he have wanted to risk it? I thought these games were s'posed to be secret."

She had a point. I kept walking until I reached the place where Stevie's body had been found. Tom had been right. It was a vacant lot, an empty space between two buildings that dead-ended at the back of another brick building. It was wide enough for a truck to park there, maybe a delivery vehicle for the store on the right. I walked over the brickwork, my gaze sweeping the area.

"What are we lookin' for?" Dot asked.

"I'm not sure." The cops would've been here and searched. What could I find that they'd missed? Prob'ly nothing. "I wonder where the body was."

"Wouldn't there be one of those chalk outlines, like in the movies?"

I grinned. "I'm pretty sure that's a Hollywood thing, Dot. Sam's never mentioned it to me."

"The brick looks darker over here."

I strolled over. It was definitely a stain with irregular edges. "Good eye."

She leaped back. "You don't mean...this is from blood? Eww."

"Could be, and there isn't a puddle. I bet some well-intentioned resident tried to clean it." I crouched down. There was no way for me to tell if it was from Stevie and it didn't matter 'cept to give me a frame of reference. I decided it was as good as any. I stood and surveyed the area. The building behind me had a wooden fence around it. No gaps, which meant Stevie hadn't come from there. The one in front of me looked like an old warehouse. The wall was solid, but there were a few windows at the top, maybe to offices located above the warehouse floor. A set of steps led up from the basement with an iron railing on the ground level. I walked around to look down. There was a heavy door at the bottom, but I could see it was padlocked from the outside. Had it been so the night Stevie was killed? Another thing to ask Sam.

A girl's voice cut the air. "Who are you? What are you doing here?"

I looked up.

A girl stood on the sidewalk. She appeared to be Mary Kate's age, maybe a little younger. Her brown hair was in two braids, one on each side of her head, and long enough to lay over her shoulders. She wore a blue gingham dress with white ankle socks and black Mary Jane shoes. Her eyes were dark pools in the bright sunlight, wide with surprise.

I stepped toward her. "My name is Betty. This is my friend, Dot. What's yours?"

As I got closer to her, I could see her deep brown peepers were rimmed with red. She'd been cryin', and recently. "Are you okay?"

She dashed a hand across her face. "You wouldn't understand. Why are you here?"

"Just lookin' around. Did you know a boy was killed here Friday night?"

Her bottom lip trembled. "Yes. Mama told me. It's awful." She looked around me at the spot near the stain.

Dot spoke up. "Did you know him?"

The girl startled. "No. What makes you say that?"

"You look sad, is all." Dot glanced at me.

A man's deep, rough voice thundered. "Virginia! What are you doin', girl? I told you not to come down here."

Virginia's eyes widened, full of pure terror.

He walked up and grasped her arm. He had to be well over six feet tall and weigh two hundred pounds if he was an ounce. Every inch of him was muscle, though. His heavily calloused hands told of hard labor, as did the corded muscles of his arms. I put his age around forty-five. His hair, almost an exact match for the girl's, was tinged with gray in the sideburns. He looked like he needed a shave. He wore pants and suspenders, but only a white undershirt, like he'd half-undressed from church. "Get on home before I break out the switch. I told you to stay away from that boy when he was alive, and I don't mean to see you mooning after him now he's gone." He gave her a push. "Now get on home."

No doubt he was Virginia's father. "Excuse me, sir. My name—"

He wheeled to face me. "I don't care what your name is. You got no business bein' here. I don't recognize you or your friend, which means you don't live in these parts."

I stepped in front of Dot, who had paled. "No, we don't. But I'm a private detective and I'd like to ask you some questions about Friday night."

"Just 'cause some no-account colored boy went and got himself shot don't give you the right to pester God-fearing folk on the Sabbath." He glowered at me. "That boy was no good, and he got what he deserved. Now get on home and don't come 'round here again." He stomped off in the direction of the houses.

Chapter Twenty-One

I watched the man stride away until he disappeared into one of the houses down the block. It was red with white shutters and white pillars on the porch. I made a note of that 'cause it was certain I'd be comin' back. I faced Dot. "Dad or uncle?"

"Father." She tapped her chin. "He was too angry for an uncle. You don't get that mad unless you're involved with raising a child. At least, I don't think so."

I got my deck of Luckys out of my handbag. "They went into the same house. He wasn't fully dressed, so they prob'ly live together. Could be an uncle who's helpin' his sister raise her kids." I lit up. "But yeah, I agree. Father." I headed for the nearest bus stop, which was at the corner of Wadsworth and Allen.

Dot peered up and down Allen. "I'll tell you somethin' else. Whatever she said, that girl was starin' at that spot on the ground and cryin'. She came over while you were checkin' out the stairwell and I watched her. She stood there a good ten seconds. You don't do that for a stranger."

"I'm not surprised she did. It was a place where someone died." The bus came and we got on.

It was crowded, and the only open seats were in the back. "Stare, yes. Cry? No." Dot slid next to the window. "She knew him, Betty. They were friends, if not more."

Dot had a good point. The death of a stranger inspired fascination. Even a sort of morbid curiosity. Tragedy turned on the waterworks. I tried to imagine Mary Kate blubbering over an unknown boy's death. I couldn't.

"Let's say you're right. How'd they meet? It's hard to imagine how two teens of such different backgrounds could be friends, much less lovers. I can't imagine either family would be happy."

"Do you think Stevie's sister would know?" Dot chewed her lip.

"Maybe. She doesn't seem to know much about what he was up to. But it's worth askin'."

We got off at the corner of East North and Fosdick so we'd be as close as possible to the Washington house. It was a Sunday afternoon, and I didn't anticipate trouble. At the same time, I didn't want to parade through the entire Fruit Belt, not with Dot at my side. It was best we get in, take care of business, and leave.

A middle-aged woman answered the door. She wore her hair in a neat bun. It was mostly dark, but had a few silver threads in it. Her eyes were sad, and her face looked old and careworn, and she wore widow's weeds. This had to be Mrs. Washington. "May I help you?" The confusion in her dark eyes was clear. She had no idea what two white girls were doin' on her front step on a Sunday afternoon.

"Yes, ma'am." I held out my business card. "I work for your daughter, Nancy."

The woman's confusion deepened, but she took my card. "Work for her? I don't understand. White folk don't work for a teenage girl like her."

Nancy appeared at the door, dressed in a black blouse and matching skirt. "Mama, this is who I told you about. She's the detective looking into Stevie's troubles." She noticed Dot next to me.

"I'm Dot Kilbride." Dot held out her hand. "I'm an old friend of Betty's. I used to work with her a lot. Pleased to meet you."

Mother and daughter seemed uncomfortable. I rushed to put them at ease. "We'd like to talk to you. It's nothing terrible. May we come in?"

Mrs. Washington recovered. "Of course. This way." She let us into a living room with a couch, two chairs, and a coffee table. The only electric light was in the corner, but the front windows let in plenty of sunlight. Or they would have, if the curtains had been open.

Mrs. Washington brushed the front of her dress. "Where are my manners?

We don't have much, but I can scrounge up a little chicory coffee. Or maybe some tea? We don't have sherry or nothing, sorry."

Sherry? Did she think we were society girls? "Please don't put yourself out. A glass of water would be swell, thanks."

Dot murmured her agreement, and we took seats on the couch. "This is a nice room you have," Dot said, using the voice she had when she wanted to put a person at ease.

"Thank you." Nancy's brown skin flushed. "Nothing as fine as what you have, I'm sure."

Dot smiled. "You haven't been to the First Ward, have you? It's not Delaware Park. Grandma Kilbride's lace doilies are the fanciest things we have. Isn't that right, Betty?"

"Neither of us are livin' in luxury, that's for sure."

Mrs. Washington came back holdin' two glasses of water. "What's all this about luxury?"

I accepted my drink. "Dot and I were tellin' Nancy that we don't live in it."

It mighta been my imagination, but Mrs. Washington seemed to relax a smidge. "What brings you over on the Lord's day? This doesn't have the feeling of a social visit."

"It's not." I took a sip of water. "From what Nancy said, I'm guessin' she told you about why she hired me."

"She did. But Stevie is dead now. Surely, you're not still interested."

"I'll work the case as long as Nancy wants me to." I glanced at my client, who nodded. "I've managed to learn a few things." I gave them the highlights of Stevie's recent doings, including where he was the night he died.

Nancy frowned. "That detective. What was his name, Mama?"

Her mother got up and fetched a different business card. "Detective Sam MacKinnon. He seemed like a nice man, but I'm sure he has more important things on his mind than the death of a teenage boy." She didn't make reference to skin color, but her implication hung in the air.

"Ma'am, Detective MacKinnon is a good friend of mine," I said. "Believe me when I tell you he takes the death of your son as seriously as he would that of a Buffalo socialite."

Her expression betrayed her doubt.

"He does," Dot said. "I know him, too."

"Do you know the man who found Stevie?" Nancy asked.

Dot touched my knee with hers, a subtle move. We'd known each other long enough that I caught her meaning. "My understanding is he's recently home from the war and having a bit of trouble adjusting."

"Do you think he could have killed my brother?"

Ouch. "They didn't find a gun on him." I hoped Nancy didn't pick up on my non-answer. I definitely didn't want her knowin' I knew Tom or was workin' for him. Not yet. Maybe not ever.

I also didn't want to examine the ethics of that decision. Not while sittin' in the Washingtons' front room. But I knew I had to face it sooner or later.

Definitely later.

I moved to set my glass down, but didn't see anything to protect the wood of the table, so I held it. "Earlier, we were at the spot where they found Stevie's body. I didn't find anything, but there was a girl there, a young white girl. She looked very distressed. Does the name Virginia mean anything to you?"

Both Washington women looked baffled. It was Nancy who spoke. "I've never heard that name. But Stevie didn't share much with us, as you know. A white girl?"

I nodded.

Mrs. Washington blinked. "I don't think I've...oh." Her hand came to her mouth. "Virginia, Ginny. It could be that's who he was talkin' to."

I waited.

She continued. "It was a while ago, at least a couple of weeks. Miz Alva, she came 'round to see us. She's my husband's sister and looks after us."

"I know Miz Alva," I said.

"Anyway, she was teasin' me about how she thought Stevie must be sweet on a girl. She'd gone to use the pay phone at Mr. Jones's store. The one we all use." She glanced at Nancy. "Stevie was there, talkin' real quiet. She didn't catch much 'cept the name Ginny and Stevie sayin' for her to wait for him at the corner and he'd come 'round tomorrow."

Nancy nodded. "I remember now. Miz Alva, she was sure Stevie had a girlfriend he wasn't sayin' nothing about. She kept going on, tryin' to guess who she was, but Mama and I kept sayin' over and over how we didn't know a girl named Ginny. I don't think Miz Alva believed us. It could be this Virginia you're talkin' about. But a white girl? Where would he meet her? Not at school."

It was logical. Ginny could be a nickname for Virginia. But since Buffalo schools were segregated, Nancy's question was a good one. Maybe Stevie had gone to that location more than once. If so, he might have run across her one night. "Do you know what corner he meant?" I asked.

Nancy and her mother shook their heads. "If anyone had seen Stevie with a girl in this neighborhood, much less a white girl, we'd know about it." Mrs. Washington sounded sure.

I didn't doubt her. I knew how I'd felt on my first trip to the Fruit Belt. Young Virginia would have been just as, if not more, uncomfortable. To me, that meant one thing.

Whatever corner she and Stevie had been meetin' at, it was closer to her home than his.

* * *

Back in the First Ward, Dot and I ambled down Mackinaw toward home. It was the middle of the afternoon, so a lot of kids were out playin'.

"How does a young White girl fall in love with a colored boy?" Dot mused. "If it was love. You know how teenagers are."

I did. Mary Kate had been head over heels three times in the past year alone. "They thought it was, and that's the important part." I swept hair off my forehead. "Well, at least one of 'em did. We think. I can't answer that question, but I intend to find out."

"A boy tryin' to meet a girl in secret?" Dot raised her eyebrows. "If that's not teenage romance, I don't know what is."

Lee walked up to us. "Who're you talkin' about?"

"You and me, silly." Dot stood on her tiptoes to give him a kiss.

He pulled her close. "You said teenage. We're practically twenty. I don't think we count."

Dot told him about our thoughts on Stevie and Virginia. "Kinda tragic, isn't it? Two families who might as well be from opposite sides of the world. I don't think his people would be any happier with him than Virginia's dad is with her. Assuming that's her father we met."

I watched my friends and felt an unexpected stab of guilt. *That coulda been Tom and me.* "It's definitely got a Romeo and Juliet air about it."

He chuckled. "What do you know? You did pick up a little Shakespeare. I'd say school, but not in this case."

Dot leaned into his hug. "If he was workin' for one of those guys you mentioned, maybe he was there on business," she said.

"Coates and Gainey. Possible." I tapped my finger on my chin. After all, I didn't know how far their crime circles extended.

Lee's grin faded as he looked at me. "Tom's at home. I looked in on him earlier."

"What'd he say?" Did I want to know?

"Nothin'. He wouldn't talk to me." Lee threw a glance over his shoulder in the direction of the Flannery house.

"I don't reckon I'll have better luck, but I might as well try." I attempted a smile, but judging from my friends' reaction, I failed. "See you later."

I had no idea what I'd say to Tom, but I owed him the attempt. I knocked on the door. "Afternoon, Mrs. Flannery. Lee tells me Tom is home. I came by to see how he's doin.'"

She let me in. "He's in his room. He wouldn't even open his door for Lee, but maybe for you he will. Let me ask." She bustled away. I heard her begging him to come out, but she returned a minute later. "I'm so sorry, Betty. I don't know what's gotten into him."

I forced a smile. "That's okay, Mrs. Flannery. He's goin' through a lot. Between his injury, comin' home, and now findin' a dead body, well, anyone would want to shut out the world. Let him know I'm here if he wants to talk, will you?"

She clasped my hand. "I know you broke off the engagement. I want you to know I'm not angry with you. He's not my boy. I've lost him and I don't know if I'll ever get him back." She crumpled.

I put my arms around her. This was the woman I'd once looked forward to calling *Mom*. Her dreams were as battered as mine. I had no idea how to fix them.

For either of us.

Chapter Twenty-Two

I felt the need for routine on Monday morning, so I went to Teddy's for breakfast. While I waited for my order, I reviewed my notes from the weekend. It wouldn't hurt if I could tie Stevie more tightly to either Coates or Gainey. I hadn't forgotten Stevie's disappearing act the day I followed him, either. The card game that happened at the scene of the shooting was too far from the Fruit Belt. Stevie musta had options closer to home if he wanted to try his hand at countin' cards. Or had he ventured farther 'cause the neighborhood gamblers knew his tricks?

The sound of someone takin' the seat across from me broke my focus. "Frank! What are you doin' here?"

He wore his hospital uniform, but it didn't detract from his killer smile or the warmth of those dark brown peepers. "I've been trying to catch up with you. I finally decided that if you weren't at your office, this was the next best place. You have to eat, and while you may be doing business elsewhere these days, this is one of your favorite places." He looked up as Judy came over with my order. "May I order a cup of coffee with milk, please? And perhaps two slices of rye toast with butter and jam?"

"Coming right up, sweetie." Judy threw me a wink and hurried off.

I quirked an eyebrow. "That's a skimpy breakfast. If you don't have the dough, I can spot you."

He grinned. "I ate at home. But it feels wrong to sit here and watch you eat." He waved at my plate. "How are you doing?"

"Keepin' busy. Idle hands and all that. Still tryin' to figure out what Stevie was up to and who killed him." I drizzled syrup on my flapjacks. "Thanks for the tip on the desk. Emmeline said your folks gave her a swell deal on it."

"I'm glad I could help. I understand they're delivering it today."

"Later this morning, I think. Are you gonna help?" I'd arrange to be in the office if that was the case.

"No, I have to work at the hospital." He paused. "That's not what I meant, though. How are *you*, personally?"

I stared into his eyes, which were a little too full of understanding for comfort. I turned my attention to my breakfast. "I'm okay."

"Why do I get the feeling that isn't entirely true?"

I stuffed food into my mouth so I'd have an excuse not to answer.

Frank accepted his java and poured some milk in the mug. He stirred it slowly. "Tom isn't any better, is he." A statement, not a question.

I mumbled in the direction of my plate. "I didn't say that."

"You didn't have to." He laid down his spoon. "Is he still drinking a lot?"

I sighed and pushed my eggs around with my fork. "And lying and gamblin' and bein' a general dope." I told Frank what I'd learned about Tom's nighttime adventures. "I knew his story about a job interview was baloney, but sheesh. It's me. I've known him since we were kids. Doesn't he owe me, and Lee, the truth?"

Frank took a drink. "My conclusion, based on what you've said, is that he's embarrassed."

"I guess, but you'd think he'd be more comfortable with people he's known forever."

"Actually, I'd wager he's even more ashamed." At my expression, he continued. "Think about it. He knows his behavior hasn't been exemplary. It's one thing to go out drinking with your friends. It's another to have your best friend and your fiancée catch you in a lie or drag you out of a bar." He glanced at my left hand. "Is that why you broke things off?"

I put my hand under the table. It was stupid. He'd already seen my bare finger. "No." I gave Frank the skinny about Tom bein' a person of interest in Stevie's death. "I thought it would be better if we kept our relationship professional. People might believe it affected my judgment, workin' for the boy I'm engaged to."

"Is that so?" He kept his voice bland, but there was no missin' the implication he didn't believe me. "You'll get back together when the case is over?"

"It depends." I snuck a look at his face. I shouldn't have. My resolve to be businesslike shrank a little at the compassion in his expression.

"On what?"

"A lot of things." I paused and cleared my throat. "You think that's it? He's upset we caught him sneakin' cookies outta the jar, so to speak?"

"Partly. The other thing is his condition." Frank took another sip.

I stared.

"Betty, you are a wonderful person. I am, perhaps, a little more fond of you than I should be considering you were engaged when we met." He gave a rueful grin. "But for a person who is so perceptive, you are being amazingly obtuse."

My expression must've given away my confusion, 'cause he said, "That means dull-witted."

"I am no such thing." I crossed my arms in front of me.

Frank held up a hand. "Not usually, but can't you see? Tom wasn't merely shot or wounded by shrapnel. He lost a limb. He left you whole in body and mind. He is returning as anything but. He sees himself as a lesser person because he is a cripple among healthy people."

"None of us have said that!"

"You don't need to." Frank pushed aside his mug. "I have seen it firsthand. Both with patients at Buffalo General and with others who have had such devastating injuries. It's a lot to come to grips with."

"Tom wouldn't think like that. You don't know him."

Frank dipped his head. "You're right. I don't. For the sake of argument, assume I'm right. He's trying to find out where he belongs. I'm not claiming he's doing a particularly good job of it."

I unclasped my arms. "You can say that again."

"But neither you nor I can possibly understand what he's feeling. You must be patient with him."

"I'm runnin' out of patience. I've got half a mind to tell him he's on his own." I picked up my fork.

He sobered. "You mustn't, however much you want to. If you ever loved him, do not leave him alone in his darkness because you will only make him worse. He needs you. And Lee, but especially you."

Frank's answer surprised me. Hadn't he just said how much he liked me? Why wouldn't he be glad I was free to date him? I studied his face. He was deadly serious. "You are one odd duck, Frank Hicks. That's for sure and for certain."

Here I was startin' to think I could finally act on my attraction to him without guilt, and he was tellin' me to stay put. I didn't know whether I liked him even more for it or if I felt rejected.

"It's not the first time someone has said that to me." He drained his mug. He wrapped his toast in a paper napkin and put some change on the table. Then he slid outta the booth and walked away.

* * *

I left Teddy's with my mind full of Frank's words. Don't leave Tom. What did that mean? He didn't even wanna see me. I thought back to the moment I handed the engagement ring back. He'd barely flinched, kinda like he'd expected it. Or that I'd done him a favor by callin' things off so he didn't look like the bad guy.

If anything, Tom was leaving me, not the other way around.

Enough of that. I had work to do. I got to the office about quarter to ten. Emmeline's desk had already been delivered. It was a pretty piece, all rose-colored wood with a delicate black inlay around the sides and top. The only visible flaw was the foot-long scratch on the side, and the legs looked fine. Emmeline had arranged all her things, including the telephone. She didn't stop workin' when I walked in. "Good morning. Do you like it?"

"It's more important that *you* like it." I headed for the inner office.

She followed. "Detective MacKinnon called."

"Swell. I need to talk to him anyway." I sat down. "What do you know about card games, specifically blackjack?"

"Not very much. Why?"

I told her my theory about Stevie and his card-counting. "I can't believe that would make him a popular guest."

"Do you think that's why those two boys were looking for him?"

"It's a good possibility." I drummed my fingers on my desktop. "The games move around, which means it's unlikely we'll find 'em at the same spot. At least not for a while. When you get to the library this afternoon, see if you can find any news articles about this racket. Or about the bare-knuckle fights that Gainey s'posedly runs."

She made a note. "If they mention locations, do you want me to research those as well?"

"Yes. I want to interview whoever I can. We also need to put a last name to Virginia."

"Who's that?"

I told her about the girl Dot and I had seen yesterday and the man who shooed her home.

"That's going to be more difficult." Emmeline frowned. "It doesn't sound like Virginia is an adult, which means any property records are in her father's name. He didn't identify himself?"

"I'm not even sure it's her dad. But I think it is."

She pursed her lips. "I might get something from the census. Assuming they lived there three years ago. You know the address?"

I gave it to her.

"I'll see what I can find."

I picked up the blower. "Say, I got another question for you. Is there a way to get from the Fruit Belt over to Wadsworth without bein' seen?"

The question clearly flummoxed her. "That's several blocks, so not by walking. Or bus. I suppose private car, but considering how few people drive, the mere fact a car would be seen defeats the purpose of secrecy."

"Think about it and let me know if you get any bright ideas." She left, and I dialed the number Sam had left. "You called?"

"How does it feel to be able to take messages and return the call in private?" he asked.

"Nifty, but that's not why you rang. What do you need?"

"Vice raided one of Alonzo Coates's gambling dens last night. Coates wasn't there. It seems he's gone to ground. The detective is a friend of mine and he knew I was interested in any connection between Stevie and Coates, so he twisted some arms." Sam paused and it sounded like he took a drag off a cigarette.

"What did you learn?" I grabbed a pad and a pencil.

"Nobody had any names. But a couple of them talked about a new kid Coates had poached from Moses Gainey's organization. Their description sounded a lot like Stevie."

I whistled. If Stevie had been sellin' out his boss, and Gainey found out, that would be bad news. "Did they say what Stevie was doin'?"

"They didn't know. But Coates and Gainey have been fighting back and forth over the Fruit Belt for a couple of years, a lot like the Germans and the French over Alsace-Lorraine." Sam took another puff. "It's not impossible that Stevie was feeding Coates inside information."

I twiddled my pencil. "But Stevie woulda been a runner, low on the ladder. What could he have offered?"

"You'd be surprised. Sometimes the best informants are the ones who seem least important. The runners and errand boys."

Not unlike servants in swanky houses.

Sam continued. "People forget to watch their mouths, and because they go everywhere, they pick up a lot of news. However."

I waited.

"One of the men who was arrested didn't think Coates considered the new boy trustworthy. He told us Coates was looking into Stevie's 'bonna-feedees.' I assume he meant bonafides."

I twiddled my pencil. "If Coates found out Stevie was a spy, how would he have reacted?"

"Whatever he did, it wouldn't have ended well for young Mr. Washington."

I made a note. "Tom came clean. The spot where Stevie was found was hosting a card game." I gave Sam the bare facts. "Who'd be runnin' that game? I don't see Coates or Gainey involved with it."

"I agree. It's out of my area, but Vice may know. Thanks for the tip."

"No sweat." I bit my lip. "Sam, what were the results of the gunpowder test on Tom's hands?"

"There was a small amount, but it could have been transfer from the body when Tom attempted first aid." Sam's voice was solemn. "We still can't find the gun. But Betty, if Stevie was in fact cheating at cards, and Tom was there, it means he has a motive. If he lost money and wanted it back…."

I didn't want to admit it, but the thought had occurred to me. "What did he do with the gun?"

"It's not impossible he got rid of it. Somehow."

If Stevie had gotten in hot water with others, he almost certainly had been up to his tricks in other places. Tom was angry at the world. His mother was holdin' his dough, and he couldn't get a job. He knew how to handle firearms. The old Tom woulda never put himself in a situation like this, and I couldn't imagine him shootin' a guy over a game.

The new Tom? I just didn't know.

Chapter Twenty-Three

I spent the rest of the morning working in the office. At least I tried. I could admit to myself, if not to anyone else, I was stumped. It seemed I had more puzzles than answers. Who was Virginia? How did Stevie get over to where he was killed? What exactly was he doin' for Moses Gainey, and how did Alonzo Coates figure into it? Had Stevie been tryin' to impress his idol? What else was Tom hidin' from me?

It was like the crime version of twenty questions.

Around noon, I decided to give my brain a break and grab a bite to eat. Maybe inspiration would come to me over a grilled cheese sandwich. I picked up my purse, but before I could leave, the phone rang. "Ahern and Associates."

"Miss Ahern, is that you? You gotta come quick. Georgie, he's got a gun."

I recognized the desperate voice. "Nancy, slow down. Are you talkin' about Georgie Vickers?"

"Yes. He's out behind a storefront on Best. He's shootin' at old tin cans. Mr. Jones, he told him to stop and give up the gun, but Georgie laughed. He said he'd shoot anyone who tried to make him." The girl sounded near tears.

It was an alarming situation for sure, but not my cup of tea. "Nancy, you need to call the police. I'm not—"

"He said the next person to get in his way would end up like Stevie!"

Doggone it. I was not about to try and talk down a teenage hoodlum who thought he was a real-life Jimmy Cagney. But I couldn't ignore the statement, either. "Listen. I'm on my way. But it'll take time. Meanwhile, you have to call the cops."

"They ain't gonna rush over here." The bitterness in her voice came through loud and clear.

"Call Detective MacKinnon." I rattled off his number. "Then, for God's sake, stay inside and away from Georgie."

She promised she would, on both counts. I rushed outta the office, pausing only to lock the door. The bus would be too slow, so I hailed a cab. "Corner of Best and Jefferson, and step on it." I slammed the door. I definitely needed a car.

The cabbie didn't turn around. "This ain't New York City, lady."

"The faster I get there, the bigger your tip." I sat back. "Now stop flappin' your gums and start drivin'."

He took me at my word and peeled away. While I clutched the door, prayin' we'd stay out of an accident, I also hoped Nancy had followed my instructions and that no one had tried to play hero and disarm Georgie.

We arrived at the corner of Best and Jefferson in what seemed like record time. I paid off the cabbie, includin' the promised tip. Nancy hadn't given me an address, but it wasn't hard to follow the noise and the sirens. The police had arrived. Less than half a block away, I saw a crowd, held back by a uniformed officer. Voices came from behind a boarded-up building that looked like it used to be a business. I recognized one voice as belonging to Sam.

"This isn't the Wild West, Georgie." Sam's voice sounded calm and reasonable. "You're not going down in a blaze of glory. Don't believe the movies. It's harder to shoot three men in rapid succession than it looks."

"I practice a lot." Georgie sounded cocky. "I can take at least one of you."

"I'm sure that will be a lot of relief to your mother when they give her your body."

"You leave my mama outta this."

I rounded the crowd to get a better look. Georgie was backed up against the wall of the building. A board set over two metal drums was next to him. Tin cans littered the ground, and I could see where the brickwork was chipped. That had to be his target. Two uniformed beat cops stood off to each side, guns drawn. Sam faced Georgie. Sam also had his pistol aimed at

Georgie's chest. The young man was waving his own weapon wildly, as if he couldn't decide where to shoot first. It was a recipe for disaster.

I thought about trying to draw Georgie's attention, but I didn't want to put Sam and his men in any more danger. Georgie was clearly an amateur, but that didn't mean he wasn't dangerous. Sam had once told me he'd rather face a pro than an armed street kid.

I found Nancy at the edge of the crowd. "What happened?" I asked as I sidled up.

"We all know Georgie likes to target practice with cans, but he's never had a pistol before." She wrung her hands. "I've always seen him with an air gun. Mr. Jones told Georgie to stop 'cause someone was like to get hurt. But Georgie just laughed and asked if the old man was offerin' to be a target. He, Georgie, said anyone who tried to take his gun away would find out what was what, just like Stevie."

"He confessed?"

Nancy's peepers were wide with fear. "Not in those exact words. Someone, I think it might have been Miz Alva, asked Georgie if he'd shot Stevie. Georgie laughed and said Stevie was a nobody, not worth killin'. But whoever done it saved Georgie the trouble of runnin' Stevie off. But he could just be talkin', right?"

It was possible. The problem was everybody in the neighborhood knew how Stevie died. Georgie could be usin' the incident to make himself look like a big man. The gun he was wavin' around might not even be the one used to kill Stevie. But until the cops could get it and do tests, no one would know.

While I'd talked to Nancy, the men had continued to jabber back and forth. I desperately wanted to talk to Sam, but I couldn't interrupt him. I needed a distraction. Something that would get Georgie to drop the gun so Sam and his fellow officers could nab him. But what?

I looked around. There were few cars on the street. But there was a truck parked not far away. I could see empty crates stacked in the bed. The driver wasn't at the wheel. He was either makin' his rounds or part of the crowd. I sprinted over to the cab and opened the door. Then I smacked the steering wheel to sound the horn. It cut the air, and most everyone, including Georgie, whipped their heads around to check. The driver came over and tried to wrestle me away. I got one more hit in before he dragged me outta the truck.

There was another rush of noise, and all the attention returned to the standoff. I pulled away from the irate driver and stood on my tiptoes. It had worked. The cops had wrestled Georgie to the ground. Sam picked up the gun he'd been waving and dropped it in a bag. Then he turned to face the crowd. When he spotted me, he shook his head.

I smiled and waved.

* * *

I sat in the passenger seat of Sam's car as he drove me downtown. I listened to his lecture for about five minutes.

"That was incredibly stupid, Betty. We had the situation under control." His voice sounded tight.

"Come on, Sam. I didn't charge into the middle of things. I didn't try, and take him from behind or interrupt what was goin' on." I shot a sideways glance at him. "I caused a ruckus is all. There was just as much chance he'd ignore it, right?"

"You're lucky Officers Wilkins and Harlington are well trained."

"How'd it go down?"

"As you intended, I'm sure. As soon as the truck's horn blared, Vickers lowered his gun and turned to check out where the noise was coming from." Sam sighed, and the hint of a grin tugged at his lips. "Harlington body-tackled Vickers, and Wilkins was able to get the gun away. Then we took him into custody." He flicked the cigarette he'd been smoking outta the window. "Don't ever do that again."

"Yes, sir." I looked at the bag holding the pistol. It looked big, but I was far from an expert. "This what was used to shoot Stevie?"

"It's the right caliber, a .38. But we won't know for sure until we run the ballistics comparison." He parked.

CHAPTER TWENTY-THREE

I nibbled my thumbnail. "The gunpowder test is gonna be useless, isn't it?"

Sam nodded. "We know Vickers was using this for target practice, so yes, the swab will come back positive." He got outta the car. "I'll let you know what we learn from him."

I scrambled out. "No way. I gotta be there."

"I cannot let you be part of the interrogation. You know that."

I grabbed Sam by the shoulder. He turned, and I let go. "Sorry. I'm not askin' to question him. But isn't there some way I can watch?"

He hesitated.

"Come on, Sam. It's me. Be a pal."

He took off his fedora and scrubbed a hand through his hair. "We have an interrogation room with one of those newfangled two-way mirrors. The captain is in Albany for a conference. I'll sneak you in so you can watch." He jabbed a finger in my direction. "No questions. No jumping the suspect when he comes into or out of the room. Any funny business and I'll arrest you for interfering with a police investigation."

I gave him a salute. "I'll be as quiet as a mouse. Thanks." Sam was prob'ly gonna ask everything I would, so I didn't have a problem with being a spectator.

He jammed his hat back on and walked away.

Sam led me to a darkened room. I'd never seen a two-way mirror before. "Are you sure he can't see me?" I asked.

"I don't understand exactly how it works, but yes. As long as you keep it dark in here." He nodded to the mirror. "It does nothing for sound, so remember what I said."

"Silent as the grave." I mimed zipping my lips.

He closed his peepers, lips moving in what might have been a silent prayer, and left.

There weren't any chairs in the room, but that was okay. I pulled out my notebook and pencil and looked through the glass. Georgie sat at a scarred wooden table, his hands cuffed in front of him, while a uniformed cop guarded the door. In less than a minute, Sam entered. He held the bag with the gun. "Welcome to the big leagues, Georgie. A Thirty-Eight Special. You're moving up in the crime world, aren't you?"

Georgie sneered. "That's right, mister poh-leece-man. You gotta respect me now."

"Except for the fact that you're in handcuffs." Sam leaned on the table. "Where'd you get the gun?"

"None of your business."

Sam walked behind him and slapped him on the back of the head. "Wrong answer. Try again."

Georgie ran his tongue over his lips. "Found it."

"Where?"

Georgie glared up.

Sam raised his hand.

"Near a dumpster over on Allen."

I pictured a map. Allen Street ran between Wadsworth, where Stevie had been found, and the Fruit Belt.

Sam must've been thinking the same because he asked, "Where on Allen?"

Georgie eyed Sam's hand, which was on the table, before muttering, "Over near Michigan, but not the corner." He studied his cuffed hands.

Sam's gaze flicked up toward the mirror. We were definitely on the same page. He returned his attention to the suspect. His next question was music to my ears. "When did you find it?"

Georgie's shoulders moved up and down. "Friday night? Saturday morning? Somethin' like that. Over the weekend."

"You gotta be more precise, Georgie."

"Well, I can't." His hard-eyed stare said he was still defiant, no matter how much he got slapped for it.

Sam changed his tactics. "What if I told you that gun was used to kill Stevie?"

I knew the lie as soon as I heard it. The tests weren't back yet. But Georgie wouldn't know.

He didn't twitch. "You can't prove that."

Sam held up his hands. "We have people who can tell us these things."

A small grin played around Georgie's mouth. "I ain't dumb, no matter what you crackers say. Don't matter if it's true, though. I didn't shoot the punk. But good riddance."

"Why do you say that?"

"Stevie was a kid who thought he was a big man." Georgie relaxed, leaning back as much as he could, and stretched his long legs under the table. "Word on the street said he was workin' for Moses Gainey as an errand boy. But he was sellin' secrets to Alonzo Coates and skimming off the bag when he delivered it to Mr. Gainey." White teeth flashed in his dark face. "That ain't good for your health. Mr. Gainey, he don't play around, if you know what I mean."

"Yeah, I do." Sam put his hands in his pockets. "There's another rumor going around, Georgie. Stevie was filching from *you*, too. Are you a big man? Maybe setting yourself up as competition for Gainey and Coates? Or proving you can be a partner?"

Georgie's expression went sullen.

"If Stevie was Gainey's boy, what if he was informing on you? That wouldn't make you happy, would it? We saw this afternoon how much you like shooting things." Sam leaned on the table again. "Tell me now, and it'll go a lot easier on you."

There was a long pause. Finally, Georgie looked up, dark eyes full of fire. "I 'spect you can pin anything on me you want. Folks like me always gonna be your huckleberry. I seen it in Alabama, Georgia, all around. You Northern crackers think you're different. You ain't. You want me to be grateful you ain't in here with a rubber hose, beatin' me? I ain't." He spit. "You gonna have to do better, mister poh-leece-man. I ain't the one you're lookin' for."

Sam stared at him. Then he motioned to the uniformed cop. "Take him back to his cell. Let him think on it."

The officer grabbed Georgie and yanked him to his feet.

I stared at him as he was pushed outta the room. The expression on his face wasn't defeated or sullen. He looked almost triumphant, like he'd won the battle. I wasn't sure he was wrong.

* * *

After the cop led Georgie away, Sam joined me in the room behind the mirror. I noted the faint dark smudges under his eyes. "Haven't you been sleeping?" I asked.

He lit a cigarette. "Insomnia. What did you think?" He waved his hand at the empty interrogation room.

"You're lucky he didn't know you were fibbing about the gun."

"Better to be lucky than good, as the saying goes." He cracked a grin.

"Remind me not to play you at cards." I leaned on the wall. "Do bluffs like that ever work?"

"Enough that I keep doing it." Sam flicked away some ash.

"Did it this time?"

"I don't know." He rubbed his chin. "Vickers stayed cool as a cucumber. That could mean he was telling the truth or maybe he's a great actor."

"We need someone who saw him pick up the gun to strike him off the list. Or for your test to be negative."

"That would be ideal." Sam exhaled a cloud of smoke. "Fingerprints won't help us on this one. We tried, but there are so many on the grip, it's useless."

I thought about what Georgie had said. "What did he mean callin' you a cracker?"

"It's a Southern term for white people. If you're thinking it doesn't sound nice, I don't believe it's supposed to."

"It doesn't sound like he had the same kind of admiration for Stevie as Stevie did for him."

"No, but that's not unusual." Sam puffed. "Stevie was a kid, a good three or four years younger than Vickers. Stevie had no accomplishments Vickers would take seriously. In addition, if he knew Stevie was playing games with Coates and Gainey, I don't think Vickers would have trusted him, either."

I tapped my chin. "That doesn't make it sound like he's got much of a motive."

"No, but this does." Sam held out a folder he'd brought in with him. "Witness statement from a canvass of the neighborhood. Two different people saw Vickers and Stevie get into an argument on different occasions. One person said it nearly came to blows."

For a moment, I couldn't think why, but then I remembered Sam's statement to Georgie. "Stevie was stealin' from his idol?"

"That's what the witness claims he overheard."

"But if he hero-worshipped Georgie, why?"

"You can't think of anything?"

I thought about Stevie. He wanted people to notice him, to take him seriously. "Georgie prob'ly isn't into high-level theft. But if Stevie wanted to show Coates or Gainey how clever he was, he mighta tried something with Georgie." I paused. "Or he was tired of Georgie puttin' him down, so he stole as an *I'll show you* thing. Look what I can do, that sort of thing."

Sam's expression conveyed his approval. "Either is possible. What is also in play is maybe Stevie thought he could take over the structure Vickers was building. It wouldn't be as big as Coates or Gainey, but he could build it. Assuming those two would tolerate the competition, which I doubt."

Any of those would be a solid reason for Georgie to kill his admirer. "Did you ever find out who else was at that card game?"

Sam pulled out his notepad. "According to your fiancé, it was him, Stevie, and three other guys identified only as Larry, Shorty, and Babyface. Larry and Shorty are white. Babyface is a Negro."

"I broke off our engagement."

Surprise flashed across Sam's puss, but he didn't say anything. "Obviously, those names aren't very helpful. We've questioned the owner of the building. He claims not to know the basement was being used for card games. He says he's the only person who has a key."

I cocked a hip. "He's lyin'. Gotta be."

Sam flipped his notepad shut. "I'm sure he is. I didn't have hours to waste listening to his denials. We questioned his employees, and they all claim to be ignorant of any wrongdoing. They also provided alibis for Friday night. We're in the process of verifying them now." He eyed me. "You realize we have a problem with all three of these suspects."

"We don't know how they got into that neighborhood without bein' seen, same as Stevie."

"We've canvassed the surrounding houses and businesses twice. Three colored men go into a mostly white area, and no one saw anything. No matter what time of day, I find that hard to believe."

I did, too. "There must be an answer. We gotta find it. Good luck with checkin' those alibis."

I left the room. I had no doubt Sam would get his answer through proper police procedure. It would be slow, though. I had an idea, and if I was right, I could get an answer faster.

Especially if I bullied Tom into helping.

Chapter Twenty-Four

Once back in the First Ward, I headed straight for the Flannery house. The weather had turned warm, and I felt a light coat of sweat on my face when I arrived. I rapped on the front door. "Afternoon, Mrs. Flannery. Is Tom here? I need to talk to him."

She wiped her hands on a towel. "I don't think that's a good idea, Betty. He still isn't in the best way."

"I understand, but this is important."

Her skin musta been dry by now, but the motion of the towel didn't stop. "He may be very unpleasant to talk to."

"I'll manage."

She sagged. "He's in the backyard."

I thanked her and went around the house. Tom sat in a battered wooden chair, his flask on the ground next to him. His chin had a healthy growth of dark stubble and I wondered how long it had been since he shaved. He wore a wrinkled t-shirt and denims, both of which looked like they were on the second day of wear. Even from a couple of feet away, I detected the rank odor of unwashed body and booze. "Hey."

He didn't answer, just continued to flick pennies into a jar about three feet away. Judging from the number of coins that found the target compared to the ones on the ground, he had good aim.

"I said hello."

"No, you said hey." Another penny sailed through the air and rattled home. He picked up the flask and took a swig.

No, he wasn't gonna make this easy. "Staying active, I see. Very productive use of time. How many times has your mom refilled that flask?"

"I do it myself." He flicked a coin. "What else am I gonna do? No one will hire me. Nobody wants a one-legged man with a high school education. Might as well drink." He swigged from the flask.

"Tom—" I reordered my words. "I can't even imagine how hard this is for you. But life isn't over, not by a long shot. You're gonna get a prosthetic leg, which means you'll get hired somewhere. Factories need workers. You gotta be patient."

"Easy for you to say." He shot me a baleful look. "How's Mr. Hollywood?"

"Stop callin' him that. Frank's a good guy." I wondered if I should continue, but I figured it couldn't hurt. "Maybe you should talk to him. He's seen a lot of wounded people, and he works at a hospital. It might be good for you."

"Cozy up to the Joe who stole my girl? No thanks." He shook the flask. "Time for a refill."

I thought about protesting, but I knew it would be useless. "I need you to come with me."

"Why?"

"We're gonna go back to where you found Stevie, the night of the card game."

With no more pennies to throw, he reached out with his crutch and gently hooked the jar between the armrest and hand grip. He dragged it toward him. He'd done this a lot 'cause he retrieved his target without spilling a single coin. "No thanks."

"I wasn't askin' for a favor."

He poured the pennies into a pile on his lap. He handed me the empty container. "Be useful and put this back over there."

"No. Get up. We're going over to that warehouse. You're gonna look at all the employees and tell me if one of 'em was at the card game the night Stevie got shot."

"Why would I do that?"

I grabbed onto the last threads of my patience and held on. Tom was actin' worse than a petulant child. "You hired me, that's why. I need this information and you're gonna come with me. It's not like you're doin' anything else at the moment."

He grabbed his crutches and heaved himself to his feet. He stumped over to me. Even slouched the way he was, he topped me by a couple of inches. He'd lost weight. He stunk to high heaven and the fire in his eyes, which were slightly red from drinkin', burned hot. "Make me."

It was an intimidation ploy. But I'd stared down guys with guns. A slightly tipsy boy missing half a leg didn't have a chance. "You think I can't?"

"I think you won't. I know you. You talk tough, but you wouldn't dare raise a finger to me."

"I'm not that girl anymore, Tom. I'm an honest-to-pete licensed private detective. I've seen a lot worse than you." I lifted my chin.

Tom called me a name, and not a very nice one.

Mrs. Flannery's voice rang out. "Thomas William Flannery. How dare you use such language in my house? And to Betty of all people." She marched over and whipped him with the towel.

I expected an outburst from him, but it didn't come.

She planted her fists on her hips. "I'm not entirely certain what's going on. I heard enough to know Betty asked for your help, and you're going to give it to her."

"I'm not feeling so good. You know that," he mumbled.

"I've tried to go easy on you and be understanding. Clearly, I've coddled you too much. It's one thing to talk like that to me, but I'll not have you calling her names." She grabbed his flask. "No more of this. You want to act like a child? I'll treat you like one. Don't smirk at me, mister." She shook a finger. "You think you're too big for me to turn over my knee? Maybe so, but you don't run as fast as you used to either. You'll feel that broom handle on your backside if you don't straighten up."

I watched as the emotions ran across Tom's face. Disbelief, anger, then shame.

"You two might not be engaged, but you'll do what Betty says or you'll find another spot to lay your head. I didn't raise an ungrateful, sullen brat." She bit her lip, two spots of color high on her cheeks. She looked at me. "He'll go with you now." She stalked back into the house.

I hadn't expected such an outburst from Mrs. Flannery. But I approved. Maybe she'd get through to her son where I hadn't.

Tom's gaze followed her, then came back to me. He swallowed hard. "Where'd you say you wanted to visit?"

"The warehouse. But you got one thing to do first."

"What?"

I turned him around. "Clean yourself up, shave, and put on fresh clothes. You smell like a drunken bum who's been sleeping in the gutter."

Chapter Twenty-Five

On the bus to Wadsworth, I watched Tom out of the corner of my eye. He took a seat across the aisle from me, even though we would have easily fit on the same one, including the crutches. He rubbed at the pink skin on his face. "You didn't have to embarrass me in front of Ma like that."

I wondered how long it had been since he shaved. "Don't blame me. You did that all by yourself." He still had the thin face of a guy who'd been sick, but clean clothes, a wash, and a comb and razor did wonders for him.

He scowled. "You think one of the guys from the card game works at the warehouse?"

"I think it's worth a look. The door to the outside was locked, which means whoever opened up needed a key. Easiest way is if he is an employee or knows one." A thought occurred to me. "How did you get there?"

"Same as we are now. Took a bus."

With the twenty-four-hour factory schedules, it would have been easy. "Was Stevie already there?"

Tom frowned in thought. "I think so, yeah. Why do you ask?"

I told him about the way Stevie had disappeared the day I followed him from the soda shop. "He had to go somewhere."

"Or someone at the store lied to you." Tom shrugged.

"It's possible, but I don't think that's the case this time." I leaned back in my seat. "The location of the card game that night isn't miles from the Fruit Belt, but it isn't right around the corner, either. Stevie coulda taken a bus, but I got the feeling he didn't want to be seen. That late, in a white neighborhood, he'd stick out. Plus, I think he had another reason for sneakin' in there." I told Tom about Virginia and the phone calls from Ginny.

He scratched his cheek. "You think they're the same girl?"

"Makes sense."

"Huh." His eyes lost focus. "A colored boy courting a White girl? Definitely two people who wouldn't want to be seen. Not together, not goin' to the same place." He paused. "Could be he used a tunnel."

I sat up. "What do you mean? There isn't a tunnel from the Fruit Belt to Wadsworth, is there?"

"Don't know." Tom gave me a lopsided grin. "It was something Lee was obsessed with when we were kids. He read about the tunnel they used when that guy shot McKinley. To get between the jail and the courthouse so people wouldn't attack him."

"That's our Lee, the history nut."

Tom chuckled, the first real laugh I'd heard from him since he came home. "It turns out there are loads of tunnels under Buffalo. Not all connected, not like a system or anything. Lee said they were used for all sorts of things, but most of 'em were early water pipes or aqueducts. We scoured the First Ward for weeks but didn't find one."

A hidden tunnel was impossibly romantic, like something out of a pulp novel. Had anyone other than Lee been the source, I'd doubt him. But I knew my friend would be all over a tale of that sort, so the idea had merit. "Is there a tunnel around the corner of Michigan and North that leads over to Wadsworth?"

Tom rubbed the wood of a crutch with his thumb. "Can't say. There isn't a map of them, not that Lee found. I'm prob'ly talkin' out of my hat. Forget I said anything." He turned away.

I couldn't, though. I wondered if Emmeline could dig anything up. I made a note to call her as soon as I could.

The bus lurched to a halt. I stood and clapped my hand on Tom's shoulder. "This is our stop."

Once on the sidewalk, I hesitated, wonderin' if I'd made the right decision by bringin' Tom.

Maybe he read my mind because he said, "I can help. I will. Swear to God."

"I'll hold you to it. We're goin' that way." I pointed, wonderin' how fast I should walk. He looked better, but I could still tell he was battlin' another hangover.

Tom solved my dilemma by setting a brisk pace. "Don't tell me you can't keep up," he called back to me.

I grumbled and jogged to catch him.

We arrived at the warehouse. I took a moment to study the building in front of us. "When you came that night, how'd you get in?"

Tom nodded toward the steps that led to the padlocked door. "Over there. Stevie told me to knock twice, pause, and three more times. Someone opened from the inside."

"Was the lock on it?"

He thought. "No, it was locked from the inside."

"Everyone else was already there?"

"Yes. I don't know why, but I got the impression I had the farthest to travel."

Now that he'd planted the seed of a tunnel entrance, I walked around the outside again. I didn't see anything I'd associate with an underground entrance. All the doors led into buildings. There weren't any manholes or other kinds of covers on the open ground. I tried to peer in the grimy windows of a clapboard building that stood at the rear of the empty space where Stevie's body had been found, but I couldn't see anything. The door was locked. A pile of crates took up most of the corner. "Does this belong to the warehouse?"

"No clue." Tom watched me with amusement on his face. "Are we goin' inside or are you gonna get on your hands and knees to examine every inch of concrete?"

"Smarty pants." I walked past him to the front door of the warehouse. "Let's go. Remember—"

"Yeah, yeah. I'm s'posed to say if I recognize anyone who was at the game." He raised his eyebrows. "I lost my leg, not my memory."

I tried to shrug off the comment as I opened the door. "Hello?" I stepped inside a small reception area. Tom followed. There was a buzzer on the counter and I pressed it.

A minute later, a portly man wearing dirty coveralls and wiping his hands with a greasy rag appeared. His gray hair was cut close, and a jowly chin covered in stubble said he hadn't shaved that morning. "Can I help you?"

I handed him a business card. "I'm lookin' for information about the card game that was here on Friday night."

"You must be mistaken. Ain't no card games here after hours." He tried to hand the card back.

"My friend here begs to differ."

The man looked at Tom. "You got the wrong address."

Either the man was ignorant or he was covering. "Who are you?" I asked.

"Gus Withers. I own this place."

I considered shaking, but his hands were filthy. "Mr. Withers, a boy was shot right outside your building on Friday night or Saturday morning." I took out my notepad.

"Cops have already talked to me 'bout that. Don't know nothing about why he was there."

I glanced at Tom. "He was at the game with my friend." I jerked my thumb at him. "I'm told Stevie went out to take a leak."

"Didn't come back," Tom added, face expressionless.

"I'm telling you, there ain't no card games held here. I lock up at six after everybody leaves." Gus stuffed his rag in his back pocket. "I don't host illegal gambling rings." His gaze flicked back to Tom's missing leg.

"Are you calling me a liar?" Tom asked, a harsh edge to his voice. "I know you want to ask. Yes, I lost it in the war. North Africa."

Gus licked his lips. "I think you've made a mistake. One building looks a lot like the rest in the dark."

"Except I came to a specific address. Yours." Tom didn't budge.

I held up my hands. "Mr. Withers. We aren't here to make trouble. Are you the only person who has keys to this place?"

"My floor manager, Davey, has a set."

"Is he here, and may we speak to him?"

Gus looked from me to Tom and back. I was sure that if I'd been on my own, he'd have told me to scram. But his tone of voice after Tom told him about bein' wounded in action let me know he was reluctant to pick a fight with a veteran. He jerked his head toward a door. "This way."

We followed him. The floor was wide open. Stacks of crates were piled high everywhere. Catwalks ringed the walls, and a second-floor office overlooked the action. It was noisy as men called to each other as they hauled some boxes to a set of wide doors where a truck was backed up, the bed half-filled. "What do you store here?"

"Machine parts." Gus pointed. "Mostly for the factories in the area. With places like GM and Bethlehem runnin' twenty-four hours a day, things break. We're the holding facility for one of the local suppliers."

I looked at the men scurrying around. A couple gave us a casual look, but most were too busy. "Where's Davey?"

"There." Gus whistled. A group of men turned around. Gus continued, "These folks want to see you."

The man who came over was a little older than Pop. Like his employer, he wore coveralls liberally streaked with dirt. The sleeves of his work shirt were rolled up to his elbows, and he had the same kind of heavy work boots Pop wore. "Yeah?"

I gave him a card. "Did you open the warehouse for a card game Friday night?"

Davey's expression turned wary. "No, ma'am." His gaze cut over to a group of workers at the nearest pallet.

"Funny." Once again, I pointed at Tom. "My friend here was at a game on your premises. If you didn't do it, who did?"

Again, that quicksilver glance. "Don't know. Maybe someone jimmied the lock."

While I'd been questioning Davey, I'd noticed Tom studying the others. He tapped my shoulder. "Him. He was there." He pointed at a middle-aged man who was supervising the loading of crates onto a forklift. He threw us a quick glance, then turned around.

"You sure?" I asked Tom.

He didn't answer, but his return look would've withered grass.

I jabbed my pencil in the man's direction. "I'd like to talk to that man, please."

"Now, just a minute," Davey stepped in front of me. "I already told you, no one was here. You got my word."

I noted the tic near his eye. "I wanna talk to him anyway."

In a flash, the guy broke from the group and sprinted toward the closest door, which happened to be the one we'd entered through. Before I could even say anything, Tom reached out with a crutch and tripped him, sending him sprawling.

He might be hungover, but his quick reaction impressed me. Maybe he meant it about bein' helpful.

Gus's face reddened. "Davey, Vic. My office. Now."

The man on the floor picked himself up and dusted off his clothes. He gave Davey a sheepish look. The two of them headed for the elevated office, trailing their boss.

Tom settled his crutches. "At least they're good for something other than holdin' a cripple up." He headed off before I could answer, leaving me to follow.

* * *

I watched Tom as he approached the stairs, alert for any sign of distress. "I'll get Gus to meet down here."

He grabbed the iron railing. "I'm jake."

"No, it's okay. No sense you heaving all the way up there."

"I said I'm fine," he snapped. Surprisingly, he was. Step by step, he hopped his way upward. The muscles in his right arm flexed and tightened with every move, and he looked far from graceful, but he did it.

I followed behind, ready to catch him at the first misstep. I kept my yap shut, though. Since Mrs. Flannery said she'd moved his bedroom downstairs, I assumed stairs were not possible for him to maneuver. Clearly, I was wrong.

146

CHAPTER TWENTY-FIVE

At the top, he paused to catch his breath.

I bit my lip. "Are you—"

His head whipped around, murder in his gaze.

"Never mind." I pointed at the open office door. "They're waitin' for us."

Gus sat behind a battered metal desk. Davey and Vic stood before him, the image of two schoolboys called before the teacher flashing in my mind. Davey and Vic were tryin' not to look guilty. To me, that made 'em look worse than if they'd done nothing. They exchanged a furtive look, one that their boss missed, but didn't fool me for a moment.

"Now." Gus folded his hands on his desk. "What's this all about?"

I gestured to Tom. "Might as well let my friend explain."

He gripped his crutches. "Friday night, you held a blackjack game here in the basement. I showed up around eleven. There were a few Joes here, including the murdered boy, Stevie Washington."

Davey swallowed. "Son, I think you're mistaken."

Tom's retort was swift. "Not hardly. I came to this address. My instructions were to come down the outside stairs and knock. He opened the door." He jerked his chin at Vic.

Vic paled. "Not me. I was home in bed. You musta confused me with someone else. If you were here at all. I'm guessin' you got them crutches as a result of somethin' that happened in the war. I don't blame you if you're usin' drink to get through it. I served in the Great War myself, and it happened to many a good man."

Color crept up Tom's neck. "Stop treatin' me like an idiot who doesn't know right from left. I'm missing a leg, not my brain. I was here, on Friday night, invited by Stevie Washington. You opened the door. There were others there as well. I didn't get last names but they were two white men named Larry and Shorty, and a Negro called Babyface."

Gus focused a hard stare on Vic. "Is that true?"

Vic gulped. "No, sir."

"Then we got a couple of problems." Gus looked from one employee to the other. "The young man has a very detailed story for a liar, and he's pretty sure of himself. Me, I don't like accusing a wounded soldier of fibbing.

That's the first thing."

Nobody said anything.

He jabbed a thick finger at Davey. "Second issue is you're the only one who's got a spare set of keys, includin' one to the door at the bottom of them steps. So." He lowered thick, dark gray eyebrows. "Which one of you is gonna be a man and 'fess up?"

Heavy silence fell in the office, and the tension was so thick, I coulda cut it with a butter knife. I fell back on Sam's old trick of staying mum and prayed one of the older men would crack under the pressure.

It took a good minute, but Davey spoke. "Sorry, Gus."

"Shut your mouth! You got your—" Vic pressed his lips together.

I knew what he'd almost said and finished the sentence. "Money. You ran the game and paid off your buddy."

Vic wilted but stayed mum.

I focused on Davey. "I need to know all the details."

He ran his hand over his head. "Few months ago, either May or June, Vic came to me. A guy he knew needed a place to hold a roving card game. At first, I said no. I didn't wanna be involved in nothing illegal. Vic assured me I didn't have to do anything 'cept loan him the keys on the second Friday of every month. I'd get a cut of the house take for my time."

I took out my notepad. "Nice work if you can get it."

Davey shot a look at his boss. "Gus, I'm real sorry. But you know Martha was in the hospital last winter and the bills are pilin' up faster than we can pay 'em. I didn't see no harm in loaning Vic the keys for one night a month. He promised they wouldn't tear nothing up, and they didn't."

Gus shook his head. "You shoulda come to me if you needed dough. I'd have worked somethin' out for you."

Davey hung his head.

I focused on Vic. "You were responsible for hosting the game. Don't bother denyin' it."

Vic's face had taken on the color of cold porridge. "I didn't have a choice."

"You always have a choice," I replied.

"Not this time." All the fight seemed to have leaked outta him. "This guy, he came to me while I was at the market with my wife."

I shot a quick look at Tom, who listened to the talk stone-faced and said nothing. But I could tell he was interested. "What was his name?" I asked.

Vic twitched. "He didn't give his name at first, but I came to know him as Charlie. He said he knew I worked for Gus and that the warehouse had a basement. He"—Vic swallowed hard—"he said he needed a place for a monthly game. Friday nights. This place would be perfect. I'd get a share. At first, I said no, but he pressed. Told me it was in Ruth's best interests if I went along. I got the message. Either I played ball or they'd go after her. I couldn't let that happen."

Gus's voice came out in a growl. "Again, why didn't you come to me?"

"I was scared. And the money was good." Vic turned an anguished expression to his boss. "Gus, I got a hundred bucks for that first night. I'd never held so much dough. Like Davey said, it was dead easy. All I had to do was open the door and leave. I came back around three in the morning and locked up. They had booze, but nothing was ever damaged, and they didn't make much of a mess. Mostly I swept up, put the table and chairs back, and that was that." He turned his face to me. "Until that kid got himself shot."

"Stevie Washington?" I asked.

He nodded.

I went over my notes. "Charlie. What does he look like?"

"Maybe mid-twenties. On the heavy side. Dark hair, cut real short, one of them buzz cuts the soldiers do." Vic paused. "He got a scar, here, on his chin." He touched his face.

It was a close enough match to the description I'd gotten of one of the guys lookin' for Stevie that day in the Fruit Belt. I turned to Tom. "Did you see Charlie at the game that night?"

Tom scrunched his eyebrows in thought. "Yes. But he wasn't playin'. He hung around the edges and kept everyone's glass full. I didn't pay too much attention to him. I was too busy with"—he paused—"my cards."

He'd been about to say somethin' else, I was sure of it. But instead of pressin' him in front of the older men, I let it pass. I turned back to Vic and

Davey. "Anythin' else I should know about these monthly games?"

Both men made noises I took for negative answers.

"One last question. How'd you get your cabbage?"

"I'd find an envelope with the dough in my locker Monday morning," Davey said. "Vic would put the keys in my mailbox so I could open on Monday."

Vic agreed. "Same. Charlie said if he needed anythin' he knew where to find me, but after that first month, I never heard from him."

I reviewed my notes. "Thank you. I appreciate your honesty."

"If you and the young man don't mind showin' yourselves out, I'd like a word with my employees." Gus's voice sounded mild, but there was a light in his eyes that made his unhappiness plain as day.

I checked with Tom, who didn't say a word and started toward the stairs.

"I'll come back if I have any more questions," I said. I headed out and shut the door behind me. Gus waited only a second before he began yellin'.

I followed Tom as he hopped down. I spared a moment of pity for Davey and Vic. But only a moment. As Gus pointed out, all they had to do was trust him and not lie.

I s'pose sometimes that's easier said than done.

Chapter Twenty-Six

Back on the sidewalk, I came up next to Tom. He fished a pack of Chesterfields outta his pocket and stuck one between his lips. "Got a light?"

I took out my lighter and flicked it.

He inhaled and pulled back. "This what you do all day?"

I took out my own deck of smokes. "There's more to do. But it's a lot of hoofin' around the city and talkin' to people."

He nodded, smoke trailing out of his nostrils. "What next?"

Now that it was just the two of us, I thought about askin' what he was gonna say back there. But I didn't. He wasn't surly. He hadn't asked for his booze. He hadn't made a mean comment. He wasn't the good-natured guy I remembered, but this was a far cry from the Joe I'd met at the train station. "I gotta follow up with Emmeline. She does my research. Then there are a few other leads I want to check on, like this mysterious girl."

"Then let's get to it." He held the Chesterfield in his lips and gripped his crutches.

For a second, I didn't have a response. "Don't you wanna go home and take a load off? I could be at this for a couple of hours yet. Your mom might expect you for dinner."

He waved me off. "No, she doesn't. I'm pretty used to these things by now." He tapped the wood with a finger.

"Tom, I—"

"You don't want me along, is that it?"

His sharp tone stung more than the words. "That's not so," I replied. "I didn't think you'd be interested."

"What else am I gonna do? Sit in my backyard and pitch pennies all day?" He took a drag off his cigarette and fixed me with a glare.

The words made me think. Tom had always been active. Overseas, even when there wasn't any fighting, there were prob'ly tasks to keep the men busy. He'd spent weeks in the hospital as he recovered. He had nothin' to keep him busy at home. Maybe that was part of the anger he didn't seem able to get rid of. "Okay. But if you get bushed and want to scram, I understand."

He jerked his head in what might have been a nod.

I ran through my tasks. "I need to find a pay phone so I can call Emmeline and get an update. Then—" I caught motion at the corner of my eye and snapped my gaze toward it.

Tom raised his eyebrows. "What gives?"

I pointed down the street. A girl had come out of a red house with white shutters that was maybe half a block away. She walked in our direction. Even from a distance, it looked like Virginia, the girl who'd been at the scene and who'd been run off by her father. "I know that girl." I slapped his shoulder. "Let's go."

I knew calling to her would run her off, so I double-timed it in her direction. Much to my surprise, Tom had little difficulty keepin' up and lagged by only a couple of steps.

We were still a good twenty feet away when she noticed us. She froze for a moment, then turned and fled to the safety of her house.

I stopped, Tom next to me. "Doggone it," I said. "If only she'd kept her head down for another minute."

"What's the problem?" He jerked his thumb. "We saw what house she went into. Go ring the bell."

I nibbled at a hangnail. "If her father's home, he isn't gonna let her talk to us."

"What's he gonna do? Assault a girl and a cripple?" Tom's voice held a note of scorn. "Let's go knock on the door. If he gets belligerent, I'll tell him I'm a wounded soldier. He might still run us off, but I've found most folks have a lot of respect. My bet? He'll keep it civil."

I thought about it. What he said made sense. "Okay."

This time, Tom stayed at my side. "You know, if I'm gonna help you out, I need my flask back."

I shot him a sideways look. "Why? You're doin' fine without it."

"In the pictures, the detective is always a hard drinker. I don't see you doin' that part. One of us has to." He gave me a grin, one of the mischievous ones I remembered. "Race you." He picked up his speed.

I watched him from behind. I wasn't sure if Tom's presence would help or hinder my investigation. But for the first time, I had hope the guy I knew wasn't completely gone.

* * *

As I climbed the porch steps behind Tom, my stomach fluttered like it held an entire flock of butterflies. What he'd said made sense, but I stayed alert, ready to turn tail as soon as things got ugly. "What are you gonna say?"

"I told you. That I'm collecting for a fund for wounded vets." He tapped the pin on his lapel, which showed a bird with its wings spread. "I'll make something up. Isn't that what you would do?"

It was. Truth be told, I was less worried about what would happen to me if Virginia's dad got belligerent. Tom put on a show, but he wasn't at the top of his game. And not just 'cause of his leg. There were the purplish smudges under his eyes and a stiff set to his mouth. He'd been on the go for most of the afternoon. This was prob'ly more activity than he'd had in months.

He rapped on the door, holding himself as straight as he could.

Virginia answered. "Yes?" Her voice sounded timid. Her gaze darted to me, and her peepers widened a smidge in recognition, but she stayed focused on Tom.

"Good afternoon." He smiled. "My name is Corporal Flannery, and I'm taking subscriptions for a relief fund for our wounded soldiers. Is your father or mother at home?"

She shook her head, the tiniest movement.

I came over. "That's okay. To be honest, it's you I want to talk to."

She darted a look at Tom. "But he said he was in the army."

"Well, that's partly true. He's a corporal. Least I think so." I checked with him.

"I didn't lose my rank when they discharged me," he said, voice flat. He inched over to let me take the lead.

"But we're not collectin' money," I continued. "I want to ask you about Stevie Washington."

"Shhh!" Virginia flapped her hand. "Not so loud."

I peeked over her shoulder. "I thought you said your parents weren't home."

"They aren't, but my granny is in the front room."

I thought. "I need to talk to you. Is there somewhere we can go?"

She bit her lip. "Yes, but I can't leave with you." She dropped her voice to a whisper. "There's a soda shop over on Allen, right across from Days Park. I'll meet you there in ten minutes." She shut the door.

Tom looked at me, a blank expression on his face. "Now what?"

I sighed. "We go, wait, and hope she isn't lyin' to us." I headed for the stairs.

He followed. "How often does that happen? The lyin', I mean."

I waited for him on the sidewalk. "More often than I care to think about."

Chapter Twenty-Seven

It was pretty easy to find the soda shop. Inside, Tom insisted on buyin' me a malt. "You didn't have to pay. This is a business expense." I held both our drinks and led him to an empty table.

He set his crutches aside and sat. "Maybe so, but I'm not gonna be seen lettin' a girl pay for me. A man's gotta have some dignity."

I started to object, but then I thought of the looks he'd gotten from other people. All of 'em had a bit of pity, although the one man had doffed his cap. Tom's expression hadn't changed, and I couldn't begin to know how he felt. But based on the person I'd known before the war, it wouldn't be good.

"Well, thank you." I sat across from him and stuck a straw in my treat.

"You still like chocolate." He'd ordered vanilla, same as always.

"Not everything has changed."

He raised an eyebrow. "The girl I left wouldn't be runnin' around the city chasing a killer."

"What can I say? Workin' at Bell taught me there was more to life."

He slurped. "How'd you get into this gig anyway?"

"You know I've always liked Sam Spade movies, right?" I told him about my first case, with Anne Linden and the sabotage with Bell. He seemed interested, so I gave a brief history of my more notable investigations, ending with the search for Private Lake's mother.

"That's how you met Hicks?" He swirled his straw.

"Yeah. We didn't get along at first, but we've become friends."

Tom grunted.

"I'm tellin' the truth, Tom. There's nothin' between us." Not that there couldn't be if I wanted it. "What about you? What's your life been like?"

He tensed. "You got my letters."

"Yeah, but the censors aren't around now. What did you leave out?"

He focused on his glass. "I'm not gonna give you a blow-by-blow account of every battle."

"That's not what I want." How could I say it? "When you got off that train, you were pretty angry."

"I don't have a right to be?" He bristled.

"You do. But"—I paused—"you seem better today."

He frowned. "I don't understand what you mean. I'm the same as I've always been."

"Yes and no." Should I say more? It might put him back in a sullen mood. But I plowed ahead. "It's only that you seem, I don't know, more like the old you, at least today. What changed?"

"I don't wanna talk about it. Not now."

I pulled back from the sting of his words.

He musta realized how harsh he'd sounded 'cause he put his hand on mine. "I'm not ready. When I am, you'll know."

We sat in an uncomfortable silence as we finished our malts. I had about decided Virginia had ditched us when the bells over the door jingled. I looked up. She stood there, scanning the people.

I waved, and she hurried over. She slid into the booth next to Tom. "I'm sorry. Granny wanted to know who was at the door, then I had to come up with a good story why I needed to leave. I can only stay for about fifteen minutes."

"Then let's get crackin'." I pulled out my notepad and pencil. "Stevie's mother told me she overheard him on the phone with someone named Ginny. Is that you?"

She nodded. "My name is Virginia Ellery. People call me Ginny all the time."

"Were you and Stevie friends?"

"You could say that." She glanced furtively around, like she was makin' sure no one would overhear us. "We were in love."

Tom raised his eyebrows.

No wonder she was skittish as a long-tailed cat in a room full of rocking chairs. And why her father had been so angry. No white man would want his daughter dating a colored boy. I wondered if Nancy knew and immediately answered my own question. She didn't. I didn't think her people would be any happier. "Is that so?"

Virginia leaned forward. "I know what you're gonna say. We're kids. I'm white, he's a Negro. It wouldn't work. But we were. He made me feel special, like no other boy I've ever known."

I thought of my own teenage sister. But arguin' with Virginia wouldn't get me the answers I needed. "How did you meet?"

"It was right in this shop. He'd come to the neighborhood on business, he said. I was here to meet one of my friends, but she didn't show." Virginia smiled at the memory. "I was sittin' in a booth, waitin' for her. That's when I noticed Stevie. He was so handsome. He had the kindest eyes, and when he talked to me, I felt so happy."

I studied her. Hair the color of dark honey, brown eyes, and a peaches and cream complexion. Virginia was a pretty girl, but younger than Mary Kate for sure. Her slim figure showed no signs of womanhood. I doubted she'd had many boyfriends, if any, in her young life. Any attention would go to her head. Maybe she'd even felt a little thrill at the idea of a forbidden love. "Did he tell you what kind of business?"

"No. He said it wasn't important. At least not something that would interest a girl." She ran her fingers over the table. "I thought it might be illegal."

"Why?"

"He was so secretive about it. Why else would he be that way?" She gazed at me, eyes wide and innocent.

I noticed Tom watchin' her. Every once in a while, he'd check out the rest of the joint. He appeared tense, like he expected her to do somethin'. *He's nervous.* Did it have to do with what he hadn't said earlier? I shelved the thought. "You think he was lyin' to you?"

"Oh no. Stevie wouldn't lie to me. Not outright anyway. He wasn't that kind of person." She spoke with a kid's simple trust. "It's not a lie if you simply don't say somethin', is it?"

Tom snorted. I didn't want to ruin this girl's innocence. "Let's back up a bit. When was the first time you met him?"

She tapped her lips. "It must have been a couple months ago. School had just ended for the summer."

"Where did you go to see him?"

"Right here." She directed her gaze to her hands. "Stevie would come and we'd share a milkshake. But then people talked, so we'd go to different places, usually up and down Allen. I asked why we didn't go to his neighborhood, but he said that wouldn't be a good idea."

I remembered the welcome I'd received in the Fruit Belt. No, this waiflike girl would not do well. "I'm guessin' your father wasn't too happy when he found out."

Tears filled Virginia's eyes. "Daddy was so mad. He's gotten angry before, but never like that. Stevie and I were down near Michigan, lookin' at the window displays. Someone must've told Daddy I was there. He marched right up, grabbed my arm, and pulled me away. He told Stevie he wouldn't stand for his daughter being with someone like him. Except Daddy used a word I'm not supposed to say."

Tom and I exchanged a look. Yeah, we knew the word. He muttered something, but I couldn't make it out. "Was that all?"

"No. Daddy said if he ever saw Stevie again, he'd kill him and no jury would convict." She gulped.

Based on Mr. Ellery's reaction when he'd seen his daughter lookin' at the spot where Stevie had died, I wasn't surprised. "Was that the last time you saw Stevie?"

"No." She wiped her nose. "I snuck out of the house last Friday after dinner. Stevie and I met right near that spot where he got shot." She took a breath. "He asked me to run away with him. He said he was about to come into a lot of money, and we could go to Canada. We'd lie about our ages, and we could get married. He told me it would be a little while, maybe a month or two, but then we could go." Tears ran down her smooth cheeks.

CHAPTER TWENTY-SEVEN

I knew what came next. "Your father found out."

"He caught me comin' back through the window," she whispered. "He said he was gonna ship me off to a convent for school. And then he got his gun. He said he was gonna find Stevie and kill him."

I tapped the pencil on my chin. "Did you see him come home?"

She sniffled. "No." Tom handed her a paper napkin, and she wiped her face. "He locked me in my room. I fell asleep after it got dark. I don't think he came home before that, though, because I would have heard him."

After dark would have been between eight thirty and nine. If Virginia was asleep, her father could easily have gotten home much later.

After he'd shot the boy she loved.

* * *

I watched Tom settle into his seat on the bus. A man had moved for us so we could sit together and closer to the front. "Are you holdin' up?"

"Why wouldn't I be?" He propped his crutches near the window.

Rush hour meant a lot of people, so I looked around to make sure no one was listenin'. "We've moved around a lot. Leaning on those sticks all day must be tiring."

"I'm used to it." Tom stared out the window.

Maybe he wanted me to shut up, but I felt compelled to talk. "Stevie and Virginia, huh? That's gotta be rough."

"Why do you say that?" He faced me.

"I dunno. They're from such different backgrounds. Her father wasn't too happy."

"He's a bigot." The heat radiated off his words. "I got to know several of the colored guys who worked in the motor pool. Their skin may be darker than ours, but that's the only difference. It's disgusting the way they get treated at home."

He was right, of course. Nancy and her brother weren't any different than me and mine. I could see a young girl like Virginia, who was prob'ly sheltered by her dad, having her head turned by a boy who paid her attention.

Even if he had different skin.

He continued. "You can't control who you love." He looked away.

I had no response to that. Unbidden, I wondered about Frank. I hadn't heard from him in a couple of days. He'd told me I needed to make up my mind. Was stayin' away part of his plan to help me do that?

Why didn't I miss him more?

After a moment, Tom faced me again. "Am I off the hook? For the murder, I mean."

If he was, that sure would solve big problems for both of us. "I'm not sure. Detective MacKinnon found gunpowder on your hands."

"From giving first aid. I didn't shoot him, Betty. The cops searched me that night and didn't find anything. Where'd I stash the damn gun?" Anger flared in his voice. "You think I hid it somewhere they didn't look? Or got someone to ditch it for me?"

I held up a hand. "I know, all right?"

"Are you on my side or not?"

Whose side was I s'posed to be on? It was a situation where one of my clients could be the person who killed the brother of another client. "I'm on the side of truth."

"What a cop-out."

I need to talk to Pop. Tonight. Caught between two clients. Caught between two boys. It was enough drama to mirror an Ingrid Bergman picture.

Tom turned away and watched the buildings as the bus rumbled from stop to stop. "Have you ever thought of gettin' a car? It'd be a lot faster. You could get a decent used one for a couple hundred bucks."

The sudden change of topic caught me off guard. "I don't know how to drive." I stared at his back.

"I could teach you."

"How?"

He turned to me. "I can't do it any more myself. Doesn't mean I can't teach you. After all, you'd be the one behind the wheel. Does your dad still have his Model T?"

"Yeah. He mostly takes the bus to work, though, because of the gas rationing."

"Then we can use his. Think about it." He shifted his stare back to the window.

* * *

I waited until dinner was done, dishes washed up, and Pop had retired to his favorite chair with his pipe before cornering him with my dilemma. "I need to talk to you." I sat cross-legged on the floor in front of him.

He lit his pipe and puffed it to life. "What is it, my darling girl?"

"I'm in a bit of a pickle." I told him about my job for Nancy, Tom hiring me, and the conflict it had created. "What do I do?"

"Let me get this straight." He exhaled a cloud of fragrant smoke toward the ceiling. "This girl, Nancy, hired you to find her brother's killer."

"Not exactly. She hired me 'cause she thought her brother was in trouble. After he died, I said I'd find out who was responsible."

Pop nodded. "Tom was found with the boy's body. He hired you to clear his name."

"Yes."

"Does Tom know about Nancy?"

I thought back to the conversation in my office. Had I told him about her? "Yes, I made that clear. And that he was a suspect until Detective MacKinnon said otherwise. I couldn't help him if he was guilty."

"If Nancy Washington was already a client, why did you take on Tom's case?"

Did he have to ask? "'Cause it's Tom. True, things are not square between us. But I can't leave him in a bind. Not when I can help him. We've been friends for ages. As long as Lee and I have been pals. Time was he'd do the same for me."

"Would he now?"

What a question. "I don't know. But that shouldn't matter. We don't do good things for people 'cause of what they can do for us, right?"

He seemed satisfied with my answer. "Tell me. Is Tom a serious suspect for this murder?"

I thought about what I knew, including what Sam had told me on the sly. "Not if I know Sam." I told him about Georgie's gun. "If that's really the murder weapon, it makes it better for Tom. Least I think so. Tom's afraid that 'cause he was involved in some shady actions, he's gonna take the rap."

"I don't know Detective MacKinnon as well as you, but I find it unlikely he'd do such shoddy work." Pop peered at me. "Here's my next question. Does Nancy know about Tom?"

I gulped. "No. I haven't told her. I was hoping I could get away with not sayin' anything."

He fixed me with a stern look. "Elizabeth Anne Ahern."

I wilted. Pop rarely used my full name. "Yes, sir?"

"Is that fair to your client?"

I stared at my toes. "No, sir."

He pointed the pipe stem at me. "Then you know what you must do."

I did. "Yes, sir. It's hard, though. I don't know what to say."

"I recommend the truth. The fact that it's hard merely reinforces that you know it's the right thing."

I hadn't expected Pop to tell me anything else. I had hoped for his advice to be more helpful than to be truthful. But it was prob'ly the easiest—and best—approach. I only needed to muster up the courage to say it.

Chapter Twenty-Eight

The next day, I was already at my desk when Emmeline arrived. "What did you find out?" I asked.

She pulled up the old kitchen chair to sit in front of me. "The roving card games have been happening all summer. It seems that as soon as Buffalo Vice detectives find and shut down one location, another one pops up. The warehouse where Stevie was killed is only the latest."

I took notes as she talked. "Do they know who's in charge?"

"I found one article that mentioned a man named Charlie Nickles. But he's never been arrested. The cops have only been able to nab the players and the people who run the locations. None of them have given up Nickles as the ringleader."

I thought of Davey and Vic. "Is it always blackjack?"

"The articles aren't that specific. There's always one or two people who open the doors and lock up afterward. But they don't know anything significant." Emmeline ripped a page from her pad. "I did look up Nickles in the phone book. There are six listings for either Charlie or C." She handed it to me.

"Good work. I don't s'pose we can tell where the next game is."

"Not definitely. But." She held up a finger. She set aside her pad and spread a map of the city on my desk. "The places that have been raided are here, here, and here. The one Tom was at is here." She made crosses on the map and numbered each one. "They appear to be moving in sort of a clockwise rotation through the neighborhoods."

I studied the marks. "That means they should be ripe to be in or near the

First Ward. Maybe the next game." Tom had been at the last one. Would he know? Unless there had been more games since then. Still, it was worth askin'. "What do you know about blackjack?"

"It's a card game." She gave a wry grin. "Sorry. I don't spend a lot of my time on things like that."

I waved her off. Tom and Lee would know. Lee might even have a clue about how one would go about countin' cards. "Did you find any information about the fights?"

She retrieved her pad and resumed her seat. "Those are definitely run by Moses Gainey. He uses a building on Best Street. The police haven't shut him down, which tells me whatever he's running isn't illegal."

"I bet there's plenty of shifty dealings there, though." I couldn't imagine otherwise. "Did you find anything to connect Stevie?"

She spread her hands. "Only the picture I showed you before. However, it seems to be true that Alonzo Coates and Gainey are going head-to-head over who should be the big cheese in the Fruit Belt. There are multiple stories that reference them trying to one-up each other."

"How?"

"Each trying to take over operations run by the other." She tapped her pad. "The fights are one of those things. So far, Gainey has maintained control."

I leaned back in my chair. "That picture tells us Stevie was involved with Gainey somehow. That's also the word on the street. Georgie told me he was selling secrets. What if he went to Coates and said he could give the inside dope that would let Coates take over the fights?"

Emmeline pursed her lips. "Gainey wouldn't like that. Not at all. But there's an alternative. What if Gainey was baiting his rival?"

"Using Stevie to give Coates bad info as a setup?"

She nodded.

"Either way, it would be bad for Stevie if he was found out." I needed to know what the deal was. "We gotta figure out how to get to the next fight."

Her jaw dropped. "Are you seriously thinking of going? Betty, that would be incredibly dangerous. A woman, and a white woman at that, walking into that kind of situation? I can't let you do that."

I held up my hands. "Don't snap your cap. I'm not plannin' on goin', at least not alone." I stood. "I need to find a bodyguard."

* * *

I called Sam to ask if he knew anything about the card games. He didn't, but he said he'd contact a buddy in Vice. Then I set about tracking down the names for C Nickles. It took all morning, but after some calls, I settled on two promising candidates. One address was close by, over on Edna. The other was halfway across the city, on Fargo. It was another warm day, blue skies with white clouds drifting by, so I decided to walk over to Edna first.

While I did, I lit a smoke and thought. One, neither of these bums were in the service. Were they both 4Fs? That would be quite the coincidence. Fortunately, I'd know right away if I'd found the person I was looking for thanks to Mr. Jones's description.

I reached my first destination and knocked. A younger man answered. He had the right color hair and eyes, and a mark on his chin, but it looked like a mole or a birthmark. Nonetheless, I handed him a business card. "Are you Charlie Nickles?"

"I am. Why do you want to know?"

"Do you know a boy named Stevie Washington?" I watched his reaction.

He shrugged, casual and unconcerned. "Never heard of him." He handed back my card.

This wasn't the right guy. "Thanks for your time." I paused. "This is none of my business, but I'm always curious when I meet a man your age."

"Why aren't I in the military?" From the resigned tone, he got that question a million times a week. "I will be soon. I had a deferment while I worked at American Shipbuilding. Then I got a hardship deferment. But that's over soon. Only a matter of time before my number comes up." He rubbed the scarred knuckles of his left hand with his right.

I'd known boys who were so eager to go fight they didn't wait to be drafted. This was not one of 'em. "My brother is an anchor clanker. I'll say a prayer for you."

He nodded his thanks and closed the door.

Tom had been one of those who enlisted. He'd wanted to serve his country. *What would he say to that guy now?* Did he think the losses he'd endured had been worth it? I could ask. Then again, I didn't really want to know.

I saw the bus at the corner and hurried to jump on before it pulled away. Tom was right about one thing: Having my own car would be swell. If I started saving now, by the time I got my license, I'd be able to buy a jalopy.

Or maybe I should finish furnishing my office and then worry about transportation.

I arrived on Fargo and made my way to the second address on my list. This house was dingier than the first one. The yard was choked with weeds, and so was the meager Victory garden. What grass there was hadn't been mowed in weeks. The concrete front walk was cracked. Dandelions pushed their way up through. The stairs had a zigzag break through 'em and one side looked lower than the other. Whoever lived here was either not good with home maintenance or didn't care.

I banged on the door. A woman in a dirty housedress and wearing battered slippers answered. Her gray hair was in curlers, and a lit cigarette dangled from her lips. "What? I'm listening to my programs."

I introduced myself and held out a business card. "I'm looking for Charlie Nickles."

She ignored the gesture. "What for?"

"I need to ask him some questions, is all. Is he home?"

The woman, Mrs. Nickles, maybe, looked me up and down. She yelled over her shoulder. "Charlie! There's a nice-lookin' young dame here to see you. Get your lazy butt off that couch and come here." She exhaled a cloud of smoke and studied me as though I was a cut of beef at the Broadway Market.

I waited for a long, uncomfortable minute. Mrs. Nickles smirked and held my gaze. I realized she was tryin' to break me down, which only strengthened my determination. I stared into her eyes and refused to budge.

Eventually, Charlie appeared. "What is it, you old bat? I told you I'm busy."

One look and I knew I'd found my man. This Charlie had to be older than

Tom. His dark hair was buzzed close, and his brown eyes were deep-set. They reminded me of pig's eyes. A broad scar shone on his chin. He was only a little taller than me, but barrel-chested. He shuffled up, his gait a little duck-footed and his bare feet flat to the ground. No wonder the military didn't want him.

Mrs. Nickles jabbed her smoke in my direction. "It isn't every day a girl shows up wanting to talk to you. If I'm lucky, she'll take you off my hands, you useless lump." She stalked off.

He shouted after her. "Talk about the pot calling the kettle black. Miserable hag."

The volume of the radio increased.

"All she does is sit and listen to that box." He shook his head. "What do you want?"

Once again, I explained who I was. "I've been told you run a roving card game in the city."

A sly light came into those piggy eyes. "What's it to you?"

"Is it true?"

He eyed me. "Why should I tell you?"

"I need dough, fast. Friend of mine said you could help out with that."

He craned his neck to look around me. "You with the cops?"

"You must be jokin'." I spread my hands. "Do I look like a dame who would be friends with the police?"

His expression turned from distrust to a leer. "I didn't think broads were into gambling."

His look made me want a shower. "Times are tough."

"Who's your friend?" After a pause, he went on. "The one who sent you my way."

"Fella by the name of Stevie Washington."

"That rat." Charlie spat.

I stepped away from the spit. "You do know him. When did you last see him?"

"Couple of weeks ago."

"Huh. I have it on good authority you went to the Fruit Belt lookin' for him. You accused him of cheatin'." I cocked my hip. "Personally, I thought he was a little young to be playin' cards with someone like you."

He leaned on the doorframe. "I take all comers, if they have the buy-in. Don't matter who they are. But no one cheats me. No one. Yeah, I went lookin' for him, but of course they closed ranks on me. Never saw the punk."

"You saw him cheat?"

"I didn't have to. You don't win that much unless you've got some scheme goin'. I search all my players for marked cards." He squinted. "I don't know how he did it, but he was up to no good. Not only is he not welcome, he's gonna pay me back every cent."

Was Charlie actin'? "Stevie was shot last Friday. Outside one of your games. He's dead."

Charlie scowled. "I'd say good, 'cept now I can't get my dough."

I raised my eyebrows. "You didn't do it? Seems like you're mad enough."

He barked a laugh. "How dumb are you? He owes me. I wouldn't kill him until he paid me back."

"Maybe you're trying to sell me a bridge in Brooklyn. You get your cash, he gives you lip, you make sure he doesn't come back to cause more trouble." I crossed my arms. "Or you did it so you look tough and no one else tries any funny business."

"Why do you care?"

"I don't wanna play somewhere the cops might show. I got enough trouble."

Again, that sly look appeared on his puss. "I didn't kill him, and I bet you can't prove I did. Can you?"

Since I didn't have an answer, I kept my yap shut.

"Didn't think so. You want in, show up at Benny's over on South Park at eleven. Password is Ike." He straightened. "As for Stevie, thanks for the tip. I guess I'll have to get my money from his partner. Shouldn't be too hard to hit up a cripple once I find him." He slammed the door in my face.

Chapter Twenty-Nine

I walked away from Charlie's house in a fog. Crippled partner? That settled it. Tom had danced around this subject long enough. He needed to spill the details. I'd go to his house—right this minute—and wring the truth outta him. What if he and Stevie had a fight about how to split the winnings? Tom coulda had that pistol in his pocket. You didn't need a leg to shoot. He could have thrown it away as he was leaving.

I took a deep breath. I needed to calm down. There were holes in Tom's story big enough to sail a destroyer through. He had been found kneeling by Stevie's body, covered in blood. Had he been lookin' for the money? Maybe the cash he claimed was his Army pay was his gambling winnings. No, that didn't make sense. He wouldn't flash that in front of his mother. He said he'd been playin' cards 'cause Mrs. Flannery wouldn't give him the dough. He wouldn't run the risk she'd take those, too.

I couldn't get around the fact Tom didn't have a gun on him that night. The cops hadn't found one. Sam had told me it was the only reason he wasn't arrested.

Georgie said he found his pistol over on Allen. It didn't make sense that Tom went all the way over there, threw it away, and then returned to the scene of the crime.

Unless the gun Georgie had wasn't the one that had been used to kill Stevie, and the murder weapon was still missin'. I'd call Sam and get the report. Or at least try to.

I'd cooled off, so I called the Flannery house. "I need to talk to Tom. Is he there?"

"I'm sorry, Betty," Mrs. Flannery said. "He left almost an hour ago. He said he was meeting someone."

I closed my eyes. Had yesterday been a short-lived blessing? "At a bar?"

"I don't know for sure, but I think not. He showered again this morning, shaved, and was neatly dressed. I don't think he'd do that if he was going out to get drunk." She paused. "He did get a phone call this morning from a man."

A man? "Who?"

"He didn't give a name, just asked to speak to Tom."

That made zero sense. "Did Tom know this person?"

"I think so. He didn't say much on the phone. After he hung up is when he told me he was getting dressed and would be out. He might not return until this evening." A gust of breath came over the line, like she'd exhaled heavily. "I do hope he's not in more trouble."

I wanted to reassure her, but I couldn't. Not in good conscience. "If he comes home, please ask him not to go anywhere until he talks to me."

"It's bad, isn't it?"

I could hear the fear in her voice. I hastened to reassure her. "I won't know until I see him. Try not to worry." I hung up.

I figured before I did anything else, I should check for messages. Findin' an answering service was somethin' I shoulda put on Emmeline's to-do list. I hadn't, and I wasn't gonna take the time to call her, so I dropped another nickel and called home. "Mom, any messages for me?"

"One." The rustle of paper came over the line. "Nancy Washington called not five minutes ago. She said she needs you to call her now at this number." Mom read it off.

It was not the communal phone I'd used in the past. I thanked my mother and dialed. But Nancy wasn't the one who answered.

"Hello?" Miz Alva said.

"This is Betty Ahern. Is Nancy there? She left a message for me."

"One moment."

I heard scuffling before a breathless Nancy spoke. "Betty? You have to come here, now."

"Slow down. What's the hurry?"

"That man is here. The one who runs the fights. He's at the Crazy Cat, talkin' about his plans for the Fruit Belt."

Moses Gainey. "How many men are with him?"

Nancy held the blower away from her and I could hear her consult Miz Alva. "Two at most. Should I go over and ask him about Stevie?"

"No!" Good mood or not, things could get ugly if Gainey was asked about whether he'd committed murder. Nancy had been helpful, but I didn't want her gettin' hurt. "I'm gonna call my friend at the police department. I'll be there as soon as I can."

"But what if he leaves?"

I chewed my thumb. "Best thing you can do right now is eavesdrop. If he skedaddles, try and find out where he's goin'. You can tell Sam and me when we get there." Assuming I could get a hold of Sam.

I could hear the reluctance in Nancy's voice as she agreed. My next call was to Sam. "What are you doin'?"

"Hunting down Moses Gainey," he replied. "So far I've come up empty at all his usual haunts."

"Then let me help you out. He's in the Fruit Belt right now. I'll take you to him if you come get me." I gave him my location and hung up before he could say anythin'.

I s'pose I could have told him exactly where Gainey was. But no way was I gonna risk bein' left behind.

* * *

I was waitin' on the curb when Sam pulled up less than twenty minutes later. "Thanks for the ride." I gave him the address.

"You could have told me that over the phone. I'd have kept you informed." The rubber squealed as he pulled away.

"I wanna be there. I promise I won't get in the way." I held up my hands. "At least I called you. He's not gonna shoot me in front of a cop."

Sam lowered his eyebrows. "There is that. And don't be too sure."

"While I've got you, did you get the results of your test? You know, on the gun?"

"Yes." He turned a corner. "It's a match for the bullets we retrieved from Stevie's body."

I told Sam my thoughts. "Don't you think that weakens the case against Tom?"

He shot me a glance. "I can't talk about an ongoing investigation. You know that."

"Then he's still a suspect."

Sam pressed his lips together.

He wasn't gonna say, which meant I had to assume Tom was still in the mix. "I know you'll find out, but he was more than just a player at that game." I shared what Charlie had said. "I figured from what he said before, he was involved, but I let it go."

Sam turned onto High Street. "You know this means I have to interview him again."

"Let me talk to him first, please?" I laid my hand on Sam's arm. "He was with me for most of the day yesterday. I think I might be able to talk him around. Make him more cooperative."

"All right. But if he doesn't call me by tomorrow morning, I won't wait any longer." Sam blew out a breath. "I don't suppose you'll stay in the car."

"Not a chance."

He turned off the ignition. "Remember your promise."

I held up two fingers. "Scout's honor."

"Since I don't think you were a Girl Scout, I'm not sure that means anything." He grabbed his fedora and got out.

Needless to say, two white people, one of 'em obviously a cop, drew a lot of side-eye looks as we walked down the street. Once again, I wondered if colored folks felt the same when they ventured out into other parts of the city. Like they were bugs under a microscope. Judging by Sam's expression, it didn't bother him. 'Course, he had a badge and a gun. "Why did we park so far away?" I asked.

"I didn't want to be right in front of our target." Sam's eyes slid back and forth as his gaze swept the street. "We'll be noticed, but no one will know exactly where we're going."

We found Gainey right where Nancy said we would. He sat at the bar inside the Crazy Cat, which turned out to be a nightclub, with people grouped around him. He wore a neat brown suit, spit-shined shoes, and a derby with a small red feather tucked into the band near the brim. From the way he spoke, he sounded like he was holding court, and maybe for these people, he was. He broke off when we entered. "Well, if it ain't the police and a pretty miss. What you all doin' in the Fruit Belt on this fine day?"

"Afternoon, Mr. Gainey." Sam lifted his hat and introduced both of us. "We heard you were here and came down for a chat. Hope you don't mind."

"Not at all." Gainey pushed his own hat back on his head and studied us through dark brown eyes. "I am a bit curious as to who gave you the tip."

A tingle ran down my spine. Gainey's words were pleasant, but his eyes held a look I didn't like. I prayed Sam wouldn't betray Nancy. She'd be in trouble for sure. I needn't have worried.

"A call from a concerned citizen," Sam said.

Gainey spread his arms. "Ain't nothing to be concerned about, as you can see. We all havin' an afternoon social, is all."

I studied the expressions of the gathered crowd. Some looked as relaxed as the crime boss claimed. Others seemed curious. A few, including the man I assumed was the store owner, flashed nervous smiles or glanced at Gainey before focusing on anything else. Not everyone was at ease.

Sam only had eyes for the boss. "I'm less interested in today and more concerned with where you were Friday night. Let's say from ten o'clock to about two Saturday morning." He rested his hands on his hips.

Gainey's puzzled expression was so exaggerated, it bordered on comical. "Why would you care 'bout that?"

"Because that's when Stevie Washington was murdered."

Confusion melted into pity. "I heard about that poor boy." Gainey's voice dripped sorrow. "But that ain't got nothin' to do with me."

I steeled my nerves and held down the frogs jumping in my stomach. "That's not what I hear."

The hard, dark-eyed gaze focused on me. "Oh? And what do you hear?"

"That Stevie was workin' for you." My voice sounded strong and clear, which gave me confidence. "I also heard he mighta been sellin' you out to your rival, Alonzo Coates. I don't s'pose that woulda made you very happy."

Gainey's expression didn't change, but he suddenly seemed less like a lord and more like Cat when he stalked a mouse. "Boy was a fool if he thought he would be able to do that."

"Then you did know him?" I asked.

"I did." Gainey showed a white-toothed smile. "You got me, Miss…Ahern, was it? Stevie, he worked for me as a runner. Carryin' my messages and such. Least, he was tryin' to. School ain't for everyone and Stevie, he needed money for his family. I'm always willin' to help a man, give him a leg up as it were. Sadly, he didn't work out."

I raised my eyebrows.

"Oh, don't be thinkin' this is some sort of confession." Gainey held up his hands. "Stevie and me, we parted ways without hard feelings. I may not have a fancy degree or nothin', but I'm a businessman. I got standards. Stevie, well, he didn't meet them. I had to let him go."

"When was that?" Sam asked.

Gainey tapped his chin and frowned. Then he snapped his fingers. "It was Friday, the mornin' of the night you asked about. I took him to breakfast and said how it wasn't gonna work. I wished him the best, and we went our separate ways. I didn't see him again."

Sam didn't move, but I knew he had the same opinion of that story as I did. Baloney. His voice remained pleasant, though. "You didn't answer my question about Friday night."

"I was with Sonya." Gainey pulled over a girl who was standin' nearby. She was in her early twenties. Her features would've made any woman weep with envy, and her clothes clung to her curves. "We spent the night cuttin' a rug down at the social hall, then we went back to my place. Didn't we, baby?" He nuzzled her neck.

Sonya murmured in agreement.

Gainey straightened. "That good enough for you, Mr. Detective?" His arm remained wrapped around Sonya's waist.

I realized her posture was stiff, not that of a woman at ease. I studied her lovely eyes. The skin around them was tight with fear. I knew instantly the man next to her, for all his loving attention, scared the pants off her.

Before I could say anythin', Sam answered. "That's perfect. Thank you." He tipped his fedora in Gainey's direction. "Oh, if I have any other questions, will I be able to find you here?"

Gainey gave another broad smile, a man who clearly thought he'd won. "Why of course, Detective. If I ain't here, they'll know where to find me. You all take care now."

I tried to make eye contact with Sonya. Before I could, Sam grabbed my arm and steered me out of the joint.

* * *

"What did you do that for?" I asked as Sam hustled me down the sidewalk.

"Because I recognized the look on your face." He checked for traffic before crossing to his car. "You had more questions. He wasn't going to answer them. I didn't want you to rile him up and become a target."

"I wouldn't do that."

"Not intentionally." He got in the car.

I did as well. "That story about bein' with Sonya smells worse than dead fish on the lake shore."

"I know." He stared toward the Crazy Cat. "We need a last name for Sonya. If we can question her on her own, she might talk. I got the sense she's scared of her boyfriend, or whatever he is."

"I know she is." An idea came to me. "Go over to Locust. I know someone who might be able to help us."

Sam hiked up an eyebrow but drove as requested.

I had him pull over in front of the Washington house. "I'll be right back." I scrambled out.

Sam did too and came around the front of the car. "I'll go with you. It'll make things a little more official."

"You don't even know what I'm gonna do."

"You're going to ask Nancy Washington if she knows Sonya's last name. If she doesn't, you're going to ask her if she can find out." He crossed his arms, a self-satisfied smirk on his puss.

He knew me better than my mother. "Fine. But don't you go bullying her." I wagged my finger at him. "She's a good girl, and she'll help me. But if you get all official, she might get scared and clam up."

"I wouldn't dream of getting in your way."

Nancy answered within moments of my knock. "Did you see him?"

"Yep, and we talked to him." I hoisted my thumb over my shoulder. "You know Detective MacKinnon, right?"

Nancy licked her lips. "You're the policeman who is tryin' to find out who killed Stevie."

He dipped his head.

"Nancy, I need a favor. May we come in?" I asked.

She hesitated but opened the door. "Mama is out, and Gram is sleeping. You gotta make it quick. They don't like white folks in the house."

I didn't bother sittin' down. Neither did Sam. "Do you know a girl named Sonya? She seems to be Moses Gainey's girlfriend."

"He has a lot of women. At least, he seems to."

"This may be his current doll." I described Sonya. "We saw her with him over at the Crazy Cat."

Nancy caught her bottom lip between her teeth. "I didn't know her name, but yeah, I've seen her around. You want me to find where she lives?"

"Her last name would be swell. Address is good if you can swing it, but don't put yourself in danger."

She nodded. "If I can't, I know Miz Alva can. She knows everybody."

"You're the bee's knees, Nancy." I hugged her.

She turned a face filled with worry to Sam. "You find out who killed my brother?"

"I'm working on it. I need to talk to Sonya on her own, so if you get a name to Betty, that will help tremendously." He checked with me.

This was the moment. "While we're on the subject, I have something important to tell you, Nancy." I swallowed. "Something I shoulda told you earlier."

She frowned. "What?"

"I have another client. His name is Tom Flannery." I glanced at Sam. "He…he's the man who was with Stevie's body in the lot."

Her gaze flicked between Sam and me. "I don't understand."

"He came to me 'cause he was afraid he'd be accused of the murder. I said I'd investigate for him. But I also told him about you." I rubbed my hands. "What I'm tryin' to say is while I've been workin' for you, to find Stevie's murderer, I've also been helpin' Tom. Which means"—I steeled my nerves—"my other client might be the guy who murdered Stevie."

She said nothing.

Sam broke in. "I understand you may feel a little betrayed, Miss Washington. I've known Betty a long time. I have no doubt that if Mr. Flannery turns out to be guilty, Miss Ahern will not interfere with his arrest."

"If that's true, why did you take his case?" Nancy asked, her peepers fixed on me.

Oh bother. "Tom and I used to be engaged. We've been friends since forever. He's recently home from the war, and he's having problems." She didn't need to hear Tom's full story. "Nancy, I honestly don't think he killed your brother. Maybe it was a mistake, but I couldn't leave him in the lurch. He needs me."

It seemed like forever before she spoke. "Thank you for being honest. I think you need to leave now."

My heart sank. "Nancy, I'm gonna get to the bottom of this. I promise."

"Detective MacKinnon, thank you as well." She went to the door and opened it. Her message was clear. We weren't wanted.

I followed her. "Nancy—"

"Goodbye, Betty."

I glanced at Sam, who gave a tiny shrug. I left. Behind me, I heard him murmur his farewell. As we walked down the path, I looked at him. "I'm not gonna stop, Sam. I'm gonna make this up to her."

Chapter Thirty

Once we were on the sidewalk, Sam faced me. "You sound very sure of yourself." He pulled out his deck of cigarettes and lit one up.

I got a Lucky and leaned in so he could give me a light. I blew out a cloud of smoke. "I've got a great record of success."

"Don't get cocky. I can't even tell you how many homicide detectives twice your age have a case they were never able to solve. It can haunt them for years." He took another drag. "What's next for you?"

"It'd be swell if you could drop me off downtown." I ashed my gasper. "As much as I'd like to keep goin', I forgot to ask Emmeline to hire an answering service. I better do that." I noticed the twinkle in his eyes. "Why do you ask?"

He gave an exaggerated shrug. "I was on my way to see Alonzo Coates when you called. Since the talk with Gainey went so well, I thought you might like to tag along." He stuck his smoke between his lips and unlocked the car. "But if you need to get back to your office, I understand."

"You stinker. I'm not gonna miss talkin' to Coates. The service can wait." I got in.

He drove over to the corner of High Street and Genessee in the northeast corner of the Fruit Belt. I wasn't surprised Coates had decided to set up shop where there'd be space between him and his rival. Good fences made good neighbors, as the saying went. In the city, several blocks would do the same.

After we parked and got out, I stopped beside a store that had a pay phone in the front. "Hold on a sec. I gotta make a call." I darted inside and dialed the number for Emmeline's desk at the library.

"You sound excited," she said after she picked up.

"Sam's taking me to see Coates. But that's not why I called. I forgot to hire an answering service before I left the office this morning. Tomorrow, would you handle that?"

"I already did. Gibson's." She gave me a number. "Any time you want to check for messages, call and give them your name. I arranged it so we both could do it."

"You're a peach." I glanced out the window at Sam, who tapped his wristwatch. "I gotta scram."

"Be careful," she said.

I joined Sam on the sidewalk. "Just once, could you park closer? My dogs are barking."

"I don't want him to see us coming. Listen. Be prepared. Coates is a different cat than his rival." He stepped aside so people could pass us. "I'm sure you noticed Gainey was smooth. Very slick and polished, despite his use of *ain't.*"

"He wants people to be impressed," I replied.

Sam nodded in approval. "Coates is more working class, or so I hear. Instead of suits, he wears dungarees and work shirts. No shiny shoes. He might look like a guy who works next to your dad at Bethlehem. Make no mistake. He'll stick a knife in you as soon as look at you."

"You're saying I should keep my lips zipped."

"If I expected that, I wouldn't have brought you. I'm telling you to be careful and not let a big smile con you into letting your guard down." He took one last puff and flicked away his cigarette.

I could have sulked at Sam sayin' I couldn't keep my mouth shut. Not in so many words, but that was what he meant. Instead, I chose to focus on the fact he trusted me enough to bring me along. "I've done this before, Sam. I'll be careful. Heck, from what I know of him, I don't think I'd even go lookin' for this guy if you weren't here."

"Atta girl." He tipped his head to tell me the direction we wanted.

We set off up Genessee at a brisk pace. The buildings here were different than over on Jefferson. There were fewer stores and more industrial-type businesses. They were close together. Sometimes, a garage or a small lot separated 'em. After a couple of blocks, Sam slowed in front of a place that looked like a mechanic's shop. A few cars were in the space next to it, which was surrounded by a chain-link fence. A large sign warning us to beware of the dog hung from the front door.

I listened. "I don't hear any barking. Do you think the sign is a gimmick?"

Sam checked his pistol. "In my experience, that usually isn't the case. Stay behind me."

We approached the front door. After a moment, Sam opened it. As soon as he did, I heard the tinkle of bells. Almost immediately, a giant black dog reared from behind the counter. The teeth in its pink mouth looked as sharp as knives. Spit flew from its jowls as it lunged and barked with enough ferocity that I figured it wanted a snack of fresh meat and was overjoyed we'd come to give it to him.

I stepped back toward the open door.

A squat, dark-skinned man with close-cut hair came from the back. "Moses, get down!" He wore faded dungarees and a shirt that had clearly been washed a couple hundred times. It was unbuttoned enough I could see a stained undershirt over a hairy chest. His eyes were coal black and beady. Scars crisscrossed his hands and a broad shiny mark, perhaps from a healed burn, showed on his right forearm. "Who're you?" He laid a hand on the dog's head.

Sam introduced us. "Are you Alonzo Coates?"

"That's me." His smile was dazzling against his skin. "A girl private dick? Now don't that beat all. You any good?"

I fought against the lump in my throat. "Why don't you hire me and find out?"

He tilted his head and studied me. To him, I wasn't an interesting insect. More like a joint of beef he was deciding how to cut up.

I continued. "Your dog's name is Moses? I don't suppose that's a coincidence. I wonder if your rival knows. If he does, he can't be all that flattered, especially if it's a reflection of what you think of him."

Coates roared with laughter. "I like you, girl. No, it most certainly ain't. As to what that bastard thinks, I don't much care." He opened the swing door, and Moses charged out. I froze. He was huge. I had no idea what kind of dog he was, but either of my younger brothers coulda ridden him like a horse. He sniffed me all over. Then he reared up on his hind legs and put his front paws on my shoulders. I staggered back and put a hand on the counter to steady myself. The dog licked my face with his enormous pink tongue. I squeezed my eyes shut. Not because I was afraid. I didn't want dog slobber in 'em.

"He likes you." Coates cackled. "All right, Moses, that's enough." He snapped his fingers, and Moses retreated. "What brings you to see me on this fine day?"

"Stevie Washington," Sam said. He pushed back his fedora and crossed his arms.

Coates rubbed Moses behind the ears. "The dead boy over on Wadsworth. I heard about him."

"Did he work for you?"

I used my sleeve to wipe my face and thought Sam was being awfully direct. Then again, takin' a roundabout path prob'ly wouldn't work with this man.

"I don't employ minors here at the garage." Coates leaned on the counter.

"I didn't mean here." Sam waved a hand to take in the dingy office.

Coates smiled broadly enough to show off a gold-capped molar. "Why, Detective. I don't rightly know what you're talkin' about."

Oh yes, you do. "That's not right, Mr. Coates," I said. "I've talked first-hand to folks who say you've been hittin' 'em up for dough. You offer protection from Gainey. Word on the street is you want a piece of your rival's action. Maybe all of it. Those same people tell me you convinced Stevie to turn traitor and work for you."

Sam's cheek twitched, but he said nothing.

"Mister Coates. I like that." The crime boss took out a knife and twirled it so the light caught the blade.

Sam tensed, and his hand went to his gun.

Coates grinned and flipped it to clean his nails. "You know, I wasn't gonna talk to you when you walked in. But since y'all so polite." He flicked dirt off the blade. "Moses Gainey ain't got no right to be boss here in Buffalo. He's not even from 'round here. Moved into town a couple of years ago from New York with his fine clothes and manners. He thinks he's better'n all of us, whatever our skin color." Coates jammed the knife into the counter with a thunk. "His boy, Stevie, came to me in July. He said he could tell me all about Gainey's operation. Mebbe help me take over." He spat on the floor.

"You must have liked that," Sam said.

"I surely did." Coates examined his fingers. "Right up until I caught the little snitch passin' information back to Gainey."

"When was that?"

Coates squinted at us. "A week ago or so? I tole him to git out and not come back, not if he knew what was healthy."

"Awfully generous of you." Sam tilted his head. "I'm surprised you didn't kill him on the spot."

"Stevie was a kid." Coates dismissed the idea with a wave. "'Sides, he hadn't passed any important dope. I'm not stupid enough to trust a fifteen-year-old boy with anything that could really hurt me. But make no mistake: Had he not run back to Daddy like I tole him to do, things woulda gotten a lot rougher."

The words were spoken in such a matter-of-fact tone, a shiver went down my spine. "Why should we believe you?"

Coates swung his gaze back to me. "Newspaper said the boy was shot."

I nodded.

"Not my style, Miss Ahern." He stretched. "Too merciful. No, had Stevie crossed me, I'd've cut him into pieces and fed him to ole Moses here." Once again, he rubbed the giant dog's head.

Now *that*, I did believe.

* * *

As soon as I got back into Sam's car, I shook. "Whoo-ee. That is one scary man."

Sam started the car and tossed his fedora in the back. "I told you."

"It was the way he talked. He sounded calm. Like he'd kill a guy before dinner and it wouldn't affect his appetite one bit."

"I find him more dangerous than Gainey." Sam pulled away from the curb. "Gainey hits you over the head with his gangster routine. Whereas Coates plays at being just folks."

"Right up until you make him mad." I thought of that gold-capped grin, the way he handled the knife, and his giant dog. Once again, I shivered. "Think he was tellin' the truth?"

"I'm not sure." Sam lit a cigarette. "He hired Stevie, yes. He would have killed him, yes. Maybe even the way he said. Heck, he might have let that beast maul the boy. Who knows?"

"That's a heck of a way to go." I took out my pad so I could write some notes. "If Stevie sold out Coates, I don't think he'd be sent home like a boy who'd snitched a pie from a windowsill, though."

"Agreed. At the very least, Stevie would've been beaten within an inch of his life."

I tapped my lips with my pencil. "Could one of Coate's other flunkies have taken matters into his own hands?"

Sam braked at a red light. "Men like Coates tend to keep control with an iron fist. That underling might find himself in hot water."

A thought occurred to me. "Would Coates sweeten the pot? Would he offer Stevie more money if he'd spy on Gainey and turn double-agent?"

"It's not impossible. Trouble is, Coates would be placing faith in a boy he knows can be bought off. It's always a risky proposition to rely on a person you know can be bought."

I played the scene in my mind. Stevie would've been in that lot, alone. Someone coulda taken him by surprise and shot him. "What if neither Gainey nor Coates knew the real truth of what Stevie was up to? He coulda been playin' both ends against the middle, making each man think he was workin' for him."

Sam glanced at me. "How would that work?"

"The light's green." I twisted in my seat as Sam pulled forward. "Gainey sent him to work for Coates. Stevie tells Coates that he works for Gainey, he's sick of being mistreated, and how would Coates like an inside man? Then he pretends to give each one information on the other, while gettin' paid from both. Basically, he lies to each one and pockets the dough."

"You're saying the person he was truly working for was himself." Sam didn't look at me as he drove, but his thoughtful expression said he was mullin' over my words. "That's a very dangerous game."

"Gainey finds out and he follows Stevie that night. He waits and when he sees Stevie come out to have a pee, he shoots him. Or Coates finds out. Same thing."

"Coates was right. It's not his style. Shooting, I mean."

I chewed the pencil. "What if he saw it as an opportunity to frame his rival?"

Sam tapped the wheel. "Complicated. But possible."

"Are we certain Gainey had nothin' to do with the card operation?" I told him about Charlie Nickles. "Could Gainey be pullin' the strings? Nickles coulda played informer."

"My gut says Nickles is on his own. Gainey wouldn't be running something as simple as back-room gambling at that level. He's a high-stakes player. From what I know, his fights are his main operation. Vice keeps trying to pin something on him, but so far they've come up empty."

I sank back in my seat. "Then I'm still lookin' at one of four people. Georgie Vickers, Coates, Gainey, or this Charlie fella."

Sam wagged a finger at me. "Don't forget the irate father. And Tom."

"Right." I rubbed my chin.

"Where to, my lady?"

"Home." I dropped my notebook and pencil back into my purse. "I gotta see a guy about a blackjack game."

Chapter Thirty-One

I had to wait until Lee got home to start my blackjack education. Tom, as a player, mighta been a better source, but his tendency to hold back key facts made Lee a better starting point. "Mom, I'm heading to the Tillotsons'. I don't know if I'll be back for dinner." I opened the front door.

Tom stood on the step, hand raised.

"What are you doin' here?" I cringed inside a bit. "Sorry. I didn't mean to sound harsh. I wasn't expecting you."

He gripped his crutches and hopped down to the sidewalk. "I thought…do you want to get dinner somewhere?" The words tumbled out.

I didn't bother to hide my surprise. A dinner invitation? That was the last thing I'd been expecting. "Are you ask'n me on a date?" I narrowed my peepers. "You're not drunk, are you?" I didn't smell booze on his breath. He'd shaved that morning. His blue button-down shirt, clean and pressed, and brown slacks, the left leg neatly pinned up, showed he'd put a little thought into his clothes. No, there was no liquid courage involved here.

"Haven't had a drop." He met my gaze with clear eyes. "We spent all day yesterday together." A pause. "I didn't mean a date. Not unless you want it to be. We don't have to go anywhere fancy. Teddy's is fine."

I could. Maybe over dinner, I could get him to open up a bit more. But I needed to talk to Lee before he went to bed. "I can't. Not that I don't want to. But I gotta work." I licked my lips. "I'm goin' to Lee's to learn about blackjack. You're welcome to come."

The angle of the setting sun cast a shadow on his face. "Sure."

We found Lee in his backyard with Dot, as usual. "Tom. Betty. What's up?" She didn't bother to hide her surprise.

Lee's face wore an expressionless mask. He and I had a wordless exchange. I read the question in his eyes: *Are you jake?* I gave a small nod.

He relaxed and flicked away his cigarette. "Do you need something?"

"Yep. You gotta teach me everything you know about blackjack." I perched on the picnic table. "I need to try and understand how Stevie's racket worked."

Lee threw a look at Dot. "There's a pack of cards in the game cabinet. Would you get them?"

She slipped inside.

He returned his focus to me. "I assume what you really want to know is how someone would cheat."

"Yes. Don't worry. I'm not about to turn into a card sharp," I said.

For the first time since Tom had come home, the two friends grinned at each other. "Betty, I don't think you could cheat if you tried," Lee said.

"No way. You're too honest." Tom made his way to the table. "I'm in."

Dot returned with the cards. "Here you go."

Lee took out the pack and shuffled as he looked at Tom. "How many players did you have that night?"

"Five."

Lee thought. "Betty, can you get a fourth person? It'll be closer to what happened. In blackjack, you have a dealer who doesn't play. I'll do that."

"Hold on." I raced back home and found Mary Kate in our bedroom. "I need you."

"I'm doin' my homework and then it's dinner."

She was the most studious of us all. But I knew her weakness. "I'll buy you a Hershey bar."

She scrambled out of her chair, schoolbooks discarded.

We went back to the Tillotsons'. "Here's our fourth."

Mary Kate beamed. "Betty told me on the way over that you're playing blackjack. Where do I sit?"

Dot rounded on me. "Your teenage sister? This game isn't appropriate for her."

"Listen, missy." I shook a finger at Mary Kate. "This is research for a case. Promise me you won't take up a life of gambling."

She made an X over her chest. "Cross my heart and hope to die."

I looked at Dot. "Satisfied?"

She rolled her eyes.

We sat at the table. Lee dealt us all two face-up cards. For himself, he had one up and one down. "Blackjack is simple. All of you are playing against me. The goal is to get as close to twenty-one as you can without going over."

"What happens if you do?" Mary Kate leaned forward. Her face shone with excitement. Askin' her might have been a mistake.

"That's called a bust, and you lose." Lee pointed. "Every card is worth face value. Jacks, queens, and kings are ten, and the ace can be one or eleven." He explained the rest of the rules.

"But how do you cheat?" Dot pursed her lips. "Everything is visible. I can't switch this seven for a queen without you all knowing."

Tom took up the explanation. "That's where counting comes in. There are fifty-two cards in the deck, four of each. Blackjack doesn't use wild cards."

"Which means you have a four in fifty-two, or about a seven percent, chance of drawing any particular card, at least at the start." Lee asked all of us if we wanted to hit. Then he dealt out the cards. "Now, Betty has two fours. Your chance of getting another four is now two in fifty-two."

Mary Kate's lips moved. "About three and a half percent, so really low. But we don't know what that card is." She pointed at the face-down one in front of Lee.

"Correct, but you do know my face-up. It's a king. Tom has a king, and so does Dot."

Her eyes were intent. "I see. The chances of that card bein' a king are also really low, as are my chances of gettin' one if I hit again."

"You'd better watch your sister, Betty." Lee shot me a look. "Yes. But you wouldn't hit, or I wouldn't recommend it. You've got eighteen now. There are a lot of cards out there. Lots of chances to bust. Let's say you all stand." He flipped his face down card, which was a seven. "You and Tom win 'cause you have more than my seventeen. I can't draw another card. Betty loses."

He swept up the cards and put them aside. "If we were really playin', she'd have hit, but never mind."

I began to see how Stevie's strategy worked. "As long as you can remember what was discarded, you can calculate the odds of gettin' a favorable card and make your bets and calls appropriately."

"Correct." Lee dealt again. "Fewer cards in the deck mean the chances of certain cards go up. Like I said, it's all probability."

We played for a bit. I didn't have the memory to keep track of things, but Mary Kate did. I could hear her whisperin' to herself, and she won more hands than any of us. She clapped her hands. "This is fun."

"You created a monster," Dot said.

"Stevie would have to be careful." I stared at the cards. "If he kept winnin', that would be suspicious. I know you've said this isn't really cheatin', not technically. But the bank can't be happy losin' all the time. Not to mention the other players. He'd have to lose a hand or two."

Tom lit a Chesterfield. "Or have a partner. He said it works better that way." His face reddened. "At least, um, well..."

I stared at him. "Mary Kate. It's time for you to scram."

* * *

I managed to run off Mary Kate by givin' her coins for two chocolate bars. Then I whirled to face Tom. "Okay, pal. I've known for a while this was more than what you said. It's time to come clean. What exactly were you and Stevie doin'?"

Lee and Dot moved away so they stood to the side of us. Not with me, but clearly not by Tom.

He spoke to the ground. "Lee, you got any whiskey?"

"Not for you." Lee's voice sounded harsh.

"Talk." I planted my fists on my hips.

Tom ran his hands over his face. He sagged. "It was mostly like I said. I met Stevie in a bar."

"And you don't remember the name."

"No. Don't ask me what a kid was doing there, either. At the time, I wasn't in a condition to wonder." He gave me a guilty look. "Anyway, Stevie told me if I wanted to make some dough, I should meet him at midnight over at that warehouse. The one you and I visited. He said he had a plan, but he could use a partner."

I crossed my arms. "Go on."

"I was still tipsy when I woke up after you and Frank dragged me home. But I made it. Stevie was there. He told me the play." Tom waved his hand. "The kid was sharp as a tack. It was pretty much what we just did. He could keep track of the cards. He chattered throughout the game. Certain words told me when to hit and when to stand. We rarely won in the same hand. Between us, we cleaned up. The plan was to split the take, seventy-thirty. He did the work, so he was gonna get the bigger share. That was jake to me."

"What went wrong?" Lee asked from his post against the house.

Tom didn't look at him. "Between hands, Stevie got up and said he needed to piss. I heard gunshots. Real faint, but I knew what they were. The others said I was imagining things. But I knew. I went outside to look for Stevie and there he was." He looked at me, eyes haunted. "I swear, Betty. That's how it happened."

"Did he really need to pee? Why not use the warehouse toilet?" I asked.

Based on Tom's blank expression, he'd not thought of that. "Maybe he thought it was Whites only. Anyway, at the time, I didn't think twice about him goin' outside. I guess he coulda been meetin' someone."

Instinct told me the story was true. "Is this why you're afraid of the cops?"

"Yeah. I could easily imagine the cops saying we argued over the money, I shot him, and was lookin' for the cash. When I saw him on the ground...." He swallowed hard, face pale. "Let's say it brought back memories. I've sunk pretty low, but I haven't reached robbin' the dead."

"Why didn't you tell us this in the first place?" Lee's voice had a harsh edge. "I understand you not takin' Dot into your confidence. But Betty and me, we're as close as family. Either one of us woulda said it was a bad idea. We want to help you. Why are you keepin' us at arm's length? Don't you trust us?"

Tom hung his head. "It's not that."

Lee pressed. "Then what is it?"

"You don't understand." Tom slammed his hands against the table.

The cards scattered, and I swept them up.

Tom didn't spare me a look. "I go out of the house, and I can hear everyone's whispers. There goes the cripple. What a shame. He had such a bright future." He ran his hands through his hair, and it stood up at wild angles. "My dad won't look at me. Every company I go to says the same thing. Gotta have two legs to do the work. You don't know what it's like."

The tips of Lee's ears turned red as Tom spoke. "Welcome to my world, pal."

Tom flinched. "Lee, I'm sorry. I didn't mean—"

"Shut up." Lee pointed at him. "I'm gonna talk and you're gonna listen. Then you're leaving." His gaze was fierce. "You've been this way for what, three, four months? Try fifteen years. Sure, it isn't too bad in the First Ward. But every time I leave this neighborhood, I gotta go through it all over again. Strangers givin' me dirty looks 'cause I'm not in uniform. Then I walk, and the scorn turns to pity. That poor boy. Isn't he brave, workin' at GM and still doin' his part."

I watched as Tom wilted under the firestorm of his friend's words. Part of me wanted to tell Lee to back off. Another part knew this was something Tom needed to hear.

"The worst was the draft board." Lee continued. "I knew I wasn't gonna be able to do infantry or even artillery. I thought maybe I'd be okay in a desk job. Turns out even the general's lackeys need two good legs."

Lee had never talked about his attempt to enlist. I hoped the sergeant had at least been kind.

He took a deep breath, getting control of his anger. "It stinks, 'cause you know you have skills. Heck, you're at least as knowledgeable as I am, better than I was when I started at GM. You worked on a tank, for cripe's sake. You'll get your shot." He stood. "When you go home tonight, stay away from the bottle. It won't help you. My dad is a prime example. Drink cost him his job and his life." Lee gripped Tom's shoulder. "You're my best friend.

More like a brother. Don't throw away what you have because you're feelin' sorry for yourself."

Tom didn't respond. He stared at his clenched fists.

Lee grabbed his cap. "I'll see you around, Betty. C'mon, Dot." He grabbed the cards and limped inside. Dot gave me a sad look and followed him.

I watched as the emotions ran across my former fiancé's face. "He's right, you know."

No response.

"There's one more thing you gotta stop."

Tom raised his head. His eyes shone, but he seemed determined not to let tears fall. "What's that?"

"Don't lie to me." I put my hand on his shoulder. "I returned your ring, but I still care about you."

"But you don't love me. How can you love half a man?"

His words hit me like a punch to the gut. The silence stretched, broken only by the sound of crickets and night birds. "Is that what you think bothers me? A missing half-leg?"

He turned away. "I can't stand seein' myself in a mirror. How can you look at me all the time and not be disgusted?" He rubbed his eyes. "Not even twenty years old and my life is over."

I ached at the pain in his voice. I'd asked for honesty. Now I was gettin' it and I half-wished I wasn't. "That's not true."

"Were you being honest when you said you didn't love Frank Hicks?"

I squirmed on my bench and felt the heat in my cheeks. "That's not a question I can answer while we're sittin' in the Tillotsons' backyard."

He didn't flinch. "Try."

"Yes." I owed that much to him. "If I get married, it'll be to a fella who is my partner. One who supports me, but also knows when to stop me from doin' somethin' foolish. I can be a little stubborn."

"You don't say," he said, voice dripping with sarcasm.

I flicked his shoulder. It made my fingers tingle. His upper arm was solid as a bar of steel. "Talk about the pot callin' the kettle black. Anyway. He's also gotta be honest. I look at you, and see anger and half-truths. I can't

love that. I want more of what you were yesterday, less of right now." Seein'
him was more painful than the looks of pity the night Frank and I dragged
him outta O'Malley's. The Tom I knew, that I remembered, wouldn't look
so beaten down.

Even if we were through, I hoped that person wasn't gone forever.

I stood. For a moment, I thought he might say somethin', but he stared at
his hands. I handed him his crutches. "Come on. I'll walk you home."

Chapter Thirty-Two

I made it to the office by nine the next morning. As usual, Emmeline was already there. The promised water cooler took up most of the corner. "When did that arrive?"

"This morning, a little after eight." She pulled out a box from the bag under her desk. "Doughnut? I bought them this morning on my way in. I know you stop at Teddy's for breakfast, but you can have a snack if you want."

I peeked in the box. Inside were plain cake doughnuts, a couple that were dusted with sugar, and some crullers. "Now we're cookin' with gas." I picked out a plain one and poured myself a cup of joe. Then I headed to my desk.

She followed me. "I found Sonya's surname. Moses Gainey's girl."

"Where?" I sat and took a bite of the treat.

"In the paper. I took them home last night." She spread the newsprint in front of me and tapped it. "Sonya Thompson. According to the photo caption, she's a singer at The Crazy Cat. She's on Gainey's arm in this snap. I can't tell where they are."

"That's the place Sam and I went to. It looked like a nightclub." I brushed my hands together to dust off the crumbs.

"It is. They have a listing in the telephone book, but not an ad. Music crosses all barriers, and jazz is very popular, so the clientele is probably mixed." She handed over a page of notes. "They don't open for business until seven tonight, but I called and asked if she was going to perform. She'll be there in a couple of hours to go over her set. I thought you might be able to catch her then."

Emmeline was a pro at sniffin' out leads over the telephone. She'd proved that on our last case when she'd called just about every hospital in the Adirondacks lookin' for dope on a woman who'd s'posedly been a patient. "What cover did you use this time?"

"A reporter." She examined the chair but chose to perch on a corner of the desk. "People either hate talking to a newswoman or love it. I said I was writing a story on local nightclub talent and wanted to interview her. The manager said the best time would be when she came in to practice."

I perused the page of notes. "Swell. I guess you've made my plans for today." I took a sip, expecting the taste of chicory. "Real coffee? Where in the world did you get that?"

She cocked her head. "Do you really want to know?"

* * *

I heard familiar male voices outside my office a little after ten. Emmeline responded with "Go in." I looked up. Lee and Tom entered. Both of 'em had shadows under their peepers. Lee clutched a cup of coffee in each hand, and an unlit Chesterfield dangled from his lips. He nodded at the chair.

Tom set his crutches aside. The wood creaked as he settled down. "I'm gonna have to see if I can get you a better seat. Every time I sit in this one, I think I'm gonna end up on the floor." He pulled out his own deck of smokes and lit one. He reached out to Lee for a mug of joe. "Thanks."

Lee handed it over, then lit his own cigarette. "Morning, Betty." He exhaled. "I wanna know where that girl got real java. Wherever it was, you'd better give her a raise."

I gaped. First off, they hadn't parted on the best of terms last night. Now they were actin' like nothin' ever happened. Second, it was the middle of a Wednesday morning. I aimed a pencil at Lee. "Why aren't you at work?" I swung it to Tom. "And what are you doin' here?"

Lee held out a hand. "Told you. Pay up."

Tom dug a quarter out of his pocket and flipped it to his friend.

I tossed the pencil on my desk. "Wanna tell me what that was about?"

Tom sipped his coffee. "Lee bet me you wouldn't even say good morning. I said you would. You have changed." He wore the same pants from last night, but a different shirt. It was mostly free of wrinkles. His hair was tousled, but his eyes were clear. More importantly, he'd shed the despair that had hung on him last night like a wet blanket.

"Fine. Good morning." I glared at each in turn. "Now, why're you two here instead of at GM or at home? Somethin' good happened 'cause you're actin' like you're best buddies again."

"I called in sick." Lee leaned against the wall. "I was up until three in the morning and barely got any sleep after I snuck back in. Tried to sneak. Mom caught me. The only thing that saved me from a whipping is the fact that I'm nineteen and the man of the house."

"Thanks again for boostin' me through my window. I'd've been a goner if I'd had to use the front door." Tom looked around for somewhere to ash his cigarette.

"You got thirty seconds to start makin' sense or I'm tossin' both of you out." I pushed a metal ashtray toward Tom. "Last night, I didn't think you two would ever talk to each other again."

Lee took a drag and exhaled a cloud of smoke. "We went to a card game. Same ringleader, different location. Poker this time."

"You what?"

Tom nodded. "It was my idea. Kinda brilliant, if I do say so myself."

I rested my forehead against my palms. "You went lookin' for a guy who prob'ly wants to beat you up for cheatin' him. You think that's smart? Did that blast knock out your brains, too?" I looked from one to the other.

I half-expected Tom to explode in anger. But he smiled.

"It's jake." Lee came over to knock ash into the tray. "You'd better start at the beginning, pal."

"It's like this." Tom set his cup on my desk. "You said you needed the dope on what Stevie was up to. I told you what I knew last night. But that doesn't help you with the guy runnin' the games. Charlie, the one who was lookin' for Stevie. After you took me home last night, I got to thinkin'. I knew the location of the next game. I called Lee and asked if he wanted to go with me."

"I wasn't keen on the idea," Lee said. "But I knew the fat head would go without me, so I said yes."

Tom made a rude gesture at his friend. "Charlie was there. Prob'ly to make sure everything ran smoothly after Stevie's death. You're right. He wasn't happy to see me. I spun him a tale. I told him I was mad at Stevie 'cause he hadn't paid me my share. Now he was dead, I needed to make it up. Then I did the thing that really got me in good."

"What's that?" I asked.

"I lost." He ashed his gasper again. "Not a lot, but enough to convince Charlie I wasn't the cheat. It made him a lot more willing to talk after we were done for the night. I asked all about Stevie, how long he'd been comin' to the games, what Charlie knew about him, and how he'd found out about Stevie's scheme."

Lee interrupted. "I knew Tom was a good liar, but he poured it on thick with Charlie. You woulda thought they'd been friends for years by the time the evening was over."

Tom grinned. The old twinkle came back into his eyes, the one he'd had before the war when he and Lee got up to their usual shenanigans.

I pushed down my flash of irritation. Neither of 'em had thought to tell me. "Did you learn anythin' useful?"

"I think so." Tom took a battered pad outta his shirt pocket. "I wrote it down when I got home. The night he died was only the third time Stevie had come to one of the games. Always blackjack, never poker. Charlie thought he was older. Like eighteen or so. Charlie figured Stevie was a 4F 'cause he was scrawny or he was another Negro the draft board didn't want."

His words reminded me of my question. "This is the second or third time I've heard of that. Why wouldn't the service want a perfectly healthy guy?"

Both of my friends grew somber. Lee answered first. "Bigotry. Sometimes, the person running the draft board doesn't want colored folks. They make up health reasons, but it really comes down to discrimination."

"Even up north?"

Lee exhaled and nodded.

Tom took a final drag from his cigarette and ground it out. "It's stupid. A bullet doesn't care what color your skin is. I had friends who were Negroes. Good guys. I woulda trusted any one of 'em with my life. In a foxhole, skin and religion don't matter."

"Aren't the services segregated?" I asked Tom.

He nodded. "The guys I knew worked the mess. Cooking, serving food, doin' dishes, that sort of thing. Necessary work, but I thought it was demeaning. Half of 'em were better shots than the white boys. Maybe this war will make the generals in Washington see what they're missing. Heck, we already got Negro pilots. Why not soldiers or seamen?"

I didn't much care for the answer, but at least I knew. "Back to Stevie. What made Charlie suspicious?"

"The dealers." Tom wrapped his hands around his mug. "They said how it seemed Stevie won a lot. He didn't win all the time. But as the dealer thought back over the evenings, Stevie clearly came out on top."

I leaned back in my chair. "Why'd Charlie keep lettin' Stevie play?"

Lee spoke up. "After the second game, Charlie went to the Fruit Belt. He was gonna confront Stevie, but he couldn't find him. Charlie decided to see if he could get Stevie to slip up during a game. Instead, Stevie got shot."

I tapped my pencil against my lips. "Charlie coulda cornered Stevie when he went out for a pee. Things got heated, and Charlie shot him. Was he there when the cops showed?"

Tom thought. "No, he'd skedaddled."

"That's when he tossed away the gun. And how Georgie Vickers wound up with it."

"Or Georgie didn't find that gun." Lee crushed out his smoke. "There's only his word. From what you've said, he doesn't sound like someone you can trust."

He had a good point.

Tom handed over his dirty page of notes. "Did we help?"

"You did. Thanks." I paused. "Why? I mean, you weren't in the best of moods last night. And you"—I looked at Lee—"I wouldn't have thought you'd go with him, not based on what you said."

"He's my best friend. I couldn't let him go alone." Lee rubbed his face. "But now I want a nap."

I brought my focus back to Tom. "Well?"

He blew out a breath. "I thought about what you said. That you wanted a partner." He locked his gaze on my eyes. "I wanna be that guy. Engaged or not, I want you to know you can count on me." He hesitated. "I wanna be useful again. I don't like myself much these days. Maybe helpin' you will change my mind."

It didn't sound like something he'd come to on his own. I glanced at Lee, who shrugged. I looked back at Tom. His eyes were mostly brown, but there was a little bit of green in them, too. "Thank you. I mean it." My heart didn't go pitter-pat when I looked at Tom. He didn't have a dimple. Instead, lookin' at him made me feel warm. Safe. Like he had my back, just like Lee and Sam. But more than that. I couldn't quite put the feeling into words.

But I knew I liked it. A lot.

Chapter Thirty-Three

Lee and Tom left soon after they finished their story. I gave them both stern instructions to go home and get some sleep.

Not that I thought there was any chance under the sun they'd obey me.

I timed my arrival at The Crazy Cat for around eleven-thirty. To further sell my cover, I held my notepad and tucked a pencil behind my ear.

The interior of the club was dim. Sonya stood up on stage behind the microphone. I didn't know the song, but I listened for a minute or two. Her voice was deep and sultry. She wore a plain dress and low heels, but it was easy to picture her in a shimmering gown of sequins, her hair all done up. I couldn't tell from where I stood if she had any makeup on. Even if she didn't, she was a beauty. The lights shone on her coal-black hair, and the dress hugged her slender, but curvy, body. Her dark brown skin glowed. Between her looks and her voice, it was little wonder Moses Gainey wanted to be seen with her.

My attention snagged on a group of men off to the side. One of 'em was Gainey. He wasn't wearing fancy duds now, just a white button-down with the sleeves rolled up and pants held up by black suspenders. I didn't recognize the other two with him. The conversation couldn't be heard over the music, but from the facial expressions, I gathered it was serious. Business matters?

They didn't seem to notice me. I took out my Kodak and maneuvered to a spot with better light. I couldn't use a flash, so I didn't know how well the pictures would come out. Hopefully, the shutter click would be drowned out by Sonya's singing. If the pictures came out legible, I'd show 'em to Sam and Melvin.

I'd taken my snaps and slipped the camera back in my purse when Sonya finished. Gainey clapped, although the other two ignored her. She gave a little curtsy and hopped off the stage. Then she held her hand over her eyebrows and looked in my direction. "Is someone there? Who are you?"

I didn't want to get closer while Gainey was there. He might recognize me. Luckily, the men packed up. Gainey planted a smacker on Sonya's lips and led the men to a door in the back. Once they were gone, I moved closer to the stage and into the light. "Miss Thompson, my name is Betty Ahern. I hoped to talk to you."

"Felix said a reporter called this morning. Was that you?" Sonya removed a pack of smokes from her purse, slipped one out, and looked around, presumably for a match.

I took out my Zippo and flicked it. "It was my associate." I lit her cigarette, something long and thin. "I'm a private detective. The reporter thing is a story in case someone butts in."

Sonya blew out a cloud of smoke. "Why would you want to talk to me, and why should I?"

"I'm investigating the murder of a young boy. I think you may have information."

Her dark eyes roved over my face as she took a drag and exhaled. "I don't know any boys."

"But you know Moses Gainey, right?"

The light in her peepers hardened. "Maybe. What's he got to do with anything?"

"The boy who was killed was named Stevie Washington. I think he worked for Mr. Gainey."

"I don't know nothing about Moses's business dealings." She pushed past me and sashayed to the bar.

I wondered if that was her natural walk or if she'd done it so much, it had become habit. "I didn't say you do." I took a seat next to her.

She waited while the bartender poured some whiskey into a glass over a couple ice cubes before walkin' away. "Yet here you are." She held up the glass. "Drink?"

"No thanks. It's a little early for me." I paused. "Did you see Stevie around? Just a kid, maybe fifteen. He prob'ly woulda been a runner or somethin'. He was too young to be anythin' else."

"I told you. I stay out of Mo's dealings." She took a sip.

This was goin' nowhere. "Sonya. Do you mind if I call you that?"

She shook her head.

"You pretend to be hard, but you can't be very old. Twenty, maybe? No older than twenty-five."

"I'm twenty-three."

"Stevie had a sister. She's not even outta high school. She loved her brother." I paused. "You got any siblings?"

"A brother and a sister. They're still in school." She swirled her drink, and the ice clinked.

"Imagine one of 'em turns up dead. Murdered. You know they mighta been into somethin' that got 'em shot. Wouldn't you want to know what happened?" I waited. When she didn't answer, I piled on. "That's what Nancy wants. What happened to her kid brother? What turned him from a sweet child into a budding criminal? I can't arrest anyone. But I can give her an answer." I didn't mention my friendship with Sam. "For Nancy's sake, help me out."

She stared at her drink. "This is gonna come back on Mo, ain't it?"

"Not if he didn't do it." I watched her. "You're scared of him."

She cast a quick look in the direction where the men had gone. "You should be, too."

The bartender had disappeared. No one was around. I leaned closer. "You can trust me. You got a swell voice. You could blow this joint and go to New York or Los Angeles. You don't need Moses Gainey."

She ran her tongue over her ruby-red lips. "Stevie was a sweet kid. I think he liked me. He used to bring me flowers backstage. Nothing fancy. Wildflowers. Maybe he picked 'em himself."

"He was in love with you?"

"I don't think so. He said he had a girl he wanted to run away with. Never told me much about her, but he'd ask me for advice." She gave a quick smile. "I told him he was too young to be workin' for Mo. But he wanted dough to buy a ring."

"As a runner?"

"At first." She downed the rest of her whiskey. "You didn't hear this from me, got it?"

"Mum's the word."

Sonya edged closer and dropped her voice to almost a whisper. "You ever heard of Alonzo Coates?"

"I know him. He and Gainey are rivals, or so I understand."

Her gaze flicked over my shoulder. "Mo's got a plan to run Coates outta Buffalo. He convinced Stevie to join Coates's crew. That way, he could feed Mo information. Mo was gonna give him a bonus once the job was done. Stevie brought an advertisement for some jeweler and asked me if they had nice goods. I said he'd never be able to afford that place. That's when Stevie told me the plan. I'm not supposed to know. I'm just the chanteuse."

I understood. Sonya was a prize, something Gainey could flash around. Not a person in her own right.

Now she did whisper. "I want to go to New York. Mo, he said not until he was done with me. He's cruel. I was stupid to tell him my dream 'cause now he'll take pleasure in keepin' me chained to him. I want out, but he needs to go first. Do you catch my drift?"

Oh boy, did I. She would love it if I'd tag Gainey for murder and send him to the pokey. "Tell me what you know."

"He had a fight with Stevie." She edged away from the bar. "I'm not sure over what, but it was big."

I moved with her. "When?"

"The day before Stevie was killed. Mo came into the club that Saturday lookin' like he had the world by a string. I asked what put him in such a good mood, and he said he'd solved a big problem. I asked if he'd worked out the fight with Stevie. He told me not to worry. Stevie wouldn't be a bother."

"Did he catch Stevie stealin' from the bag, or was it somethin' else?"

"I don't know."

Sonya prob'ly didn't have more detail. Gainey woulda been careful to keep her in the dark. I tried anyway. "Could Stevie have sold Gainey out? You know, turned double-agent for Coates?"

"Stevie was smart. He mighta thought he could get away with a plan like that. But he'd have been playin' with a stick of dynamite lit at both ends." Her dark eyes pleaded with me. "I can't say more. Please, go. And don't come back here again."

Chapter Thirty-Four

After I left Sonya, I stopped at a diner to grab lunch and go through my notes. If Stevie wanted dough, not only to buy a ring for his girl but maybe get outta Buffalo, he'd have grabbed it from wherever he could. Poor deluded kid. The plan never woulda worked. There was still the fact that Georgie Vickers had the gun, though.

First things first. I'd talk to Virginia again and see just how mad her father had been.

The thought of Virginia led me to the question I'd shoved to the back of my brain. How'd Stevie gotten all the way to Wadsworth without bein' seen? Between Sam and me, we were certain he hadn't walked or taken a bus.

I finished up my lunch and headed back to the Fruit Belt. I went to the last place I'd seen Stevie the day I'd tailed him. I faced the strip of dirt. Nothing but a dead-end alley, the buildings lined with trash cans.

My attention focused on the square of cement near the sidewalk. Why one patch? Why not the whole strip? Or, why not dirt all the way to the sidewalk? I went to the other side of the building where there was a similar empty space. On that side, the entire area was natural ground that had been walked on so often, only a few hardy weeds managed to take hold.

I went back and knelt down. I ran my hand over all the edges of the cement and brushed debris away. On the second pass, I spied a notch. It was small. At first glance, it could be taken for a chip in the concrete. But the edges were smooth and worn. I wiggled my two fingers in and lifted.

The square grated and shifted just enough that I could grab the edge with my other hand. I lifted it. It swung up on industrial-sized hinges.

Underneath was lined with steel. There was a handle bolted in place. I peered down into the black.

No way was I gonna drop down into a black hole when I didn't know what waited for me at the bottom. "I need to start carryin' a flashlight." I brushed off my hands.

Luckily, the shop across the street was a hardware store. I jogged over, found what I wanted, paid, and returned to the hole. I aimed my light down. The ground was dry. "Here goes nothing." I made my way down some metal rungs but left the cover up. It would blow the secrecy, but I wasn't gonna trap myself underground.

Once my feet were on the ground, I shone my light in an arc. It was a good-sized tunnel. I didn't have to crouch over, and by holdin' my arms out, I could tell it was fairly wide. It was lined with cement that was water-stained but dry. "I guess Lee and Tom were right. There *are* tunnels under Buffalo." I took a couple of steps. I oughta let someone know where I was goin'. But who? I had no idea if Sam was at headquarters. Dot was at work. Frank was at the hospital. Lee and Tom were prob'ly out toasting their success. It was after noon, so Emmeline was at the library. I took a deep breath. I'd turn back at the first sign of trouble.

I'd left the entrance open. There was a good chance some curious neighborhood resident would investigate or call the cops.

After about ten yards, I heard a skittering behind me. Someone tryin' to hide his footsteps? I sped up. The skittering followed. I broke into a jog, my only thought to get to an exit before the person behind me caught up. My feet hit a pile of bricks and I tripped. The flashlight tumbled outta my hand. The sound stopped at my head, and I felt a light tickle on my outstretched arm. I looked up. A rat sniffed my hand. "Eww, get off!" He sped away.

I examined my palms. They were a little scraped from the fall, but nothin' serious. Then I looked at the pile I'd fallen over. A few of the bricks had fallen away and exposed a corner of a metal box. I moved the rest of the pile, then I grabbed my flashlight. A metal strongbox had been hidden under the bricks. It wasn't locked. I lifted it out and opened it. Stacks of greenbacks nestled inside, along with a satchel, a canteen half full of water, a map of

Ontario, and a train schedule. "Where'd you think you were goin', Stevie?" I pawed through the rations. I didn't find an engagement ring. Either he hadn't bought it yet, or he'd hidden it somewhere else. Or given it to her already.

I closed the box and put it back. I shone my light ahead of me. Nothing. I kept walking. The tunnel felt empty, like an abandoned house. I passed another set of rungs, but when I climbed and tried the lid, it didn't budge.

Eventually, I reached a third set of rungs that led to another cover. Hopefully it wasn't locked. If it didn't move, I'd go back.

I climbed up, tucked the flashlight in my purse, and pushed. The cover gave way reluctantly, with the scrape of metal on metal. I heaved myself up and out.

I was in the lot off Wadsworth where Stevie had been shot. The cover was a metal circle, like a manhole in a street. It was behind the stack of crates, which meant I wouldn't be seen unless someone was walkin' right by. It was also why I hadn't seen it when I was there with Tom.

I looked at my hands and knees. There were streaks of rust, dirt, and blood on 'em, but I'd looked worse. I stepped out from behind the crates. A man holdin' a clipboard in one hand and a lit cigarette stopped, mouth open. He wore coveralls, a long-sleeve shirt, and heavy shoes.

"Excuse me." I handed over a business card. "May I use your telephone?"

* * *

The officer I spoke to at headquarters promised to find Sam and send him to my location. He arrived about twenty minutes later. He parked at the curb and came over. "I leave you alone for the morning, and this is what you get yourself into?"

"Well, hello to you, too." I pointed at the crates. "I think I found how Stevie got here from the Fruit Belt without bein' seen."

Sam went over to the open hole, put his fedora on the ground, and peered down. "Hand me your light."

I did.

He finished his inspection. "This'll do it." He stood up and brushed dirt from his slacks. "You walked the whole way?"

"Yep. It's a straight shot."

"Didn't it occur to you that it might be dangerous?"

I crossed my arms. "Yes, it did. I thought about callin' you. But what if it was just a hole in the ground? I didn't want to waste your time. And I didn't have anyone else who could come help me."

He pinched the bridge of his nose. "You find anything else?"

I told him about the metal box with the cash. "I think this was Stevie's hidey-hole. He was stockin' up for a trip."

"Stevie or someone else. Was there anything in the box with his name on it?" Sam headed for his car.

"No. I assumed 'cause that's where I saw Stevie disappear." I gave Sam the details of the day Nancy and I had followed him.

He reached in his car and got on the radio. "Send two units over to—" He looked at me.

"The empty area next to 452 Michigan."

He read back the address. "They should find the entrance to a tunnel and a metal box a ways inside. Take it and cordon off the area. I want interviews with all business owners in the neighborhood. See what they can tell us. And find out who owns that strip of dirt."

"This would not only give Stevie a way to get to his card games, but to see his girl. Maybe even a place they could be alone, away from pryin' eyes." I leaned on the car.

"Not very romantic, but it is private."

I wasn't my idea of a place to take your sweetheart, but for two kids lookin' to be alone, it worked. "What's with the tunnel?"

Sam lit a smoke. "Buffalo has them all over the place. They aren't connected, like a network or anything. Some of them are old waterways, from the days before modern pipes. Some are from Prohibition and were used by bootleggers. There's an old story about one that leads from the jail to the courthouse. They used it to bring Leon Czolgosz, the guy who shot McKinley, to court. Some say it was built for that purpose, but that's probably an old wives' tale."

"They were right." Wait until I told Lee and Tom.

Sam drew down his eyebrows. "Who?"

"When they were kids, Lee and Tom looked for tunnels all over the First Ward. They never found one." I looked down the lot. "Sometimes kid stories are true."

Sam rubbed his lip. "Where was Stevie going? And with who?"

"I know who might be able to tell us." I walked backward down the street. "If you come with me, I won't have to call you again."

Chapter Thirty-Five

I led Sam to Wadsworth and the Ellery house and knocked on the front door. Mr. Ellery, dressed in work pants and his undershirt, answered. "What do you want?"

I handed him my business card. "Is Virginia here? We'd like to talk to her."

He ignored my offering. "She ain't home from school. Are you that girl detective? The one I saw over where the colored kid died?"

"That's me."

He made a dismissive noise in his throat. "Get off my porch. I don't wanna talk to you."

Sam came up and showed his badge. "Do you want to talk to me? Here's a hint. Say yes."

Mr. Ellery growled but came outside. "What?"

Sam tipped his head toward me, an indication I should speak first. "Had you ever met Stevie Washington?" I asked.

"Once." Mr. Ellery scuffed his shoe on the planking. "I caught him and Ginny walkin' home one night. They were holdin' hands. They stopped in front of that tree over there. Then he kissed her. My little girl. Kissed by a—"

Sam broke in. "I assume you said something."

"You're darn right I did." Mr. Ellery's face purpled. "First off, Ginny is only thirteen. She doesn't have any business kissin' anyone. Second, I guess those folks are okay. But not for my girl. She's too young to date and certainly not one of *them*."

Before this case, I'd not had much interaction with colored people. I thought of what Tom had said last night. It didn't make any sense to me. People oughta be people. 'Course I'd never understood when an Irish parent got upset their daughter fell in love with an Italian, either. "She was in love. Doesn't that count for somethin'?"

He snorted. "You don't understand." He addressed Sam. "You got kids?"

"No, I haven't been lucky enough on that front." Sam pushed back his fedora.

That earned another grunt. "Then you don't get it either." Mr. Ellery pounded a thick finger from his left hand into his right palm. "Kids don't always know what's good for 'em. It's up to parents to make 'em understand. By whatever means necessary."

I thought of my folks. Thank goodness Pop didn't take after this fat head. "You realize that doesn't sound too good for you." I crossed my arms. "Did you beat your girl until she got the message?"

He recoiled. "I wouldn't do that. I would wring that punk's scrawny neck to make *him* understand, though. Wouldn't even blink."

"Good thing for you Stevie was shot, not strangled."

It took a moment for him to process my words. "You…me…you think *I* killed that whelp?"

Sam didn't blink. "Do you own a gun, Mr. Ellery?"

"I'm not gonna answer that." He moved toward the door.

Sam stopped him. "Yes, you are. Either here or down at the station. You just said you'd have murdered Stevie without a second thought. I'll ask again. Do you own a gun?"

Mr. Ellery shot us a baleful stare. "Yes."

"What kind?"

The glare intensified. "A .45."

"Get it."

Mr. Ellery disappeared inside. He returned a couple of minutes later, holding a heavy handgun. He thrust it at Sam.

Sam looked it over. He flipped open the chamber, which was empty. He sniffed the barrel. "You don't keep it very clean, do you?"

"I don't use it much. My pa had it from his time out West. It's more of a keepsake."

Sam handed it back. "Where were you last Friday night into Saturday morning?"

Mr. Ellery clutched his pistol. "I was workin' the night shift. My boss'll tell you."

Sam gave him a pleasant smile. "We'll ask. Don't worry."

"You do that." Mr. Ellery snarled and slammed the door.

* * *

Sam and I walked back to his car. "Do you believe him?" I asked.

He cupped his hand around a cigarette and lit it. "Maybe. Do I think he would have killed Stevie? Absolutely." He held out his Zippo, the one with the shamrock I'd given him long ago. "But by shooting him? I'm less convinced."

"What was with the gun? You know it isn't the murder weapon."

"It never hurts to make someone nervous." Sam held out his lighter.

I pulled out a Lucky and leaned forward for a light. Then I took a drag and exhaled. "I'spose Mr. Ellery mighta had two pistols, but I think he's more the type to use his fists."

Sam snapped the Zippo shut. "I agree. Not only that, Georgie Vickers claims to have found the gun two blocks in the opposite direction. I don't see Nate Ellery voluntarily going to the Fruit Belt. Or throwing away his weapon, especially if he didn't think anyone would suspect him."

"Unless he wanted to frame someone or at least push suspicion that way." I raised my eyebrows. "Wait, you don't think Georgie is tellin' the truth?"

"I think it's very convenient he found it where he did. I've walked the street." He flicked ash to the sidewalk. "The lot where Georgie says he found the .38 is taken up by a dumpster. There's no way he found it on the ground."

"Unless he climbed inside." I ashed my smoke. "I don't know of many people who'd go crawlin' around the trash for fun."

"I don't either. I'll be talking to him again."

I eyed Sam. "He's still in jail?"

211

"Based on the fact he had an argument with the victim and was in possession of the murder weapon, we booked him. But the case is weak. While the DA would love to get this one off the books, he agrees. I think Georgie will be released by the weekend, if not sooner." He puffed. "The DA doesn't want trouble, especially in an election year."

"Would there be problems?"

Sam nodded. "Buffalo isn't immune to racial tensions. The DA wants votes, not riots."

I hadn't thought about it much, but Sam was right. "Georgie's off the hook?"

"I didn't say that." Sam flicked ash again. "We'll be keeping a close eye on him. From outside the jail." He eyed me. "How's Tom?"

It took me a second to follow the sharp turn in the subject. "Okay, I guess. One day he's fine, the next he's crawled in the bottle. It's confusing and frustrating."

"He took the end of your engagement hard."

"How did you know about that?" Sam and I didn't talk about our personal lives often. Had he noticed I wasn't wearin' my ring?"

"Tom told me."

"When did you talk to him?"

"Yesterday." Sam took a final drag of his smoke and flipped it into the gutter. "I dropped by to go over his story one more time."

"And?" My heart froze.

"I don't have enough to arrest him." Sam scuffed the sidewalk. "I don't have enough to clear him, either. He definitely had motive and opportunity. It's still not impossible he hid the gun and got rid of it later."

I didn't like it. I didn't think Sam did, either, but it was his job.

He put his hands in his pockets and looked at me. "Tom looked sober to me. I asked how he was doing, and we talked about some other things. It was a conversation a young man should have with his father, but I get the feeling Mr. Flannery isn't the type."

"You could say that."

"He told me you'd returned his ring."

I folded my arms tight against my chest. "I don't see how that's any business of yours."

"Tom Flannery is in pain, and I don't mean physical. He reminds me of a friend of my father's, who came back from the Great War shattered." Another beat of silence. "Why'd you break it off?"

Trust Sam to call a spade a spade. "Fact is, I don't know if I want to get married. Maybe someday. But not now. Tom left, and I went to work at Bell 'cause I wanted to do my part. But that got me out of the house. It made me start to think there was more than gettin' hitched and havin' babies. Now I'm doin' this." I spread my arms wide. "I wanna be my own woman for a while. The world is bigger than it was before the war. I wanna explore it."

"I see." He rubbed his chin. "There's nothing wrong with that. Have you told Tom what you said to me? Or Frank, for that matter?"

"No."

"Because you feel guilty?"

"No!" I wrapped my arms around myself again. What did I mean? "Dot and Lee, they're happy. In fact, they're talkin' about gettin' hitched. I don't see why I have to be like her. And why is it anybody's business?"

"No one's saying you do. Here's what I think." He stepped closer. "You do feel guilty. A little bit. It's fine to want something different than your friend. You and Dot are not the same person. But you owe it to both those young men to be honest."

"I haven't lied to either of 'em."

"You're stringing them along. Each one thinks he might have a shot. And that"—Sam jabbed a finger at me—"is unworthy of you. You insist on people being honest with you. I think it's time you think about whether you've been lying to them. Even if it's been unintentional." He got into his car.

I stood on the sidewalk. I hadn't thought of it like that. But now that Sam had brought it up, I couldn't look at it any other way.

Chapter Thirty-Six

Sam offered to drive me back downtown, but I said no. I needed to clear my head. I'd do that better if I could wander around. Since it was still light out and the neighborhood wasn't particularly rough, Sam drove off and left me alone.

While I walked, I smoked another Lucky. It was a good thing I wasn't s'posed to be payin' attention, 'cause I barely saw my surroundings. I hadn't meant to play games with either Tom or Frank. If I set my feelings about gettin' married aside, how did I feel about each one?

Of course, I had a soft spot for Tom. We'd known each other forever. I knew he loved me, and yes, I felt a lot of affection toward him. Sadness, too. I knew some girls would be shallow enough to dump a guy who'd lost a limb, but I didn't care about Tom's injury. Truly. I wasn't afraid of hard work. Whatever Tom couldn't do, I'd handle without a problem. Or I'd get someone to help, like Lee or Pop.

The problem was I didn't know Tom these days. Was he the angry drunk, mad at the world and itchin' for a fight? Or was he the Joe who'd been in my office this morning, the mostly clean-cut boy who wanted to be useful? What would he be like a month or a year from now? The flip-flop back and forth was enough to make me dizzy.

Then there was Frank. I knew who he was. At least I thought I did. He was educated, smart, caring, and handsome as a movie star. He was fond of me. He made my heart flutter. But if I was bein' honest, was that pitter-pat love or just a reaction to a good-looking guy?

I checked my watch. It was almost four thirty. I didn't know if Frank was workin' today or what shift. Since I was already poundin' the streets, there was no harm in goin' to see.

Once in his neighborhood, I walked from the bus stop down to his apartment building. The manager was out front. "You again." His smile was a little too understanding. "He's home. Door's open, so go on up."

"Thanks." I hadn't wasted a trip. My knock sounded a little hesitant, almost as though I wanted an excuse to leave without seein' him.

It was loud enough. "Betty. How nice to see you." Frank leaned on the door. He was still dressed in his orderly uniform. "What brings you over here? Is there another problem with Tom?"

"No, least not that I'm aware of." I fidgeted with my purse strap. "I said we'd go to dinner. Instead, you wound up dragging Tom home from a bar. I'd like to make good on my promise."

His deep brown eyes were serious. "Are you sure you have time?"

"Tonight's as good as any. This place you mentioned, do we need reservations?" I hoped not. We coulda found somewhere else to eat, but I wanted a quiet spot since I planned to hash things out with him.

"No. Give me a few minutes to change." He stepped back.

"I'll wait here."

He disappeared.

Unable to restrain my curiosity, I took a couple steps inside his apartment and looked around. It was clean, but plain. He hadn't used any of his parents' swanky furniture to decorate. It looked exactly like what it was: the apartment of a single guy. I spotted a full bookcase against the far wall. I wandered over. There were books of poetry, some religious stuff on Saint Francis of Assisi and St. Claire, a Bible with a worn cover, and a couple of novels. I pulled out F. Scott Fitzgerald's *The Great Gatsby* and skimmed the pages. This set of shelves was the only bit of Frank's personality in the entire place.

"I thought you said you'd wait outside." His voice behind me made me jump.

"You know me. Curious as the proverbial cat."

He nodded. "You want to borrow it?"

I replaced the book. "Nah. I was lookin', that's all."

"I didn't know you liked *Gatsby*." He came closer.

I backed up. "I don't. I'm not much of a reader."

"That's right. You're a movie fan." His gaze was a little too…something. Knowing? He had to have noticed I didn't want to be close to him. Was he offended? "Shall we go? The restaurant is only a couple of blocks away."

We walked in silence. The leaves on the trees lining the street had not yet turned. The afternoon sunlight filtered through them. Frank kept a respectful distance. He didn't reach for my hand, but he didn't look offended, either.

At the restaurant, the waiter showed us to a table in the back. He held out my chair, and Frank waited until I was seated to take his own place. "I think we'll skip cocktails. Two glasses of water, please."

The waiter murmured a response, put two menus down, and left.

I skimmed the list. "What's good?"

"I like the chicken with roasted potatoes." Frank hadn't picked up his menu. "If they were able to get a good cut of beef, the New York steak is also excellent."

The waiter returned with our water and took our order. I went with the chicken. "Thanks again for this." I waved my hand around. "It's been a busy couple of days."

"How are your investigations coming along?" He sipped from his glass.

I brought him up to speed, right up to the visit with Mr. Ellery this afternoon.

"A tunnel?" Frank took one of the dinner rolls, cut it apart, and spread it with butter. "Makes you wonder how Stevie found it."

I held my knife over the butter. "What do you mean?"

"Either he went looking for it or someone knew about it and told him." He took a bite. "It doesn't seem like something Stevie would stumble on. But if this Gainey person had given him a job that job required getting from one place to another in secret, he might also have told Stevie about the tunnel."

It was an interesting point. "The entry is in that dirt lot. It's a question of which building it belongs to. Emmeline or I can find that out from city records."

"It also sounds like Tom is off the hook." Frank smeared butter on the second half of his roll.

"You'd think so, but Sam won't say it. Until he does, I gotta assume Tom's a suspect." I laid aside my bread.

Frank once again gave me that too-knowing look. "Betty, what's wrong? There's something on your mind, I can tell."

I was saved by our food arriving. While the waiter arranged our plates, I marshaled my thoughts. "Frank, this is swell. Dinner, I mean. But, I don't want you thinkin' this is a date or anything. I'll pay for my share." I studied his face. The hint of his dimple lurked. He wasn't makin' this easy, but I took a breath. "Fact is, I like you. As a friend. You've been great these past few months. But I broke off my engagement, and I don't really wanna get into anything serious right now. I like my freedom. I'm sorry if I've led you to think there was more to us than friendship."

He cut his meat. "Not to mention you're conflicted about Tom."

"This isn't about him."

"Oh, but it is." Frank raised his eyebrows. "Betty, I understand. You need time to decide who you want to be. Part of that includes what role Tom plays in your life. It's not any different for him."

"How do you know how Tom feels?"

He stalled for time by takin' another drink. "I've spoken to him. I admit, the first couple of times were rough, but I think we've come to a detenté." He grinned. "A peaceful agreement."

"How did you find him?"

Frank laughed. "I walked him home from a bar. I knew his address. All I needed was a phone book." His expression grew solemn. "He's trying to figure out his new life, too." He speared another bite with his fork.

I was too taken aback to respond. Why was it that the men around me seemed to understand my feelings better than I did?

Chapter Thirty-Seven

I dawdled over breakfast at Teddy's the next morning. My thoughts were consumed by Frank and Tom. I'd cleared the air with Frank last night. Now I had to talk to Tom. No doubt I'd been thinkin' mainly of how he affected me. I hadn't given a single moment to how my actions could hurt him. I'd been pretty selfish. The realization burst my balloon of indignation.

Judy must've sensed my discomfort 'cause she mostly left me alone and stopped by my table only to make sure my coffee mug was full.

As soon as I walked into the office, Emmeline sprang up. "Where have you been? It's almost ten." She took one look at me and hurried around the desk. "Are you okay?"

"I'm jake. Why would you ask?"

"Because you look like someone killed your cat. Sit." She herded me over to a chair in the corner. It hadn't been there yesterday, so most likely it was something she'd brought in that morning. Then she bustled over to the percolator and returned with a steaming cup of java. "Here. Now tell me what's wrong."

It didn't have anything to do with business, so a part of me wanted to brush her off. On the other hand, the opinion of someone not closely involved might be helpful. I filled her in on my talk with Sam yesterday and the evening with Frank. "I really put my foot in it, huh? Frank and Tom must hate me."

"Oh, I don't know about that." She pursed her lips and resumed her seat. "After all, Frank did insist on paying for that meal last night."

"Then Tom does. I don't want either of 'em to feel that way."

She nodded in sympathy. "I won't blow sunshine up your skirt and tell you everything's fine. However. I don't believe either of those boys dislikes you. Not based on how they've acted. They might be frustrated, but that's part of life."

"Good. They can feel like me for a change."

She cocked her head. "Have you spoken to Tom about this?"

"I didn't go to his house last night. I didn't think it was a good idea."

She tilted her head the other way. "Seems to me what's important is what you do now. You were honest with Frank last night. Do the same with Tom."

She made it sound so easy. "I will, as soon as I can." I slugged down some joe. "You looked awful excited when I walked in. What's shakin'?"

She turned back to the papers on her desk and grabbed one. "Remember we were wondering how Gainey or Coates would have gotten to the lot on Wadsworth?"

"Right. They would've stood out, same as Stevie, no matter the time of day."

"What if they took the same route he did?"

I blinked. "Stevie told them about the tunnel?"

"He would have to had to tell Coates, I think. From what I've been able to determine, he mainly works the strip on Genessee. He lives on Grey, which is only a block or two away from his garage. Even within the Fruit Belt, there are little sub-neighborhoods, it seems. But Stevie would not have had to tell Gainey about the tunnel."

I heard the suppressed glee in her voice. The piece of paper she'd handed me was a map of Michigan Avenue, right near the entrance to Stevie's tunnel. She'd written notes in the margins, and I squinted to read 'em. "Does this say what I think it does?"

"I just got off the phone with a man at city records." She pointed. "If you think it says Moses Gainey owns the property where the tunnel entrance is located, then yes, it does."

* * *

219

Emmeline and I rode the bus back to the corner of Jefferson and High. Before we left the office, I called Mr. Jones. After explaining why Nancy was sore at me, I enlisted his help to get her to meet us at his store.

It was a little after eleven when we reached our destination. As we walked inside, Nancy nearly dropped her bag of groceries. "I thought I told you to stay away."

I held up my hands, palms facing her. "Actually, you said I should leave, which I did. I need your assistance, so I'm back."

She whirled to face Mr. Jones. "Did you know she'd be here?"

"I did," the old man said. "She explained what happened. Put yourself in her shoes, girl. What would you do if someone you'd been friends with for your whole life asked you for help?"

Nancy's eyes shone. "She said she'd help find the person who killed my brother. What if her friend is guilty?"

I moved forward. "Nancy, I swear. If it turns out Tom is guilty, I'll give him over to the cops. But I don't think he is." I took another step. "That means Stevie's killer is still on the loose. I can catch him, but I need you. Please."

Nancy gave Emmeline a side-eye. "Who's she?"

"My associate." I introduced them.

Nancy didn't seem convinced this new person was on her side, but she turned to me. "Seems like you got a lot of people. What do you need me for?"

"I think I found out how Stevie got over to Wadsworth." I filled her in. "In our research, we learned Gainey owns the property with the tunnel entrance. He prob'ly knows about it. If your brother might have told Coates, 'specially if he was two-timing Gainey."

Nancy seemed to understand. "Either man coulda followed Stevie to the card game."

I aimed a finger at her. "I want to know whether Gainey was a regular at the store."

A little crease appeared between Nancy's eyes. "Those folks won't talk to a white woman."

"That's why I need you." I patted her shoulder. "If you still wanna help, that is."

She bit her lip and looked at Mr. Jones, who gave an encouraging nod. She turned back to me. "All right. I'll do it for Stevie. But you'd better be right about this Tom fella."

She had no idea how much I hoped I was.

It was almost ten blocks, but the three of us walked the over to the store on Michigan. Nancy took a deep breath before she went in, Emmeline and me hot on her heels.

The inside looked like every mom and pop corner store I'd been in. Canned goods lined the shelves. There was a small selection of vegetables, includin' things I'd never heard of. I fingered a large, leafy plant. "What are collard greens?"

"It's something we make as a side dish. We can grow 'em in our Victory gardens, but they don't like the winters up here much." Nancy moved through the aisles. "Grace, Thelma. How are ya?"

Two colored girls chatted behind the register. Both were about Nancy's height. They wore matching pinafore dresses, one red, one blue. The other thing that matched was the distrustful light in their eyes when they saw Emmeline and me. "What are they doin' here?" one girl asked.

Nancy made the introductions. Grace wore the red dress, Thelma the blue. "I hired Betty to find out what happened to Stevie. I mean, I know he was shot, but she's gonna find out who did it. The other girl is her partner."

Grace gave me a slow once-over. "That right? You care that much about a boy from 'round here?"

"It's my job. I'm a licensed private detective." I handed over a business card.

Thelma snatched it. "So you only interested 'cause you gettin' paid. Figures." She handed the card to her friend.

I swallowed a retort. Of course these girls were suspicious. I wondered how many white folks came into this store on a daily basis. Prob'ly none. If a total stranger showed up in the First Ward claiming to give a fig about the people who lived there, I'd think twice myself. "I don't think people oughta go around shootin' other people. No matter their skin color, or religion, or whatever."

Grace and Thelma checked with each other. Then they focused on Nancy. "That true?" Grace asked.

"That's why I hired her," Nancy said.

The other two exchanged a look. Thelma shrugged, and Grace faced me. "What do you wanna know?"

"Do you know the man who owns this store?" I rummaged in my purse for the picture I'd snapped at the club.

Thelma leaned on the counter. "He got money."

I handed over the photo. Despite the low light, it hadn't come out too bad. "That's him, the one in the hat. You recognize him?"

Thelma squinted as she studied the image. She shook her head. "Never seen him." She handed the snap to Grace.

She pursed her lips. "He looks kinda familiar. He's never been in the store, but I mighta seen him outside." She gave it back to me.

I motioned to Emmeline, who handed over a newspaper photo of Alonzo Coates. "What about this man?" she asked.

The girls looked at it. "Never seen that one." Thelma gave the cutting back as Grace murmured her agreement.

I took out my notepad and pencil. "Where'd you see the guy who you think was Moses Gainey? He owns this store and the lot it's on."

Grace tapped her chin. "He was on the sidewalk, over to that corner." She pointed to the alley where the tunnel entrance was. "I didn't think much of him, although he was dressed a bit better than most of the folks 'round here. He was lookin' up and down the street, then he stepped outta sight. I went out a minute later for my break, and he was gone."

"Gone as in he walked away?" I shot a glance at Emmeline.

Grace shook her head. "Gone as in not around."

Emmeline spoke up. "That didn't puzzle you?"

The look Grace gave showed her disdain. "It don't pay to be too curious. Man was there, then he wasn't. He coulda gotten into a car or gone into another building."

CHAPTER THIRTY-SEVEN

Thelma said something under her breath and snickered.

I decided I didn't wanna know what she said. I had a hunch it wasn't all that nice. "Did you hear a car?"

"No." Grace lifted her shoulders. "Like I said, I try not to be nosy."

I checked with Nancy, who spread her hands. "Thanks very much for your time," I said. "If you think of anythin' else, it'd be very helpful if you'd call me. If you lose the card, Nancy knows my number." I grabbed Emmeline and hustled her out.

Nancy stayed behind. "I'll be a minute," she called.

Back on the sidewalk, Emmeline pulled away from me. "Those girls knew more. Why'd you leave?"

"'Cause they weren't gonna say anything to us." I put away my notepad. "Maybe they'll call. Or they'll tell Nancy. But couldn't you tell they didn't trust us?"

Emmeline crossed her arms. "Yes, but that hardly matters. I'm used to it."

Her words surprised me. "You are?"

"Once people find out I'm Jewish, they treat me differently." At my look, she hastened to add, "Not everyone. Not you. My parents tell me America is better than a lot of places in Europe, but many people still automatically think I'm rich because I'm a Jew. The Klan likes to blame Jews for a lot of problems. Even Henry Ford writes in his paper about how all society's problems are the fault of the Jews."

She mighta tried to keep the bitterness out of her voice, but I heard it. "I'm sorry. I don't personally know how you feel, but I bet my grandparents do."

For a moment, it looked like she didn't believe me, but then her expression softened. "No Irish need apply."

"A lot of folks don't have a high opinion of Catholics, either. Pop says they think our first loyalty is to the Pope."

She tilted her head. "Is that why you take the cases you do? The ones no one else will touch?"

I hadn't thought about it like that. "I think everyone deserves a fair shake. If I can help, I will."

Nancy came out of the store. "I told Grace and Thelma they weren't very nice to you, and they should be sorry."

"I thought you didn't much care for me 'cause I worked for Tom?" I shouldered my purse.

She folded her arms. "When you first told me, I didn't. But I guess Mr. Jones was right. You wouldn't have turned your friend away." She sighed. "As much as I don't wanna believe you, I do. If he's guilty, you'll turn him in."

"Thank you." I wanted to say more, but best leave it simple. That's what Pop would tell me.

"They did say one thing." Nancy fell in beside me as I walked to the corner. "The man in the photograph you had. What did you say his name was?"

"Moses Gainey."

"That time on the corner wasn't the only time Grace saw him. He came into the store with another man."

My pulse quickened. "They know who?"

"No. It wasn't the other man you showed 'em. But it was another guy in the picture." Nancy held her hand out.

I gave it to her.

She tapped the man sitting to Gainey's right. His face was in profile. Sitting, he was shorter than Gainey. "This one. Grace said she didn't hear his name. But Gainey asked about the progress on solving a problem. This man said it would be taken care of before the end of the weekend."

"When was that?" Emmeline asked.

Nancy clutched the photo. "The Wednesday before Stevie got killed." Her eyes filled with tears.

I had no doubt that Moses Gainey had a lot of problems. But Sam would tell me that it was too coincidental to hear a problem about to be solved only two days before Stevie's death, 'specially given what we suspected.

I heartily agreed.

Chapter Thirty-Eight

Emmeline had to get to the library, so she skedaddled as soon as she said goodbye to Nancy. I took off for Jefferson, Nancy on my heels. "Where do you think you're goin'?" she asked.

"Since I'm here, I figured I'd talk to Mr. Jones again." I made the left turn. "Detective MacKinnon still hasn't been able to match that key from Stevie's pocket to anything. Mr. Jones might be able to help me."

But when I arrived at Mr. Jones's store, Georgie and his boys were clustered outside, blocking the sidewalk. One of 'em tapped Georgie on the shoulder. His eyes narrowed when he saw me. "Nancy, what you doin' bringin' that white girl around here?" He pulled a switchblade from the back pocket of his dungarees. "Girl, I told you before you ain't welcome here. Do I hafta make myself clear?"

Nancy grabbed my arm. "Run. Before he gets too close."

I shook her off. I watched as Georgie approached, the knife held loosely in his right hand. He swaggered as he came nearer. It was a show for his boys and for Nancy, I realized. I could tell by the way he held the blade he wasn't a good fighter. Even on one leg, Tom coulda taken him. Lee would knock him flat.

Both of 'em, and Sean, had taught me knife-fighting basics. Not so I could get into a scuffle, but in case I found myself in this kind of scrap. "You don't wanna do this, Georgie." I held up my hands. "Let Nancy and me by, and no harm done."

He leered. "I've never been with a cracker before. Think I'll make you my first."

Nancy whimpered and tugged again.

I pushed her off to the side. "I'm no easy target just 'cause I'm white. You've never been to the First Ward, huh? We're as tough as you are. Maybe tougher."

The smarmy grin turned to a snarl. Georgie lunged clumsily. I stepped aside. I tried to keep his gang in view. If they decided to get involved, I was in trouble. For now, they seemed to be content to watch and egg their leader on.

Georgie held the knife in front of him and swiped at my middle. Again, it was fairly easy to dodge. I could tell my moves were makin' him angry. For a third time, he waved the switchblade wildly.

I danced out of the way.

"If you're so tough, stand still and fight me." He waved at his gang. "Y'all stay back. This is between me and her. I can handle a skinny white girl." He came at me again, this time stabbing the spot where he expected me to go.

Instead, I darted close to him. I brought my knee up into his private parts and jabbed hard into his middle. He clutched his groin, and the air whooshed out of him like a spent balloon. He staggered past me. As he did, I rabbit-punched him in the kidney. "Like this?"

Behind me, I heard the unmistakable sound of a shotgun being racked. I froze, and my blood ran cold.

"I done told you, Georgie Vickers, I'm not gonna stand for your antics." Mr. Jones's voice cracked like a whip. I moved back. The old man came to stand beside me, gun pointed at my attacker, who was still doubled over tryin' to catch his breath. "You all right, Miss Betty? I'd'a come out with Lizzie earlier"—he patted the shotgun's stock—"but you looked like you was handlin' yourself just fine."

"He didn't even come close, Mr. Jones. But I thank you for your help."

Miz Alva came outside. "You boys oughta be ashamed. Wait until I tell your mommas what you been up to."

Mr. Jones swung around to face the group of boys, who'd fallen dead quiet. "Any of you got anythin' you'd like to say?"

They fled.

He faced Georgie again. "Should I call the cops, or do you want me to run him off?"

"In a sec." I took a step forward but stayed out of Georgie's reach. "The pistol. You said you found it. That true?"

Georgie muttered something under his breath.

Miz Alva took one step and whacked him over the shoulder with her purse. "You keep a civil tongue in that mouth, boy. Where'd you find the gun?"

"In the dumpster, like I said." George sidled away from the older woman. "Well, not really in it. More on the ground next to it, like."

I crossed my arms over my chest. "When?"

"Saturday afternoon." He shot another glance at Miz Alva and her enormous handbag and edged away again. "I was walkin' down Allen. I'd gone over there to see a pal of mine. We played some pinball and had a soda. As I went by the space with the dumpster, I saw it, the gun."

"Why'd you pick it up?"

"My ma took the one I had." He licked his lips. "She said she wasn't gonna stand for me gettin' dragged to the cop shop 'cause I'd accidentally hurt someone with my stupidity. She said just 'cause the draft board didn't want me was no reason I couldn't get an honest job." He rolled his eyes. "She gets on that tune a lot lately. I didn't pay her no mind. When I saw the gun, I picked it up. I didn't plan on her findin' this one."

"It didn't strike you as odd, a pistol lyin' on the ground?" I asked. Georgie wasn't too bright. Maybe the Army knew what it was doin' when they turned him away. He prob'ly woulda shot one of his fellow soldiers as easily as a German.

He shrugged.

I fixed him with a hard stare. "You didn't like Stevie much, did you?"

"He was a pill." George rubbed his nose. "He followed me all the time, braggin' about what a tough guy he was. I laughed at him. Last time I saw him, he took a swing at me and said how some day I'd be sorry I hadn't taken him seriously. He'd be the man and I'd be at his heels, beggin' for attention. He said he'd take my boys away from me." He snorted.

"That make you mad?"

George gave me a look.

"Maybe you wanted to put him in his place?" I pressed. "I think you took that gun over to Wadsworth, ambushed Stevie when he came outside, and read him the riot act. He got outta hand and you shot him."

Georgie's eyes got wide like a panicked horse I'd seen once in a western picture. "I didn't shoot him. Yeah, I threatened him a couple of times with my old pistol. I told him to grow up, and then maybe I'd take him seriously. But I wasn't anywhere near that empty lot."

None of the others had moved. Miz Alva had puffed up a little when Georgie mentioned his threat, but that was it. "Where were you?"

His gaze flicked to Miz Alva. "It's private."

She narrowed her peepers.

I wanted to laugh. Given the way Georgie watched her, Miz Alva mighta scared him more than his own mother and Lizzie the shotgun combined. "Georgie, I'll be square with you. You're either gonna tell me or the cops. You think Miz Alva is harsh? Wait until Detective MacKinnon gets his mitts on you." I knew Sam wouldn't rough him up, not really. Georgie didn't.

Again, the nervous look. "I was with Angela Powers Friday night, okay? She's a girl I know. We went to the movies, but, uh, we didn't stay. We"—he swallowed—"we went to The Carlton Club for dancing and drinks."

Mr. Jones cackled. "I know The Carlton. Lots of dark corners in there. Good for other things, too. Way I hear it, you wouldn't be the first to win Miss Angela's favor." •

I swear Georgie blushed. I checked with Nancy. "Do you know Angela?"

"No. That is, I know who she is. But she's older than me." Nancy sounded slightly envious. "Her clothes are the bee's knees. I think she looks like Josephine Baker. The boys are all mad about her."

I was familiar enough with the actress to wonder if Angela agreed with the comparison. I doubted her clothes were as outrageous as the pictures I'd seen in newspaper stories about Baker's shows in France. I looked back at Georgie. "I need Angela's address and phone number."

"Mr. Jones knows 'em." Miz Alva bulled forward and grabbed Georgie by the ear. "You come with me. We gonna have a talk about the way a young man should behave." She nodded toward me. "Best you get to talkin' to Angela soon 'cause after I'm done with this one"—she gave Georgie a shake—"I'll be speakin' to her. There may be a war on, but that don't mean we don't do things proper." She marched off, Georgie at her side.

I followed Mr. Jones into his store. "I always thought that Mrs. O'Shea was tough. She's a widow lady who lives on my street. I've seen her have grown men cowering in their shoes. Now that I've met Miz Alva, I'm not so sure."

"Every neighborhood's got a Miz Alva, it seems." He took a sheet of paper and wrote an address on it. "That's where Angela lives. It ain't far from here. Tell her Miz Alva sent you, and she's more likely to talk."

"Thanks." A thought came to me. "You said Stevie used to work for you. Did you ever give him a key to the store?"

He shook his head. "Police asked me the same thing. But I never asked Stevie to open or lock up the place. That detective showed me the key, but it don't look like anything I've ever seen. Sorry."

I thanked him again. Outside, I lit up a Lucky. I'd talk to Angela, but I figured she'd back up Georgie's story. I needed to find out what that key belonged to. Instinct told me once I did that, things would get a lot clearer.

Chapter Thirty-Nine

I sent Nancy home, since she admitted she was too intimidated by the older girl to be much use. I needed someone from the neighborhood to come with me, so I made arrangements to meet Miz Alva at the corner of Orange and High streets, which was right near Angela's home.

In my gut, I felt my best suspects were Coates and Gainey. What exactly had Stevie been up to? I had an idea how to find out. Neither Tom nor Lee would like it, but hopefully I would be able to convince them to go along. But I had to cross Charlie and Mr. Ellery off the list. I'd take 'em one at a time.

I s'pose Tom was still a suspect, too. I didn't want to think about that.

I ground out my cigarette as Miz Alva came up. "You'd better ask Angela your questions first. I'm likely to go on for a while once I get started." She cocked her head. "Weren't you wearing a ring when I first met you?"

She was observant. "I broke it off," I said.

"I assume the boy is overseas. Ain't that a little hard on him?"

"He was. Not anymore." I squirmed, but I'd spent enough time with her that I figured she wouldn't leave me alone until I gave her the story. I did, but only the barest details.

"You ain't the type to cut a man loose 'cause he drinks too much." She pinned me with her stare. "You met someone else."

"Yes, but that had nothing to do with my decision to call it off with Tom."

She sighed. "Child, why you lyin' to yourself? You ain't the first girl caught between two men. You gotta ask yourself which is gonna help you the most in your life. Which one can you give your heart and soul? There ain't no half-way in marriage." She shook a finger at me. "The problem is you, not those boys. I can see you're one of them newfangled girls. You got a little taste of independence and now you ain't so sure you wanna give it up."

I threw my hands up. "You make that sound like a bad thing."

"It ain't, but you can't have your cake and eat it too. Tryin' to do that is cruel to those boys and yourself. And if that's who you were, I don't think you'd be helpin' Nancy the way you are." She gave an emphatic nod. "Now let's go talk to Miss Angela."

At the Powers house, I let Miz Alva take the lead. I stood a step below her as she knocked. Not a timid one, either.

The girl who answered the door was a beauty. Tall and slender, with jet black hair, liquid brown eyes, and perfect skin. It bein' the middle of the day, she didn't wear makeup, and she didn't need any. She wore a white button-down shirt with a Peter Pan collar and a dark blue skirt. It was a very proper outfit, but Angela still gave off a come-hither air. I could immediately see why a boy would be at her beck and call.

Miz Alva waved a hand at me. "Angela, this is Betty Ahern. She's lookin' into who killed Nancy's brother Stevie. She has some questions for you."

"Why should I answer them?" Even Angela's voice was sexy. Low and melodic, and a little smoky. It was more suited to a nightclub than a chat on a front porch.

Miz Alva's generous bosom swelled. "Because I told you to. Now, Miss Ahern. Ask your questions."

"Do you know Georgie Vickers?" I asked.

Angela eyed the older woman. "We run around a bit."

"Were you with him last Friday night at The Carlton Club?"

"For a while."

Had George sold me a bill of goods? "How long?"

"From about nine to eleven." A teasing smile appeared on Angela's full lips. "After that, we went somewhere else. We were there for the rest of the night."

I could feel the heat in my cheeks, and I hoped I wasn't blushing. "Doing what?"

I must've been, 'cause she laughed, a rich, throaty sound. "Do you really wanna know?"

I decided I didn't. "Nancy was concerned her brother was up to no good. Was it with Georgie?"

Angela tossed her head. "Stevie was a child. He hero-worshipped Georgie. For the life of me, I don't know why. Georgie is fun, but he's no role model. I heard a rumor Stevie wanted dough to impress some White girl. Fool boy. Word on the street is Stevie found a better source of money than Georgie and his gang." She shrugged. "Least that's what my friend Nellie told me."

"Why would she know?"

Again, Angela's slim shoulders moved up and down. "When she's bored, she steps out with a guy who works the fight rings for Mo Gainey. She told me she saw Stevie at the fights a couple of times. One of Gainey's men gave him instructions, so she figures Stevie was a runner."

"The man, what's his name?"

"Leroy. Nellie says he organizes things. You know, he books the fighters, shows up, makes sure things run smooth." She studied her nails. "Anything else?"

"No, that's all for now." I handed her a business card. "If you think of anything else, I'd appreciate a phone call." I looked at Miz Alva. "She's all yours, ma'am. I can find my way back to a bus stop."

It might've been my imagination, but Angela paled when Miz Alva suggested they go inside for a talk. I didn't blame her.

Chapter Forty

With Georgie off the list, my next target was Charlie Nickles and his card games. I thought about the pros and cons for him. He knew Stevie was at the game. Charlie wouldn't have looked outta place in the neighborhood. He could have easily followed Stevie to the lot and killed him after an argument gone bad.

There were two big things that argued against Charlie. Killing Stevie didn't get his dough back. Not unless Stevie had it on him when he died, and I doubted that, since the games were still goin'. Also, I doubted Charlie woulda shot anyone. He would beat someone to death or strangle him during a fight. But usin' a gun showed a level of cold-blooded intent I hadn't felt when I talked to him the first time.

Should I confront him? I might be wrong. Any number of people would slap me silly if they knew what I was thinkin'. On the other hand, it was the middle of the day, and Charlie lived with his mother. If she was home, would he attack me? I could call Sam, but he wasn't my bodyguard.

I decided to go, but first I phoned Emmeline at the library and told her my plan.

"Are you sure about this?" she asked.

"No, but I gotta do something. I have my pocketknife. I'll make sure to talk to him outside where folks might see or hear us. There were people around when I visited last time. He'd have to be dumber than a box of rocks to try anything." I hoped.

She sighed. "I'll give you an hour. If you don't call me back, I'm sending in the cops."

I checked my watch. It was quarter to two and it would take me ten minutes to walk to Charlie's house. Plenty of time. "Deal."

On my way over, I thought about how I'd get my answer. I didn't much care if Charlie incriminated himself or put himself in the clear. But how was I gonna do it? I could lie about how Stevie was killed. But if Charlie was guilty surely he'd be smart enough to play along.

How would Sam Spade or Philip Marlowe handle it? Better yet, what would Nick Charles do? He was the sneaky one who didn't rely on his fists.

Nick would lay a trap.

Charlie ran card games. He believed Stevie cheated. Stevie'd worked with Tom at least once, and he had some knowledge of how the trick was done. Charlie didn't. Could I use that?

Maybe.

I spied a pay phone and called the Flannery house. I breathed a sigh of relief when Tom answered. "You told me you wanted to be useful," I said. "Did you mean it?"

"Of course I did."

"Good. Are you doin' anything right now?"

"Yeah, I got ballroom dance lessons in fifteen minutes." His old humor had returned, which I took for a good sign. "What do you need?"

"I'm at the drugstore on the corner of Fargo and Porter. How fast can you get here?"

"Unless they've changed the bus schedules, between ten and twenty minutes."

"See you then." I hung up without waiting for an answer. I knew it was a little rude, but I also hoped it would stoke his curiosity.

It must have, because he got to the store in fifteen minutes. "What are you up to now?"

"I'm about to spring a trap on Charlie. It'll either prove he killed Stevie or knock him outta the suspect pool."

Tom rubbed the wood of his crutches. "Are you sure that's smart? Confrontin' a guy who might be a killer?"

"That's why I called you." I held up a hand to forestall any objections. "I don't need you to be a tough guy. If we play it right, I'll know the score. If Charlie's guilty, I'll call Sam and let him make the collar."

Tom seemed to think it over. "What's the plan?"

I told him.

He rubbed his chin. "That oughta work. I assume we're goin' to his house."

I took a moment to study him. He was still thin, but he didn't look quite as haunted and sullen as he had when he'd gotten off the train. I could still see it in his eyes, though. They held the light of someone who'd seen much more than a nineteen-year-old kid should have. At the same time, there was a hint of determination that I hadn't noticed before. Things had changed for him.

It was a conversation for another time.

I led him to Charlie's house. His mother, once again dressed in a shapeless, faded housedress and ratty slippers, stood by the mailbox, flippin' through what had to be today's delivery. This time, the cigarette in her mouth was unlit. She squinted at us. "You're the dame who was here before."

"Yes. Is Charlie here?" I caught the faint whiff of booze, sharp and cheap.

She rolled her eyes. "Charlie! That girl is back."

He shuffled outside. "What are you yellin' about now, hag?"

His mother jerked her thumb at us. "Visitors. It's the same one as last time. She's too pretty to be one of your hussies. You owe her money?" She snorted. "Not like you have any."

"Shut up." He hitched up his pants. "Now what?"

Mrs. Nickles skirted him and went inside, muttering the whole way.

Charlie must've heard her. "Stupid broad. Throw me out? Like you've got any dough." He shook his head. "Talk fast. I got things to do."

I doubted that, but let it slide. "I brought someone who has a beef with you."

Charlie eyed Tom. "Never seen you before in my life."

"You sure did. Last Friday," said Tom. "At your card game off Wadsworth. Don't play me for a sap."

Charlie tugged his waistband again. "Fine, I remember. What's your problem?"

"Stevie Washington," said Tom. "Punk owes me money."

Charlie's laugh reminded me of a donkey. "I thought you said you were there. You oughtta know Stevie is dead."

"I do. I want my dough back. Since I can't collect from him, I'm comin' to you."

"I don't offer insurance or nothing." Charlie hooked his thumbs in his belt. "What makes you think I got it?"

"Cops didn't find any on his body." Tom shifted his grip on his crutches. "I figure you stripped him after you did the deed. I want my stake back. It's all I got."

"And if you don't get it?"

"I'll go to the cops." Tom waited a beat. "So far, I've put it off, but that can change."

"The fuzz already know about the gambling. Far as I can tell, they only bother me when they don't have nothing better to do. Or when the brass wants to look good before an election." Charlie grinned. "As for anything you saw, well, you came with a full flask. I'm sure you saw a lotta things that weren't there."

As the exchange went on, I watched Charlie. He was too relaxed. He'd copped to the gambling ring without blinking an eye, even seemed to think it was a good joke between him and the police. The mention of anything else shoulda put him on edge. But as per the plan, I kept my lips zipped and let it play out.

"Maybe I did," Tom said. "But I recognize a man with a .22 when I see one."

This was the key. Reports of the shooting had not mentioned the caliber of the gun.

Charlie scoffed. "A .22? A pea shooter like that ain't gonna kill no one."

Tom didn't move. "If you shoot a guy in the head, it will."

The reports had also not mentioned where Stevie's wounds were. A lot depended on Charlie's reaction.

He gave another braying laugh. "Buddy, you got me all wrong. First off, if I wanted the cabbage, I wouldn't kill the kid. Brass knuckles, now, that's a possibility. Not only that, I ain't dumb enough to get close to someone if I did decide to shoot him." He shook his head. "Seems to me you think I'm an easy mark. Sorry to disappoint. Even if I had your dough, I wouldn't give it back." He slapped his leg. "The next time you want to try blackmail, check your facts before you hit up your mark. 'Cause you look stupid." He jerked his head, waddled to the house, and slammed the door.

Tom watched him. "Are we done?"

"Seems like it." I turned and headed back to the bus stop. Charlie was not a master criminal, and he wasn't Laurence Olivier either. I lit a cigarette.

Tom pulled one out of his own deck and stopped so I could light it. He took a drag and exhaled. "Did you learn anything?"

"Charlie Nickles is a small-time crook, but he's no killer."

"What does that mean for you?"

I leaned against the telephone pole at the corner. "I cross him off the list." I flicked ash onto the sidewalk and headed for a phone so I could check in with Emmeline before she called in the cavalry. I turned back to Tom. "You a boxing fan?"

"It's okay, I guess. I'd rather go to a ball game. Why?"

"If you still want to be helpful, I was thinkin' you and I could go to the fights."

* * *

I cornered Lee right after dinner. He was unimpressed with my plan. I understood, but he shoulda known me better by now.

"You want to go where?" he asked. He lifted a cigarette and lighter, but in his shock, didn't complete the action.

"I need to go to the bare-knuckle fights Moses Gainey runs in the Fruit Belt." I glanced at Tom for support. I couldn't read his expression. Before the war, he'd been an open book. Now, well, it was anybody's guess what thoughts were goin' through his head.

Lee shot a glare at his friend. "You on board with this harebrained idea?"

Tom lowered himself into an Adirondack chair. "She says she needs to talk to this Gainey. Seems logical to go where you know he'll be instead of runnin' all over town."

"But a fight?"

"Dames go to the fights." Tom rubbed his left thigh. "Joe Louis made boxing respectable. Popular, even. I hear women like it as much as their men."

Lee stuffed his Chesterfield back in the pack. "This isn't a boxing match at the Garden, with rules and stuff. It's a bare-knuckle brawl in a warehouse in Buffalo. That's no place for a girl."

"She's gonna go anyway." Tom fixed me with a flat stare. "Won't you?"

I said nothing.

"Exactly." He turned his attention back to Lee. "We might as well go with her and keep her outta trouble as best we can."

Lee scrubbed his hands through his hair. "This is gonna sound mean, but I gotta say it. You aren't the guy you used to be. What good will you be if it gets rough?"

Tom continued to rub his leg. "I can handle myself."

I wondered if it hurt. I'd read stories, and heard from Pop, about people who lost limbs experiencing phantom pain from the missing leg or arm or whatever. Is that why Tom kept rubbin' his thigh like he was tryin' to work out a charley horse? I focused on Lee. "Quit yappin'. If you don't wanna go, fine. Both of you stay home. I'll ask Sam."

That made the boys give me dirty looks.

"Yes, 'cause bringin' a guy who is obviously a cop will work so well. The criminals who are there will open right up." Tom didn't have to roll his eyes. His low opinion of the idea was clear in his sarcastic tone. "Say it. Even if Lee or I refuse to help, you'll go anyway."

I lifted my chin. "I'm a licensed private detective. I go where the case takes me. Right now, that's Moses Gainey's fight ring."

Tom looked at Lee. "See?" Tom pointed at me. "At least she's honest enough to come clean. I'll give her that, even if I think this is a dumb idea."

I crossed my arms. "Hey!"

"When's the event?" Lee asked.

I thought. "Friday nights. That's the story I'm hearin'. It's in the Fruit Belt. I forget the exact address, but it's one of Gainey's warehouses. I got it written down at the office."

Tom grabbed his crutches and heaved himself up. "Good. Call me tomorrow." He settled the armrests and jerked his chin toward Lee. "You in?"

Lee ran his hands over his face and through his hair again, makin' in look like he'd just rolled outta bed. "A girl and a cripple. Of course I'm comin'. I only hope I can keep you two in one piece."

I clapped my hand on his shoulder. "You're a-okay, Lee. I knew we could count on you."

"Whatever you do, don't tell Dot." He grabbed his things and went inside.

Chapter Forty-One

Friday morning, I went to Teddy's for breakfast as usual. In the bright light of the September sunshine, I could admit I worried about Tom. Lee was right. If things got ugly, what could a one-legged Joe do? Hit someone with his crutch? I didn't doubt it would hurt. I also knew Gainey and his boys would be armed with something a lot more serious. A knife, if not a gun. Maybe Tom had gotten good at ground fighting. Gainey's men wouldn't give him the chance.

"You look pensive."

I looked up as Frank slid into the booth across from me. "Good morning. What are you doin' here?" I asked.

He leaned his arms on the table and smiled, dimple in full view. "Checking in with you." He leaned back as Judy brought him a thick white mug of steaming coffee. He nodded his thanks. "You're a creature of habit, Betty. You always have breakfast at Teddy's." He cautiously sipped. "I'm not sure that's a good trait for a detective."

"No one's gonna jump me in a diner."

"The people in Chicago wouldn't agree with you."

"Buffalo isn't the Windy City. And I'm not chasin' down the Mafia."

He raised his eyebrows. "I hardly think you're investigating a garden club, either."

I shoveled eggs into my mouth to avoid answerin'. But when I looked up, he was studyin' me, a knowing look in his eyes. "What?"

"Nothing." He took another drink. "How's Tom?"

The sudden shift took me by surprise. "Why do you ask?"

"I'm concerned about him. He's as wounded as the people I work with." Frank held up a hand. "Oh, he's not clinically unhinged. But I work at the hospital because I want to care for those in need. It doesn't matter to me whether that person is a patient or not."

"Truth be told, I'm worried." I told Frank about Tom's recent behavior. "He was always up for a spot of mischief. Him and Lee. But there was a boyishness to it, if you understand me. Now he's…" I searched for the right word. "Hard. Almost reckless. Like he's got something to prove."

"Perhaps he does." Frank set down his mug. "Tom is like you, Betty. He doesn't want pity."

"I don't pity him."

"I'm sure you don't. But." He held up a finger. "Look at things from his point of view. He's seen war. Violence on a level you and I can only imagine. He's lost friends, comrades. You keep saying he's not the boy you knew. You're right. Tom is not a boy anymore. Of course he's harder. Life has made him that way. Or is trying to."

"You sound like one of those docs at the hospital. A head shrinker."

"I've spent enough time there to pick up a thing or two."

I pushed my food around on my plate. "I can't figure him out. Like last night. You shoulda heard him. He sounded like…" Again, I fumbled for the right thing to say. "He sounded like Philip Marlowe. A wise guy."

"How do you feel about that?"

I didn't want to admit my attraction. Not to Frank. As a Quaker, he'd think I was nuts. Or worse. I half-laughed, tryin' to stall. "Now you really sound like a doc."

Frank didn't smile. "The one thing you've never been is indecisive. Why now? Are you afraid of hurting my feelings?"

I knew how Frank felt. He'd admitted it. "Yes." It came out almost as a whisper. I lifted my head. The truth was that although Frank believed in me, he'd never insist on comin' with me into a dangerous situation. Last night, Tom did.

I expected Frank to be hurt, if not angry. But all he did was nod and grab my hand. "We're men, Betty. We want honesty. Remember that." He got up and left.

***

I announced my intention to go to the fight as soon as I arrived in the office. I expected Emmeline to argue with me, or at least question my judgment.

"It makes sense." She drummed her fingers on her desk. "You're sure of the location and time?"

"There's always been one on Friday night before. We have the address from the newspaper. I s'pose they could move it, but I think it'd be a lot harder to move a boxing match than a card game." She had a point, though. It would be a good idea to confirm. I knew exactly who to call. I went to the back office, closed the door, and picked up the phone. "Melvin. What's shakin'?"

"Heya, Toots." The sounds of a busy newsroom filled the background. "Same story, different day. What's up with you?"

"Listen." I grabbed a pad. "Remember those bare-knuckle fights Moses Gainey runs?"

"I do."

"I need a favor. Can you confirm there's one tonight and it'll be held at the same place?"

"Probably. Why?"

"I'm goin'. I need to see Gainey."

It took a couple of seconds for Melvin to reply. "Betty, I don't think that's a good idea. You're a smart investigator, and I don't doubt your ability to protect yourself." He used my name, somethin' he never did. He must be serious. "Gainey is no one to mess with."

"Don't worry. I'm takin' Lee and Tom."

"Two boys, one with a serious injury? Why not ask Detective MacKinnon to go with you?"

"I can't." I tapped my pencil. "They'll peg him for a cop the minute we walk in the door. "I want to blend in, not stand out."

"What about me?"

I was touched, but Melvin would be just as outta his league as me alone. "Have you ever been in a fight? A street fight?"

"No."

"Tom and Lee have. I know Tom's not your idea of the perfect backup, but he's savvy, and he's been in a war zone. He's not gonna let me get hurt." My words came without thought, but I was certain they were true. What it would cost him, that was my worry.

A heavy breath came over the line. "Let me ask around and I'll call you back."

"Thanks, Melvin. Remember how I said there prob'ly wasn't a story here?"

"Yeah."

I swiveled my chair to face the back wall. "I'm pretty sure I was wrong."

Chapter Forty-Two

elvin called me back midafternoon and confirmed the dope for that night's fight. "You're set on going, huh. No way to talk you out of it?"

"None. Thanks." I hung up the blower.

While I'd waited, I'd made a list of what I needed to do. I'd eliminated Charlie and Georgie from my suspects. I needed more on Mr. Ellery. He musta been furious to learn his daughter planned on runnin' off with a boy like Stevie. How furious?

I needed to know exactly what Stevie had done for Gainey. Had he been a willing plant in Coates's organization? Had Coates found out? What about that key? Sam still hadn't matched it to anything.

After dinner, I went to Tom's house. "You ready?"

He shrugged into a worn jacket. "As I'll ever be." He fumbled with his cap and dropped it on the floor.

I bent to pick it up. While I did, I thought I saw him slip something into his pocket. I stood and handed him the cap. "What was that?"

"What?"

"You put something in your jacket."

"Yeah, my hand." He held it up. "You ready?"

"Gimme a sec. I want to check the address one more time." I'd brought a bag with a strap long enough to wear across my body. I took out my notebook and flipped to the page I wanted. As I did, a photograph fluttered to the ground.

Tom pointed. "What is that?"

I handed it to him. "Sam found a key in Stevie's pocket when they took his body to the morgue. It doesn't fit any door or lock at the Washington home or at any other place where Stevie spent time."

Tom studied it. "Looks like the keys to the equipment sheds we had in the Army."

I perked up. "You had sheds in North Africa?"

"Not there." He handed it back. "When I was in basic training in Kentucky, there were equipment sheds on base. Some of 'em had padlocks. That looks like the type of key."

It was an intriguing idea. As far as I knew, there weren't any sheds at Stevie's house or Mr. Jones's store. But maybe something had a padlock. I'd ask Sam tomorrow. "Let's meet Lee and split. Fight starts in half an hour."

Lee once again borrowed a truck. He insisted it was not a night he wanted to rely on the bus. I put the crutches in the bed and sat in the middle. Tom squeezed in beside me. Lee had started the engine by the time Tom closed the door.

"What'd you tell your mom?" I asked. "She musta asked about the truck."

He backed out. "I told her Les at work had asked me to take a look at the engine 'cause it was rattling. So don't put me in the hospital—or worse—or else you're gonna have to explain why I lied."

"It'll be jake." The plan was to observe and maybe ask some questions. But I knew things could go sideways lickety-split.

"I still can't believe a girl and a cripple are doin' this," Lee muttered.

"Excuse me." Tom held up a finger. "A girl and *two* cripples."

Lee called him a name that, under normal circumstances, he wouldn't have used in front of me.

The warehouse on Best where Gainey held the fights had a parking lot. It was mostly full when we arrived, but Lee found a spot. We paid our money at the door and found a place to stand just as the announcer started his spiel.

Tom put his hand in his pocket. "Where's Gainey?"

I scanned the crowd. "There. The tall, well-dressed man sitting ringside on the right."

The crowd was full of roughly dressed working men, so Gainey was easy to spot. He wore a swell-looking suit, black, with a white shirt and a black tie. The bowler with the red feather covered his head. A deep red rose graced his lapel. It matched the one in the hair of the beautiful woman on his arm. It wasn't Sonya. They sat in the only two chairs I could see. Two hulking men stood behind them. I assumed they were the muscle for the night.

Lee lit a Chesterfield. "I wonder where he gets the fighters."

"The two in the ring gotta be too old for the draft." Tom pointed. "Between guys like that, boys under 18, and those who are 4F, I bet he has plenty."

I watched the two men in the ring, each bouncing in a different corner. They were heavy-bodied and well-muscled, but Tom was right. While not as old as Pop, they had to be in their forties. One of 'em had a shiner. They didn't wear gloves, but their hands were wrapped with something, prob'ly tape.

The bell rang, and the fighters came together. The crowd roared its approval, but I was more interested in Gainey. He split his attention between the woman beside him and the fight.

The first bout ended in a knockout. Two more fighters, this time young lightweights, took their places. Their bout went on a little longer, but Gainey paid less attention. Maybe he only liked the heavyweight matches. I took a couple chances to study the crowd. Lee had been right. I wasn't the only woman in the place, although I did look like the youngest.

At the end of the fourth fight, Gainey stood. He kissed the woman's hand. Then he motioned to his two goons, and they headed for the door, leaving her behind.

I slapped Lee and Tom on their shoulders. "Gainey's gone outside. Now's our chance."

* * *

Outside, I scanned the street. Where had Gainey and his thugs gone? There was little sound. Pools of light from the streetlights punctured the night. I strained to hear, but no voices echoed through the darkness.

Lee tapped my shoulder. "There." He pointed.

I could barely see the three figures standing by a post with a busted light. The orange tip of a cigarette glowed. They were the right shape for Gainey and his pals. I walked closer, making sure I made as little noise as possible.

Lee and Tom kept tight on my sides, maybe a step ahead of me. I expected Lee to be stealthy, but Tom surprised me. He made very little sound as he stayed on my right, yet he had no problem maintaining speed. His body looked tense, and his gaze never stopped moving all around the area in front of him. He might be wounded, but he looked alert and ready for action. A soldier on his guard.

Which is exactly what he was.

Eventually, the group under the light noticed us. Gainey reached out a hand to keep the other two in place. "Who's there?"

Lee, Tom, and I stopped a good ten feet away. Close enough to be seen, but far enough away to scramble if things got ugly. "Betty Ahern," I said.

Gainey's pearly whites practically glowed. "If it ain't the girl detective." He looked at the others. "And two friends. I thought you was inside still. You all like the show tonight?"

A shiver ran down my spine, like someone had dropped a piece of ice in my shirt. We hadn't blended in as much as I'd hoped.

The boys didn't move.

I twitched my shoulders. "It was okay. I'm not a big fan of boxing, although describing your operation as a boxing match might be goin' overboard. I'm surprised the police haven't shut you down."

"I'm a legitimate businessman. Got a license and everything." Gainey's teeth gleamed. "Folks wanna bet on the side, that's no business of mine. You make a little coin tonight?"

I didn't take my eyes off Gainey and hoped the boys were watching the muscle men. "I don't gamble."

"Then why you all in the Fruit Belt? Not a place for white folks to be roaming around at night."

"I wanted to talk to you."

"'Bout what?"

I watched him. "Stevie Washington."

Gainey's laugh shattered the air. "You sure are interested in that kid. What now?"

For the first time, I wondered if this had been a bad idea. I shifted, comforted by my friends next to me. "I've learned Stevie was workin' for you as a runner, which you told me before. Rumor has it he was stealin' from you. That couldn't have made you happy."

Gainey's smile stayed in place. "It wouldn't, if it were true."

"Then it's not?"

"I ain't gonna detail my business to no white girl, no matter what she calls herself."

"Fair enough." I hadn't really expected him to answer. Then again, he hadn't denied it either. The dough in Stevie's stash had come from somewhere. "I also heard you planted him in your rival's organization. That would be Alonzo Coates."

"I know who you're talking about." Gainey flicked a quick look at his goons. "You need intelligence if you're gonna have a war. Your friend there carries himself like a soldier boy, even if he only got one leg. He knows."

Tom didn't flinch.

"What if that wasn't Stevie's plan?" I asked.

This time, Gainey's smile faded. "I don't know what you talkin' about."

"I think Stevie double-crossed you." I watched Gainey like a hawk. "He got into bed with Coates and sold *him* information about *you*. Add that to skimming from the money bags, and I think you'd be hot under the collar. Enough to kill him."

"Oh, you do?" Gainey's voice sounded soft, but it called up the image of a snake, coiled and ready to strike. "Didn't your mama teach you to stay outta other people's business? Girl could get herself hurt bad pokin' her nose in where it didn't belong." He stepped forward.

I took half a step back. Tom and Lee closed ranks. Lee took his switchblade outta his pocket and flicked it open.

Gainey pulled a pistol from under his coat and chuckled. "Look at you. Bringin' a knife to a gunfight." The two mooks followed suit.

Tom's crutch clattered to the ground. "This more your speed?"

I looked at him. He'd let his right crutch fall away, but relyin' on one prop didn't seem to bother his balance. He held a handgun in his right hand. It looked a lot like the one used to kill Marian Carstairs, whose death I had solved in my last case. I had a million questions, but I held my breath.

The goons checked with their boss, uncertain of the next move. Gainey ran his tongue over his lips.

"You said I looked like a soldier boy, Mr. Gainey. You were right." Tom spoke in a measured voice, calm and confident. Facing three armed men didn't seem to bother him. "A soldier never goes to war unprepared. If you and your boys are wonderin' if I can shoot, I had the best marksmanship score in my company, third-best in the division."

I shot a quick look at Lee. He covered his surprise well, but I could read his face. He was stunned.

"Betty asked a simple question," Tom continued. "I suggest you either answer her or we say goodnight and part on peaceful terms."

Gainey's men shuffled their feet. One of 'em leaned in to whisper, but Gainey jerked his head away. "The bags were light. Stevie told me it wasn't him. I gave him a second chance with Coates. Stevie knew how to sell a story, so I sent him in on the sly. That's all I'm gonna say." He tilted his head. "You playin' a dangerous game, Miss Ahern. Better take care you ain't found here without your friends." He snapped his fingers, turned, and walked away. The two big men walked backward, watchin' us until they were safely outta range. Then they turned, and the three of 'em faded into the night.

* * *

Lee waited until we were back in the truck to snap his cap. "What the hell was that?" He turned to Tom, his gaze fierce.

I stayed silent.

Tom shrugged. "A Walther P38. The Jerries are replacing the old Lugers with 'em." He pulled it out of his pocket and held it up. "We take 'em as souvenirs." He put it back.

A German soldier wouldn't willingly give up his pistol. I didn't want to think about where Tom and his buddies got their keepsakes.

Lee saved me from askin'. "You aimin' to blow your hand off next, stashing a thing like that in your jacket pocket?"

Tom's shoulders twitched again. "Don't be a knucklehead. The safety is on."

"What was all that guff about bein' a sharpshooter?"

"I never said that. I said I had the best marksmanship scores in my company, and that's a fact." Tom locked his peepers on mine. "'Course I qualified with an M1, which is a rifle. Not a handgun. But that fella, Gainey, didn't need to know that."

Crammed on the bench seat of the truck, I was keenly aware of Tom's upper leg pressed against mine. This was as close as we'd been since he came home. I felt my heart tighten and my breath catch. The pistol didn't bother me, nor did Tom's casual handling of it. With his background, it was natural he'd hold a gun as easily as Lee wielded that switchblade.

Beside me, Lee continued to grumble under his breath as he drove home. The words he used weren't fit for polite company, but they were right for the current circumstances.

No, what got under my skin was I didn't know how I felt about what I said next. "You would have shot him. Gainey."

Lee stopped muttering, and his body tensed.

Tom's eyes never left my face. They were deep black, like bottomless wells. Not dead and soulless, but they also held no trace of mischief or warmth.

I couldn't read his expression. "Am I wrong?"

He didn't move. "Let's just be glad it didn't come to that."

Chapter Forty-Three

I woke up the next morning with my head stuffed full of conflicting thoughts and emotions. What happened the previous night? Not the events. I had that straight. Tom had shown himself as a completely different guy. Again. He seemed to have left behind the angry, bitter, wounded version of himself, as well as his hopelessness. At least temporarily. I'd been prepared for him to be protective, not only of me but of his best friend.

I had not expected the cool, collected tough guy who didn't flinch at a potentially violent situation.

I sat on my front stoop, and Cat meandered over and hopped in my lap. He washed his paws, and I ran my hand over his fur. I replayed the confrontation with Gainey and his men. Not to analyze his words, but to review my own reactions. Lee had acted exactly as I figured he would. I knew him well enough that I'd spotted the tension in his face and shoulders. He'd recognized he was outmatched. But he'd promised to help me, and he was gonna stick it out, stay as calm as possible, and hope like heck I could talk our way outta trouble.

I'd expected the same outta Tom, but that wasn't what I got. He'd been intense. Focused on his target, not relying on me at all. The crack about his shooting skills meant nothing at the time, but as I sat there, soaking up the autumn sun, my cat a warm lump next to my chest, I knew he'd have taken out all three of his marks without batting an eye.

I shivered. It shoulda scared me to death, but it didn't. I'd been far more afraid of the angry, drunk Tom than I was of the tough guy I'd been with last night. That was a guy I wanted with me if I got into a jam.

More than that, I *liked* him.

"Cat, I must be outta my mind." I curled his tail around my fingers. "How could a girl be attracted to someone who'd shoot a man?"

Philip Marlowe didn't have problems gettin' dames, though.

"Don't get me wrong"—I continued to stroke Cat's soft fur—"I like Frank well enough. He certainly is attractive. But I don't think he's the guy for me. He and I can be pals, though."

Cat blinked, whatever that meant.

I took a deep breath. Since it was Saturday, I'd normally not go to the office. Right now, I felt that was the best place to be. I thought about sticking Cat in a bag and takin' him with me for company, but I didn't think he'd appreciate that. I let Mom know where I was goin' and left.

Once there, I flipped on the lights. I set the percolator to brew a pot of Emmeline's coffee and went to my desk. I spread out all my photos and reviewed my notes. I hadn't learned anything that cleared either Coates or Gainey, 'specially after last night. Trouble was, I hadn't learned anything, either. Not that I didn't already know. I fetched a cup of joe and returned to my desk.

"It's gotta be a triangle," I said. "Gainey and Coates at two points, Stevie in the middle. He had to have done somethin' big to get himself killed. But what?" Sam said one of the men I'd seen with Gainey at The Black Cat was a known associate of Coates's. Was he there to spy on Gainey or check on Stevie? Could be both.

Could be he told his boss Stevie was a plant.

Two sharp raps came from the doorway. "Knock, knock," Tom said.

I looked up to see him standing in the doorway. His clothes were neat, a pair of dungarees, a button-down work shirt, and a medium-weight jacket. The left leg of his pants was neatly pinned up and he wore a work boot on his right. He stood straight, not hunched over the crutches like when he first got home. His posture made him look taller.

He was the person I remembered—but not. "What are you doin' here?"

"I went over to your house. Your mom said you'd come here to do some work." He pointed at the empty chair. "Do you mind?"

"Sorry. Have a seat." I watched as he moved. "You look good."

"Not like a drunk, you mean." He lowered himself and set the crutches aside.

"I didn't say that."

"You don't have to." He rubbed his left thigh. "Whatcha doin'?"

"Goin' over my notes and adding things from last night." I bit my lip. "You didn't bring the Walther, did you?"

"I left it at home, locked up." He tilted his head. "Does it make you nervous? Me carryin' a gun?"

"No, I…never mind."

He nodded at the piles of paper. "It's Saturday. Don't private detectives get the weekends off?"

"There's so much to think through." I ran my hand through my hair. "The connection between Stevie, Gainey, and Coates is a little clearer, but fuzzy around the edges."

"Want some help?"

I cut my gaze to his face. He looked sincere. "Why would you give up a Saturday?"

"I told you the other day. What else am I gonna do?" Again, he ran his hands over his leg. The movement came off as unconscious, like he wasn't aware he did it.

I blurted out the question. "Does it hurt?" His eyebrows bunched together, and I continued. "Your leg. You keep rubbin' it." I held my breath and hoped I hadn't touched a nerve.

He looked down. "Not like you might think. The part that's left doesn't hurt at all. Sometimes I think it's still there, you know?" He swallowed. "They told me about that when I was in the hospital. People who've had a limb amputated get these ghost pains, I guess you'd call 'em. I think my leg is whole, but when I look down…." He clenched his hands.

It was more than he'd said to me before. "I'm sorry." It sounded like a whisper to me, but Tom jerked his head up.

"Nothin' for you to be sorry about."

"Pop served in the Great War. He doesn't talk about it much. He told me once a lot of guys never do."

"He came over a few days ago. You know my dad. He's sympathetic, but he doesn't know what to say. Yours?" Tom gave a weak laugh. "He's a good listener. And good with advice. It helped a lot, him bein' there for me."

The visit would have been about when Tom started bein' more calm. *Thank you, Pop.* Maybe I shouldn't say anything, but I couldn't help myself. "If you ever want to talk to me, I'll listen. It's not like I've been in war, but I've seen dead bodies now. I won't get squeamish. Prob'ly."

For a moment, I didn't think he'd say anything. He stared at his hands. "A shell hit the Sherman I was driving. My gunner and my loader, they were killed immediately. A piece of shrapnel went through my leg." His hands shook a little. "I passed out. When I woke up in the field hospital…"

"Tom, I didn't mean to pry."

"No, I want to." He flattened his palms. "The doc told me they couldn't save it. But they'd amputated below the knee. I knew I was lucky. A lot more than the others. I didn't want to see it that way. I was afraid—" He looked up. "I was afraid you'd leave me for sure. I knew you were keen on the detective thing. I figured this"—he waved at his leg—"was a good excuse for you to leave with a clear conscience. You can't be a professional and care for an invalid husband."

"Oh, Tom." His words cut me to the heart. "I wouldn't do that to you. Heck, haven't we been friends with Lee since we were kids? He's not an invalid, and you aren't either."

"Then why'd you break off our engagement? Don't tell me 'to keep it professional' 'cause that's bull."

I licked my lips. "I'm not sure what I want. Until I figure it out, it wouldn't be fair to leave you hangin' out there, like a kite on a string."

To my surprise, he simply nodded. "Fair enough. We've always been honest with each other. I guess now's not the time to give that up."

I studied him. "How's this? Let's get past this case. Then we can talk."

He nodded. "Now, tell me what's holdin' you up."

I felt a weight lift from my shoulders. I told him my thoughts about Stevie,

Gainey, and Coates. "If Sam's right, and he usually is, Coates and Gainey were playin' the same spy game."

"'Cept Coates's guy would know about Stevie's true mission." Tom looked at the ceiling. "What if Stevie really went over to Coates? Add that to suspected theft, and Gainey would be madder than a wet cat."

I sorted through the papers on my desk. I picked up the picture of the key that had been in Stevie's pocket. "You said this looked like a shed key." I held it out.

"More like a padlock." He took it. "They used locks on the doors to the supply shed that are heavier than a regular padlock."

"None of which Stevie had access to."

"That you know of." He put the picture on my desk. "What you need to figure out is where he'd keep such a thing if he didn't want anyone to stumble on it by accident. Like you did in the tunnel when you found his stash."

"But everywhere Stevie went…" My voice trailed off. Everywhere was public. Except one place. One place no one from the Fruit Belt would ever go or see.

Tom cocked his head. "You got a look in your eye. Like you just had a brainwave."

I told him about Ginny Ellis. "He could easily get her to promise not to snoop. Gainey wouldn't go to her house. Neither would Coates."

"A white girl's home?" Tom snorted. "No one from Stevie's life would set foot there. Even if they thought of it, which they prob'ly wouldn't. But is there a shed at the Ellery home?"

I pushed my chair back and stood. "Wanna come with me and find out?"

Chapter Forty-Four

I called Sam and asked him to meet us at the Ellery house with the mystery key. Tom didn't question my ability to summon a police detective. As we rode the bus, he gave me a slanted grin. "You thought any more about those driving lessons?"

"Every time I gotta take the bus."

When we arrived, Sam loitered on the sidewalk, smoking. He flicked away the cigarette when he saw us. "This better be good. It's Saturday morning, and I was chasing down a lead." Sam extended a hand. "Mr. Flannery, good to see you again. You're looking better."

"Yes, sir. Thank you." Tom shook. "I appreciate your help."

"Least I could do to thank you for your service."

I narrowed my eyes. They were too friendly for cop and suspect. "Why do I get the feeling there's more goin' on between you two than I know? I thought Tom wasn't out of the picture."

"Mind your own beeswax, missy." Sam pulled a bag from his pocket and shook out the key. "What's so important you dragged me over here?"

I brought him up to speed on the theory I'd worked out with Tom. "I figured you'd want to be on the scene if we were right."

Sam nodded. "Get a girl no one knows about to hold the goods. Clever. Then again, we knew Stevie wasn't a dummy." He tugged his jacket. "Ring the bell, Betty."

Sam and I mounted the steps while Tom waited on the sidewalk. Ginny answered the door promptly. "May I help you?" She sized up Sam and me.

"Good morning," I said. "Sorry to bother you this early in the morning. I hope you remember me."

She gave a timid nod. "You're the private detective, the one looking for Stevie's murderer." Her gaze flicked to Sam. "And you're the police detective. You've been here before."

He nodded.

Ginny returned her gaze to me. "What do you want?"

"Stevie had a key in his pocket when he died. This one." I held out my hand. Sam dropped the key in it, and I showed it to Ginny. "Do you recognize it?"

The muscle at the corner of her eye twitched. "No."

"You sure?" I raised my eyebrows. "We, Detective MacKinnon and I, think Stevie asked you to hold something for him. Wherever he hid it, this is the key."

"I don't know what you're talking about." Her voice wavered. "I've never seen that key in my life."

"Miss Ellery." Sam wore his best *trust me* expression. "You aren't in trouble. I'll ask again. Did Stevie ask you to hide something?"

Mr. Ellery appeared behind his daughter. "Virginia, what is goin' on? You know I'm sleepin.'" He halted at the sight of Sam and me. "What are you doin' here?"

"Hello, Mr. Ellery," I said.

Mr. Ellery's peepers narrowed. "The girl detective. I've got nothin' to say to you. Now scram."

"Perhaps you have something to tell me." Sam flashed his badge. "We were asking your daughter about this key. Do you know it?"

A flicker of recognition crossed Mr. Ellery's face, then his expression went blank. "Nope."

Sam musta caught it too because he pressed. "See, here's the thing." Once again, he went over our idea. "Your daughter is a child. If this key unlocks the hiding place holding critical evidence, she'll get her hand slapped. You could be arrested for obstructing a police investigation. Maybe even withholding evidence."

I had no idea if that was true, but I reminded myself never to play poker with Sam.

Mr. Ellery's face turned an interesting shade of purple. "You think that… boy asked my girl to hide something? You must be outta your tree. Ginny would never do a favor for a kid like that."

"Daddy, I loved him!" The words burst from Ginny as tears ran down her cheeks.

Mr. Ellery raised his hand. "You bite your tongue, girl, or you'll get what's comin' to you."

Sam stepped forward and grabbed his wrist. "I wouldn't do that. Not in front of me." He looked at Ginny. "Last chance. Do you recognize that key?"

Ginny bit her lip as she looked from one person to the other. A frightened rabbit searching for an escape.

Behind us, Tom cleared his throat. "There's a shed in the back. It's got a lock I think would be exactly the type you're lookin' for."

"How dare you snoop on my property," Mr. Ellery growled as he yanked his hand free, pushed past Sam and me, and leapt down the steps to tower over Tom.

Tom stood his ground. "I can see it clearly from right here, sir. It's not snooping if it's in plain sight. It's hard to hide a garden shed."

Mr. Ellery clenched his fists, and I could tell he was working up to a punch. I could only hope Tom was payin' attention. Then again, given how he'd reacted when Lee and I surprised him on the sidewalk the other night, he prob'ly spent most of his waking time on alert now.

"Mr. Ellery, I advise you to get a grip on your temper." Sam hustled down to position himself between them. "Mr. Flannery. Where's this shed?"

Tom tipped his head. "In the back. Right up against the fence line."

Sam snapped his fingers. I tossed him the key. Wordlessly, he headed for the shed. Tom and I followed, leaving Mr. Ellery and his daughter on the front walk.

Sam fitted the key into the lock and twisted. With a click, it gave way. He yanked the door open with a squeal of rusty hinges. "What do you keep in here?" he asked Mr. Ellery.

Mr. Ellery followed us across the yard. "Junk, mostly. Broken tools, stuff like that. Used to have a little workshop, but I ain't been in there for a while.

With the war on, I can't get materials."

I picked my way among a collection of shovels, saws with broken teeth, and some other things. I lifted a cracked flowerpot. "There." Underneath was a school composition book. The cover was dirty, but it was readable. I picked it up. Stevie Washington's name was written on the cover. I shot a look at Sam. "It's his."

Sam turned to Mr. Ellery. "Get your daughter over here."

Mr. Ellery beckoned, and Ginny came to stand beside him.

I came out and held up the book. "When did Stevie give this to you?"

She snuck a peek at her father, but he said nothing, his expression carved from wood. "A month ago, maybe two. Stevie, he said it had important information in it. He didn't want anyone to find it. He said it could get him in a lot of trouble. So I hid it in the shed." She edged away from her father. "I gave him the extra key so he could get it when he needed to. I knew Daddy never went in there."

Sam thumbed through the pages. "Do you know what's written in it?"

She shook her head. "I looked once, but it didn't make any sense to me."

He gave a hard look at Mr. Ellery, then at Ginny. "I'll be taking this. If I have more questions, or if Miss Ahern does, I assume you both will be more than willing to answer them."

They nodded.

"Mr. Ellery. I gather from your reaction earlier that you didn't approve of Stevie." Sam pulled out his notebook and a pencil. "Mind telling me where you were Friday last between ten at night and three in the morning?"

Mr. Ellery tried for a bit of bluster. "Why?"

Tom spoke. "Because if you thought your daughter was with a boy you didn't like, you might have taken steps to break them up." He paused. "If you couldn't talk the couple out of it, you might have resorted to more direct action."

The red faded from Mr. Ellery's face. "If you're thinking I shot the little… upstart, I didn't."

I moved to stand next to Tom. "Then you won't have a problem telling Detective MacKinnon where you were."

Mr. Ellery shuffled his feet. "I picked up an extra shift at the plant. My supervisor will tell you. I was there all night."

"Good. I'll be checking on that." Sam tipped his fedora. "Miss Ellery, sorry to have upset you." He took off.

Tom and I exchanged a look. "Thanks for your help, Virginia." We hurried off.

We met Sam on the sidewalk a couple houses up the street. "Good catch, Mr. Flannery," he said as he lit a cigarette.

Tom glanced at me. "When noticing details is the difference between livin' and gettin' shot, you learn to keep your eyes peeled."

"Indeed." Sam exhaled. "Come on. We'll get lunch and see exactly what Stevie was hiding. My treat. I'll even drive."

"Gee," I said as we followed Sam to his car. "That's real swell of you."

Chapter Forty-Five

Sam took us to a neighborhood diner. We all slid in, Sam with his back against the wall. He propped Tom's crutches next to him.

Tom and I sat next to each other across from Sam. Tom unzipped his jacket. "What's in the notebook?"

"Not as much as you think." Sam slid it across the table.

Tom opened it and flipped to the first page. The entire sheet was covered with dots and dashes. "It's a visual representation of Morse code."

Sam asked the waitress for three cups of coffee and told her we needed another minute to order. After she left, he said, "That was my suspicion. Now to find someone who knows Morse because I don't."

More time lost. I stamped down my frustration. "I don't either."

"I do." Tom looked up. "I need a piece of paper and something to write with."

Sam ripped a sheet from his notebook and passed it over, along with his pencil.

I raised my eyebrows. "Do all soldiers learn?"

"No." Tom's eyes moved back and forth as he read the code, his right hand jotting down the translation. "I had a buddy in the signal corps who taught me." He paused. "It's all numbers. Look."

Sam and I craned our necks to inspect the writing. "Swell," I said. "Numbers of what?"

Our coffee arrived. We ordered some sandwiches, but I wasn't thinkin' about food. I suspected the others weren't, either.

Tom chewed the pencil for a few seconds. "Jesus. This kid was smart."

I folded my hands and glared. "There's no need to take the Lord's name in vain." I heard Sam's muffled laugh, but when I looked up, he was busy with his joe.

"Well, he was. It's an A1Z26 cipher." Tom looked at me. I must've had a blank expression, 'cause he hurried on. "It's a very basic code. Each letter of the alphabet is assigned a number: A is one, B is two, and so on." He switched his focus to Sam. "Can I have another sheet?"

Wordlessly, Sam ripped off another piece of paper and handed it over.

Tom turned it sideways and wrote the alphabet. Then he wrote numbers underneath, one through twenty-six. "Replace every number with the corresponding letter. Here, this is the word *the*."

I pointed. "And that's Gainey."

"You got it. Easy as pie."

"Wonderful." Sam took a drink. "It'll only take us days to translate the entire book."

"Naw, Betty and I can do it in a few hours. I can translate the Morse, and she can do the cipher." Tom looked at me. "You game?"

Suddenly, I was very aware of him. He smelled like soap and the leathery lemon of Aqua Velva. Warmth radiated from his body. His face was inches away from mine, and a lock of brown hair tumbled over his forehead. His eyes weren't as deep brown as Frank's, but there was a jagged ring of green around each pupil that I'd never paid much attention to. His skin was tanner than when he'd left, and there was a new smattering of freckles across the bridge of his nose. My heart thudded against my ribs, and my breathing became quick and shallow.

The pupils of his eyes shrank, the green more prominent. Was he feeling the same way I did?

There was a lump in my throat. "Sure." My voice sounded croaky to me. Did they think it did, too?

Out of the corner of my eye, I saw Sam grin. When I turned my attention to him, the twinkle in his eyes was a little too knowing. "What?" I asked.

"Nothing," he said and took a bite of his sandwich. "It's almost eleven-thirty. If I drive you two back to Betty's office, how long do you need?"

Tom licked his lips, then tore his gaze away from my face. He flipped through the notebook. "A few hours."

I wanted to press my hands to my cheeks. They were on fire. I had to be blushing something fierce. Fortunately, Sam and Tom let it pass without comment.

"Finish your lunches. I'll catch up to you around three." Sam pointed. "You might not get through all of that, but it'll be enough to get us headed in the right direction."

"Sounds like a good plan." I applied myself to my food. Next to me, I heard Tom murmur his agreement. As I ate, I told myself I was feeling that way 'cause I was excited about the breakthrough. Tom had nothing to do with it. I felt the same way when Frank was around. It meant nothing.

I couldn't convince myself it was true.

* * *

It was close to twelve thirty when Tom and I arrived back at my office. "You want coffee?" I asked as I unlocked the door.

"No. Water would be good, though." He maneuvered behind me. "That chair still by your desk?"

"Yeah. Let me get you a glass." I tucked the notebook under my arm so I could hold the water.

Tom reached out and took it. "My hands still work, Betty. I can carry this. Just bring the water." He moved into my office.

I got the drinks and went after him. He'd pulled up the chair so we could sit face to face. "Here." I put the cup of water at his hand.

He moved it out of the way. "Thanks. Got paper and a pencil I can use?"

"Right here." I took out both and gave them to him.

"You have the cipher key I wrote out in the diner?"

I got it out of my purse and waved it.

"Good. I'll decode the Morse on a fresh sheet. Then you can use the cipher key to do the rest." He wrote rapidly, his strokes bold and sharp.

I watched. "Your handwriting is different."

263

He didn't look up. "Don't tell me you can't read it."

"I didn't say it was sloppy, just different. Faster. Sharper, I guess."

He didn't stop. "Except for my letters home, I didn't have a lot of time. Whatever I wrote when I was overseas had to be quick and easy to read."

It made sense. "Remember the penmanship prize you won in fourth grade?"

That made him look up. "Mrs. Dutwiler. What a dragon lady. But she liked me."

"'Course she did. You and Lee. Always the teacher's pets." I leaned back. "They liked him 'cause he was a good student. You, well, I'm not really sure how you charmed 'em all."

He wiggled his eyebrows. "I was a lovable scamp. Not the best student, but my personality won 'em over."

"It drove Dot and me crazy. Always bein' compared to you two."

"You were just jealous." He returned to work.

I didn't have a response. Mostly 'cause it was true. After a minute or two, Tom passed over the first sheet, and I got to work. We didn't talk much, the only sound the scratch of our pencils and the rustle of paper.

Tom stretched. "What have you got?"

"A mess. Stevie *was* playin' both ends against the middle. Gainey thought Stevie was workin' for him, and so did Coates. Look." I spun my translations around. I didn't know if reading upside down was a skill Tom had picked up, but he'd learned code, so who knew? "There are some numbers, dates and such. He kept a record of everything he did for either of 'em. Sam said one of the men in the photo I took, the one of Gainey in the The Crazy Cat, worked for Coates."

"He woulda been on the spot to let his boss know that Stevie was sellin' them out." Tom swore under his breath. "Talk about playin' with fire. The only question was who would catch him first."

I frowned. "Your mother told you not to swear in front of me."

His answering grin could only be called sly. "My mom isn't here." He jabbed a finger at me. "You worked in a factory. Guys or dolls, that's a setting where colorful language is a given. You may not use the words, not regularly, but you've heard 'em. I bet it doesn't even bother you."

I ducked my head as the heat crept up my neck.

Tom's laughter was rich and warm. "You're no Sunday school teacher, Betty Ahern. Admit it."

"Back to business." I cleared my throat. "Based on this, Gainey and Coates both have motive. Let's see if we can get one of 'em out of the picture."

* * *

A few hours later, a knock on the door made me look up.

Sam was there, right on time. "I see you're hard at work. Any results?"

"Lots." I really needed a second chair. "Emmeline isn't here. Grab her seat, drag it in, and we'll show you."

Once he did, Tom and I talked for a good twenty minutes, showing him our findings. "Bottom line," I said, "Stevie was in hot water, whether he knew it or not."

"He played a dangerous game, that's for sure." Sam flipped sheets back and forth as he read.

I passed him the photograph I'd taken in The Crazy Cat. "You're sure this guy works for Coates?"

"Positive. He was picked up by Vice earlier this year with Coates, but there wasn't enough evidence to arrest him." Sam tossed the picture back.

"Tom was right." I sat back. "He was a mole. He'd have found out about Stevie and told Coates."

"That would be ugly." Tom rubbed his left leg. "Either Coates or Gainey mighta shot Stevie. God knows they'd want to if they found out what he was doin'."

I tapped my pencil on the blotter. "Question is, which one? And how do we find out?"

We all stared at each other. Sam and I locked eyes. "You thinking what I am?" he asked.

"We have to lure both of 'em out and see who shows," I said.

Tom tilted his head. "How do you figure that? Gainey owns the tunnel property, right? Why not focus on him?"

"Stevie coulda told Coates about it." I drummed my fingers on the chair arm. "There's an entrance halfway between Gainey's property and Wadsworth, where Stevie was killed. I couldn't get the entry open, but maybe that's 'cause Coates blocked it up. He wouldn't have to get anywhere near his rival to show up unannounced."

Sam rubbed his chin. "I want to draw them to a location we choose."

"You want to pick the battleground." Tom's gaze grew unfocused. "If you're plannin' an ambush, you want the enemy to come to you on favorable turf."

Sam shot him a look. "Not the words I would have used, but yes."

"The vacant lot on Wadsworth?" I asked.

Sam shook his head. "Too public. I don't want to run the risk of civilians getting caught in any crossfire."

I ran through all the locations I'd visited over the last week. "What about that empty lot next to where the fights were held? I bet Gainey owns it." I looked at Tom. "I doubt any real business goes on there. All the neighboring buildings looked abandoned. Plus, it's not that far from Coates's automotive garage, so he prob'ly won't feel exposed."

"Definitely a good possibility." He rubbed his chin. "Yeah, I like it. It's got good cover, but also good sightlines. You'll see whoever is coming before he spots you."

"Now we need the bait," Sam said.

A tiny thought took root in my brain. "I have an idea. But you aren't gonna like it, either of you."

The men looked at each other. Sam waved a hand to indicate I should continue.

"Gainey and Coates know me. They know I've been lookin' into Stevie's death." I paused. "I'll leave both of 'em a message that I've found out what Stevie was up to, but I'm willing to sell my silence, since Nancy can't pay my fee. I'll arrange to meet Coates at ten tonight in that lot, and Gainey at an hour later. Then I'll get one of 'em to 'fess up to the murder. Sam, you can slap the cuffs on."

Tom's response was swift. "No. Absolutely not. What if the killer decides to shoot you instead of payin'?"

"That's why Sam will be there." I used my most reasonable voice. "I've been in tight places before, Tom. It'll be jake."

"Why can't one of Sam's officers be the bait?"

"Because as soon as Gainey, or Coates, sees a cop, he'll split." Sam's voice was bland, but his expression betrayed his discomfort. "I'm with Tom on this one, Betty. It's very risky. Whoever shows up may decide to kill you from the shadows. I can't bring anyone with me, not to an unsanctioned stakeout."

"Then I'll stand where they won't be able to see me until they come into view." Truth be told, I wasn't keen on turnin' myself into a shooting gallery tin target, but I couldn't see any other way. Even a plainclothes officer would be a stranger and, therefore, suspicious. "Sam, you'll be right there. This may be our only shot."

Tom leaned forward. "Detective. You can't possibly—"

Sam held up a hand. "I already said I wasn't fond of the idea. But I don't see any other way. We need to lull our killer into a false sense of security. An apparently unarmed and unaccompanied woman will do that." He aimed a finger at me. "But you stay hidden until I arrive. Do not put a toe into the line of fire. Understand me?"

"Yes, sir." I glanced at Tom, whose face was scrunched up, thunderclouds in his eyes. He'd pulled a gun on Gainey and knew this was no game. Now he fully understood the job I'd chosen. Whether he liked it or not.

Chapter Forty-Six

om insisted on coming with me to both The Crazy Cat, where we knew Gainey spent time, and Coates's garage. "For heaven's sake, I'm only leaving messages," I said.

"I'm not getting in your way."

"But you'll scare 'em off."

He faced me, his expression dead serious. "Moses Gainey will remember the man who drew a gun on him and his boys. I don't think that'll frighten anyone. If anything, me being here makes 'em take you seriously."

I left the same sealed note with the bartender and a mechanic. I'd finished my investigation, and I knew Stevie's game. For a cut, I was willing to keep my yap shut and tell the cops I'd come up empty.

Tom and I rode the bus from the Fruit Belt back to the First Ward. "Now what do we do?" he asked.

"I go home, change, and I'll meet Sam tonight. You, well, stay up and fret if you want." I chewed my thumbnail.

"I'm going with you."

I scowled. "No, you're not. Tom, stumping along beside me in broad daylight is one thing. Tonight will be different. I might have to move quickly. I don't want to hurt your feelings, 'specially since you've done good work. But you keep sayin' mobility isn't your strong suit."

"If you're wonderin' if I can be quiet, trust me. I learned how to do that in basic training. I thought you'd realized that by now."

He didn't understand. Still the same mule-headed Irish boy. "It's more than that."

"Look." He grabbed my shoulders. "We're not gonna argue about this. I promise I'll stay outta your way. As soon as I see Detective MacKinnon, the show is yours. But don't ask me to stay behind while the…while you put yourself in harm's way. If you don't understand why I can't, then you don't know me at all."

I stared into his peepers. The green was sharper, giving them a fierceness. Was this the way he looked before battle? His grip was firm, but not painful. I wondered if he needed to do this to prove something to himself. Perhaps that moment of drunken honesty had been his rock bottom. If so, didn't I owe it to him to help him finish climbin' outta his hole?

"Okay." I pulled his hands off and held them maybe a moment longer than necessary. They were warm and his skin callused. Again, my heartbeat sped up. *The anticipation of tonight*, I told myself. "But once you see Sam, you stay put."

He nodded. "Deal."

He'd given in easily. Somethin' was up.

* * *

Ten o'clock. I peered around the corner of the warehouse on Best into the empty lot. The space was almost vacant. A pile of pallets occupied one corner, and a few boxes took up the other. I didn't see any other entrances, which meant he'd come from the street or the building. I'd dressed in shades of gray, to blend in with the shadows. I'd be hard to see until I wanted to be. I could only hope I hadn't missed anything.

I felt a light touch on my shoulder and jumped nearly a foot in the air. I turned to see Tom behind me. He'd also dressed in muted colors. Between the softer sole of his shoe and the rubber caps on the wooden crutches, I hadn't heard a peep. "I told you to wait around the corner," I hissed.

"I said I'd leave when I saw Detective MacKinnon. I don't. Where is he?" He craned his neck to see around me.

"I don't know." I hadn't seen Sam when I arrived. It worried me a little, but I wasn't gonna let Tom know that. "It's good you can't see him. If he can hide from a trained soldier, a thug like Gainey or Coates won't have a chance. We don't want to spook the mark."

"You didn't arrange a signal?"

"Of course we did. We haven't needed it yet." I grabbed his arm and pulled him, nearly knocking him over. "Keep your voice down. You want someone to hear you?"

Frank rounded the corner. "Hear who?"

I clenched my fists. "What the he—heck are you doin' here?"

"I called him." Tom didn't look at me. "I thought you'd need all the help you could get. This feels like a battle plan that's already gone belly up."

Frank's stubborn expression was plain, even in the low light. "We aren't going to leave you undefended. Tom and I talked. We felt it would be dangerous, not to mention ungentlemanly, if we let you out here alone."

Oh, for the love of Pete. "I'm not alone. Sam is gonna be here any minute, if he's not already." We were bein' too loud. "Someone's gonna hear you and you'll blow the sting."

Tom's face paled. "Too late."

I heard the unmistakable click of a gun being cocked. Slowly, I turned. Coates stood not ten feet away. I raised my hands. "Evening. Nice night, isn't it?"

Coate's smile was cold. "You ain't foolin' me, Miss Ahern. Three white folk ain't out in the Fruit Belt for a nighttime stroll." He twitched the muzzle of the gun. "Over here. I wanna keep an eye on you. All of you."

We followed orders. Frank and I kept our hands at shoulder height. Tom couldn't, of course. Not and stay upright.

It seemed Coates didn't care. "Lemme see your hands."

"You can see 'em just fine where they are." Tom's voice didn't quaver. He had to be afraid, but not a trace showed on his face.

Coates sneered. "You keep 'em right there, then." He jabbed the gun forward. "Looks like I got here in plenty of time to take care of all of you."

There was enough light for me to recognize a .38 Special. "Tom and Frank have nothing to do with this."

"I ain't talkin' 'bout them. Word is you invited Mo Gainey. Glad I arrived first." Coates grinned. "Thanks for the opportunity."

"To get rid of your rival." Doggone it. I shoulda thought of that.

"Kill two birds with one stone. Get rid of you *and* Gainey. With the boy gone, ain't no one standin' in the way of me takin' over." He gave a predatory smile. "I even get to frame Gainey for all of it."

"I told you. You pay me enough and I'll keep quiet."

Coates spat. "You don't fool me. You the righteous type. You aren't gonna keep your mouth shut."

"Why'd you shoot Stevie?" I tried to keep my voice level. I needed to buy time. *Sam, where are you?*

"Double-crossed me, didn't he?" Coates raised his eyebrows. "I ain't dumb. Put my own man on the inside of Gainey's crew. He told me the real score. Kid shoulda known I'd check up on him."

"You told me you wouldn't have shot him." All I could do was play for time. "You woulda made it painful."

"Most folks know that. Gainey's got the quick trigger finger. I even had my man tip off Gainey, told him Stevie had really switched to my gang." The light glinted off his gold tooth. "I didn't care how the kid went down, arrested or dead. I wanted him gone."

I had to face facts. For whatever reason, Sam wasn't comin'. I needed a new plan.

Frank stood at my left. He wasn't gonna do much to help. Tom had positioned himself on my right. Had he brought his Walther? If he'd had it at the fights, surely he had it now. But I didn't see a telltale bulge or lump in his jacket. Maybe if I went for Coates's feet, Tom could take him out with a swing of a crutch.

I stepped closer to him and tried to catch his eye.

Tom didn't spare me a glance. "How'd you know where Stevie would be that night?"

"Kid was smart, but he had a big mouth." Coates's gaze flicked to the street, but never left us long enough to make him vulnerable. "Bragged about his card trick and his tunnel to one of my boys. All I had to do was wait for him."

"Then it was only a question of who got to him first. You or Gainey," I said. Poor Stevie.

"You got it, girl." Coates glanced at Frank. "I'm familiar with the man with the sticks, but who are you?"

"I'm a friend of Betty's. I came to escort her safely home." Frank also seemed unconcerned with the situation. Maybe he thought he could talk this guy down, like one of the patients at the hospital. Fat chance of that.

Coates guffawed. "Look at you, all polite and proper."

"You can't shoot all three of us at once." I tried for a bluff. "The cops are on the way. Your next stop is the city jail."

"I don't think so." He cocked the gun. "Been real nice talkin' to y'all. You seem like nice folks, but 'course you understand I can't let you live."

What happened next was a whirl of sound and motion. Gunshots split the air. Frank shoved me to the ground behind Tom, and I landed on the paving stones with a grunt.

Chapter Forty-Seven

I looked up. Tom stood like a statue, gun in hand. A thin wisp of smoke trailed up from the barrel. Coates was crumpled on the ground in front of him. He'd dropped his .38, and it had skittered a few feet from his splayed hand.

Tom didn't move. "You okay?"

I'd skinned my palms on the stone and torn my pants in the fall. A thin line of blood dribbled from a cut on my knee. "A couple of scrapes is all. Is he dead?" I looked around. Still no police. What had happened to Sam?

"Coates hasn't moved, but I'm not gonna get close and look." Tom's gaze flicked to me. "Check on Frank."

Frank. I scrambled over to him. He lay facedown on the cobblestones not far from where I'd fallen. "Frank, you all right? Talk to me." I shook him gently and tried to roll him over. His shirt was wet and warm.

I pulled my hand away. Blood. "Frank! Say something, please." I heaved and he rolled over.

His front was soaked. How had that happened? I replayed the scene. He'd shoved me aside just as Coates fired. Whether he'd been aimin' for me or Tom's shot made him miss, it didn't matter.

Frank had taken the bullet he believed was meant for me.

"Please. Wake up. Come on. Sam will be here any minute." This wouldn't have happened if Sam had been here like he promised. I patted Frank's face. "Tom, you gotta help me. He's been shot. We gotta do something. It's too far to the nearest pay phone."

I sensed Tom come over and lower himself to the ground behind me.

Frank's eyes fluttered open. "Betty." A bubble of blood swelled and burst at the corner of his mouth.

I leaned in. "I'm here. It's gonna be jake. You hang on." I laid my hand over where I thought the wound was. "Tom, I need your shirt." I pressed my hands to Frank's chest.

Tom didn't move.

"Betty." Frank's voice was so faint.

I put my face right next to his. "Don't say anything. Save your strength."

He blinked. "It's…too late." He closed his eyes, and his voice trailed off.

"Hush, now." Where was Sam?

Frank's eyes opened. "You and Tom…need." He took a shallow breath. "Don't forget…I…" He went still.

"No. Frank. No, no, no, no, no. Tom, help me." My voice echoed off the brick buildings. Frank lay motionless under my hands. "You musta seen things like this before. Do something."

"I have." Tom's voice came out of the dark, heavy and solemn. "That's how I know there's nothin' to do."

"No, there's gotta be a way to save him. Lee, he told me about some new-fangled thing. You push a guy's chest to restart his heart." I pushed randomly. No response.

Tom's arms, strong yet gentle, wrapped around me, and he pulled me away. "He's gone, Betty. I'm sorry."

I wailed. That couldn't be the case. But deep down, I knew Tom told the truth. Frank's eyes, always so warm and inviting, had taken on a vacant stare. The dimple that flashed when he smiled was invisible. It might have been my imagination, but his cheeks looked blue and waxy, not rosy and healthy like they always did. "Frank! You dumb sap, why'd you have to go and do that?" I shoulda told him how I felt. He'd have stayed home, where he was safe.

Tom tightened his embrace. "Because he loved you, Betty."

It was too much. I buried my face in Tom's chest and wept like a baby.

* * *

Frank Hicks was dead.

The rest of the night passed like a dream. The air was neither warm nor cold. Sam arrived at some point. I heard his voice like he was talkin' through water. The words sorry, delayed, and incident came through my fog but meant nothing. He gave up and went over to Tom.

I stared at the men who'd arrived to take care of Frank's body. They draped it with a sheet, put it on a stretcher, and put it into the back of the meat wagon. I didn't know when they had arrived. They just appeared.

A patrol officer helped me wipe as much of Frank's blood off my hands as he could. There was nothing to be done about my clothes. I stood there, not limp, but not stiff, either. I couldn't erase the vision of Frank's body, lying on the stones, motionless.

I felt the weight of a hand on my shoulder and looked up.

Sam took my hand. "One of the officers is going to take you and Mr. Flannery home. Your statements can wait."

"I gotta go tell Frank's parents. They'll wonder where he is when he doesn't see them tomorrow." My voice sounded odd to my ears. Like it came from someone else. "It's Sunday. He always has dinner with his folks."

"I'll take care of that personally." Sam led me over to a waiting car. "You go home and rest."

"Promise?" I grasped his hand. "You won't send some dope who didn't even know Frank, right? 'Cause if you can't, I gotta do it."

He made an X over his chest. "Cross my heart. I'm going right now." He shifted his gaze to Tom. "Get her home. For now, tell Mrs. Ahern only what she needs to know. Make sure Betty stays warm and goes to bed. She's in shock."

"Yes, sir." Tom loaded his crutches into the back seat. "I've seen it before. I'll take care of her. Her mom isn't the hysterical type. She'll know what to do."

"Good man." Sam clapped him on the shoulder and nudged me to get in. Tom followed. Then Sam closed the door.

I didn't notice a thing as the officer drove us home. The yellow-bellied conchie, that's what people called Frank. He had more guts than all of them put together. "They wouldn't call him a coward now," I muttered in a dead sort of voice.

Tom grasped my hand. "He was as brave as any guy I served with."

His words didn't make it better. But considering he'd made the same accusation only a few days ago, challenged Frank to a fistfight, and then taunted him when he wouldn't engage, it was something.

Small, but something.

Tom opened his door. "We're here."

I blinked. We were? How'd that happen? The shooting had been on the other side of Buffalo. We couldn't be in the First Ward already. But we were. Pop was there, helping me out. "Oh, my darling girl. Come on, let's get you inside. Thank you, Officer. I've got her."

He led me into the house. Mom's face was white as paper, but her voice sounded as brisk as ever. 'Come on. Joe, a small glass of whiskey, I think. Then a hot bath and bed." She led me to the kitchen. I didn't fight.

I could hear Tom's voice behind me. Then Pop's. I didn't care what they were saying. I'd never care about anything again.

Frank Hicks was dead.

Mom pressed a glass to my lips. I swallowed and coughed. The whiskey burned, but it didn't lift the fog. I drank obediently. She brought me to the bathroom, where I let her take off my clothes, fill the tub with hot water, and give me a good scrub. She dressed me in a clean nightgown and tucked me in bed.

"Mom?" My voice sounded small, like a little girl's.

The mattress sagged beneath her as she sat. "Yes?"

"Don't go. I don't want to be alone in the dark."

She brushed my hair aside. "I'll stay right here if you want me to."

"All night?"

She pressed her lips to my forehead. "As long as you need me."

I nestled my head on her lap. I hadn't done that for ages, not since I was a kid and sick with the flu. In the hustle and bustle of growing up, I thought I'd moved past the need to have someone hold me tight and keep the monsters away. I knew better now. I'd never outgrow it. Not when life could kick me

right back to bein' ten and wantin' my mother to keep me safe.
Because Frank Hicks was dead.

Chapter Forty-Eight

It was a couple of days before I could screw up the guts to go visit Frank's parents. The store was closed, so I walked up the stairs to their apartment and knocked. Mrs. Hicks, dressed in widow's weeds, threw her arms around me the moment she opened the door. "Oh, Betty. Come in. Would you like some tea?"

The tension I'd been holding since I got off the trolley fled. I had been afraid Mrs. Hicks held me responsible for their son's death. He had been comin' to rescue me, after all. But it didn't seem like she did. Maybe it was a Quaker thing. "Tea would be great. Is Mr. Hicks here?"

"He's out. He hasn't been able to stay put, since...." She left me in a sitting room filled with comfortable-looking furniture covered in floral fabric. A photograph with a black ribbon drew my attention, and I picked it up. It was a portrait of Frank. He looked younger, but not by much. Taken after he graduated from St. Bonaventure's College? Or high school? His face was full of laughter and the promise of youth. I put it down gently.

Mrs. Hicks bustled in holding a tray containing the tea things. "It was taken after Frank finished college. That boy. He didn't know what he was going to do with a degree, but he so enjoyed his years with the Franciscans. Then the war happened and, well, perhaps he'd have found something afterwards. Now..." Her voice failed, and she sniffed. "Please, sit. Would you like milk or sugar? I have a little of both."

"Plain is fine, ma'am. I don't want to be any bother." I sat on the couch and stared at my lap. "Not more than I have been."

She handed me a delicate cup with flowers on it. "Whatever do you mean?"

"It's…I'm real sorry about what happened. If it wasn't for me, Frank would be here." She looked puzzled, and I stumbled on. "He went after me. That's the only reason he was in that lot in the first place. I wouldn't blame you if you'd taken one look at me and told me to scram." My teacup rattled against the saucer in my trembling hand. A little tea sloshed out.

Mrs. Hicks took a seat next to me. She took the cup away and held my hands. "My dear girl. Didn't you know anything about my son?"

My eyes filled with tears, and I half-laughed. "He marched to his own drummer, that was for sure."

"That he did." She squeezed. "From the time he was a little boy, he could be as stubborn as a mule. Once he got an idea into his head, he had to see it through. Did he ever tell you the story of how he rescued some baby kittens and nursed them? Their mother had disappeared, maybe killed, and he took pity on the poor things. It didn't matter how many people told him they'd never make it. He fed them milk from his fingers every day. He was so proud of himself. Not one of them died."

"Sounds just like him."

She patted my hand. "Then you know once he got it into his head he had to do something, he did it. You needed him, he went to you."

She wasn't helping. The tears rolled down my cheeks. "I didn't want him there. I knew it would be dangerous. I'd called my friend in the police. Frank didn't need to come. Tom shouldn't have brought him. I told him to leave. I killed him."

Mrs. Hicks let me cry. Eventually, she said, "Betty, you didn't do any such thing. The only person responsible for Frank's death was the man who pulled the trigger of the gun. No, I think you feel guilty about something else. What is it?"

A mother's intuition was better than any detective work. "You know Frank and I didn't get off on the right foot."

She smiled.

"But eventually, we got to know each other, and I liked him. He was funny, and smart, and kind. And easy to look at."

"Yes, I know. He was an adorable child who grew into a handsome man."

"I knew he was sweet on me. I thought maybe I felt the same way about him. But—"

"Yes, Frank told me about your young man. The one who was in the Army, who came home on crutches. Tom is his name?"

I nodded. "I'd been tellin' myself that I didn't know which of 'em, Frank or Tom, I liked more. But I knew all along. I just didn't wanna admit it. Fact is, things never woulda worked between Frank and me. I'm not ready to marry Tom, but I shoulda told Frank what my heart was sayin' all along. I wouldn't have been happy with him, not for a lifetime."

"Don't you think he knew that?" She took a wispy linen handkerchief and wiped my cheeks. "Frank was no fool. He realized as soon as Tom came home that he didn't stand a chance. He loved you anyway. He went to you that night knowing he wouldn't fight, not like Tom, but determined to do what he could to protect you."

"I wish I'd have told him. That we could be pals, but that was all. I thought I had more time."

She wrapped me in a motherly hug. "You told him through your actions, Betty. That was enough for him."

Chapter Forty-Nine

Tuesday morning, I stopped at Teddy's for breakfast as usual. Emmeline and I were meeting later to go over the books, finish the billing for the Washington case, and write our report for Nancy. Despite everything that had happened, we had business to conduct. With any luck, there'd also be new cases waiting for me. If I stayed busy, I could put off facing Tom and sayin' what I had to.

Judy was setting my plate down when I saw him coming toward me. I hadn't seen him in two days. His gait was awkward, and he held a cane in his left hand. I stared. "You have two feet."

"Good morning to you, too." He lifted his left pant leg and tapped the steel prosthetic with the cane. "Got it yesterday. How's it look?"

"Swell." I bit my lip. "Wanna join me?"

"Be glad to." He slid into the booth. "Coffee, black. Eggs over easy, side of bacon, and rye toast, please."

"Got it." Judy wrote down the order. Then she bent to whisper in my ear. "Another cutie. You need to learn to share." She hustled away.

I was glad I couldn't see my face. "How's it feel?" When Tom looked confused, I added, "The new leg."

His expression cleared. "Fine. Docs think I'll be able to lose the cane eventually. I'll have therapy for a while, but it'll be jake." He stared at his hands.

I studied him. He was clean, and his clothes were neat. A clear light shone from his eyes. "You off the sauce?"

"I haven't had a drink in days." He winced. "I should say, I haven't been drunk in days. I had a stiff one when I got home Saturday night."

After the shooting. "Are you okay with what you did?"

He sipped his coffee. "I did what I had to do."

Just like I'd known he would. And he'd do it again. "I'm gonna write up my final report when I get to the office later and settle your bill."

"What do I owe you?" He took out his wallet. "Mom handed over my dough."

I held up my hand. "Don't worry about it. You saved my behind. I think we'll call it square. Besides, I still want driving lessons."

"I haven't forgotten." He smiled, the one I remembered. The slightly mischievous grin that brought you into the joke. "Then at least let me buy your breakfast."

"Okay."

Uncomfortable silence settled over us. Judy brought his food. After she left, I watched him eat. "Are you gonna get in trouble? Over Coates, I mean. Sam must know you didn't kill Stevie."

Tom broke the yolks of his eggs with his toast. "I'm in the clear. Detective MacKinnon said, based on the scene and my statement, it was self-defense." He forked some egg onto the toast and took a bite. After he swallowed, he said, "They gotta keep my Walther for evidence until the investigation is over, but I'll get it back."

The question burst from my lips. "Why'd you bring Frank?"

"I wondered when you'd ask that." He put down his fork. "You don't go into battle alone."

"He was a Quaker. He wouldn't do anything. You should have left him behind and brought Lee."

Tom's answering look was somber. "Frank didn't do anything?" He sighed. "He was s'posed to look after you, Betty. So I could focus on the task at hand."

"Sam and I had it planned out. You didn't have to be there."

Tom raised his eyebrows. "I learned early on in the war. The plan never survives first contact with the enemy. What do you imagine woulda happened if Frank and I hadn't come Saturday night? Personally, I don't wanna think about it. 'Cause I doubt we'd be sittin' in Teddy's having breakfast."

My cheeks warmed. "Sam would have shown."

"Not until it was too late." Tom's voice was blunt. "He got called to another scene earlier. That's why he wasn't there. He couldn't send someone else 'cause it wasn't an official op. In the Army, we called that…never mind. But it was a real mess." He blew out a breath. "I'm sorry about the way it turned out. Frank was a good guy."

"How do you know?" I heard the bitterness in my voice. I hated it, but there it was. "You barely knew him."

Tom dropped his gaze to his plate. "I've been a real jerk since I got home. Three guys helped me pull my head outta my a…rear end. One was your dad. One was Detective MacKinnon." He looked up. "The third was Frank."

I blinked.

"He knew both of us better than we knew ourselves." Tom paused. "He wanted me to tell you not to feel bad. If things turned out ugly."

I took a slug of my joe. It sounded like Frank. Tom resumed eating. After a minute or two, I spoke again. "Where does that leave us?"

Tom wiped his mouth with a napkin and pushed aside his plate. "I know how I feel." He took something out of his pocket and laid it on the table.

I stared at my engagement ring. The diamond twinkled in the overhead light. Did I want it back? I lifted my gaze to Tom. He didn't make my heart go pitter-pat. Even before the war. Our love had been between two kids who didn't know anything else. We'd been friends forever. 'Course we'd get married.

The boy—no, the *man*—across from me didn't make my heart go pitter-pat, either. He made it speed up and pound against my ribs. Bein' close to him made my stomach swoop as though I'd jumped off a building. I thought back to how I'd felt next to him as we worked on Stevie's code, how his arms had protected me the night Frank died. How when it came right down to it, Tom was the one I wanted beside me. He was solid, dependable, and supportive.

He made me feel safe.

But.

"Tom." I clasped my hands in my lap. "We don't know each other anymore." He opened his mouth, and I held up a hand. "Let me finish. We've both changed. I think before we rush back into what we were, we should get to know each other for who we are. Raw emotion isn't enough. It might turn out we're great pals, but would be awful lovers. I wouldn't want that for either of us. Would you?"

Tom thought a moment. "No, I wouldn't." He swept up the ring. "You don't mind if I keep this, though, do you? Just in case?" He gave me one of his lopsided grins.

"Be my guest." His words warmed me from the inside.

Judy arrived with more coffee. "Want a top off?" she asked Tom. He nodded, and she refilled his mug. She glanced at me.

I nodded and she did the same. I kept my gaze on Tom. "You still lookin' for a job?"

He drank and nodded. "Sure am. Got any ideas?"

I aimed for a careless tone, although my heart was beating like the bass drum in a marching band. "You're a pretty smart fella. Good in a tight spot and can keep your head when things go sideways. I could use someone like that."

"Is that right?" Again, the crooked grin. "You don't wanna see my resumé?"

"Consider Saturday night your interview." I lifted my mug. "If you want the job, you're hired."

A Note from the Author

There really is a collection of tunnels under Buffalo. Note that I say "collection," not "network." Many of the tunnels are unconnected and were made at different times in the city's history to serve different needs. Some pre-date modern water and sewer networks and were used to deliver water to houses. These are largely unused today but still accessible. Some provided a way to walk from one building to another during the cold winter months. Others were used during Prohibition, both for transporting illegal alcohol and storing it. One leads from the City jail to the County courthouse and was in fact used to transport Leon Czolgosz, the man who assassinated President William McKinley, so angry mobs could not attack him. There is a story that the tunnel was dug expressly for this purpose but that is most likely an urban legend.

The tunnel that Betty discovers in this book is fictional. But within this history, it very well could have existed.

Acknowledgements

A long time ago, I said, "I'll never write a historical novel." Six books later, I have to eat my words many times over. Just goes to show you: In this business, never say "never."

As always, there are many people to thank.

To my critique group: Annette Dashofy, Jeff Boarts, and Peter WJ Hayes. This time, these writers helped me write my most emotional book ever (at least I think so) and pushed me to really dig deep on this one.

To my father, Gary Lederman, who continues to answer my frantic questions and who keeps me supplied with story ideas by sending stories of Buffalo's history.

To Susan Helene Gottfried for her eagle-eyed editing and helping me smooth out the rough prose and bumpiness in the story. If you like stories about people growing into who they can be, check out her Tales from the Sheep Farm novels.

To the Dames of Detection, Shawn Reilly Simmons, Verena Rose, and Deb Well, for your unending support of Betty and her story.

To the readers who love these stories, especially Mark Baker of Carstairs Considers, who has championed this series from the beginning.

To Sisters in Crime and Pennwriters, the blog communities at Jungle Red Writers, Wicked Authors, and Chicks on the Case, and the friends I've made through them. Community is key no matter what you do and the crime fiction community is one of the best.

To my husband, Paul: through the ups and downs we're still partners in life. Love you.

About the Author

Liz Milliron is the Shamus-nominated author of the Laurel Highlands mystery series, starring a Pennsylvania State Trooper and a Fayette County public defender in the scenic Laurel Highlands of southwest Pennsylvania. She is also the author of the Homefront Mysteries, set in Buffalo, NY in the early years of WWII. The series features Betty Ahern, a Rosie the Riveter turned Sam Spade. Her short fiction has been published in multiple anthologies including *Murder Most International, Blood on the Bayou,* and *Murder Most Historical.* Liz is a past president of the Pittsburgh Chapter of Sisters in Crime and the current Vice President, as well as the Education Liaison for the National Board of Sisters in Crime. She is a member of International Thriller Writers, Pennwriters and the Historical Novel Society. Liz splits her time between homes in Pittsburgh and the Laurel Highlands, where she lives with her husband and a very spoiled retired-racer greyhound.

https://lizmilliron.com

https://www.facebook.com/LizMilliron

Also by Liz Milliron

<u>The Homefront Mysteries</u>
The Enemy We Don't Know
The Stories We Tell
The Lessons We Learn
The Truth We Hide
The Secrets We Keep

<u>The Laurel Highlands Mysteries</u>
Saving the Guilty
Thicker Than Water
Lie Down with Dogs
Harm Not the Earth
Broken Trust
Heaven Has No Rage
Root of All Evil

<u>The Jackson Davis Mysteries</u>
Shattered Sight